Gratest Ever After

CARISSA MAY

Gratest Ever After

Editing by Britt at Paperback Proofreader and Kristen Hamilton at Kristen's Red Pen

Proofreading by Jaime I. at TLC Editorial Services

Cover design by Monika de los Rios at riocovers on Fiverr

For anyone who's ever stopped believing in happily ever afters.

And to my exes.
Thanks for being exes.

authors note

Dear Reader,

Thank you for choosing my debut novel, Gratest Ever After, as your next read.

While this is a book with a happy ending and lots of laughs along the way, it also addresses heavier topics. If you'd like to avoid potential spoilers, stop reading here. Otherwise, I'd like to provide you with on page content warnings for anxiety and panic attacks, domestic abuse (emotional, physical, and mental), gaslighting, car accident, hospitalization, open door content, and death of parent (off page). Gratest Ever After is intended for audiences 18 years and older.

If any of these are potentially sensitive for you, please be gentle with yourself while reading. I did my best to handle the above with the utmost respect and compassion. If you find yourself in the pages of this book, please know that you are seen, understood, and loved so very much.

With love,

Carissa May

one

I'd come to accept that happily ever afters didn't exist. They were just something that Hallmark, Disney, and our parents brainwashed us with in order to sprinkle some magic into our otherwise boring lives. Maybe once upon a time I appreciated that, even wished for it, but I knew better now. Magic could be dark. If I knew then what I knew now, maybe I wouldn't be so broken.

Why, then, did I decide to start reading another romance novel? Was I hoping this would be the one happily ever after to prove me wrong? That it wouldn't make me roll my eyes and want to toss it across the room? I struggled to believe anyone — fictional or real — could fall so madly and completely in love that quickly. No man of my dreams would make me easily forget he'd hurt me with some persistent groveling and sappy Hallmark moves.

Trust me, I spoke from experience. But then again, I hadn't met a fictional character who'd gone through what I had...yet. Not that I'd want to. The main character in a book about my life would probably just piss me off. Maybe if I came across a book with a happy ending I could relate to, my confidence would be restored.

Until then, I'd keep denying that happily ever afters were possible.

Now, I wasn't expecting my knight in shining armor to toss pebbles at my window. I was *not* waiting for an embarrassing meet-cute to happen. One where I bumped into the town's most loved citizen leaving the grocery store and spilled a box of tampons all over the sidewalk. I was not looking for an ex-boyfriend to see me flirting at a bar with someone new and instantly regret letting me go.

Certainly not *that*.

I pulled the laces tight on my sneakers, popped my AirPods in, started up my next audiobook, and headed out the back door. The sun hadn't come up yet, so the summer heat wasn't in full effect, but the humidity was tangible. It was as if a set of hands were gripping anyone who dared step outside around the neck. I clawed at my throat just thinking about it, finding no actual hands squeezing me, and let out a small breath of relief.

Relax, Maddie. It's summer, not a personal attack on you.

Trying to keep my strides light so as to not call attention to myself, I winced as the gravel crunched beneath my feet as I jogged past my dad's black Range Rover. Another perk to leaving before the sun was fully up — I didn't have to see him. And usually, by the time I was back, his car was gone. I increased the volume of my audiobook, letting my favorite narrator's voice transport me elsewhere, and felt instantly at ease.

Before long, a thin layer of sweat was dripping down the nape of my neck and traveling south with abandon. I swiped the back of my hand across my forehead in an effort to control what I could. Summer never ceased to remind me I was at its mercy, threatening to blind me with my own sweat. *Kick a girl while she's down, why don't you.* Did I mention I hated this time of year? I only stepped outside if I had absolutely no other option — in this case, avoiding my father — and it suited me just fine.

"Oh, come on," I groaned after only a few short minutes, shoving my dead AirPods into my sports bra. I stopped on the road and pulled my phone out of the waistband of my shorts, pausing my book at a particularly spicy chapter. I was sure my neighbors would rather hear my early 2000s pop playlist than the graphic narration of a couple getting it on in the storage closet at work at six o'clock in the morning. With the volume set to high, I let the music take over the silence that surrounded me.

I didn't even like running. I'd never been an overly "active" person. My therapist, Heather, suggested I get a hobby that encouraged me to physically get out of the house, so I settled on running. A few months ago, I downloaded one of those apps that could apparently take you from the couch to the Olympics in a matter of weeks, and I hadn't stopped since.

I would never be an Olympian, of that there was no doubt. In fact, the app practically yelled at me the first few weeks because I didn't keep up with their times. I still wasn't. So I stopped using the app and decided as long as I was moving, I was doing just fine. Anything that got my heart racing in my chest while curbing my anxiety was a win I would claim.

The rev of a motorcycle broke me out of my thoughts, and I froze on the sidewalk. In a matter of seconds, all the blood in my body drained to my toes, rendering me numb and causing me to trip over my feet. I avoided a face plant, landing on my hands and knees, but wasn't able to prevent the concrete from tearing my skin to shreds. I rolled over to the grass, gritting my teeth as my knees stung from the movement. My heartbeat competed with the rumble of the engine as it grew nearer and more overwhelming. I clenched my right hand into a fist, slamming it against my chest to jumpstart my lungs. When the motorcycle roared past and I saw it wasn't *his*, I exhaled, drawing my knees to my chest and dropping my head between them.

"Are you all right?" a voice shouted, penetrating my spiraling thoughts. I jerked my head back up and stared at the rider, wide-eyed. I didn't realize he'd stopped. My heart slowed as I watched him take off his helmet, revealing a full head of salt-and-pepper hair. He had to be close to my dad's age. *It wasn't him*, I forced my brain to acknowledge. "I didn't mean to scare you."

"You didn't," I snapped, finally looking down to examine myself. My knees were cut open and blood trickled down my shins. I turned my hands over, noting the dirt and scratches covering my palms. "I'm fine."

I looked over when I noticed him approaching in my periphery. Gripping the grass in my fingers, I focused on the dampness from the morning dew and not on the bike or its owner. I must have looked wary because he stopped where he was and scratched at his jaw, watching me as one would watch a stricken doe.

"I said I'm fine," I grumbled, climbing to my feet despite the pain flaring on my skin. The walk back home was going to be fun.

"You should really clean that before it gets infected." He winced, waving a hand haphazardly toward my knees. What was he? A doctor? "Do you live close by? I can give you a ride back."

I had to bite back a scoff at his question. Surely he could see the error in his ways, asking a stranger to get on the back of his bike. He probably wanted to murder me.

"I said I was fine," I insisted, a little louder this time, as I slowly backed away from the man and headed in the direction I'd come. He seemed friendly enough, with a big belly and rosy cheeks, almost like Santa Claus, but it didn't matter. I wouldn't get back on a bike if my life depended on it.

Once I made it around the corner and out of the man's view, I stopped to lean against a tree. I pulled my shirt over my head, leaving me in my black sports bra, and pressed it lightly against my knees to stanch the bleeding. *Oh my god*. The pain teetered from a sting to a full-fledged burn. I probably should have taken Mr. Stranger Danger up on his offer for a ride...but I couldn't. The fact that I'd evaded a panic attack was shocking enough, and I didn't want to push it.

"Stupid noise-canceling AirPods, why couldn't you have died

five minutes later?" I mumbled angrily to myself. "No. Stupid *Griffin* for ruining everything."

It always circled back to Griffin. What I would have given to go back in time and never met him. I shook my head and focused on steering my mind away from him, then continued the walk back home. As I turned into the empty driveway, I looked down at my phone, checking the time. Dad must have left earlier than normal. I felt the tightness in my chest slowly loosen as I took in a deep, steadying breath.

The house was dark and quiet as I made my way to the main bathroom. Stripping out of my clothes, I turned on the shower and stepped inside. I winced in pain as I scrubbed my scrapes and washed off the sweat from my morning run, cursing my earlier decision to leave the comfort of my bed. Covered in goosebumps and recognizing the effects of my shock wearing off, I stepped out, wrapped a towel around myself, and grabbed our first-aid kit from the cabinet.

Back on my bed, after what felt like a lifetime but was realistically an hour, tops, I took stock of my banged-up knees. A dry laugh escaped my lips and bounced off the walls of my lavender bedroom. I looked like a five-year-old who fell off her bike going too quickly down the driveway. Opening the metal kit, I got to work applying ointment and covering the roughest-looking cuts with bandages. I sighed. The last thing I wanted was more scars covering my body.

Despite the day only starting, I was ready for it to be over. I stood up and walked over to my closet, standing there for a minute with my fisted hands at my hips. I sighed again and pulled a random sundress off the clothes rail, watching in slow motion as the hanger caught and two boxes, filled with my best and worst memories, fell from the top shelf. I cursed and jumped away from the floral-print boxes, their contents spilling on the floor.

"Shit," I gasped, slipping the dress over my head. I sat down on the floor, tucking my feet to the side to avoid putting pressure on my scraped skin.

I looked at the mess of notebooks and trinkets that scattered the floor. With shaking hands, I picked up the journal closest to me. The one that started it all. Running my fingers over the purple cover, I traced the stitched butterflies and choked back tears. This journal was the last gift my mom ever gave me before she died. It was for my thirteenth birthday, and she'd given it to me early, claiming she was too excited. In hindsight, she would've known the chances of her making it to my actual birthday were slim.

You're about to be a teenager, Madison, she'd said. Her voice had been weak and throaty, but filled with so much hope. *And you're going to go on so many adventures. I want you to have a place to write it all down. This way, when you're my age and your daughter turns thirteen, you can reminisce about what you went through and go easier on her.*

I filled that journal by the end of the summer with letters to her, keeping her up to date with everything that was going on in my life. I had to buy a new one before the next school year started. Every night before bed, I'd pull it out and fill her in on my day and ask all the questions I would have asked her if she were still here. But once I started college and met Olivia, the letters to my mom became more sporadic. There just were some things you didn't want to tell your mother...even if she'd never hear it.

After placing all the journals addressed to her back into their respective box, I moved on to the next. These were the journals that I started after my best friend, Olivia, left. They were addressed to her. Apparently, I had a habit of writing to people I lost in one way or another. But these journals were different from the ones I wrote to my mother. They contained my darkest moments. I shoved all those journals back into their box, afraid that if I touched them too long, the darkness of my past would jump out of the pages and try to finish what it started.

I grabbed my travel souvenirs, a small jewelry box with an

embroidered *M* on it, movie ticket stubs, and some of my favorite photos and put them back in the box with Olivia's journals. Before closing the lid, I lifted one of the photos of Olivia and me, smiling at how happy the two of us were. Her brother, Nate, had snapped this photo when we were visiting their parents for Thanksgiving. We definitely had too much wine (and mashed potatoes, by the look of my unbuttoned jeans) and were holding each other up as we smiled big, toothy grins, eyes unfocused and...*happy*. This was the last photo we took together before everything changed. Before Griffin planted himself in my life like a ticking bomb, waiting for the perfect moment to destroy everything that had ever meant something to me.

It'd been two years since I last saw her, and my heart still hadn't fully healed. But to be honest, I don't think it ever could. Olivia was more than just a best friend to me; she was my other half, and she threw all of that away. How could someone I considered a sister just up and walk away when I needed her most? I put the photo back in the box and picked up the jewelry box, tracing the letter *M* with my thumb. My heart raced as it trailed along the letter, the thread soft and worn beneath the pad of my finger. Before I could stop myself, I lifted the lid by its blue ribbon tab and pushed the charm bracelet inside to the side, grabbing the folded piece of paper tucked beneath it.

I flattened the worn receipt, unable to decipher what it was from the faded ink, and turned it over. My eyes scanned the words written in black permanent marker, still as clear as the day Nate wrote them two years ago. I settled against the doorframe, feeling my heart shatter all over again. This had been my last chance at safety, the last life preserver on the sinking ship of my life. And I was too stubborn to realize it. Too blinded by my heart to see what was actually happening.

Tears streamed down my face as I wrapped my arms around my legs and buried my face between my skinned knees. A hand hovered in my mind's eye, ticking off all the ways I had failed. I was living with my dad. *Thumb.* I gave up on my dream of becoming a published author. *Forefinger.* I was in the same exact place I was in a year ago when everything happened. *Middle.* I still couldn't see or hear a motorcycle without falling apart, couldn't trust or accept help from anyone, and still found silence suffocating and terrifying. The imaginary hand waved its spirit fingers frantically in the face of my despair. I swiped at the tears that streaked my cheeks with the hem of my dress and closed my eyes, focusing on my breathing.

If Heather were here, she'd be disagreeing with everything I was thinking and feeling. She'd be telling me in her most practiced and professional tone that I *was* making progress and the fact that I didn't shut down and let the panic take over when I found myself face-to-face with a motorcycle was huge. I was glad she wasn't here to witness this sad scene, though; I wouldn't want her to see me this way. Sure, she'd coaxed me out of worse breakdowns, always with those kind, knowing eyes, but my day had already sunk down the proverbial drain. I didn't need to add insult to injury.

I rolled my neck and shoulders out, my eyes circling the room before landing on the calendar hanging over my desk. There it was. The dreaded date circled in red. *How has it already been almost a year since the accident?* Looking down at the two floral boxes that contained my past, I realized I'd never amount to anything if I stayed here. No, I had to go. Scrambling to my feet, I ran over to my phone and did a search of the address Nate had written on the back of the receipt, finding it was only a three-hour drive.

I pinned my focus on my desk, knowing that if I opened my laptop, I'd be faced with a blank document. The same blank document I'd been staring at for the last six months, hoping for something creative to magically transfer from my mind to my keyboard. Maybe I just needed to be in a new environment, surrounded by new people. Maybe then I could start being who I wanted to be. Maybe then I'd be able to write again.

Only one way to find out.

two

I took in a deep breath through my belly and exhaled through my mouth, trying to convince the elephant sitting on my chest to kindly get off.

You're fine, Maddie. Everything will be okay.

I shook the jitters from my hands and brushed off the remnants of my memory-box meltdown. I knew if I waited too long, I'd change my mind, so I grabbed my duffle bag and packed what I could. Purse, tote bag, laptop, and planner spilling from my arms, I took one last look at my room. Satisfied, I shut off the light and left.

Three hours later, I stood on Nate's front porch in Briar Oakes. Now that the adrenaline had all but worn off, a zillion possibilities of what could happen flooded my mind. I was trying to come up with what I'd say to him, but when the door opened, it wasn't Nate.

I could tell that Tyler recognized me immediately. I recognized him, too, as it was hard to forget the nights Olivia and I had spent dancing before Nate would appear, Tyler often at his side, to bring us home. He blinked as if to check that I was real, and then gave me a half smile and mumbled something about calling Nate, leaving me standing in the doorway alone. When he returned, he had a four-digit code scribbled on a blue sticky note and a message from Nate saying that I could stay as long as I needed. Nate was away for work for the next few weeks and Tyler had only stopped in to feed the cat. Tyler was just as quiet and professional as I remembered, but he was nice enough to give me a quick tour of the house and didn't question my reluctance to step foot inside any of the more lived-in rooms. The lack of personal touches throughout the home made me feel more comfortable, safer.

He gave me a single nod and said goodbye a short while later, leaving me to unpack in the spare room. As soon as I heard the front door snick shut, signaling I was alone in the house — apart from the cat I'd yet to meet — I fell back on the bed and let my mind reel.

"Nope, I can't do this," I whispered, sitting back up. On autopilot, I fumbled for my phone and jabbed the familiar contact from my list, putting it on speaker and resting it carefully in my lap like the lifeline it was. My body began to overheat from the panic coursing its way through my body. "Please pick up, Heather."

"Maddie?" Heather's voice was gentle, but I could still sense the concern in it. "Is everything okay?"

"No," I managed to get out. "I'm having a panic attack. Or I'm going to, I guess. I don't really know what I'm feeling. I'm freaking out. I don't know what to do. What do I do?"

"Okay, we'll get through this together," she said, and what sounded like a door slid open and closed in the background. I'd come to appreciate her willingness to take these unscheduled appointments over the last several months. I sought comfort in her melodic voice and trusted her guidance, but I wished more than anything they weren't necessary. "Where are you?"

"Connecticut." I dropped my hand to my thigh, the softness of my light cotton dress underneath my fingertips anchoring me to the present. I closed my eyes as I traced the scars through the fabric; a reminder that I'd survived. If I could make it through that,

I could make it through this. "I sort of made an impulsive decision to visit an old friend — well, I don't know if *friend* is the right word to use. But now that I'm here...what if I made a mistake?"

"That's a very valid feeling, Maddie. Can I ask you a question?" I nodded despite knowing Heather couldn't see, not able to get a sound out with the way my throat was tightening. "What's the worst that could happen?"

The familiar question seemed to ground me, almost pulling the corners of my mouth into a smile. I knew I'd gotten into the habit of jumping to the worst-case scenario, and it prevented me from doing anything for *me*. Anything that reminded me of who I was *before*. Hell, I couldn't even walk to the mailbox without crumbling. When I'd first started seeing Heather, she'd provided me with some prompts to help offset my anxiety attacks. I remembered the way my eyes rolled when she suggested it, not thinking it'd actually work, but I surprised myself. It was amazing what you could do when you didn't let your thoughts take over.

"I'm not sure," I said with a grave sigh, trying to hold myself together. These episodes still happened frequently, but more often than not, they were less intense. Anxiety medication helped, but I still had to work to stop my thoughts from distorting reality. "I guess he would make me leave, and I'll have come here for nothing."

"I take it we're not talking about Olivia?" she asked, and I groaned at the sound of her name. Even after two years, a new crack managed to grace my heart every time I heard her name.

"No." I flexed my hand and tipped my head back. "Her older brother, Nate."

"I see." And this time, Heather paused. I waited, gnawing on my lower lip, my stomach twisting in nerves. "You haven't spoken much about Nate, only that he was around a lot when you were in college. Is he the type of person who'd send you away?"

"No." I let a small grin escape. "He would never. It would go against everything he is."

"Okay, so since that possibility is ruled out, what's the best that could happen?"

"I guess he would be happy to see me." I pulled my shoulders away from my ears and gave it some thought. "Or at least let me stay, no questions asked."

"And what's most likely to happen?"

"Probably that." As my mouth formed the words, the elephant sitting on my chest inched off, leaving room for a lighter, more forgiving feeling. The one that always seemed to flood me after I voiced my fears. I knew Nate would hear what I had to say, and sure, my fear of disappointing him was greater than my fear of rejection. But could any of it be worse than it already was?

"I'm curious as to why you chose to go to him and not Olivia."

"Because she abandoned me when I needed her most, but Nate...he always made sure that I was safe and knew I could turn to him," I murmured into the phone, my voice cracking. I hated the words just as much as I hated the constant battle with myself over whether I was angry with her or grateful that she'd walked out two years ago. "And if I was going to do something as drastic as leaving, then I needed to go somewhere that I felt safe. I needed to be with someone that I knew would have my back versus someone who had hurt me before."

"Sounds like he took on an older brother role. Would you say that?"

"An older brother..." For whatever reason, the words tasted bitter and wrong on my tongue. I'd referred to him as that in the past and it'd never felt wrong, so why did it now? "No, definitely not. He was more like a...bodyguard? I don't know. He just cared about me, I guess."

"And what sparked your decision to leave?" Heather asked, and I let out a soft sigh.

"You're all about asking the hard questions, huh?" I rubbed my hand up and down my left thigh. "I was cleaning out my closet and came across a few boxes of — " I stopped myself, careful not to mention the journals, which I still wasn't ready to share " — just some things from my past. As I was going through them, I started looking back on this last year and realized how much I hadn't done. Sorry, Heather, I didn't even think to ask. Do you have time for this? It's honestly not a big deal, and I'm sure you're busy. I'm not freaking out anymore, so...yay! Right?"

"No deflecting. You were saying?"

"Right, okay. Thanks," I grumbled, raising a palm to my cheek and feeling the blush travel south to my neck and chest. Heather definitely didn't shy away from calling me out on my crap. "These boxes...I haven't added anything to them since I came home after... after everything. I've done nothing worth keeping as a memory." I choked back a sob, a tear finally slipping down my cheek. "And I knew that if I stayed with my dad, I never would. I love him and am grateful for his support this past year, but no part of waking up in my childhood bedroom every day was inspiring me to go after it, you know? I was suffocating."

A faint knocking in the background interrupted us.

"Excuse me for a moment, Maddie," Heather said softly before placing me on mute. I tapped my fingers nervously against my chin as I waited, trying to not let the panic I managed to stifle escalate again.

"Sorry about that," Heather said, returning after a few moments. "My next appointment arrived early, but I have a few minutes before I have to go. Let's continue what we were discussing."

I let out a watery laugh and even though, again, I knew she couldn't see me, I smiled into the sunlit room and hoped she could feel it. "Holding those things in my hands, seeing what I once deemed worthy of keeping," I continued, "it reminded me of the person I used to be. Of the person I always thought I'd become."

Heather asked a few more questions, and the more I answered, the lighter the pressure on my chest became. "Thank you so much," I said, taking the call off speaker and holding it up to my ear. "I'll try to call again soon. With a bit more notice next time. Hopefully."

"I'll hold you to that. You know I'm always here for you, Maddie. Just remember, your thoughts and feelings aren't predictive of what's actually going to happen."

"I know, you're right," I sighed. "I need to remember that."

"You're stronger than you think." I heard a drawer open on her end, then the clunking sound of a book being flipped open. "I have an opening Monday morning. I'd like to have a follow-up call with you if you're available."

"Why?" I questioned. Our appointments had grown farther apart this summer, thanks to a successful combination of medication and my determination to be Perfectly Fine. Our next one wasn't scheduled until the one-year anniversary of the accident. I thought I was making progress. Did this one phone call set me back?

"I can hear you overthinking through the line." She laughed lightly, and it took everything not to look around. Her ability to read my mind was uncanny. "This doesn't mean anything bad, Maddie. Going to therapy is important even when we're doing well. But you're making some big decisions and stepping outside of your comfort zone."

"Yeah, that makes sense. Hold on a sec." I stood and left the room, the hardwood floor cold on my bare feet. Opening my bag that I'd set on the kitchen counter, I grabbed my planner and a pen. "What time?"

Where is this cat? I'd resorted to checking inside cabinets, searching under furniture, and even inside the garbage can to find my four-legged roommate. I was starting to think Tyler had made the whole thing up so he could escape any lingering awkwardness.

Standing up from just checking under the sofa, I brushed off my knees, noticing the bandages had held up pretty well, and then triple-checked that the front door was locked. I froze when I heard a familiar sound echo off the walls, turning to follow it to the kitchen. I groaned, taking a few steps over to where my phone sat on the island. Before I even saw the name flashing across my screen, I knew it was my dad. Only two people had my phone number, and it was unlikely that my therapist was already calling me back.

I wasn't ready to talk to him yet.

I declined the call and slipped my phone into the pocket of my dress, making my way over to the kitchen cabinets. I opened each one to see if there was anything I could use to make myself dinner, but all I could find were a few mugs, spices, and mixing bowls. The cabinet under the sink was filled with cleaning supplies. Finding the pantry, I opened the door and pulled out a box of cereal, hoping there'd be some milk left in the fridge. To my surprise, it was decently stocked with milk, eggs, and a shit ton of cheese. *Interesting.*

I poured myself a bowl of Cheerios and felt my body relax just the slightest. This was good. I survived the drive here, I survived knocking on Nate's door, I survived his friend at the door, and now I would survive dinner. All I had to do was make it through each day as if it were some giant checklist and I'd be okay.

I finished my cereal in record time. I couldn't believe how hungry I was, but then I thought back to this morning. My run, my *fall*, my epiphany, the drive here — yep, that would do it. I put my bowl away and hobbled down to my room where I unpacked my essentials: sound machine and phone charger. I caved and texted my dad to let him know where I'd gone and that I had arrived safely. *That should buy me a few days.* After turning off my phone, I dug around in my bag, trying to find a pair of pajamas, only...shit, I didn't pack any, did I?

Shoving the two boxes of journals onto the top shelf in the closet, I grabbed my toiletry bag before I trekked down the hallway to the laundry room. When I stepped inside, I nearly stumbled back and had to grab hold of the door handle to steady myself. Nate was *everywhere*. His clothes in the hamper, which would now be mixed with mine as I peeled off my dress. His lived-in slippers by the far wall that even had the imprint of his feet etched into the wool. A pair of mismatched socks tucked into a pair of sneakers. It was...a lot. I took a few steps back, still in my bra and underwear, and went to turn out the light when a stack of folded clothes caught my attention. Without giving it a second thought, I snatched one of his shirts and a pair of athletic shorts and put them on.

That hyped-up feeling of being in someone else's space overcame me, not to mention that I was wearing this *specific* someone's clothes. I took my time getting to the bathroom, nervous that I'd find something that might hint at what Nate had been up to the past few years. But not to my surprise, the white walls were bare, containing not a single framed photo or piece of art.

When I padded into the bathroom, I caught my reflection in the mirror, gaping at the walk-in shower. I bet that thing could hold ten people at once and there'd still be space left over! I let my fingers trail along the white countertop and across the two sinks as I crossed the marble floor. I turned around, eyeing the white freestanding tub. *God, are those jets? I bet that thing is magical.* Imagining myself soaking in it — a book in hand, surrounded by candles — was enough to put me at ease.

Dropping my toiletry bag onto the counter, I grimaced at my disheveled appearance in the mirror. My shoulder-length honey-blonde hair was a tangled mess from driving with the windows open, and I had dark circles under my eyes. Would Nate even recognize me? My eyes wandered to the scar above my right eyebrow next, and then down to the one that curved along my chin. I looked like a trainwreck.

I brought the hem of his shirt up to my nose, inhaling the scent of laundry detergent and a hint of something else...was that butter? *What are you* doing, *Maddie?* I glanced down at where it fell just above my knees. Had Nate always been this large? I hiked up his shorts and tied them tightly around my waist, not keen on risking yet another mishap.

I met my reflection again, chuckling at how ridiculous I looked dwarfed in his clothes. But despite feeling ridiculous and slightly embarrassed at myself, I gave his shirt one more sniff. Standing there, in Nate's clothes, savoring his scent, I didn't feel scared. I felt safe. If only I could bottle this smell up in a can and use it as an air freshener or somehow get it made into a candle...No, that would be weird. *Seriously, what is wrong with me?*

After brushing my teeth, I rested my toothbrush on the counter and, seeing my yellow one next to his green, was reminded that I was actually in Nate's house. My ex-best friend's older brother's house. This was real.

Oh my god, Nate and I would be sharing a bathroom.

I'd read just enough romance novels to know that this would ultimately end in disaster. At some point, one of us would walk in on the other while they were naked, or there would be a case of explosive diarrhea with no toilet paper in sight and the need to call for help would arise. Whenever he came home, I'd have to make a Target run to buy some air fresheners.

Gripping the hem of Nate's shirt, I twisted it in my fingers as the panic started bubbling in my stomach. What the hell was I doing? Not in a million years did I ever think I'd pack my bags, get in my car, and leave in hopes of crashing in a guy's house I hadn't seen or spoken to in two years.

Breathe, Madison. You'll be fine. Everything will be okay.

three

"*You* must be Tuna. You're a wily little thing," I said as I stood in the doorway of Nate's office, eyeing the large gray cat perched on the window seat after I spent a good chunk of the morning trying to find him since I was unsuccessful last night. I had no interest in entering Nate's space, but when Tyler mentioned that I'd have to take care of his cat, I figured I should at least introduce myself. Tuna's yellow eyes connected with mine instantly, and I felt the urge to step out of the office. *His* office. I didn't hate animals, but if I had to choose a pet to live with, it certainly wouldn't be a cat. Especially not *that* cat; he looked like he wanted to take down the world, starting with me.

Tyler had pointed out Tuna's care instructions taped to the fridge before hightailing it out of here yesterday. All I had to do was feed him and make sure his litter box was kept clean throughout the day. Otherwise, he liked to be left alone.

At least we had that in common.

"I'm Maddie." Wonderful, now I was talking to a cat? I took another step into the office, taking in the space. Aside from Tuna's pillow on the window seat that overlooked the backyard, all that seemed to occupy the room was a large desk centered between two built-in shelving units and a brown leather chair in the corner. I walked over to the shelves, taking note of the random knickknacks that I was sure were Olivia's doing. There was a miniature globe, several dusty cookbooks, a candle...was that vanilla bean? I picked it up and gave it a quick sniff, trying to imagine a scenario in which Nate would ever light a candle. I let out a raspy laugh and could've sworn the cat was judging me as I continued my perusal. Standing proud in all shapes and sizes and scattered across the highest shelf were half a dozen framed selfies of Olivia making silly faces and a ceramic cat sporting devil horns.

"Looks like you and Olivia weren't exactly friends," I stated, brushing some dust off the figurine. Ignoring the pang in my chest from seeing the photos of her, I looked over my shoulder at the cat tracking my every move. He hissed in return. "Noted. Well, you don't have to worry about me, pal. I'll stick to my room if you stick to yours."

Deciding it was time to make use of that glorious shower, I crossed the hallway to the bathroom. Shrugging out of Nate's clothes, I stepped in and was pleasantly surprised to find it well stocked and, luckily for me since I *also* forgot to pack my shower products, Nate didn't use those dreaded 3-in-1 combo bottles.

"Oh, this smells good." I placed my head under the showerhead and let the scent of rosemary and mint body wash surround me.

I wonder if he always smelled like this. I tried to think back to one of the last times Olivia, Nate, and I were together, but I couldn't remember. As I lathered my body with his soap, an image of Nate doing the same flashed in my mind. His hands roaming over his body, soap bubbles trailing down his chest as the water washed it away.

My eyes shot open and darted around the room as if I'd been caught. *Woah*. That was...a brand-new feeling.

Now more than awake, I slipped out of the shower and back into Nate's clothes. I wasn't planning on leaving the house and no one else was here to see, so what did it matter what I wore? I grabbed my Kindle from my duffle and made my way to the kitchen to feed Tuna. The soft pitter-patter of his paws sounded on the hardwood floor as soon as I opened the pantry door to grab a can of his food. Once again, he looked at me, unimpressed in a way only cats could pull off, as I attempted to dump the contents into his bowl while burrowing my nose into the crook of my arm to keep from gagging. I barely got my hand away from the dish before Tuna dove in. *That* felt altogether too difficult of a task. Standing up straight, I sighed and glanced around Nate's house, finally getting a good look at it.

The entire front half of the house consisted of the living room, kitchen, and dining room, all open-concept and drenched in natural light. A large fireplace framed by two windows took up most of the wall, surrounded by white shiplap and a floating cedar mantle. A television was centered above it, and the intrusive image of Nate in an outfit just like the one I wore now, lounging on his recliner with a drink in hand, assaulted my mind. I wondered if we had the same favorites on Netflix and — nope, not going there.

I pushed myself back into the kitchen to *really* take it in this time. A white farmhouse sink centered under a window that looked out over the yard and out toward the wooded area behind his fence. Two floating cedar shelves hung on either side of the window, something that felt almost like the main feature of the space. I pulled one of the six black stools away from the island and audibly scoffed when I saw what lay in the middle: an empty wooden fruit bowl. Now we were talking. This one touch gave me so much unexplainable satisfaction. He might've had a kitchen that belonged in a magazine and kept everything sparkly and clean, but he still fell for the same design traps we all did.

Tuna meowed at me, and I took that as his way of saying thank you. Before I could further humiliate myself and reply with a "you're welcome," he turned down the hallway and sashayed toward Nate's office. Ready to get my own productive day started,

I jumped onto the living room couch and stretched my legs out in front of me, propping them up on the coffee table. Turning on my Kindle, I opened my current read and melted into comfort.

The clock read 10:30 p.m. when I finished my book. I placed my Kindle on the coffee table where I rested my feet and sighed. It was a workplace enemies-to-lovers romance where the characters were competing for the same promotion. I surprised myself a few times by laughing out loud at some of the banter between the characters but was ultimately still disappointed in the end.

Not wanting to jump into another book, I got off the couch and turned out the light, only to skid to a stop as a set of headlights shone through the living room window. Dropping to the floor, I hissed, "Shit, shit, *shit*!" Tuna was at my side in an instant, nuzzling his head against my body. I looked down at the ball of gray fur, unsure of how to react.

The sound of tires crunching along the gravel of the driveway rang in my ears, and I lost the ability to breathe. Who the hell could it be? Nate wasn't supposed to be back for a few weeks. My fingers shook as I gripped the hem of my shirt tightly until I felt Tuna nudge me, bumping his forehead against my clenched fist. "Thank you," I whispered. His soft fur and the way his purring felt against my skin did the impossible job of easing my panic. I loosened my grip and tentatively rested my hand on Tuna's head, scratching behind his ears.

I was trying not to let the fact that he was letting me touch him be a big deal, but I was getting the feeling that he knew I needed to be comforted. Or maybe he was just as scared as I was. "Any chance you're some secret guard dog or something? Because if that's a murderer outside — "

The sound of footsteps on the front porch silenced me. The

ache in my belly intensified and I bit the inside of my cheek hard, tasting blood instantly. Knowing that I was in plain sight of the front door, I crawled into the kitchen, ignoring the pain from my scrapes. I reached the cabinet under the kitchen sink, not looking back to see if Tuna was following, and swung open the door. I grabbed the first thing my hands landed on, a can of Lysol, and took a deep breath, jumping to my feet and nearly stomping on Tuna's tail. Hunched over, I scurried over to the front door, plastering myself against the wall and out of sight.

I glanced over at the coffee table, seeing my cell phone resting on a stack of books. Before I could even debate running over to grab it, the doorknob jiggled and my knees almost gave out. Biting back a scream, I held my breath as whoever was outside punched in the code to the door. The keypad dinged, and I covered my mouth with my free hand as I gripped the can of Lysol tighter, holding it out in front of me with my finger on the trigger.

This was it. I was ready to attack.

The door slowly opened and my heart just about leaped from my chest. I pressed my back against the wall harder, as if it could absorb me. Not wanting to look away from the opened door that was inches away from crushing me, I paused to wonder if Tuna was still with me. I hoped that he'd run off and taken shelter. If not, that was his problem.

The person, clearly a man, didn't even bother to turn around or check to see if anyone was home before closing the door. I watched as they opened the top drawer of the entryway table and rummaged through it before shutting it and moving on. I guess he didn't see anything valuable there. What was he expecting, car keys? Sorry bud, but those were in my purse. *Crap, my purse.* I turned my head to the kitchen where my bag sat open on the counter.

Whoever this man was didn't appear to be in any rush. Shouldn't he be storming through the house, in search of the bedrooms? Instead, he stood there with his back to me, surveying the living room. Maybe it was his first home robbery? I watched as he turned, and I tried to melt myself into the wall some more, praying I had become invisible.

I was so focused on the intruder that I failed to notice Tuna at my feet, who was purring loudly as he weaved between my legs. Dang it, why didn't he run away before? Afraid that he would give me away, I tried sliding him to the side with my foot, which he clearly did not like because, all at once, he hissed and I screamed.

Shit.

As he turned toward me, I squeezed my eyes shut, pushed off the wall, and sprayed. The scent of lemon and cleaning solution filled the air as I continued to scream at the top of my lungs. I opened my eyes and watched as Tuna leaped into the air and scurried down the hallway, his paws slipping on the wood floor the entire way. *Oh sure, now you decide to run.*

"What the hell, Maddie?" a voice yelled into the darkness between coughs. My eyes widened into saucers, then narrowed on the intruder as he waved his hands frantically in front of his face. How did he know my name?

I kept my finger pressed on the trigger, prepared to empty the entire contents of the can on him. My screeching, mixed with the sound of him stumbling and knocking into the end table, filled the room. But when the light switched on in the living room, I stilled.

"Shit," I yelled, dropping the can of Lysol at my feet. I ran to the kitchen, grabbed the dish towel that was hanging off the handle of the oven, and soaked it under the faucet. "Shit, shit, shit. I am *so* sorry!"

Dripping towel in tow, I hurried over to where Nate was leaning against the couch, sputtering wet coughs and rubbing his eyes raw. I pulled his hands down and shoved the towel in them, silently motioning him to apply pressure. If I'd learned anything from the shitstorm that was my life, it was how to react in a crisis — even one of my own making. And while I hadn't had the opportunity to actually enact any of my hypothetical emergency situations, I'd spent the better part of a year daydreaming about them. This was my time to shine.

"Are you okay?" I mouthed, and when he dipped his chin and nodded, I grabbed his arm and pulled him down the hallway, ignoring the fact that my fingers barely wrapped around his bicep. Bursting into the bathroom, I winced as the door banged against the wall and let go of him. I planted my hands on his back, pausing at the feel of the hard muscles under my fingertips. *Stay focused, Maddie.* Shaking my head, I shoved him into the shower, fully clothed, and turned on the water.

"Open your eyes, you need to flush them out," I demanded, standing on my tiptoes to better reach his head. I gripped him by the hair and tilted his head back, forcing his face into the stream of water. "Oh my god, what have I done? Should we call poison control or is that only for ingestion? Was your mouth open? Do you taste any lemon? Or was it lavender? Oh my god. Maybe we should call just in case. Do you know the number? Answer me!"

The panic in my chest was crushing my lungs, and I fell to the tiled floor of the shower, letting the water rain down on me. *Great.* There was Nate, who was probably going blind as he stood next to me, while I just sat here like a drenched rat. I hugged my knees to my chest and buried my face between them, feeling the water-logged Band-Aids start to peel off under my hands.

Breathe.

"Maddie?" Nate's deep voice reached me, sounding muffled and tinny like I was trapped underwater. I guess I was, in a way, if the spray soaking through my clothes was any indication. The water shut off and everything went quiet. His classic black Vans, soggy from the shower and squelching as he turned, came toe to toe with my bare feet. I took in a ragged breath as he crouched down in front of me. The past five minutes played on a loop on the back of my eyelids. The headlights. The panic. The darkness. The keypad beeping. The footsteps. The Lysol.

My first thought had been, "What if he's found me?"

Everything always came back to *him*.

If that were the case, the headlights would have been a single light. I would've heard the rev of an engine, always loud and showy. The footsteps would've been from clunky boots, not sneakers. The doorknob would have been broken off the door, not patiently punching in a code. The Lysol would've been knocked out of my hands. His hands would have been...

On me.

I could feel it.

Hands on my shoulders.

I jolted back to the now, pushing myself back off the floor.

The shower tiles slammed against my back.

I was trapped.

I gasped, unable to get air into my lungs.

The shower was off, but it still felt like I was drowning.

"Whoa, sorry," Nate said, his voice hitching. He shot up and backed away from me. I could hear the alarm in his voice, but what came out of his mouth next almost sounded gentle, understanding. "It's okay, Maddie. I'm here. You're safe. You're always safe with me, remember?"

Everything went quiet again, and I tried focusing on my breathing, but the silence was suffocating. I tried to find a sound to latch on to, but couldn't. *You're safe*, his voice repeated in my mind. *You're always safe with me.* My panic seemed to hydroplane, and despite begging my body to let those words spoken in his voice soothe me, I knew I was already too far gone to come back.

Nate cleared his throat, and I lifted my head to peer over my knees. He was standing in the corner of the walk-in shower, the farthest spot from me. I allowed my eyes to trail the length of his body from his jeans, soaked and clinging to his legs, to the way his shirt had ridden up in the pandemonium, revealing a slice of tanned skin. Before I could trail my eyes up any higher, he asked, "Are you okay?"

My eyes jumped up to his. Geez, he was tall. How had I never noticed that before? But then, I didn't think I'd ever been in this position before either — me on the floor, curled up in a ball, and him standing over me. *In his shower.* He scratched the beard that covered his jaw with his other hand. Well, *that* was new. I wasn't used to seeing him so...manly? I watched as he pried an elastic band off his wrist, slicked back his hair, and pulled it into a bun.

"What?" I asked, my voice breathy and hoarse. I really needed a drink of water.

"What just happened?" He crossed his arms over his chest, and I tried to ignore the way his wet shirt clung to his body, further stretching over that inch of bare skin above his jeans. My eyes locked on the ridges of his muscles, and my breath hitched for an entirely different reason.

"I just — " I paused, closing my eyes and shaking my head. "I thought you were a burglar or something. What are you doing here?"

"I live here," he said as he kicked off his shoes, which were probably ruined now. I looked up at his face, taking in his swollen red eyes. "What are you doing here?"

"Dinglehopper," I whispered, knowing that by saying that one word it was equivalent to saying a thousand.

I looked up at him, watching as he processed what I said, knowing that when we created the code word, we made the rule that no more questions would be asked. His throat bobbed and his eyes, filled with understanding, softened on mine. He took in my current state, crumpled up into a ball in the corner of the shower, and relief washed through me as not a speck of pity was found on his face. I'd never felt so...small.

"Okay," he finally said, his eyes flitting to the scar just above my right eyebrow and then to the one on my chin. Pain and what looked like regret flashed in his eyes the moment he saw them. *Please don't ask about them.* I wasn't ready to talk about it. Not with him.

Thankfully, he said nothing more as he stood there, unsure of what to do. I tugged on my shorts, covering as much of me as I could. *Crap, I'm in his clothes.* His eyes lingered on my ankle, taking in the gruesome scar that curved like a *J.* Thank goodness his shorts covered the scrapes on my knees, otherwise, he would probably think I had escaped some haunted house.

"Is that my shirt?" he questioned, gesturing to my outfit. Completely catching me off guard, I couldn't help but chuckle.

"And your shorts."

"And why exactly are you wear — "

"I'm so sorry about attacking you," I said in a rush, cutting him off. How was I supposed to answer that question anyway? *Oh, these? Sorry, but I saw them in your laundry room and they just looked so comfortable and smelled delicious and I had one of the best night's sleep in them...so could I have a new set to sleep in tonight since these are now ruined?* Yeah, right. He'd regret ever giving me his address. I took a deep breath and rose to my feet, my eyes coming perfectly level with his chest. "Are *you* okay?"

"I'll be fine," he shrugged. "I think I rinsed most of it out."

"Maybe you should go to the hospital?" I suggested.

"Nah, I'll be fine." His eyes grazed over my scars once more. He didn't hide the torment in his features quite as well this time. "What happened?"

"Don't worry about it," I muttered, stepping out of the shower.

I walked across the bathroom and grabbed a towel, wrapping it around me before tossing another to Nate. He caught it with one hand and managed to pull off his wet shirt with the other. My lips parted as I took in his bare chest. My god, I had never seen a body like that before. Sure, Griffin was built, and even his muscles had muscles, but that was mostly thanks to spending the majority of his spare time at the gym. Nate, though...he was a *man.* I took in the light brown hair dusting his chest, and I gripped my stomach, hoping to tamp down the burning sensation I suddenly felt in my core.

I knew I was ogling, but I couldn't be stopped. I hardly knew what to do with myself as I stood there, dumbly taking in his chest, stomach, the hair trailing off beneath the band of his jeans, and — nope, *no*. Not going any further. I shot my eyes back up to his face, noticing he was standing there with a crooked smile. Yeah, I was caught.

Nate emerged from the shower and stepped closer. It took everything in me to ignore the reflex to step back. In its place, something delicate fluttered in my belly. Feeling a blush spread across my cheeks and down my neck, I backed myself to the door and gripped the doorknob.

"Goodnight, Nate," I whispered as I turned and walked out of the bathroom before I could really drive my embarrassment home.

four

The sun shining through a tiny crack in the blinds woke me from my dreamless night's sleep. I rolled over to my side and slapped my sound machine, turning off the white noise that filled the room. I noticed Tuna curled up in a ball at the foot of the bed. Had he slept there all night? How did he get in here? My bedroom door was closed, so did Nate let him in? Oh my god, if Nate let him in, that meant he saw me sleeping. I looked down at my legs, tangled around the sheets, and groaned. Hopefully he didn't see anything with the lights off. When I got back into my room after escaping the dreaded Lysol aftermath, I finished unpacking my clothes and found a pair of running shorts and my sports bra, figuring they'd be comfier to sleep in than one of my dresses.

Not wanting to wake Tuna, I untangled myself from the covers and crawled out of bed. I stumbled over to the mirror that was fastened above the dresser and yawned, letting the wood's rough surface under my palms pull me from my sleepy haze. Rustling in the kitchen grew louder, reminding me again that I was no longer alone.

Oh my god, Nate is back.

And I had a panic attack in front of him. In the shower. With him. Holy. Shit. How was I supposed to explain *that*?

I leaned into the dresser, my fingers gripping the edge tightly. I wondered how long I could hide in here. Would he believe me if I said I had the flu? Would he leave me alone and never speak to me again? I glanced at the window and considered sneaking out. I could have my stuff packed up at record speed and find somewhere else to stay. He'd never know.

"I know you're awake," Nate singsonged from the kitchen, inappropriately cheerful for seven in the morning. I always liked Nate's voice. When he spoke, it instilled a sense of confidence in you. I was so used to my dad's sharp tone and the roughness of Griffin's voice that Nate's was refreshing. Soothing. "Breakfast will be ready in a few minutes."

Breakfast? Nate was making me breakfast. In his house. Where I was staying. We were living in the same house. Our bedrooms were only separated by a small hallway. We were going to share a bathroom. The realizations continued to sink in, and I gasped. Tuna sat up immediately, startled by the noise, and watched as I moved about the room.

"We're okay," I whispered, walking over and taking a seat on the bed next to him. He rolled onto his back and rested against me, his fur soft against my thighs. Still not sure how he felt about me touching him, I hesitantly placed my hand on his stomach and rubbed. His purr was deep and vibrated through my palm, putting a small smile on my face. Part of me was starting to wonder if this cat was an emotional support animal in his past life. He was so aware of my emotions and seemed to know exactly what to do to make me feel like I wasn't alone.

"Maddie," Nate shouted again and my hand stilled on Tuna's stomach. "You can't hide in there forever."

I wanted to shout back, "Sure, I can!" But he was right. I crossed the room and changed into the first dress I saw hanging in the closet. *Okay, Maddie. All you have to do is make it through breakfast, then you can come back to your room and figure out what comes next.*

"Wish me luck," I said, then sauntered out of the room, leaving Tuna behind. I swore I heard a meow of encouragement as I turned down the hallway.

"I didn't think that'd actually work," Nate said when I rounded the corner into the kitchen, sounding impressed with himself. The spatula fell from his hand, clattering to the floor, as his eyes landed on my legs. His jaw flexed so subtly I might've imagined it, and then his eyes came up to meet mine. Normally I got self-conscious when people stared at my legs, worried that they'd see something I wanted to keep hidden, but with Nate's eyes on me now, I felt...pretty.

His smile vanished when his attention caught on the scars on my face, then dropped to my scraped knees. Perfect. He took a step forward, his hands clenched into fists at his sides. "I'm going to kill him."

"It's not what it looks like." I held my hands up in front of me and took a step back, regretting the move when I remembered those were cut up, too. Sighing, I clasped my hands behind my back. Why did I have a knack for making things exponentially worse?

"Am I wrong?" he challenged, folding his arms over his chest.

"I fell and scraped my knees while I was out for a run," I cringed at how that sounded more like a cover-up than the truth. "I swear."

A silence fell over us as he watched me curiously. I glanced around the kitchen, eyeing the assortment of food spread out over the counter. Everything from crispy bacon to pancakes, sausages and scrambled eggs, French toast, and by the looks of it, Nate had been mid-omelet flip before I walked in. Behind him, a coffee pot hissed as it spewed out coffee.

"What's all this?" I asked, refusing to make eye contact.

"I wasn't sure what you liked, so I made a little bit of everything."

"You cooked all this?" I asked in utter disbelief, gesturing to everything laid out between us. I took a seat on a stool, eyes trained on the food. Everything smelled absolutely amazing; my mouth watered.

"I am a chef, Madds," he said, sliding an empty plate in front of me. *Madds.* Leaning forward, I let my hair fall, creating a shield between us to hide the flush in my cheeks. "Have what you want. The coffee should be ready soon."

"I don't drink caffeine," I said as I loaded my plate up with French toast. Was that cinnamon sugar sprinkled on top? My god, it was like he knew the way to my heart and delivered. "Spikes my anxiety."

Still not wanting to chance looking at him, I decided to focus on his clothes. A pair of gray sweatpants hung low on his waist and, not wanting to focus too long on what was level with the counter, I quickly moved on up to the white shirt that clung tightly to his muscles. Yes, muscles. I could literally see the grooves of his abs through the material. Even though I saw them yesterday, bare and glistening in all their glory, it was still a shock to me that he looked like this. He wasn't the lanky guy I remembered anymore. Shirts that fit like that should be illegal.

His hands moved to the counter, and right there, attached to his white-knuckle grip, were those prominent veins that the book boyfriends I always melted over had. I didn't know what looked more delicious — the never-ending carbs and sugar in front of me or those veins.

Not wanting these thoughts to take hold, I moved my eyes to his face, taking in his well-kept beard. His hair fell just above his shoulders and was a mess of perfect waves, his natural amber high-lights reflecting under the kitchen lights. How did he transform from a gangly guy to this gruff, husky, manly man in the two years since I last saw him? Skipping past his mouth, I continued upward and froze.

"Oh my god," I gasped, tipping back on the legs of my stool and clutching my throat. "You look terrible."

"Thanks." He chuckled, turning back to the stovetop. "Just what every guy wants to hear."

"Shit." I slapped my palm against my forehead, repeating what I'd said in my head. "I didn't mean *you* look terrible. You look amazing, actually."

Nate glanced over his shoulder, raising an eyebrow curiously at me, and my face felt like it was engulfed in flames. Why couldn't I be one of those people who blushed *under* their skin?

"I didn't mean that you look amazing in *that* way, you know, like in an 'I can't stop looking at you' sort of way," I grumbled, resting my elbows on the counter and burying my face in my hands. "I just meant that your eyes look terrible. So bad, actually. Ugh, why do I keep making this worse?"

I peeked through my fingers, unsure I wanted to see his expression. Nate was silent, but his lips were pressed together and his shoulders were shaking a tad. If he started laughing now, I would have to join in, and then I'd probably never stop. I didn't always have the most typical (or appropriate) stress responses. Instead, though, he walked over to the cabinet above the coffee machine and reached up, grabbing a black mug from the top shelf. I took the opportunity to clear my head, realizing that I'd been practically drooling over a guy I had no business drooling over, and focused my attention on the room beside us.

Instead of a formal dining room, a large white table was placed in front of a window seat with upholstered chairs on each end and a large bench on the opposite side. Built-in cedar bookshelves lining either side of the window seat were empty. Immediately my mind started to race with all the books I could fill them with. Looking down at the feast set out before me, I wondered why Nate didn't utilize that room instead of the kitchen.

"Why are you home?" I asked, desperate to change the topic of conversation. "Tyler said you were going to be away for a few weeks."

"Yeah." He leaned against the kitchen sink, mug in hand. "I was supposed to be."

"I'm sorry." I shook my head, feeling like an idiot. When I decided to pack up and come here, I didn't think about how it might impact Nate. "I can leave. I'm sure I can find somewhere else to stay."

"You want to leave?" His shoulders fell just the slightest and his gaze fell to the steam rising off his coffee. He brought the mug to his lips, and the way his throat bobbed as he swallowed had me mirroring the action. Yeah, I needed to find a new place to live immediately. I didn't think I could survive living here when every move Nate made caused my heart to stutter for some unknown reason.

"Not really," I said, letting out a breath. A movement to my left caught my attention, and I turned my head to see Tuna poking his way out of the doorway. Just the boost I needed. I brought my attention back to Nate as I said, "But I don't want to get in the way or anything. I'm sure I can find somewhere else to stay, maybe someone in town has a room to rent? Yeah, I can do that. I'll do that."

"Maddie." He sighed, placing his mug on the counter next to him. I kept my focus on the spot where his lips touched it. "Don't do this."

"Don't do what?" I asked, my voice cracking. "I'm not doing anything."

"Why are you here?" He sighed, yet again. I couldn't help but think maybe my presence wasn't welcomed.

"There's supposed to be no questions asked." My eyes flicked back to him as I spoke rather sharply. "Do I need to remind you of the rules of dinglehopper?"

"No," he said, scratching his jaw through his beard. "I'm just trying to understand how we got here, after not hearing from you for two years."

"I've been crashing with my dad for the past year. He's been helping me — " I cut myself off, unsure. I sat up straight, trying to figure out what I wanted to say. How to word this without revealing too much, but still enough. I took a deep breath and exhaled loudly. "It just wasn't working out anymore."

He lifted a brow in question, resting his arms over his chest, and remained silent. I watched him place his hands back on the counter, gripping the edge tighter than before.

"I found your address out of the blue. I didn't really think beyond getting in my car, driving here, and knocking on your front door. Tyler was here; he gave me the code to your house." I kept my gaze on his hands as I continued, "He said he called you and let you know that I was here?"

"Yeah." He nodded, watching me intently. He seemed to be analyzing my every breath and movement. I fidgeted in my seat, trying to find something to focus on. Tuna finally crossed the threshold into the kitchen and greedily ate his breakfast. Had he been watching me this whole time?

"Why are you home early again?" I asked, desperate to divert the conversation. "You never answered me."

"I'm going to be honest with you," he said, tilting his head side to side as if carefully choosing his words. "Tyler called me as soon as you showed up. He told me you were here and he was...concerned."

"Concerned?"

"He said he had a bad feeling. He didn't want to ask too many questions, afraid that you'd leave if he did." He closed his eyes and sucked in a breath. "I had to come home. I wrapped up the episode I was filming and backed out of this festival I was scheduled for. I know you didn't use the code word, but I had this feeling that you needed me. I had to make sure you were safe."

"I don't need *you*," I said harshly, and Nate's eyes shot open. I felt the fire in me start to bubble up; the same fire that appeared whenever anyone showed they cared. "I needed a place to stay."

Nate continued to study me from across the kitchen. I was regretting what came out of my mouth, but didn't have the courage to take it back. He shook his head at me in...was that disappointment? He opened one of the kitchen drawers, pulled out a roll of aluminum foil, and slid it across the counter.

"I'm going to take a shower and get to work," he said, avoiding my gaze as he moved about the kitchen. Great, I pissed him off. "Wrap up the food when you're done and put it in the fridge. I'll be in my office the rest of the morning editing if you need me."

"I won't," I muttered as Nate walked out of the kitchen. There was a pause in his step where he must have heard me before he continued down the hallway.

five

I hid in my room for the rest of the day. Tuna didn't even keep me company, not that I blamed him. I'd been pretty terrible to his human. I tried to be productive, attempting to read rather than replay our conversation, but all I could think about was the way he reacted when I said I didn't need him.

A soft sound at my door distracted me from my thoughts. Assuming it was Tuna, I hurried over and yanked the door open, eyes searching the floor. Except where I was expecting a ball of gray fur to be, I found Nate's feet.

"Oh," I gasped, bringing my hand to my chest and taking a step back. "Sorry, I thought you were Tuna."

"I'm assuming these are yours?" Nate asked, holding out a pile of neatly folded clothes. They were the ones I'd thrown into his hamper what felt like weeks ago.

"Uh, yeah." My cheeks flushed as I grabbed the pile of clothes from him, careful not to let our fingers brush. The thought of Nate touching my dirty underwear made me want to crawl under my bed and never come out. I managed to say thank you, hoping he could hear the sincerity in my voice and know that I wasn't the asshole he talked to earlier.

We continued to stand there, only an open doorway separating us, remaining silent. Why didn't he walk away? Would it be rude if I shut the door in his face? No, I couldn't do that. He just cleaned and folded my freaking underwear, for Christ's sake.

"So..." I started nervously. "I was thinking of ordering in tonight. Did you — I mean...I can order — " I took a deep breath. "You made me breakfast."

"I did." The corner of Nate's mouth curved into a grin. He scratched at his chin, his thumb grazing his lower lip. My eyes followed the movement, of course. "I can also cook you dinner."

"N-no," I said, snapping my eyes to his, startled by how suddenly close we were. I sucked in a breath, letting my next words rush out of me in a long exhale. "You've done enough, let me repay you. Do you still like Indian? I'm sure I can find a place that'll deliver. But if you don't want that, we can order pizza. Or how about Thai? No, I'm not in the mood for that. But if you are — "

"Madds," he interrupted, that crooked smile still on his face. "Pizza sounds great. There's a place in town that has the best grandma's pie."

"Perfect." I turned on my heel and tossed my clothes onto my bed, trying to not let the fact that Nate remembered my favorite style of pizza affect me. Walking over to my dresser, I grabbed my wallet out of my purse and pulled out some cash to give him. "Do you mind ordering?"

"Sure, but it's on me," Nate said, reaching out and closing my hand over my money. I jumped at his touch, jerking my hand back. Nate seemed to startle at my reaction, following my hand as I clutched it against my chest.

"Let me know when it's here," I whispered, turning my back to him. "I'm going to put these clothes away."

Nate didn't linger, and the door swooshed shut behind him with a click. Sighing, I sat down on the bed and ran my hands along the folded clothes, noticing that there was more here than I put in. Pulling my dress off the top, I found the clothes I'd borrowed from Nate underneath. I bit down on my lip to stifle a smile.

A little less than an hour later, Nate was shouting from down the hall that the pizza was here. Not taking my eyes off my Kindle, I rolled out of bed and made my way to the kitchen. I inhaled the scent of fresh tomato sauce and cheese that filled the room, and my stomach growled.

"This looks delicious." I smiled, finally looking up from the screen.

"Wait until you taste it." Nate winked and I coughed, clearing my throat. I brought my Kindle back up to my face, trying to hide my blush again. Why the hell did he keep winking at me? He let out a low chuckle, then took a seat on a stool.

I grabbed a plate and a slice and walked around the counter to join him, leaving one barstool between us. The sound of us chewing filled the silence, and I was grateful that I wasn't one of those people who couldn't stand the sound of people eating. But even still, I felt the need to say something. Nate was letting me stay at his house, made me breakfast, and now ordered dinner for us. I couldn't sit here and ignore him.

"So..." I trailed off, wiping my face with a napkin before angling my body toward him. "What have you been up to since the last time I saw you?"

"I've been busy traveling the East Coast for my YouTube channel." He shrugged like that wasn't something to be proud of, reaching across the counter to grab another slice. "And then I started my own food truck business a little over a year ago. For the most part, it's parked on Main Street in front of the town's gazebo; you can't miss it. When I'm traveling locally, I'm able to keep it there and my friends help run it. Otherwise, I try to take it with me."

"A food truck?" I questioned.

I knew all about the YouTube channel. When Nate was in college, he started it up for fun and would review the crazy things his roommates ate on campus. It didn't take long for his videos to go viral, and from there, he started reviewing street fairs, festivals, and local restaurants. I guess his channel still did well if he was traveling for it. It never even crossed my mind to keep up with Nate's Gratest Food Finds, and I wanted to slap myself for not thinking about it. I'd thought about Nate over the years, and his sister, of course. Somewhere along the way, though, thinking about Olivia had become too painful.

But a food truck? I wasn't expecting that.

"Is that what you meant this morning when you said you were a chef?" I asked, picking at the crust on my plate.

"Yeah." He swallowed a mouthful of pizza. "I was surprised that you didn't comment on that, to be honest. I went to culinary school shortly after — " He broke off, taking in the way my back stiffened at his words. "I wanted to see if I could do what all the restaurants I was reviewing were doing. Turns out I can make a killer grilled cheese, so I started up Nate's Grates. You should stop by and try one while you're in town."

"Yeah, maybe." I offered him what I hoped was a convincing smile, knowing I probably wouldn't. "I don't know how long I'm planning on staying anyway."

"You can stay as long as you need, Madds." He reached out to place his hand over mine, but I pulled it down to my lap before he could. If he noticed, he didn't say anything. "You're always welcome here. Just..." He was silent for a beat, so I looked at him, taking in how nervous he had become. "Can you do me a favor?"

"What?"

"Don't leave without saying goodbye," he said softly. So soft that I wasn't sure he said it.

"I won't," I promised.

"What about you?" Nate asked, hesitantly. "How's your writing coming along?"

"It's not. I haven't written anything in years. I can't even remember the last time I did, to be honest. It might have been before Olivia left." I sighed, continuing to pick at my pizza crust. "That's actually one of the reasons why I'm here. I'm hoping a change of scenery might spark some inspiration."

"Anything I can help with?" He kept his attention on me. "You can brainstorm with me if you want."

"I don't know." I hesitated. Griffin wasn't exactly supportive of my writing, so it was strange hearing those words come out of Nate's mouth. "I can't write, anyway, so it would be a waste of your time."

"Why do you think you can't write?" Nate asked the dreaded question.

Heather and I had been over this many times in our sessions. The fact that I hadn't been able to come up with anything had been haunting me for months. I gave myself the first six months after the accident to recover, heal, and work on myself, and then I started focusing on my writing again. I'd have ideas flash across my mind every now and again but was quick to shut them down.

"I used to be able to create a beginning, middle, and end in a matter of seconds. I could envision the happily ever after in the blink of an eye. But now?" I shook my head, heavy from disappointment. "All I can think of are the ways a person can be hurt. There are many, in case you were wondering." I let out a laugh that I knew sounded more self-deprecating than anything.

"What happened to the girl who believed so deeply in happily ever afters?" Nate nudged me with his elbow, his soft chuckle tickling my shoulder.

"Her ex happened," I muttered, scrunching up my face in disgust. Disgust at myself, disgust at Griffin, disgust at everything I allowed to happen. "That's what."

"Ex as in..." I saw him scratch the back of his neck out of the corner of my eye. "As in the past?"

"That's typically what an ex means, Nate."

"Sounds like maybe you got your happily ever after, after all."

I paused, tilting my head to the side. I hadn't thought of it like that. Had I been living my happily ever after this whole time without knowing it? I thought about the past year filled with doctors' appointments, physical therapy, and the fear of doing anything — leaving the house, checking the mailbox, answering the phone. My panic attacks were just the cherry on top.

"I'd hardly call this a happily ever after." I shook my head. "Even if I prefer being alone than with him."

"I know I said no questions asked," he said, his eyes flashing to the scars on my face briefly. "But I'm worried about you. You know you can talk to me about anything, right? I don't want to force anything out of you, so if I overstep, call me out on it. I won't take it personally. But if you decide to share what happened, you'll find no judgment here, Madds."

"Can we stop talking about this, please?" I asked, looking up at Nate through my lashes. I offered him a quick smile so he'd know I'd heard him, and was grateful he was trying.

"Of course." He opened his mouth as if to say more, but then pressed his lips into a thin line. He stood up, gathered the garbage between us, and stacked it onto his plate. "Do you want another slice?"

"No, I'm stuffed." I stood up but lingered by the counter. Why was doing something so simple as talking *this* exhausting? "Thank you again for dinner."

"It was nothing." He smiled, but this one didn't quite reach his eyes like his others had. "What are your plans for tomorrow?"

"I don't know." *Surviving*, I wanted to say. "Maybe I'll venture out into the real world and go for a run. I can't stay hidden in your house forever." But as soon as the words escaped my lips, my heart started to race. I didn't know Briar Oakes or its residents. What if something triggered an episode? I didn't know anybody here. "Actually, do you mind if we exchange phone numbers?"

"I haven't changed mine," Nate said, the tips of his ears turning a pastel pink. I couldn't think of a reason why that would embarrass him though. I couldn't think of anything that would. This was a guy who had his shit together.

"I got a new phone and number," I said, tapping my unpolished nails along the countertop. "It's in my room, though, so can I just give you mine? You can send me a text so I have yours."

"Yeah, sure," Nate said as he pulled his phone out of his back pocket. I quickly recited my number to him, giving him strict instructions not to give it to anyone. "Are you planning on going into town?"

"No," I replied, fighting back a yawn. "I'll probably just run around here."

"Sounds good." He scratched the back of his neck, his eyes darting to the floor. "If you go into town, can you give me a heads up?"

His question set me on edge. "Why?"

"No reason." He shrugged. "Just thought I could show you around and introduce you to some people."

I nodded, even though I felt like that wasn't the complete truth. Why did it seem like he was hiding something? Was there something in town that he didn't want me seeing? Or someone? *No, Maddie, you're thinking too far into this. Not everyone has some ulterior motive.* "I think I'm going to go take a shower and call it an early night. See you tomorrow?"

"You know where I live." His eyes shut and he cringed slightly, and I swore I saw him mouth the words back to himself.

"Goodnight, Nate."

"Sweet dreams, Maddie."

six

I didn't sleep well last night, and knowing the only way to cure my restlessness was by going for a run, I laced up my sneakers and slipped out the front door. Nate wasn't home when I woke up, but he had left me a note on the refrigerator letting me know that he'd be out of town for the day. Putting my AirPods in, I took my phone out of the waistband of my shorts and turned it on, only to feel it buzz for a solid minute as notifications poured in.

I had seven missed calls from my father, in addition to the ones I'd been ignoring from the past few days. Stepping off the porch steps and hitting the street, I started the call. With each ring, my heart thumped louder. I picked up my pace, falling into a comfortable jog as I waited for my dad to answer.

"Madison?" The way he said my name as if it were a question, sounded like he wasn't sure I'd be the person on the other line. His voice sent a wave of guilt through me. I didn't respond. *Couldn't*. When I heard the fear in his voice, everything in me went numb. "Is that you?"

"Hi." My voice was barely over a whisper. "I'm sor — "

"Thank god, Maddie." The use of my nickname felt like a punch to my heart. He'd never called me Maddie, not once in my

27 years. I was strictly Madison. "I thought maybe it was an EMT calling from your phone again."

I stopped on the pavement at the mention of the accident. We never spoke about it. He tried to get me to open up about what happened after I came home from the hospital, but I always shut that conversation down. I never knew for sure how he found out about it, but I guess I had my answer now. I swallowed the lump in my throat, convinced that it was permanently there now. I tried to imagine what that would've been like; receiving a phone call, seeing your daughter's name flash across your screen, hearing a stranger's voice on the other end, and then being told your daughter was in an accident.

"I texted you that I was safe."

"Where are you?" His voice was gaining strength, and I took a deep breath. "And what are you doing? You sound out of breath."

"Running," I replied even though I'd stopped, wiping the sweat off my forehead with the back of my hand.

"I've been trying to reach you for days, Madison. Days."

"I know." I could feel the tears threatening to spill from my eyes. "I'm sorry."

"Where are you?" he asked again, his voice stern. I knew I couldn't avoid the question anymore.

"I'm on a writer's retreat," I lied.

"A writer's retreat?" he questioned, not sounding convinced. "What the hell are you talking about?"

"I thought changing up my routine would do me some good. Heather was the one who suggested it." I felt bad keeping the truth from him, but mentioning therapy always boosted Dad's confidence in my choices.

"And where exactly is that?" He was starting to sound impatient.

"Briar Oakes, Connecticut," I said, then rushed to add, "I promise I'm safe," before he could get the chance to ask for more details.

"Madison." His sigh was as heavy as the frustration in his voice. "Don't ever ignore my calls, okay? I can't go through that again." I heard all the words he didn't say, and it broke me.

"I'm sorry," I whispered, choking back the tears. My dad had never come close to showing that he loved me with his words before, preferring to shower me with gifts and provide me with financial support instead, so hearing the panic in his voice made my chest feel tight. "Just...don't ask me to come home. Not yet, at least."

He grumbled when his office phone rang in the background, and the sounds of shuffling filled my ear. "Fine." He sighed, sounding defeated. "Do you still have my credit card? Don't worry about finding a job, I'll support you while you figure things out. Use it for whatever you need, Madison. I have to take this call, I'm sorry."

"It's okay," I said quietly. I had a decent amount of money saved up from my blogging days, but it was nice to have that extra security. "Thank you."

"And Madison," he said, stopping me from disconnecting. "I want you to text me every now and then. I don't care what. It can even be one of those little smiley face things you love. I need to know that you're okay."

"Sure." I looked around, taking in the fairytale-esque charm of Nate's neighborhood. I stood to the side of the road with my hands on my hips when he ended the call, grateful for the oak trees lining the road serving as a canopy, wondering if my dad would hold me to this promise.

When I got back to the house, everything was quiet. Not even the soft ticking of a clock filled the silence. Being in his house was... weird. Even back when Olivia and I lived together, I never got to see his place. His apartment was in the same city then, but far enough away that we wouldn't go out of our way to drop by. Seeing where Nate spent his free time, where he ate his dinner, and where he took a shower...it turned him into an actual person. And back then, I'd only ever known Nathaniel West as a "bodyguard" of sorts.

He was very protective of Olivia when we were in college and always insisted on being her designated driver when she went out. That protectiveness quickly spilled over to me once she and I grew closer. He was adamant about protecting his little sister from getting hurt in any way, which meant keeping me safe, too. Because if something happened to me, Olivia couldn't handle it.

Outside of the nights spent in the passenger seat of his car trying to convince him to stop at a drive-through on the way home from whatever party or bar he'd picked us up from, I didn't really know him. I had no clue what he liked to do for fun, who his friends were, what his favorite song was, or if he preferred to binge-watch an entire series on Netflix in one shot or spread it out over a period of time. Now I wondered what his bedroom looked like. Was it just as bare as the rest of the house? Did he have dirty laundry thrown across the floor? Did he hang his clothes or fold them? Was his bed always made? Was his mattress firm or soft? Ugh, why was I thinking about his mattress?

When I first arrived, I wanted to keep everything Nate-related out of sight so that it didn't feel like I was staying in his house. But now that Nate was home and there was no hiding his existence, I found myself itching to take a closer look. You could find out a lot about a person by snooping through their things.

I walked down the hallway, pausing in front of his bedroom door. My heart was already racing in my chest as I contemplated going in. Curiosity winning, I reached forward and gripped the doorknob. I could open the door a crack, poke my head through, glance around, and then move on with my life. I wouldn't technically be going in, so I wasn't really crossing any lines. *Right?*

I loosened my grip on the handle when the subtle sound of paws against the hardwood floor stole my attention. I looked over my shoulder and there was Tuna, creeping out of Nate's office and heading my way. He stopped a few feet away and kept his glowing eyes on me, waiting for me to make my next move before he... attacked? I didn't know what angle he was playing. I turned back to the door, tightened my grip around the handle, and was startled when Tuna hissed.

"Okay," I said, holding my hands up in surrender and stepping away. "I won't do it."

With nothing else to do, I needed to fill my time somehow before I eventually gave in and barged into his bedroom. Since I didn't bring any books with me aside from what was downloaded to my Kindle, I used my phone to google the local library's address. Going back to my room, I got cleaned up, grabbed my purse and keys, and got in my Jeep.

The library was empty aside from a few moms talking in the children's section, so I took my time perusing the shelves. To the left of the check-out desk, a wall of shelves held their newest arrivals. Not reading the synopsis on the back of any as I preferred to go in blind, I grabbed the first three books with enticing covers and tucked them in my arms. I doubled back and grabbed a few more for good measure from the romance section, balancing them on top of my stack and heading for the front counter.

"Hello," I said softly as I approached the librarian at the desk. The nameplate on the desk indicated she was Lorraine. "I'd like to check out these books, but I don't have a library card. I'm new to town."

"Well, then we must get you one." She beamed at me as she took the books from my outstretched hands. "I just need a proof of address and we're good to go."

"Oh," I said, deflated. Well, there went that idea. Maybe there was a bookstore nearby? "I don't have one. I'm just visiting a friend for a bit. I'm sorry, I can put the books back."

"How exciting! I'm hoping Briar Oakes has been nothing but welcoming so far. I have no doubt you'll love it here," she gushed as she started scanning the books. "Who are you visiting?"

"Nate," I said, wondering if that was the name he went by here. "Nathaniel West."

"Oh!" she gasped, clapping her hands in front of her in delight. "Our Nathaniel is so wonderful. Don't worry about opening an account, I can check them out under his name."

"Are you sure?" I questioned. I'd been to plenty of libraries before and they never let you do this. My hometown library wouldn't even let me check out a book under my own name if I didn't have my card with me. "I don't want to break any rules."

"Oh, sweetie." She smiled at me and reached across the desk to grab my hand. I glanced down, raising my eyebrows in alarm. "I'm just glad he finally found someone."

"Oh, we're not...I mean, he's not — " I managed to pull my hand free from her grip, feeling flustered. "We're just friends."

"Hey, Margaret," Lorraine shouted over her shoulder. Another woman, who appeared to be in her late fifties, popped her head out from behind a cart of books. "Can you believe it? Our Nathaniel finally found himself a pretty lady. Come take a look at how gorgeous she is."

Our Nathaniel. Oh my god, how did I get myself into this situation? I held back a laugh, not wanting to seem rude.

"Aren't you just the sweetest little thing," Margaret gushed. I looked around as she stood up and walked over to the desk. "I tried setting my niece up with him once, but he was always too busy with that fancy business of his. How'd you manage to lock him down?"

"Please, no. It's not like that," I begged, starting to regret coming here. This was why I preferred never to leave the house. "Seriously, we're just friends. If you can even call us that. He's just doing me a favor."

"Oh, no need to be bashful with us, sweetheart. Boy, you sure do like to read a lot, let me get a bag for you to carry these in." A grin took over her face as she placed the books into a canvas bag. "You just tell him we said hello and that we miss him. It's been a while since he's visited."

"Sure. You got it." I smiled sheepishly, grabbing the bag of books from her and beelining to the door.

Once I was in the safety of my Jeep, I tossed my books onto the passenger's seat. *What the fuck.* Knowing how quickly rumors spread in small towns, I wondered if I should give Nate a warning. I pulled out my phone and typed a new message.

> Me: Just a heads up, the librarians know I'm staying with you and are most likely planning our wedding as we speak.

> Nate: You went to the library? You said you'd text me if you were going to head into town.

> Me: Sorry, I forgot.

I bit down on my lip, nerves bubbling inside me. The text bubbles appeared, then disappeared, then appeared again, before disappearing entirely. Was he mad at me? Not being able to handle it, I sent him another text.

> Me: I just wanted to warn you. I read a lot of small-town fiction books, so I have an idea of how fast rumors spread lol.

> Nate: Nothing's going on between us.

> Me: I know... Just figured I'd let you know in case people come running to you asking for details.

> Nate: lol. You read too many books.

> Nate: Are you heading back to the house or planning on exploring Briar Oakes some more?

Me: Back to your house. I've done enough peopling today.

Knowing I was staying in for the rest of the day, I changed back into Nate's clothes and made myself comfortable on the couch in the living room. Tuna walked into the room, his collar jingling as he hopped onto the arm of the couch. When I opened my book and turned the page, his beady yellow eyes narrowed as if he were judging my book choice. He made a show of "testing out" new spots on the couch before eventually curling into a ball at my feet. This cat needed to make up his mind on whether he liked me or not.

The keypad on the front door pinged and I tilted my head to find Nate walking in, placing his keys down next to mine. He hadn't noticed I was on the couch yet, and I watched as he shook his hair out of its bun. My heart raced, watching him run his hands through his waves and then placing them on his hips.

"Rough day?" I asked. He jolted and turned his head sharply in my direction, his eyes lingering on the clothes I was wearing. My stomach somersaulted as I tugged on my shorts, making sure I was fully covered.

"I didn't realize you were in here," he said, walking into the kitchen and grabbing a glass from the cabinet. My eyes tracked him as he went to the fridge, filling the glass with water. I swallowed, my mouth suddenly dry, as he drained its contents. "I thought you'd be asleep."

"It's six o'clock, Nate."

He shrugged, and I continued to watch him, unsure of what else to say. Luckily, he spoke first.

"Well, I'm going to take a shower." He winked, and I covered my face with my book as heat flared in my cheeks. "Save me a slice of the pizza from last night, all right?"

Keeping my book over my face, I gave him a thumbs up. *A thumbs up?* Out of all the things I could've done, I chose to do that. It's like I could only survive on awkward moments. I didn't relax until I heard the bathroom door close and the water start. But even then, I couldn't get my mind off the fact that Nate was in there. Taking a shower. Naked.

My heart picked up as I imagined myself standing next to him, squeezing his body wash into the palm of my hand. The way his muscled chest would tense underneath my touch as I lathered his body. A soft sigh escaped my lips as I imagined my fingers lightly trailing down his stomach, following the trail of hair until I met his — *What the hell is wrong with me?* I sat up straighter and dropped my head into my hands, pulling my hair at its roots.

I was about fifty pages into my book when Nate emerged from the bathroom and made his way down the hallway. His footsteps grew closer until they stopped, and he took a seat next to me. And then my jaw dropped. Nate was on the couch next to me in gray sweatpants, but aside from that, he wore nothing.

My eyes trailed over his waist and up his chest, admiring each dip and curve of muscle. He chuckled, fully aware that I was ogling him, and leaned forward to grab something off the coffee table. His muscles flexed as he adjusted himself to face me, trying to get comfortable on the couch that suddenly felt so much smaller than it was. Small droplets of water fell from his wet hair and rolled down his body. I followed them down until they absorbed into the waistband of his sweats. I bit down on my lip, lost in a fantasy of licking each droplet off his body.

"You okay?" Nate asked, snapping me back to the present.

"Hmm?" I mumbled, taking in his forest green eyes and how they seemed to sparkle as they looked back at me. *Fuck, Maddie, you need to get a hold of yourself. He's not a piece of meat to salivate over.*

"You've got a little" — he gestured to the corner of his mouth with his thumb — "something right there."

I swiped my mouth with the back of my hand, my eyes widening as I felt the drool on my skin. *Oh, you've got to be kidding me.*

"Thanks," I groaned.

"Do you mind if I play a video game?"

"Go for it."

"Sorry I missed you this morning," Nate said as he turned on the television. "I had to leave early to grab Nate's Grates for a last-minute festival a few towns over." He scratched at his beard before turning to look at me. "I felt bad leaving when you just got here, but I figured you might have wanted some time alone to get settled and more comfortable."

"Thank you," I said softly.

"How was your day?" Nate asked as he propped his feet up on the coffee table, crossing them at the ankles.

"It was okay." I shrugged, looking back at my book. "Not any worse than any other day. How was yours?"

"Interesting." He let out a laugh that I felt vibrate through the couch. "Found out I have a mystery girlfriend. My phone's never gone off as much as it has today."

"I told you!" I shrieked, slamming my book down on my lap, leading Nate to laugh even harder. "Oh geez, I am so sorry, Nate. Is this going to cause issues for you?"

"Issues?" he questioned, raising a brow. "Why would this cause an issue for me?"

"I don't know." I shook my head, feeling my pulse skyrocket. *Great, here comes the word vomit.* "I haven't seen you in years, Nate. Do you have a girlfriend? Or someone you like? Oh god, you don't need to answer that. But what if by me going to the library, I ruined that for you? Now everyone is going to think you're off the market when you're not and it's all my fault. I'm ruining your life."

"Maddie, stop," he said, unable to control his laughter. "One, I don't have a girlfriend. And two, you are not ruining anything."

"Are you sure?" I asked, unable to hide the panic in my voice. "The last thing I want is to screw things up by being here."

"Positive," he said, but then tensed and flipped the controller in his hand a few times. "There is, however, something I haven't told you."

"Oh no," I gasped, my hand coming to my mouth. "Do you have a child?"

"What? No!" He looked at me like I had two heads, but at least he looked less uncomfortable. Nate put his game on pause, placing the controller on the table, before turning to face me. "But I do have a sister."

"Um, yeah." I blinked a few times. "I'm aware."

"And she opened her own coffee shop in town and lives in the studio apartment above it," he rushed out. "And she's nosy. It won't be long before she hears that I have a 'girlfriend' and starts snooping."

Olivia was *here*? Was that why Nate wanted me to tell him if I went into town? *Oh my god, Olivia is here.* Coming here was hard enough, and now I might run into Olivia too? I wasn't sure I was ready for this or if I ever would be. I sat up, avoiding any eye contact with the half-naked man sitting next to me. Tuna hissed at my movement and, forgetting the little gremlin was there, I jumped a foot in the air.

"Tuna, get out of here," Nate sighed, lifting him from my side and placing him on the floor.

"He doesn't have to leave," I said, standing up. "I'm going to go to bed."

"No, stay. You said it yourself, it's still early." Nate wrapped his hand loosely around my wrist, his thumb pressing into my pulse point. I inhaled sharply, pulling away from his touch, and took a step back, forgetting that Tuna sat at my feet.

I screamed as I fell backward, my butt taking the brunt of the fall. Nate lunged forward, cupping the back of my head to keep it from hitting the corner of the end table. I gasped, my eyes locking with his, and my stomach flip-flopped as his fingers lightly massaged my scalp.

"You good?" he asked, his voice barely above a whisper.

"Yeah." I pushed his hand away and climbed to my feet. I winced at the pain that shot through my tailbone, knowing it'd hurt like hell in the morning. "I'm fine."

"Maddie — "

"I said I'm fine," I cut him off as I grabbed my book off the couch and hurried down the hall to my room.

I was *not* fine.

seven

Collapsing into bed, I buried my face into my pillow and let out a groan, kicking my feet against the mattress. *Why was I such a horrible person?* Nate's been so warm and hospitable and how did I repay him? By storming out of the room the second he said something that took me by surprise.

It wasn't his fault that everything overwhelmed me.

Olivia was here. I was inevitably going to run into her at some point. And now, thanks to my visit to the library, she probably knew I was here too. Would she knock on Nate's door to see if we could pick up where we left off? Is that something I even wanted? Would she believe the rumor that I was dating her brother? I pressed the pillow harder into my face, stifling another groan. Even if I wanted to rekindle our friendship, it couldn't happen now. Not if she believed I broke the ultimate girl code.

Rolling out of bed, I dragged my feet to the door and poked my head into the hallway. I could see the back of Nate's head as he rested against the couch. He stared up at the ceiling, his hands clasped behind his neck and let out a sigh.

"Nate?" I asked hesitantly as I stepped out of my room, twisting the hem of my shirt in my hands.

He turned his head sharply at the sound of my voice, sitting up straight. "You okay?"

"Yeah," I took a deep breath and continued down the hallway, stopping once I stood in front of the television. The game he was playing was paused in the same place as before, his controller resting on the coffee table between us. "I'm really sorry, Nate."

"It's fi — "

"No." I kept my eyes on him as I took a deep breath. "You've been so kind to me and I...haven't been. Hearing that Olivia was here took me by surprise and I shouldn't have reacted the way I did."

"I should have told you as soon as I came home, I'm sorry." He leaned forward, resting his elbows on his knees. "But I was scared you'd leave because of it."

"You have nothing to apologize for," I shook my head and walked around the table, taking the seat I had abandoned before. "So, she finally did it? She opened a coffee shop."

"She did," he beamed, sounding so proud of his sister. A wave of warmth spread through me as he continued, "You should check it out, once you're ready. It's on the corner of Main, across from where I set up the truck."

"Yeah," I glanced down at my lap, twisting the hem of my shirt around my fingers. "Maybe."

Groaning, I slapped aimlessly at my sound machine. Images from last night of Nate shirtless with water dripping down his chest flooded my mind, spurring me out of bed and to my closet, hurrying to grab the first dress I could find. I needed to get out before seeing him again, because who knew what I'd do — or fantasize about — next. Being near him was confusing. Slipping out of my pajamas and into my clothes, I rushed over to my door and paused. What if Nate was in the hallway? Or worse, what if he was in the kitchen making breakfast again?

I opened the door and poked my head out. Every door was closed and the house was silent, so chances were he was still sleeping or left early again. Needing to get out of here, I bolted to the front door and grabbed my boots from where they sat next to Nate's now-dry Vans. Once I was safely on the front porch with the door closed behind me, I slipped my boots on and did a double-take when I saw the behemoth truck parked in the driveway.

I walked from one side of the truck to the other, counting not one, not two, but *four* tires. There were four tires on the back! What did he need this for? When I got to the tailgate, I looked at the trailer attached to it. It was on the simpler side, with matte black paint and wood accents. The concession window was closed and to the right of it was his logo. A white circle outlined in orange with a grilled cheese cartoon in the center, surrounded by the words Nate's Grates. Crisp and professional.

"Like what you see?" My heart somersaulted at the booming voice coming from the house. I turned sharply, pressing my back against the trailer and running through my options. He'd clearly spotted me.

"Shit," I breathed, peering at Nate standing barefoot on the porch, wearing a pair of jeans and a black short-sleeved shirt. His hair was pulled back into a tight bun, making my heart do funny things inside my chest. He leaned against the railing, a satisfied grin on his face. "You need to quit sneaking up on me."

Yes, well done. Solid, carefree choice, Maddie. He definitely wouldn't know you were just devouring him with your eyes. Again.

"I have never snuck up on you." I could see his eyes roll from where I stood. "The night *you* attacked *me*, I was walking into *my* house. If anything, you were the one who snuck up on me."

"Whatever." I waved him off, making my way around the Beast truck to my own considerably smaller vehicle. "I'm going out."

"Where are you going?" My stomach clenched at his question out of habit, but his words didn't hold any of the contempt I associated them with, so I brushed the feeling off. I climbed into the driver's seat, closing the door behind me without giving him an answer.

When I pulled into the nearest Target parking lot twenty-five minutes later, my phone chimed in the cupholder, reminding me that I had an appointment with Heather. I parked and pulled up her contact, putting it on speaker when it started to ring. As I waited for her to answer, I tapped my fingers nervously along the steering wheel. I should have picked up an iced coffee or something on my way over so I'd be able to keep my hands busy.

"Good morning, Maddie." Heather's voice was always so animated and cheerful. I wondered how much caffeine it took for her to reach that point. "How are we doing this morning?"

"I'm okay," I recited. "A lot's happened since we last talked."

"Is there anything specific you want to focus on?" I always liked that she started off our sessions like this, putting it on me to decide the direction we'd take. It made me feel in control when my thoughts and emotions didn't allow me to be.

"Olivia is in town," I said, feeling a weight lift off my shoulders. "I found out last night."

"How does that make you feel?" I let out a soft chuckle at Heather's cliché question.

"I'm still trying to figure that out." I sighed. "When Nate told me, I...freaked out. It's like any time something surprises me or I feel anyone getting close, the only way I can think to protect myself is to be a bitch. I did go back and apologize to Nate shortly after and all was fine." I took a deep breath before continuing. "She opened up her dream coffee shop about a year ago and lives above it."

"Do you plan on seeing her?"

"I'm bound to run into her eventually, so I might as well get it over with, right?"

"That's entirely up to you," Heather said. And although I knew she was right, sometimes I wished she would decide for me. "I know Olivia has always been a sore subject, but if you were to go and see her, what would you hope the outcome would be?"

"I don't know." I paused to really think it over. "I don't think I'm angry with her anymore, but it still hurts to know that she could walk out on our friendship so easily. Maybe if I saw her, I could get some sort of closure?" I shrugged despite Heather not being able to see. "When Nate told me about her coffee shop, I almost cried. We always talked about her dream of opening her café and mine of writing a book...but she actually *did* it. As proud as I am of her, I also felt sick to my stomach hearing that she was able to make her dream a reality, and I..."

"You what?" Heather probed.

"It'll be a year since the accident next week." I tried to convince the tears lining my lids to dry. "And what do I have to show for it? Nothing. Olivia managed to start a business while I made a mess of my life."

"You have made so much progress, Maddie, and I'm not just talking about your physical recovery," she chastised. I wish I could let myself believe it. "And you're starting to reach out for help when you need it, which is huge. You called me when you arrived at your friend's house, feeling the early signs of a panic attack, and you were able to work through it. That is a huge accomplishment."

"But I can't write," I reminded her.

"Just because you're having difficulty finding inspiration doesn't mean you aren't making progress."

"I used to be able to look at a stranger and envision their story. Now...I just don't know anymore." I thought back to what I'd said to Nate the other day about no longer being able to envision happily ever afters.

"And why do you think that is?"

"Because of Griffin." I let the tears fall, not bothering to wipe them away. "He was my first shot at love and look how that turned out. He took everything from me, Heather, *everything*."

"Losing someone who doesn't treat you the way you deserve or with respect is not a loss. The second you walked away, you took everything back." Deep down I knew Heather was right, but I didn't want to believe it. "If you could go back and change what happened, what would that look like?"

"I don't know," I groaned, running a hand through my hair and drumming my fingers on the steering wheel. "I can't think of that."

"Just pretend," she said, her voice calm. "When you think back to your relationship — "

"I don't," I interrupted, but she repeated herself as if I said nothing.

"When you think back on your relationship and everything that happened flashes through your mind — "

"It doesn't flash through," I interrupted, again. "It takes over."

"Madison, please, just listen to me." Her voice remained calm. "If you were to create your own happily ever after, what would it look like?"

I let out a groan and looked up at the ceiling.

"Would you still be with Griffin?"

"Hell no." I didn't even hesitate. "That would be worse than what actually happened."

If I were seated in her office right now, she'd be putting her pen down, leaning back in her chair, and smiling proudly at me. She'd call this a breakthrough.

"Let's dive deeper in our next session. I feel like we're starting to get somewhere with this."

"No, don't go!" I protested. Looking at the time on the dashboard, I couldn't believe forty-five minutes had passed by already. How was it already time for our session to end? I still didn't have my answers. "I still can't write."

"Are you sure?" she questioned. "Because I think you can."

"The blank document on my laptop says otherwise."

"Maybe you need to focus less on the happily ever after and focus on what you know and feel." What the hell did she mean by that? "I'm going to leave you with some homework. I know you work hard at keeping your painful memories away, but I want you to welcome them the next time you feel them creep forward. Open the door and let them in, then change what happens."

"I can try." I sniffled, wiping my nose with the back of my hand.

"You've got this, Maddie," she said, and I caught myself smiling in the rearview mirror at her reassurance. "And don't hesitate to call or text me. I'm always here for you. I'll speak to you next week."

"Thank you," I said and hung up the phone.

The homework that Heather assigned weighed heavily on my mind. Our next session was next week, but the roiling in my stomach made me question whether that was a mistake. Too much too soon. Ultimately, I knew it would be good for me to face my past, but I'd done so well at hiding from it. What if I couldn't handle it?

Latte Da! sat on the corner of Main Street and overlooked the park. Although I grew up in a small town in New Jersey, it didn't have the small-town feel. Everyone was always in a rush commuting to the city and made it a point to keep to themselves. Briar Oakes had everything within walking distance. It was quiet, minus the birds chirping and children laughing. I bet the people smiled and said hello when you walked past them. I pictured myself sitting at one of the tables along the wall of windows, people-watching and creating stories about them in my head.

Wait, what?

I hadn't done that in forever, even though it used to be my favorite thing. I spent the majority of my teenage years at the mall, sitting outside with my Starbucks in hand, eyeing people as they came and went. I'd imagine who they were, where they lived, their personalities, and their deepest, darkest secrets. When I met Olivia in college, it became a game of ours. We would stand at the bar and come up with the craziest lives for people. And once we started drinking, we'd be bent over in laughter at the insane things the other came up with.

A soft chime of bells rang over my head and the smell of ground coffee beans and fresh pastries welcomed me as I walked into Latte Da!, but nothing felt as sweet as the gush of cool air from the air conditioning. I approached the counter and looked over the menu hanging above on the wall, taking deep breaths with each item I read.

What was I thinking showing up at Olivia's coffee shop like this? I was *never* impulsive. Heather always told me that I could do hard things, but now that I was here...what would I even say when I saw her? Now I remembered why I never did anything without thinking it through.

"Welcome to Latte Da!, or should I say Briar Oakes? I don't think I've seen you around here before," the barista said enthusiastically, pulling my attention away from the menu. He looked to be about seventeen years old, had acne scattered across his forehead and chin, and desperately needed a haircut. I was glad to see the awkward stages of teenagehood still existed. "What can I get started for you today?"

"I'll have an iced decaf vanilla latte, nonfat milk, and a dash of cinnamon, please." I smiled at him, hoping I looked friendly instead of nervous. His focus was on the register in front of him. When he gave me the total, I handed him my credit card and waited patiently while he processed the payment.

"And can I get your name for the order?"

"Maddie?" a familiar voice answered for me, causing my stomach to twist into a nervous knot. I looked behind the barista to see if it really was her. Olivia let the door she just came out of swing shut behind her. "Sweet baby cheeses, is that really you?"

I nodded, smiling nervously at her.

She released an ear-splitting shriek, jumping up and down and clapping her hands excitedly. I laughed as she rounded the counter and threw her body against mine, wrapping her arms around me in a hug. "What are you doing here?"

"Can't. Breathe," I gasped, wriggling out of her grip. My heart pounded in my chest at her reaction. Was she really happy to see me? "Let. Go."

Finally, her hands untangled from my neck and dropped to grab mine tightly. I winced as the scabs on my palms stung beneath her touch but made sure to keep my face clear and scowl-free. I couldn't believe she was happy to see me. I slipped my hands out of hers carefully and took a step back. Now what?

I glanced around the coffee shop and at how *Olivia* it was. Nothing matched, yet everything worked perfectly together. The two farthest walls were lined with black-framed windows featuring the same white brick as outside. There was a staircase that was painted bubblegum pink leading up to a small loft, its railings painted a dark teal. That same color covered the wall behind the counter, where she had four chalkboard signs displaying the menu. Matte black tables filled the cafe with yellow suede chairs, mostly occupied by teenagers laughing and scrolling on their phones.

"Please don't take this the wrong way," Olivia said, and I stilled at the hesitancy in her voice. The barista called out my name and she grabbed my latte from him, handing it to me before pulling me off to the side to sit down. "But why exactly are you here? I never thought I'd see you again, and I'm still in shock that you're now here, in my coffee shop."

"It's a long story." I exhaled shakily. "I came across some things in my closet from when we were in college. It basically pushed me to make a spur-of-the-moment decision. I packed all my stuff and left."

"From where?"

"Home." I paused, looking down at my fingers twisting the hem of my dress. "With my dad."

I could tell she wanted to ask more, and I was surprised to see her holding back. Olivia always spoke what was on her mind. I looked at her and noticed she was avoiding looking at me too, picking at her nail polish. She was nervous. I took comfort in that, knowing that I wasn't the only one who felt uncomfortable. How were you supposed to act when you came face-to-face with your ex-best friend after two years of not speaking?

"Just spit it out, Liv," I sighed, reaching over and dusting some of the paint chips off her legs.

"I'm sorry, this is just weird. It's been a long time and — "

"And who's fault is that?" The words burst from me before I could stop them. Her body stiffened and I wanted to apologize immediately. Ugh, I was making a mess out of this. This was *not* how you won your best friend back. And it took me until right now to realize that was what I wanted out of this. I didn't want closure or answers more than I wanted her back in my life.

"That's beside the point." She looked up at me and I saw the hurt in her eyes. "I don't know what to say or do. I'm afraid I'll say the wrong thing and you'll just get up and leave."

"No, that's your job," I muttered under my breath. "I never left."

Olivia reached across our table, grabbed my latte, and took a sip. "No wonder you're being a grouch; this is decaf."

"Sorry," I whispered, taking my cup back from her. I swiped at the condensation with my thumb as I avoided her gaze. I could practically feel her eyes assessing me. "I shouldn't be talking to you that way. I'm just — "

"Something's different about you," Olivia interrupted me, looking down at her ruined manicure. "I can't put my finger on it, but...something's off."

"A lot can happen in two years." I huffed a dry laugh. "A lot *did* happen."

"Is..." Only two painted nails remained, but she continued to hack at them as she gathered the rest of her sentence. "Is Griffin here?"

I shook my head.

"Where is he?"

"I don't know, I haven't seen him in almost a year," I murmured, dropping my head into my hands. "I can't talk about this right now."

"But you will tell me, right?" There was something in her voice that made me look at her, but I couldn't put my finger on it. I had no idea what was going on in her head; that was something I had long ago given up on. It honestly terrified me. I always joked that her head was filled with a combination of Pop Rocks, sparkles, and caffeine. I missed the chaos.

"Yeah, I will." I gave her a small smile. "You're not mad at me?"

"Mad at you?" She laughed and reached out to grab my hands in hers. I let out another shaky breath. "Maddie, if anything, I should be asking you that question. I was a terrible friend and don't you dare deny it." She let go of my hand to point at me, wiggling her dainty finger in my face. "There were so many times that I wanted to come back or to call you, but I was scared. I wasn't a very supportive friend."

So that was what I'd heard in her voice. Guilt. But there was something else, too. She sounded scared. Like she didn't believe she'd ever get the chance to sit and talk to me again. All these years had gone by, and she'd been here regretting it all?

Sure, I'd admit it. I was mad initially. Hurt. Broken. Betrayed. I couldn't believe that my best friend would be so quick to pack up and leave all because she didn't like my boyfriend. I always assumed that meant she didn't care about me in the same way. See me like a sister in the way I did her.

"Olivia," I started, but she held her hand up between us.

"No, I can't believe I did that to you. I'd thought leaving would help. Maybe if I wasn't around to see what he was doing, that would mean it wasn't happening." Her lip started to wobble, so I stood up and pulled her to her feet, wrapping her in a hug. She still smelled the way I remembered, but the scent of coffee beans was stronger and the vanilla sweeter. "You needed me, and instead of being there for you, I left. What kind of friend does that?" She was breathing into my ear now, and my cheek was wet from her tears. I was glad the group of kids had left soon after I arrived or this would have been quite the show.

"It doesn't matter. Shh, it's okay." I rubbed her back, hoping to ease the flow of her tears. I'd had enough of those in the past few years. Coming here was supposed to be an escape from the past, a chance to move on. "Let's talk about something else. Anything else." I gave her a soft smile.

"Sure." She nodded. I had a feeling she'd agree to anything just to guarantee I wouldn't disappear. I took a step back to get a better look at her, taking in the lavender hair, green eyes, and colorful outfit. I couldn't help but smile at her floral skirt and bold striped shirt, and the fact she was still rocking mismatched patterns. She was an adult-sized five-year-old, unapologetically herself.

"Holy macaroni, this is not how I pictured my day going." She giggled, then took a step back to take me in, tripping over my scars. The smile on her face vanished as her eyes trailed from my forehead down to my chin. I stood frozen as her eyes moved to my scraped knees, now scabbed over. Thank goodness my boots covered up the scars from my surgery. She took a step forward, her hands now clenched into fists. "I'm going to kill him."

"Funny," I smirked, rocking back on the heels of my boots. "Your brother had the same reaction."

"My brother?" Olivia whisper-shouted. Before I could start to explain, she let out a high-pitched squeal. "No way! *You're* the girl he's — "

"Well, here's something I thought I'd never see again," Nate's voice boomed from behind us.

eight

I wobbled on my feet, working to catch my balance. Nate reached out, his grip firm but gentle as he steadied me. I quickly shrugged him off me and glanced at Olivia. She side-eyed Nate's hands, which were now flexing at his sides, and I tipped my head back to look at the ceiling with a soft groan.

"What did I say about sneaking up on me?" I asked irritably, glaring at him and trying to distract from how my skin buzzed under his touch. It had to be a static shock. People didn't go around zapping others every time they touched.

"You snuck up on me!" He shot his hands out at his side, clearly frustrated that we were having this conversation again. "Do I need to remind you of what my face looked like two days ago? Will that convince you?"

"Wait," Olivia said, looking between us. "How long have you been back, Nate? I thought you were supposed to be in Vermont. I mean, I did think it was weird that your food truck was suddenly gone when I opened yesterday. And what happened to your face?"

I looked up at him, grateful that his eyes were no longer blood-shot and irritated. I'd never forgive myself for that.

"That's a great story." His lips curved into a crooked grin, his eyes fixed on me. "Do you want to tell her or should I?"

"How about neither of us do and we forget it happened?" I took a sip of my iced coffee, closing my eyes in delight. How an iced drink could feel so warm and cozy was beyond me. This coffee was pure magic. "Wow, this is delicious, Olivia."

"Hold up, don't change the subject." She put her hand on mine and stopped me from taking another sip. "I'm having a real hard time following along here. When did you get home?" She turned her focus to Nate, who stared at her hand on mine. "You were supposed to be gone for two more weeks."

"Change of plans." He shrugged, sending a wink my way, and of course, my cheeks flushed. *Please tell me Olivia didn't catch that.*

"I think I'm going to leave; we can catch up another time, Liv, okay?" I slipped my hand out from her grasp and turned, only to be blocked by Nate. "Please move, Nate."

"No one is leaving until I get an explanation," Olivia shouted, and we both tipped our heads down like scolded children. "Sit down, both of you."

For someone so small and bubbly, she could be terrifying. We sat down and knocked knees, and it really started to feel like we'd been called to the principal's office. I wiggled in my seat, pulling down my dress with shaky fingers to cover up as much skin as I could. Olivia's eyes jumped to where our legs touched, and despite feeling like I should, I couldn't pull away.

Olivia stared at us, waiting for someone to start talking. At first, I wasn't going to say anything, but the more I thought about it, the more I worried about what Nate would say if he spoke first. I needed to be in control of this situation, but what would I even say? I sat in silence, my leg bouncing. Nate's knee bumped my thigh, the denim of his dark jeans rough against my bare skin, and it was enough to still me. I felt the calm breeze over me.

"I got here a few days ago, but Nate wasn't home. Tyler let me in," I said quickly and risked a glance at Nate, whose eyes, unreadable under a creased brow, were pinned on where our legs touched. "Nate came home the next day. I was going to bed when I heard someone pulling into the driveway, and I freaked out."

"That's an understatement," he huffed. I glared at him, but when he turned his gaze back to mine, I suddenly found the ring of condensation on the table very interesting.

"Ignore him." I waved my hand in the air, dismissing what he said and focusing on Olivia, who was trying her hardest to keep up. "When I heard someone on the porch trying to open the door — "

"I wasn't *trying* to open the door," he interrupted, angling his body toward me. His left knee dragged along my thigh as he repositioned himself so that I was now seated in the V of his legs. I swallowed, trying to ignore that spark again. "I was coming home. Into *my* house."

"Let me finish," I said through clenched teeth. "So I grabbed the first thing I could find, which happened to be a can of Lysol."

"Because the first thing you happened to see was something kept under the sink, hidden inside a cabinet," he said sarcastically, sliding his hands down his jeans. I tracked the movement, wondering how his hands would feel sliding down my thighs instead. Biting down on my lip, I gripped my dress between my fingers and willed those thoughts out of my mind. "I find that *very* hard to believe."

His hands stopped next to where I was gripping my dress, and my heart skipped a beat as his pinky slowly reached out, brushing mine. I coughed loudly, shifting in my seat and putting some distance between us. What the hell was he doing? I didn't even want to look at Olivia. I could only imagine what she'd think.

I looked over at Nate to silently plea with him to stop, only to see his eyes move from where my hands were to my face. A puzzled expression flashed across his face as he tilted his head slightly, looking at me as if he were trying to figure something out. No, trying to figure *me* out. *Yeah, good luck with that.*

"Oh my god," I groaned. "You know, I felt bad about spraying you in the face, but now I'm starting to think those red eyes suited you. Really made your eyes pop."

"Wait, wait." Olivia was choking back a laugh and not even bothering to hide it. "You attacked him with Lysol? Holy macaroni, I wish I could've seen it. Did he scream like a little girl?"

"No," I said, my stomach dropping as I replayed that night. The fear, the screaming, the shower, the way his hands felt on me... the shower. "He was silent. He'd be such a boring kill."

"Thanks," Nate muttered, crossing his arms. I turned my attention back to Olivia and not to those arms that were barely contained in his short sleeves.

"Anyway, that's pretty much it." I clapped my hands together, ignoring the huff of air coming out of Nate beside me. "Once he turned on the lights and I saw it was him, I apologized, and that was it."

"Why didn't you tell me you were coming back?" Olivia asked Nate. "Or that she was in town?"

"Because I didn't think I had to?" he mused as he stood up, placing his hands on his hips.

"So," Olivia smirked, crossing her arms over her chest. My eyes flicked to the way her fingers tapped along her forearms. "When did you two start dating?"

I choked on my coffee, wiping my chin with the back of my arm. "Oh, we're not — "

"She's not my girlfriend, Liv." Nate's hands fisted at his hips. *Woah, okay then.*

"Bullfrog." She rolled her eyes. "Do you think I haven't been watching you guys find a way to touch each other any chance you could get? And the winking, Nate? Really? C'mon, even you can do better than that."

"We're not dating," he repeated, his voice firm and words final. His eyes lingered on me for a moment longer before taking a few steps back. "I better get going, enjoy your day, ladies. I'll see you at home, Maddie."

Home.

I tried not to let the use of that word affect me. Tried to ignore the buzzing in my ears. I didn't want to watch him walk toward the door, but my eyes betrayed me. When a butt like that walked away, you had no choice but to watch. He must have sensed my eyes on him because before he pushed the door open, he turned and grinned.

"Yeah, right," Olivia snorted, turning to face me. "You two can deny it all you want, but I'm on to you."

Olivia's attention switched to her phone, tapping away on the screen. With her being distracted, I watched as Nate strolled across the street and back to his truck, where he began to unhitch his trailer. *We're not dating.* The way he'd said the words, as if something like that would never happen nor could ever be a possibility, hit me harder than I thought it would.

"So...are you just dropping by or are you staying for a while?" Olivia asked, snapping me out of my daze.

"I'll be here until inspiration strikes." I gave her an unconvincing smile. "Which could be forever."

"Inspiration for what?" Olivia perked up, leaning her elbows on the tabletop, her large eyes on mine. "Let me help!"

"I'm trying to get back into writing but every time I try, I come up blank." I pursed my lips, looking down at my hands.

"Why don't you write a romance? It can center around new beginnings, small towns, old friends...old friend's brothers..." Olivia said, wiggling her eyebrows at me.

I gasped, choking yet again on my coffee. Oh god, was it coming out of my nose? I reached across to the table next to us and fumbled for a wad of napkins, holding it to my face.

"You okay?" she asked, her eyes growing wide. "I'm CPR certified, but I am not confident."

"I'm not in cardiac arrest," I retorted, my voice hoarse as I wiped the tears that were now streaming down my chin. "It just went down the wrong pipe."

I stared at Olivia, replaying her words in my head. Oh, she knew *exactly* what she was doing. My "homework assignment" came to mind then. Heather wanted me to change my ending, to think of a happily ever after for myself. But how was I supposed to do that? I couldn't write a fictional person's happily ever after; how could I be expected to write my own? The only way to achieve that goal was if I'd never met Griffin, but she didn't want me to change the beginning of my story.

Maybe you need to focus less on the happily ever after and focus on what you know and feel.

"You know..." I started, an idea taking shape in my mind. "You might be on to something."

"I know." She rolled her eyes. "I already told you — "

"No, not about me and Nate." I shook my head. "But writing a book about my relationship..." I hesitated, before finally saying, "With Griffin."

"Huh?"

Focus on what you know...

"I have to go," I said urgently, standing up and grabbing my iced latte. "Want to come over later? Nate's going to be at his friend's house for his weekly video game night. What a nerd."

"You want me to come over?" she asked, ignoring my thinly veiled jab at her brother. She must've been surprised if she was passing on a chance to team up against him.

"Yes, I want to show you something," I replied, heading for the door. "Seven o'clock? We can order in."

"Sure...?" Olivia responded, watching me dart out the door.

"Hey, get down from there!" I shouted as I walked into my

room, finding Tuna perched on top of my dresser next to the boxes of journals. The cat, startled by my outburst, hissed in response. Taking a cautious step forward, I put my palms up, hoping it conveyed I meant no harm. "Just let me grab those boxes."

When I was somewhat confident he wouldn't claw at me, I snatched them down and held them close to my chest. Tuna seemed to relax when I backed away, realizing I wasn't going to touch him. What the hell was his problem? He was all comforting and supportive when I was losing my shit, but now he was acting as if I were an intruder in his home.

I left Tuna in my room and strolled into the kitchen. Placing the boxes on the island and taking a seat in front of them, I dropped my head into my hands and closed my eyes, hoping they might disappear. When I lifted my head, those damn boxes still stared straight at me. There were many times over the past year when I contemplated showing the journals to my dad, but I always chickened out. They held my deepest, darkest secrets. Every little truth, every feeling, and every thought I ever had were forever engraved on those pages. Truth was, I hadn't read them since.

My fingers itched to pull the boxes closer, to peek inside, but I wasn't sure I was ready. *Maybe you need to focus less on the happily ever after and focus on what you know and feel.* Taking a deep breath, I reached for the box that contained the journals to my mother and pulled out the first baby blue notebook in the pile.

"Here goes nothing," I whispered, letting out a deep breath as I flipped through the pages until I landed on the entry from the night that started it all.

Three hours later, the chime of the doorbell ringing pulled me back to the kitchen. My heart raced in my chest as I glanced at the time on the microwave: 6:50 p.m. I had an inkling I knew who'd be on the other side of the door, but that didn't stop me from padding into the living room, cracking the blinds, and peering out the window. Olivia stood on the porch, glancing around nervously, a bag of takeout in her hand.

"Hey," I said as I opened the door, not bothering to hide the relief in my voice. "I'm surprised you knocked and didn't just come in. I figured you had the code to the door."

"Didn't wanna freak you out and get myself sprayed with Lysol," she teased, stepping past me and into the house. Totally at ease, she kicked off her shoes and made for the kitchen, dropping the bag of food on the counter. "I had Thai delivered to the shop and then rode it over. Hope that's okay?"

"Rode it over?"

"Yeah, still don't drive," she said casually as she took two sets of silverware out of one of the drawers. When we first met, Olivia told me the story of how she'd gotten her license like everyone else while in high school, but after getting into an accident one summer, she refused to get behind the wheel again. She still had her license, just in case, but only used it for identification purposes. "It's not so bad, but it did take me a while to figure out how to pedal with heels on."

"Yeah, I noticed those death traps." I laughed, glancing at the Barbie pink stilettos lying on the floor next to my Doc Martens. "I can't believe you stand around on your feet all day in those. Don't they hurt?"

"Fashion is pain, Maddie."

"Don't you mean beauty is pain?"

"Tomato, tomahto." She snorted and grabbed her container of chicken Pad Thai, and then meandered over to the couch before shouting over the back of it, "So, what did you want to show me?"

I glanced at my phone that rested beside me, seeing that only two minutes had passed since the last time I checked. This had been the longest hour known to date, and I was itching in my skin. I ran my thumb over my thigh, feeling the raised scars through the thin material of my dress. *Swipe up, inhale. Swipe down, exhale.* Olivia sat next to me on the couch, the box of journals opened between us, and the last of the journals written to her in her hands. If I was going to publish my story for any stranger to read, I might as well get used to someone close to me reading it, and Olivia was the best person to start with. Knowing that Nate would be out of the house tonight, it was the perfect opportunity. I wasn't ready for him to know all the details of my relationship, and I couldn't risk him overhearing Olivia and me talk about my past.

"Are you sure?" Olivia had asked skeptically when I'd told her my plan of writing my story and wanting her to read the journals. "I don't want to read something that you forgot you put in there."

"They're all addressed to you," I admitted, not taking my eyes off the floral box on her lap. Her fingers tapped along the edges, mimicking the rapid beat of my heart. "So you might as well. It's everything I would have told you if — "

"If I hadn't left," she finished for me. Her shoulders dropped as she looked away.

"If we hadn't stopped talking," I corrected her. "At first I was angry you left, but now...I'm glad you did and you'll see why."

We spent the last hour sitting there, wiping away tears between pages. I asked her not to ask questions until she read everything, but now that I saw she was on the last entry, I wasn't sure I was any more ready for what she had to say now than I'd been at the beginning. She slowly closed the journal and slid it back into the box between us; the only sound in my ears was the thumping of my heart.

"Say something," I pleaded. "I can't handle silence."

"I have no idea what to say." Her voice was quiet as she struggled to formulate words.

"Anything," I whispered as I angled my body toward her,

tucking my right foot under me. "I don't even care if it's something totally unrelated."

She nodded her head and took a deep inhale, and then reached over to grab my hand and give it a squeeze. "I knew something was off with him. Then you show up, scars on your face and no life left in your eyes, and...I knew something bad happened." She gestured to the box of journals. "But this?"

"I...survived?" I tried to come across as confident, but it sounded more like a question. I continued to rub my thumb over my dress; the scars a physical reminder that I *did* survive.

"Your last entry was less than a year ago," Olivia noted, finally lifting her head to look at me. I winced, taking in her glossy green eyes. They always turned a shade lighter when she was emotional. I hated that I was making her sad.

"I wrote about the accident three months after it happened." I swallowed, trying to push the words out quickly. My therapist had suggested I write down what happened since I wasn't comfortable talking about it out loud yet. When I did eventually have the courage to talk about it, I may have tweaked the truth a bit. It's not that I didn't trust Heather, I just wasn't ready to reveal everything. "It'll be a year next week."

"Holy macaroni." She sighed, tossing her lavender hair over her shoulder as she slouched back on the couch. I let out a soft laugh at the fact that Olivia, at the age of twenty-seven, still couldn't curse. "I can only imagine how your dad reacted when you told him. Did he throw Griffin's pathetic butt in jail? Please tell me he did."

"No." I let go of her hand and brought one of the cushions up to my chest, squeezing it close. "You're the only one who knows the truth."

"What?" she shrieked, jumping to her feet. "Are you kidding me, Maddie?"

I refused to look up at her.

"You're telling me that Griffin is just out there living his life like nothing happened?" I watched as she paced the floor in front of me. "That he could do that to you and just go about business as usual? Why didn't you say anything?"

"I just couldn't, all right?" I swiped my cheek with the back of my hand, smearing the tears. "He knows we broke up and that there was an accident, but that's it."

"But why?" She sat back down next to me, tugging the pillow from my arms and holding my hands once more.

"I don't know...it's embarrassing." I lifted a shoulder and sniffed. "If I'd told him, then I would've had to face Griffin in court. And I wasn't ready for that. I know it's such a dumb reason, but I was scared. I still am."

"Well, I think writing this book will be amazing," she said, picking up on my mounting stress. "And therapeutic."

"Only problem is I have no idea how to spin this so I get my happily ever after." I grabbed the box that contained the journals addressed to my mom, scanning the spines until I found the notebook that documented where I met Griffin.

"What are you talking about?" She laughed. "You need to kill him off."

"Obviously that's the first thing that came to mind, too, but the more I thought about it, the more I realized it wouldn't make a difference."

"Write what you know, and by the time you get to the end, maybe you'll have it figured out." I watched as she pursed her lips, deep in thought. "It's kind of like a relationship, come to think of it. You fall for a guy without knowing how things will turn out, but you go for it anyway."

"When did you become so insightful?" I laughed, lightly shoving her with my shoulder.

"Who knows?" She sighed and glanced down at her phone. "I hate to cut this night short, but I have to open up shop tomorrow. I should probably be getting back home."

"No worries," I said, gathering up the box and tucking it under my arm. "Want me to give you a ride back?"

"No, it's okay." She offered me a shy, hesitant smile. "I'm glad you're here, Maddie."

"Me too."

Once Olivia left and I was back in the safety of my room, I changed into Nate's clothes and crawled under the covers. With my sound machine on, I tossed and turned in my bed, unable to get comfortable. Turning on the light, I pulled my laptop out of my bag and grabbed my box of journals.

Setting them on the bed in front of me, I opened up the dreaded blank document and began typing. There was a soft scratch at my door, and I darted up to let Tuna in. I watched as he hopped onto my bed, curling into a ball next to my opened laptop. Sitting back down, I crossed my legs and leaned forward, opening to the page where I met Griffin, and began typing.

Part of me was excited to finally explore this urge to write, but another part of me was terrified. Terrified to relive the time in my life when I'd fallen in love with a monster disguised as a man.

title to be determined
By Madison Williams

Olivia and I are trying a new bar out tonight. The Big House opened a few months ago and is just a few blocks over from our apartment. We've gone past it a few times, but there's always such a long wait to get in, so we never saw the point. Until tonight.

Since it's an unusually warm night for February, I cave and tell Olivia we can go. The Big House has a jail theme and they definitely nailed it. The windows have bars over them, the walls are all exposed brick and gloomy dankness. The first thing I notice when we get here is the ceiling with exposed pipes — I'm a sucker for that industrial design look. Black leather couches line one of the walls with small wooden tables, and I can already feel how comfortable they'll be after we spend an hour or two dancing in these shoes. I scan the bar and giggle at how borderline cheesy it all is. The back wall behind the line of red barstools is decked out with hanging handcuffs, jail cell keys looped around rusty-looking nails, and framed mugshots line the walls.

"Who are you texting?" I lean over and nudge Olivia, whose face is buried in her phone, her sunshine yellow-painted nails tapping quickly on the screen. We picked one of the dark wood high-top tables farthest from the DJ so we could chat. Not that my best friend is doing anything other than ignoring me.

"Nate." She clicks her tongue. "You know how he can be."

"Oh, lay off him, Liv." I nudge her again. "You're lucky you have someone who cares so much about you. My dad hasn't called me in over a month."

Nate is *always* around, and I often find myself slightly jealous over it. I don't have siblings, so I missed out on that protective brother thing.

"Yeah, yeah." She lets out a sigh, placing her phone face down on the table. "I just wish he'd let me breathe a little."

"He has good reason, though." I lean one elbow on the table, scanning the room. I can still remember the moment I found out about Tyler's sister vividly.

"Your brother is coming to get us?" I'd giggled as we'd stumbled out of Olivia's classmate's apartment. It had been our first time going out together, and I'd already known it wouldn't be the last. Olivia was fun. I'd grabbed a hold of the banister at the top of the stairs, trying to hold myself upright. "Is he cute?"

"Ew, gross!" Olivia swatted my arm, causing me to fall off-balance. The fact that Olivia could drink her weight in vodka and still walk perfectly in heels would always be a mystery to me.

My ankle gave out and I gasped, unable to stop myself from going face-first down the stairs. Bracing myself for impact, I squeezed my eyes shut. But instead of feeling the rough concrete tear up my skin, I felt something warm and soft around my bare midriff. Opening my eyes, I glanced down to see an arm wrapped around my stomach, and a large hand on my waist.

"I got you," a comforting voice whispered in my ear, and I melted against whoever it belonged to. "You're safe, don't worry."

"Whoa." I went to turn around but stopped, closing my eyes as I instantly regretted the movement. "Slow down, Earth. I've got nothing to hold on to."

"Here." His hand moved from my waist, wrapping loosely

around my wrist instead, to bring it to his chest. My fingers glided over the soft cotton of his shirt, only stopping when they felt the heart beating rapidly beneath it. "You can hold on to me."

I opened my eyes, only for my breath to get caught in my throat as I found myself locked into the richest green eyes I'd ever seen.

"Is that better?" he asked, and I dropped my gaze to the crooked grin on his clean-shaven face.

"Nate," Olivia snapped, pushing my hand off her brother's chest. "I may have agreed to let you babysit me every time I go out, but I didn't give you permission to flirt with my new best friend." She pointed a finger at me. "Same goes for you, Maddie." Now she was shaking her finger back and forth between the two of us. I swallowed, trying to hold down the drinks I had earlier. "I won't have an issue never talking to either of you again."

"I'm not babysitting you." Nate turned his attention to her, but kept his arm around me, supporting my weight. "I'm just trying to prevent what happened to Tiffany from — "

"Happening to me," Olivia finished his sentence. "I know."

"Who's Tiffany?" I asked, bringing Nate's attention back to me. "Is she your girlfriend?"

"She's my best friend Tyler's sister." I zoned in on the way Nate's throat bobbed as he swallowed. "She was drugged, raped, and killed after going to a party one night. I was with him when he got the call that they found her unconscious in her bed." He turned back to Olivia. "And I'm going to do everything in my power to make sure that never happens to you." His eyes were back on mine. Could everyone just stop moving? "Either of you."

"You're such a good brother," I said in one dragged-out breath.

"Can you walk?" Nate asked me, loosening his grip from around my waist. I took one step forward and everything started to tilt. Before I could grab a hold of the banister, Nate hooked his arms behind my knees and lifted me, carrying me to his car with Olivia following behind.

"I can still hear the panic in Nate's voice when he called to tell me about Tiffany," Olivia shudders as if trying to shake her own memory away. "If anything happened to Nate, I don't know what I'd do. I give Tyler major props."

As soon as I heard that story, I knew I couldn't complain when Nate would come off strong or overprotective. Who wouldn't be when their little sister is away at college? So when he demands that he be the one to pick us up *every single time* we go out, I keep my mouth shut. He gave us a code word — dinglehopper — to text him anytime we feel uncomfortable and he'll be there, no questions asked. When I first heard it, I laughed, but Olivia loves Disney, so he wanted to make it something she'll remember.

Olivia, on the other hand, hates it. Whenever she has to text Nate with an update, she gets next-level crabby. And if he ever gets protective over me, forget it. Olivia is a force that can't be reckoned with. I don't mind, though. Sometimes I even like it. I'm an only child with a father who only shows he cares with money, so having someone who looks out for me is comforting. I'll never admit that to her though.

"Why don't you just invite him? Poor guy has to be our designated driver every weekend, he might as well have some fun while he's at it."

"What?" Olivia's gaze moves from her phone to my face. "You're not getting the hots for him, are you?"

"Oh, come on." I sigh. "Don't start with this again."

"If I invite Nate and he comes, then I'm not going to have any fun tonight and you know it." She drops her attention back to her phone, tapping away. "He'll scare off any guy who comes near me."

"That's not true." I snatch her phone from her hands, tired of being ignored. "Nate is the furthest thing from intimidating."

"Fine, maybe you're right," she huffs, grabbing her phone back and slipping it into her purse. "But he'll give me that judgmental, disapproving look he always does when I bring home a guy."

Ever since I met Olivia, she's been single. Too focused on her dream of opening a coffee shop, she doesn't want to waste any of her time on a relationship. Plus, it *is* kind of hard to find a guy when your older brother is always lurking around, waiting to stop anyone who pursues you.

"I think he prefers to not actually know what we're up to," she says, dragging us away from the table and closer to where the DJ is. "He only wants to make sure what happened to Tiff doesn't happen to us."

Olivia insisted that I wear her black velvet minidress and, surprised that she even owns something in a solid color, I agreed. My hair, which I usually leave down in my natural waves, is pulled back into two French braids. She hates it when I wear my hair this way because she says it makes me look like I am still in high school and no one will believe that we are of age. My new Doc Marten boots are laced up loosely, and I have my oversized denim jacket draped over my shoulders.

Olivia is wearing her signature mismatched style — a distressed pair of jeans, a polka dot shirt, and a purple-and-pink striped cardigan. She's always doing something adventurous with her hair, and the flavor of this month is an icy blonde bob with the underside layer dyed blue. It's fierce and earns her many double-takes. Everything about Olivia is bold though; from her looks to her personality. She's so sure of herself, which is something I envy. I don't think I'm a boring person, but she's kind of right about my hair, among other things. I've always been too scared to take the leap.

"The bartender to the left keeps staring at you," Olivia says into my ear over some throwback song. "He's kinda cute."

She pulls back and drops low to the floor, rising and doing a silly twist that she somehow pulls off. Olivia loves to dance and makes a dance floor even where there isn't one. Seriously, it doesn't matter where we are; if there's a DJ or even if she's just humming along to a song in her head, she's always dragging me into a two-step or whatever other ridiculous move with her. Without Olivia,

I'm just the girl standing on the sidelines, counting down the minutes until she can go home.

She has this rule that until we turn thirty, we shouldn't pay for our drinks, so she always finds us the perfect guys to flirt with for the night. Her reasoning is full of holes, but it's all in good fun. The two guys who bought us a round tonight are standing nearby, watching us as we move to the beat.

"Yeah, right." I laugh, throwing my head back as one of my favorite songs comes on. I don't even bother looking at whoever she's talking about.

"Hey, I have an idea!" Olivia squeals as she turns to face the bar. "You should go get us some shots."

"Are you crazy?" I say through clenched teeth, grabbing her arm so she faces me.

"Please." She pouts her lips in a way I can't say no to. I groan as she puts her hands on my shoulders and turns me toward the bar. "He hasn't taken his eyes off you since we walked in. I'm doing you a favor."

I want to protest. I want to complain. I want to beg her not to make me. Because that's what I always do. But to be honest, I kind of want to go up to him. Olivia is always the one being stared at, whistled at, and flirted with. So hearing that someone is looking at me instead of her makes me feel special. This is a first, and I'm not sure what to make of it.

My breath catches in my throat, and my stomach drops like I'm on a rollercoaster, flying down a three-hundred-foot drop. He is *way* more than kind of cute, what the hell was Olivia talking about? Everything about him screams tall, dark, and handsome. He has dark brown hair and stubble that frames his square jaw.

He's looking right at me, holding me captive. Even if I could look away, I don't want to. I don't want this feeling to go away. Because what if I never experience this again? These things never happen to me. No one ever looks at me like that. Like they are addicted. No, that's always saved for Olivia.

Feeling a blush heat my face, I drop my eyes from his and they land on his arms. Are those arms? No, they can't be. They have to be the same size as the Hulk's. Why aren't they green? They should be green. Then maybe I wouldn't be practically foaming at the mouth in the middle of the bar. I swallow as my eyes slowly take in his dark tan skin, absorbing every tattooed inch. Part of me wonders where else he has them.

"Good golly," Olivia hollers, snapping me out of my trance. "Just watching you two eye-banging is getting me all hot and bothered. Please, do me a favor and get your cute tush over there."

"Come on," I groan, turning back toward her. "You know you're the one who's good at flirting. He'll just think I'm an idiot."

"No, you *come on*," she says, mimicking my whiny voice too well. She glances over my shoulder in the direction of the bartender, and her eyes light up. "Just go." She gives me a little shove forward. "You need a confidence boost. You're hot, Maddie. Pretend to be me if you need to, but just have fun for once."

I turn and shoot her a glare over my shoulder, but then take her advice and try to channel my inner Olivia.

"Hey." I try to sound seductive as I lean against the bar, pushing my boobs up subtly with my arms. Why didn't I try harder to squeeze my push-up bra under this dress?

Olivia is always so straightforward with guys, which is something that I wish I was with anybody. I spend more time obsessing over whether the person I'm talking to is enjoying themselves, trying to be the person they think I am, and then beating myself up mentally afterward. I hope he can't hear my foot tapping on the hardwood floor beneath me.

His eyes drop to my chest and then slowly drag their way up as if it takes all the effort in the world. I smile and say, "My friend said you've been watching me?" *Ugh, that didn't sound flirty or confident at all.* I am already failing at this.

"Kind of hard not to." His voice is powerful and it lures me in. He smirks and I swear my heart skips a beat. This bartender isn't the type of guy I normally go for, but I do have to admit he's hot. He has that bad boy vibe going that makes you want him to do bad boy things to you. I look up at him quickly before he can notice me checking him out. His eyes are dark and intense, and they look almost hungry, as I stand in front of him.

He leans in closer, resting his elbows on the bar, that same smirk on his face, and asks, "Can I see some ID?"

"Why?" I cross my arms now, trying to hide my shaking hands and the fact that I can barely breathe. Why am I so nervous? "They checked my ID at the door."

"Give me your ID." His voice sends a burning shiver rippling down my back, stopping at the base of my spine. I eye his outstretched hand and wonder how it would feel against my skin. I gently slide my ID into the palm of his hand, my fingers lingering there and mingling with his.

"So do I pass?" I ask, unsure what to think as he reads over my information.

Way to go, Maddie. Now he'll definitely think it's a fake.

"Hello, Madison," he says as he slides my license in front of me, pulling his hand back as I reach for it. I swear my name has never sounded so alluring. I stare at his lips for an elaborate amount of time.

"Maddie," I correct him, clearing my throat.

"Celebrating anything tonight or is this just a girls' night out?"

"Both?" A soft, nervous laugh escapes my mouth and he raises an eyebrow at me. "You'll think it's stupid."

"Try me," he challenges, and I watch as the veins in his arms bulge as he crosses them over his chest.

"It's National Carrot Cake Day," I quickly say, covering my face with my hands. "Ugh, I can't believe I said that."

"I'm sorry, it's what?" He laughs, and the sound has me peeking through my fingers. God, that laugh is intoxicating. How can I make him do it again?

"My friend loves to find any reason to celebrate." I shrug,

unable to take my eyes off his chest, muscles straining against the thin fabric of his shirt. "And today just happens to be carrot cake day."

"That's the best answer I've heard." I stare at the grin that takes over his entire face and have to remind myself to breathe. I feel my smile growing larger, too. I want to tell him never to stop, but he does sooner than I hope. "Do you like carrot cake?"

"It's my favorite." My voice shrinks as I think back to all the times my mother and I spent in the kitchen baking together. "My mom would make it for my birthday every year. It was the best."

"Well..." I watch as his fingers tap against the countertop before he gestures to the two shot glasses in front of me. When the hell did he pour those? "Consider this my gift, then. Happy National Carrot Cake Day, Maddie."

"Thank you," I say quietly, looking down. The way my name sounds on his lips makes me want to giggle in excitement, so I bite down on my lower lip. My pulse quickens as he reaches over and places his thumb on my chin, pulling down so that my lip is freed from the grip of my teeth. I stand there, frozen despite my skin burning beneath his touch. The noise of the bar drifts away as if we're the only two people standing there, in a world of our own. I always read about moments like this in my books, but I never thought one might actually happen to me. But here I am, completely lost in this moment, proving that theory wrong.

"Don't do that." He's captivating, and I cling to every syllable that escapes his lips. "Your mouth is too perfect."

Before I can respond, Olivia is at my side squealing, "Yay, shots!"

His hand slips from my face and I swallow, unable to take my eyes off his, my chin still tingling where his thumb had rested just seconds before. There is something about the way he looks at me that makes me feel important. Like I'm worthy of attention. I don't know if it's something I could get used to, but I'm willing to find out. The longer we hold each other's gaze, the more I feel like he's testing me, and I don't want to be the first to look away.

"Nice to meet you, Maddie," he finally says. I give him a smile and he hustles over to the other end of the bar, a chill seeping through my bones as he walks away.

"I take it that went well?" Olivia giggles.

"Maybe?" I say as I down both shots before grabbing her arm and walking us back to the dance floor. If he's going to watch me, I'm determined to make it worth his while.

Maybe that's where Olivia's confidence comes from — a mix of whiskey and boys.

It is a little after two in the morning when Nate shows up. I watch from inside as Olivia climbs into her brother's car, then I turn my attention back to the bartender. The longer I wait for him, the more I start to second-guess myself. What if he isn't single? What if he's a murderer? I don't even know his name. I back up against the wall and close my eyes. I feel someone lean up against the wall next to me and my eyes open.

"I wasn't sure you'd stick around," the bartender says, looking down at me. "My bike is parked around back. Want a ride?"

He would drive a motorcycle. If I wasn't so focused on trying to remember how to breathe, I would laugh.

"I think I'm just gonna head home," I say, avoiding eye contact as I attempt to walk away. Without Olivia nearby, all my confidence has vanished.

"I don't think so," he says sharply, grabbing my wrist and pulling me back against the wall. The fire I felt on my chin when he touched me earlier now burns under his fingers. He stands in front of me, his legs straddling mine, as he places one hand on either side of my face, caging me in. My eyes widen, and my heart pounds in my chest. I'm taken aback by the authority in his voice, but also *very* turned on.

Being this close to his forearms, I take in his tattoos. I can't quite make out the intricate designs that cover his skin, but he has a full sleeve on each arm.

"And you are?" I finally ask as I look up at his face, noticing him grinning down at me. He has this look on him, like watching me admire his tattoos makes him proud.

"Griffin," he whispers into my ear, his breath making me tingle in places I didn't know I could. His lips graze against my neck and I go weak in the knees. He moves one hand from the wall and places it around my waist, supporting my weight as he pulls me against him. *Okay, so this is happening.* I move my hands to his chest as his lips crash against mine before he pulls away. "And you're coming home with me tonight."

"The hell she is," a familiar voice booms, causing me to jump back. Forgetting that I'm an inch away from the wall, I slam against it and groan. With my hand massaging the back of my head, I look past Griffin and see Nate standing with Olivia at his side. My eyes dart to the way his hands open and close into fists at his side. "Let's go, Maddie."

"Is that your brother?" Griffin asks, not irked in the slightest.

"Something like that," I grumble, pushing off the wall. As soon as the words escape my mouth, I notice a change in Nate. His eyes soften and look as if he's been punched in the gut. But as quickly as I notice, it's gone, and his eyes darken as he looks at Griffin.

"I'll see you around, Maddie," Griffin says. His hand wraps around my wrist again, stopping me in my tracks. I swallow nervously, glancing at Nate whose eyes are fixed on where Griffin touches me. Tugging on my arm, he pulls me back to him so my chest is pressed to his, and I let out a gasp. I shudder as his thumb traces my lower lip.

"Don't count on it," Nate mutters, loud enough to snap me

out of the trance. My cheeks heat as I take a step back, and Olivia rushes to my side, lacing her hand in mine.

Nate's ushering us through the doors when I look over my shoulder, but he's gone. I hate that my heart shatters a little that he isn't there watching me walk away, unable to keep his eyes off me. One taste of attention and I apparently can't get enough.

title to be determined
By Madison Williams

From the moment I wake up till the second I go to sleep, Griffin consumes me. All I can hear is his voice. All I can think about is the way he felt against me. I've never had it this bad before. I've had my crushes, sure, but none felt this intense.

Since I've never shown this kind of interest in a guy, Olivia is just as eager as I am to run into him again. I think she likes seeing this side of me — the fun, flirty, confident, and determined Maddie that even *I* never knew existed.

Thanks to Nate's overprotective outburst last weekend, Griffin and I didn't get to exchange numbers. I tried to find him on social media, but with only knowing his first name, I came up blank in all my searches. Going back to the bar he works at is the only way to see him again.

But he isn't here.

I'm tempted to ask the bartender working tonight about him, but I can't find the courage.

"Do you want to go home?" Olivia offers, stirring the olive in her martini with a toothpick. "I don't like Mopey Maddie."

"I am not mopey." I plaster a smile on my face, hoping it's convincing. "But no, let's stay. Who knows, maybe he'll show up."

So we wait. We flirt with strangers, drink too much, dance too hard, and sing at the top of our lungs, all in the hopes of distracting me from this crushing disappointment. But even the cheap pizza and cookies we grab before Nate comes to take us home can't fill the empty feeling inside me when I accept that he'll never show.

Ugh, Nate. If he had just minded his own business, I wouldn't be feeling this way.

When he picks us up, I can't even look at him. He opens the passenger-side door for me like he always does, but I push past him and climb into the back, taking Olivia's usual seat. Olivia, without questioning it, hops right into the front and starts playing with the radio. Feeling his gaze on me through the rearview mirror, I spend the ride looking out the window. When Nate pulls up in front of our apartment, I hop out of the car and run into our building before he can say anything. I know I'm being a brat, but I didn't ask him to interfere, and now I'm pissed off.

A few days go by when I decide to stop by the coffee shop Olivia works at. My plan is for an afternoon pick-me-up to try and push past the wall I've hit with outlining my newest book idea. In need of some fresh air, I decide against taking my car, knowing the few blocks to the coffee shop will finally get me to stop obsessing over Griffin.

Why can't I forget about him? I mean, I know *nothing* about him aside from his name and where he works. So why is he taking up so much real estate in my head? Is it only because he showed interest in me? No, I can't be that pathetic. I like to think it's because I'm bothered that Nate shut it down, and I want to piss him off by going after him even more. Blaming someone else for my embarrassing mental state feels better, no matter how immature it might be.

"Wow," Olivia says as I walk up to the register. "I can't even remember the last time I saw you in sneakers. What's the special occasion?"

"Needed to clear my head." I shrug, looking down at my feet. "I'll take my usual."

Olivia gasps as she hands me my iced vanilla latte, looking at something behind me.

"What?" I take a sip of my drink, not even flinching. I am used to her theatrics.

"Is that Mr. Hotty Bartender?"

Now *that* gets my attention.

"What?" I shriek, turning sharply toward the windows. My heart leaps in my chest as the feelings inside overwhelm me. Not only have I found the person I've been looking for, but he's staring right back at me, looking just as relieved at the coincidence.

Griffin is sitting on his parked bike with helmet in hand, holding my stare. He's *here*. I've been thinking about him for the past week, but now that he's right there in front of me...

"What do I do?" I whisper to Olivia, my eyes still trapped by his gaze. I nervously take a sip of my latte, hoping it'll distract me from my heart pounding in my chest. I've never done this before, but something tells me that I shouldn't come across too eager. Even though that's exactly how I feel. All I want to do is shove my drink into Olivia's hands and run out the door. But then what?

Olivia squeals behind me as Griffin gestures for me to come outside.

"I can't do this." I panic, breaking free from his gaze and looking at Olivia.

"Yes, you can," she insists, grabbing my latte and spinning me around. "Don't you dare mess this up."

I pause in the open door, digging deep for even an ounce of confidence, before stepping onto the sidewalk. A sly grin creeps across his face as I step forward and...*Oh, shit*. Butterflies don't even come close to describing the feeling in my stomach as his eyes devour me. It's more like a stampede of elephants. Does he know how nervous he makes me? How completely clueless I am when it comes to guys?

"Are you stalking me?" I laugh as I make my way over to him.

"No," he says, his voice rougher than I remember, and I swallow, unable to control the rapid beat of my heart. "Just incredibly lucky."

"I went back to The Big House on Friday." The words slip out, and I press the palm of my hand to my forehead. *Ugh, why did I admit that?* "You weren't there."

"I had the night off." He chuckles and flashes that dangerous grin at me again. I let my hair cascade across my face to hide my blush, but he leans forward and tucks it behind my ear. My breath catches as his knuckles brush against my cheek. "Had I known you'd be there, I would've shown up."

"Oh," I say quietly, taking a deep breath as I look back up at him. I am definitely screwing this up. *Come on, Maddie, think of something to say. You're acting like you've never talked to a guy before.*

"Come on." He pats the seat behind him, grabbing a second helmet off the back of his bike. "Let's go for a ride."

"On that?" I take a step back, side-eyeing the death-on-wheels he's sitting so casually against. I've never been on a motorcycle before, and I'm not sure I have any plans of ever checking that off my bucket list, especially not with someone I barely know.

"You'll be fine," he says, reaching out to grab my hand. His calloused thumb slowly runs along the length of my own, and I shiver.

It feels like a scene out of a movie as I let him pull me closer, trying not to react as he places the helmet on my head; his fingers lightly grazing my skin as he clasps the buckle under my chin. I swallow hard as his thumb traces my jawline before he pulls away, smirking.

"What?" I grumble. Can he see my legs turning to jelly before his very eyes? I shake my hair out and bend down to tie my shoe, eager for a distraction. "Do I look that ridiculous?"

"The opposite." I startle as he revs the engine. "Get on."

I climb on behind, pressing my body against his as I straddle him. *Now what?* Looking on either side of me, I don't see any handles to hold on to. I lift my hands, my fingers shaking, and hesitantly rest them on his back. His body vibrates as he laughs, his head shaking side to side in front of me. He reaches behind and grabs a hold of my arms, wrapping them around his waist. I swallow over the lump in my throat as he pulls me closer still, my front now flush with his back. The smell of leather and tobacco overwhelms me as I rest against his black leather jacket. I am certain that if I look back, Olivia will be jumping up and down inside the coffee shop.

"Hold on tight," he shouts as he revs the throttle. I squeeze even tighter and feel Griffin's shoulders shake from laughter as he pulls away from the curb and into traffic.

I've never thought of myself as an adrenaline junkie before, but there is just something so liberating about riding on the back of a bike through the city. Or maybe it's just because my body is pressed against his, my legs straddling him as we fly down the road.

title to be determined
By Madison Williams

Griffin Jones has, without a doubt, completely stolen my heart, my mind, and more often than not, my ability to breathe.

He hasn't mentioned what this is between us, and I haven't found the courage to ask him. I'm not really sure what we're doing, to be honest. All I know is that we can't keep our hands off each other. Olivia always rolls her eyes at me when I come home with tangled hair, swollen lips, and wrinkled clothes. But even though she rolls her eyes at me, she knows that Griffin and I haven't taken *that* step yet.

Olivia doesn't like Griffin, despite her being the reason we're together. Whenever he leaves our apartment, on the rare occasion when he doesn't stay over, she gives me this look that makes me wish we weren't roommates.

"I hate the way he looks at you," Olivia would say. "It's like he wants to devour you."

"You're crazy." I'd always laugh, shaking my head at her theatrics. "Maybe you should stop watching vampire movies with me so much."

She's been coming home later and later, hoping to avoid him

or hoping that we're already in bed asleep. When we wake up in the morning, she's usually already gone. I try not to think that Griffin could be driving a wedge between us, but it's becoming more and more difficult.

So imagine my surprise when I find out that Olivia and Griffin are working together to throw me a surprise party. I expertly extracted the secret and demanded Griffin spill some details, but I won't let Olivia know. I don't want to give her another reason to not like him.

Today's my twenty-fifth birthday, and Griffin's picking me up early for a surprise adventure before the *surprise* surprise. Normally, I spend my birthday with Olivia and we go shopping, dance around the apartment, order takeout, and end the day with my favorite: carrot cake. Being a girl set on routine, I'm an anxious mess.

"Can you tell me what we're doing *now*?" I plead as I try smoothing down my hair. We just went on a long ride outside the city, and I can only imagine how windswept my hair is. If I knew what today would have entailed, I would've pulled my hair back into a braid to tame it.

"You'll see." He grips my hand and pulls me close against his body, crushing his mouth against mine. His kisses are always rough, and I can only imagine what they look like to people passing by. I melt into his chest as his hands guide mine to his waist, letting go just so he can place his on the small of my back. A shiver runs down my spine as his other hand tangles itself in my hair, his teeth grazing my bottom lip.

"Griffin, come on," I manage between kisses. His hand slides from my lower back to my leggings, where he grips my butt. "People are watching."

"So?" He pulls back to look at me. There's a hunger in his eyes that only means one thing. I squeal as he lifts me up and sits me on his bike. "Let them watch."

"Stop," I breathe as I manage to evade his next kiss, but his lips only move to my neck. He nibbles on my ear, and I let out a soft moan. Griffin growls in response, stepping between my legs. "I want to know what you were dying to show me, please?"

"Fine." He tugs on his jeans as he adjusts himself, and my cheeks heat as I glance down, registering the effect I have on him. "But when we get back to your place later, we're finishing this."

"Griffin," I groan, already missing the absence of his body against mine. "Please don't push it."

"You're killing me, babe."

"I'm sorry." I sigh, resting my head against his chest. To be honest, I'm not sure why I'm dragging out the inevitable. It's not that I don't want him, because trust me, I *really* do. But I like the anticipation. I like the tension and buildup. I like having something to look forward to with him. Once that's gone, there's no getting it back. "And besides, I can't be late to my own party."

"Sure you can." He laughs, placing one last kiss on my neck.

It takes us almost two hours to complete the hike, but in our defense, we stop to take a lot of breaks. When we reach the end of the trail, my jaw drops as I take in the beautiful skyline. Despite living here since I graduated high school, I never took the time to appreciate the beauty of what I call home. I'm always so preoccupied with my daily routine, my schedules, and checking off the next item on my to-do list.

Griffin comes up behind me and wraps his arms around my chest, pressing my back against his front. I smile as he rests his chin on top of my head, feeling as if I can stay here forever, wrapped in his strong arms. Closing my eyes, I let the breeze whisper across my face as I focus on the sound of his steady breaths and how he always smells like crisp leather and smoke.

"Happy birthday, Maddie," he whispers in my ear, planting a soft kiss on my earlobe. I feel him chuckle against me when goosebumps erupt over my skin. Griffin loves the effect he has on me and my inability to hide it.

We stay at the end of the trail for what feels like forever. Other people come and go, but we're so locked into each other that we don't notice. Griffin does that to me. I become so absorbed in him that the world around me disappears. Maybe I'm falling too hard and moving too fast, but how am I supposed to know? He's the first guy I've really ever dated. We eventually pull ourselves off each other and to his bike so that I can get ready for my party.

When I walk into The Big House, I do my best to act surprised. Gold balloons line the ceiling with matching ribbons draping down, confetti covers every inch of the bar and tabletops, there's a candy table against one of the walls, and my favorite music is blasting. After I say a few hellos and accept about a dozen happy birthdays, Olivia pulls me aside and hands me a champagne-colored sequin dress to change into. It falls mid-thigh and clings to my body, has a deep V-neck that makes it impossible to wear with a bra, and sheer sleeves with rhinestones that end at my elbows.

"This dress is perfect," I squeal as I turn to face Olivia in the bathroom of the bar. I run my fingers over the crystals that look like they're floating on my arms and smile. "Thank you so much!"

"There's something I have to tell you though." She bites her lip and turns her attention away from me, hesitating. "There was a mix-up with the cake."

"What do you mean?" My stomach drops at her words. With just one look at Olivia, I know instantly what it is. *Carrot cake.*

"I put Griffin in charge of the cake. I am so sorry. I should have known better. I feel like the absolute worst friend ever."

"It's fine." I square my shoulders in hopes that it'll ease the disappointment from the pit of my stomach. Turning to face the mirror, I try on different smiles to help pull me back into party mode. "It's just cake."

"Are you sure?" She doesn't sound convinced.

"Positive." I link my arm with hers and pull her toward the door, not wanting to continue this conversation. The bigger deal we make out of this, the more likely I'll break. "Come on, let's dance."

We spend the next hour dancing, letting the music transport us somewhere else. We don't care that everyone else is standing around, enjoying the free booze and food rather than joining us. We're used to this. It feels like a normal Saturday night for us, aside from the fact that we no longer need to flirt for our drinks anymore. To be honest, I would have been fine with just going to the bar like usual. They didn't have to close it down and fill it with our friends. All I need is Griffin and Olivia.

"I have to pee," Olivia shouts in my ear. "I'll be right back."

Standing awkwardly in the middle of the bar, I twist my fingers as I try to find Griffin. First, I glance at the bar, hoping to see him there, but when I don't, my heart speeds up. Where is he? Biting my lip, I turn on my heel and gasp when I'm pulled against someone's body.

"Finally." Griffin's breath is hot on my neck. His hands land on my shoulders and slide their way down the rhinestones on my arms until they reach my wrists. "I thought I'd never get you to myself tonight."

He spins me around and walks us backward until my heels touch the wall. His gaze drifts to my chest, and I watch as he licks his lower lip. I'm aware of every part of his body that touches mine and how it feels like small flames between our skin. He moves his hands from my wrists and reaches behind me, grabbing my butt with one hand so hard that I gasp. His other hand moves to the back of my neck, angling my head back.

My breath is heavy as I whisper, "Kiss me."

He crashes his lips against mine, hungrier than I've ever felt them before. I pull away, gasping for air as he moves his mouth to my chin, kissing along my jawline until he reaches my ear. His kisses tend to make my mind go fuzzy, and I need to get some fresh air before we get carried away. The room feels twenty degrees warmer than it did a few minutes ago as Griffin's lips skim down my neck to my collarbone.

"We need to go." I manage to pull his head back up to mine,

pressing my forehead against his and closing my eyes to catch my breath. When I open them and lock my eyes with his, they're the darkest I've ever seen them. "Now."

"But your party," he pouts, mimicking me from earlier today. "You can't miss your party."

"I made my appearance, everyone's seen me." I shrug and pull his mouth to mine one more time. I suck his bottom lip into my mouth, letting my teeth graze against it as I slowly pull back. Grabbing my hand, Griffin pulls me toward the entrance. Knowing I'll need it, I snatch some champagne on the way out and tip the glass back, letting the bubbles fizzle down my throat. "Oh, wait! I forgot my purse."

"I'll meet you out front," Griffin says, planting another demanding kiss on my lips. His voice is raspy and needy, as if walking away from me is the hardest thing in the world. "Keep those dirty thoughts in your head, okay? I don't want you changing your mind."

After ditching the empty champagne flute and grabbing my purse from where I stashed it, I head to the door. I pull my phone out of my bag and open a text to Olivia, ready to type out an apology for leaving when I almost trip over my feet. My phone falls from my hands but is caught before it hits the floor.

"Oh my god, thank you," I say, my hand flying to my chest in relief before I grab my phone from their hand. Looking up, I find myself in front of Nate. "Oh, it's you. What are you doing here?"

"Hey, umm. Happy birthday, Madds." He smiles and scratches the back of his neck. Did Olivia invite him? I want to ask, but I'm distracted by the wrapped gift in his outstretched hand. He got me a present? I take the wrapped box from him and rotate it in my hands.

"You got me a gift?" I question, looking up at him. "Why?"

"You're my little sister's best friend," he says the words evenly, but then looks down at his shoes. I catch the tips of his ears stinging red and bite my tongue. I follow his gaze down to his black Vans, watching as he shifts on his feet. I don't think I've ever seen Nate nervous. "If you're happy, then she's happy."

"Oh." I look back up at him, watching as he runs a hand through his short wavy hair. The lighting in the bar accentuates the streaks of gold and amber in his hair, something I've never noticed before. He has the type of natural highlights that any girl would kill for. The air feels different as I stand in front of him, and maybe it's the alcohol talking, but I ask, "Are you sure that's it?"

"What else would it be?"

"I don't know," I say, looking up at him through my lashes playfully. Yup, I blame the champagne. What am I doing? Just a few minutes ago I was ready to drag Griffin into the alley, and now I'm lingering in the bar, having far too much fun teasing Nate.

I turn the present over in my hands, admiring the polka dot wrapping paper that covers it. Not wanting to wait any longer, I pull on the pink ribbon and tear off the paper. When I see the fabric jewelry box, I gasp. My fingers brush over the embroidered M on the lid before lifting it and finding a dainty bracelet inside. I trace the charms dangling from the gold chain, my fingers shaking as they pass over different charms: a bookstack, an open book, a steaming cup, a cursive M, and...my breath catches as I land on a fork.

"It's perfect," I whisper, blinking back tears. How did he manage to pick out the perfect gift? Every charm on this bracelet was so personal and...*that fork*. How did he find a dinglehopper? It's so...*us*. Did he have this custom-made? I have so many questions, but I can't find the words to ask them.

The rev of Griffin's bike echoes in the vestibule of the bar, bringing me back to reality. I peer around Nate's shoulder, seeing him pull up along the curb. With shaking fingers, I place the bracelet back into the box and shove it into my purse where Griffin won't find it. I'm not sure why I have this thought, but I don't have time to unpack it. "I have to go."

"You're leaving?" he asks, reaching out and placing his hand on my arm to stop me. His thumb swipes along the rhinestones of my dress, causing goosebumps to flare up my arm. I shrug out of his hold, trying not to think about my reaction to his touch.

"Tell Olivia I'm sorry," I say as I push past him, ignoring the jolt of electricity I felt when my shoulder brushed his arm.

When I reach Griffin's bike, he hands me my helmet silently.

"Everything okay?" I ask before putting the helmet on. When he doesn't answer, I reach over and place my hand on his shoulder, trying to turn him toward me. "Hey, what's wrong?"

"Who were you talking to?" he asks, staring straight ahead. His voice is sharp and almost accusatory. I glance to where his hands are gripping the handles with white knuckles.

"Olivia's brother," I say, looking back at the bar, expecting to see Nate still standing there, but he's gone. "Why?"

"Did you tell him to come?" His head turns in my direction, and the look in his eyes has me taking a step back. I've never seen them so dark. The goosebumps return to my arms, but for an entirely different reason this time.

"No." I run my hand up and down my arm as though trying to smooth out my skin. "I had no idea he was coming; I swear."

"I hate that guy." My attention flashes to his hands again. Before I can open my mouth to reassure him that he has nothing to worry about, Griffin asks, "What did he say to you?"

"Happy birthday?" I say with a nervous laugh, hating how it comes out more like a question than a fact. I'm becoming more and more confused, but it's almost like I'm watching this argument from a bird's eye.

"Are you sure?" he asks, and I nod, barely able to breathe. Griffin keeps his eyes on mine as he reaches out for my hand. His fingers overlap mine tightly, tugging me to his side. "You look far too beautiful tonight, sorry for not wanting to share."

I grin, relief washing over me at the sound of his tone, back to normal and filled with mischief. *This* is the Griffin I know. "Take me home and you won't have to worry about sharing, then."

He takes the helmet from my hand and places it on my head, his thumb tracing my lower lip before letting go. "Get on the bike, Maddie."

nine

I woke up with my journals fanned out around me, my laptop opened, and my sound machine blaring. Shooting up in bed, I quickly shoved them back into their box, not worrying about their order. How could I have been so stupid as to fall asleep with them out in the open? What if Nate had come in and seen them? Glancing around, I saw Tuna stretched out on the floor beneath the window and relaxed. Nate wouldn't have come in except to let Tuna out.

I reached back inside and grabbed the jewelry box, taking the charm bracelet out. I unclasped it and fastened it around my wrist, feeling my pulse flutter beneath it. Lifting it to my face, I looked at the dainty charms that dangled from it. I still couldn't believe how much it shined despite being tucked away and hidden for so many years. I hadn't let myself think about its significance until the words started pouring out of me last night. Even back then, it was clear that Nate had always seen me for exactly who I was. I could see that now.

Huh. Surely that's progress, right?

I glanced at my phone and saw that it was almost one in the afternoon. Hopping out of bed, I threw on a dress and grabbed my library book off the dresser, deciding I'd spend the rest of the day curled up on the porch swing.

Hours later, and I couldn't focus on a single thing in the pages of my paperback. Swaying in the shade of an old oak, I let myself imagine how much homier Nate's house could be if he put a little effort into it. My mind flooded with so many plans to turn this house into a dream, and I had to stop myself before I did something crazy like get in my Jeep and drive to HomeGoods. There was no point in dreaming when I had no clue how long I'd even be here.

Would I stay until I finished writing my book? Would I stay in Briar Oakes forever? I knew I couldn't just throw myself at Nate like that and become his permanent roommate. This had to be temporary. I shook my head and opened my book, sliding the library receipt I was using as a bookmark down the page as I read. I settled into the swing and began rocking, letting the words on the page transport me to another place and transform me into someone else.

A flash of bright lights beamed on the porch, blinding me and making me aware of how late it'd gotten. Dropping my book onto my lap, I slid down and lay flat on the swing, eyes wide and alert. The sound of tires rolling over the gravel driveway silenced the crickets and cicadas. I hoped that whoever was out there couldn't see me. My heart pounded in my chest, and I gripped the edge of the swing.

"You're fine, Maddie," I whispered to myself as I closed my eyes. "Just breathe."

"Maddie?" I heard a deep voice call out into the darkness. The beating of my heart was so loud in my chest, and I was too focused on my breathing to tell if I recognized the voice. Every sound became warbled, and my brain screamed *danger*.

Gravel crunching beneath someone's feet rang in my ears. The thumping of footsteps on the porch overwhelmed me. It was as if the sound pressed down on me, suffocating and preventing me from getting up. I twisted side to side on the swing and covered my face with my arms, trying to get rid of this feeling.

Breathe, Maddie, just breathe.

"Maddie," the same voice from before said my name again, but this time it sounded like shouting. Why did they know my name? The footsteps grew quicker and louder as if they were running. And then they stopped.

I squeezed my eyes shut tighter as I kept my arms crossed over them, muttering for the man to go away. He kept saying my name, over and over, as if trying to get me out of this attack I was in. The voice was closer but softer than before. Almost a whisper in my ear. Whoever this person was, he needed to go away. What if I opened my eyes and it was Griffin? A sob escaped my lips, and I wished whoever it was would just do whatever they came for and leave.

Hands.

There were hands on my wrists.

They were pulling me.

I tried backing up, but I was lying down.

There was nowhere to go.

I was trapped.

I gasped.

I gave in.

My arms were lowered and placed at my side.

"Maddie." The voice was in my ear again. His hands were still on my wrists. "It's Nate. I'm here. You're safe."

Nate? No, it couldn't be. I'd recognize his voice. I'd recognize his truck. But those lights, they were so bright. I'd let my panic overwhelm my senses. My eyes fluttered open and I turned my head, taking in the concerned forest green eyes that stared back at me.

You're safe.

I was safe.

"Nate!" I gasped, and before I processed what I was doing, I propelled myself off the swing and into his arms. I heard and felt the air knock out of him as I collided into him. Nate's arms wrapped around me protectively, making it impossible for him to stop us from tumbling backward onto the porch floor. "It's you."

Nate was still beneath me and I was too afraid to lift my head from where I had it tucked into his neck to see if he was okay. *Oh my god, what if I knocked him out?* I focused on my breathing, hoping that it would bring me back to my senses, but as soon as I took a deep breath in, Nate's scent overtook me. His arms tightened around me and I sighed in relief, feeling my body melt against his. There was something about being in Nate's arms that felt oddly like home.

Holy crap, this felt good. One of Nate's hands trailed up my back and tangled itself in my hair, lightly massaging my scalp, fusing my body to his. Strong and warm, I let myself imagine them —

"Oh my god," I gasped, coming out of the trance I was under. I pushed myself off him and crab-walked until my back hit the door. My hand flew to my mouth as I registered the fact that my entire body was just pressed against his. His eyes darted to my leg and narrowed. I looked down, noticing that my dress had slid its way up toward my hip. Quickly, I grabbed the hem of my dress and pulled it down. "I am *so* sorry."

"What just happened, Maddie?" he asked hesitantly as he sat up, looking me straight in the eyes.

Yeah, I'm wondering the same thing.

His eyebrows pulled together, and I swallowed as I felt his eyes trail down my body and land on my right leg, trembling against the planks of the porch. Nate pursed his lips as he stretched his legs out, putting just enough pressure against mine to stop me from shaking. I glanced up at his face, watching as his lip twitched at the corner. Seeing him fight back a smile, eyes warm and genuine, was like a balm over my nerves, and I sighed deeply.

My teeth raked over my bottom lip as I tried to think of a way out of that question. This was now the second time I had what I classified as a level-ten panic attack in front of him. I bet when Nate told me to just "say the word" and he'd come get me, he never thought it would result in this.

"I was reading a book," I said, trying to mask the way I was falling apart on the inside. I turned my attention away from him and focused on my book which was now flat on the ground with my bookmark off to the side. "Ugh, now I lost my place."

"Are you seriously worried about your book right now, Madds?" He gently nudged his foot against mine. I looked over and saw the same unreadable expression still plastered across his face. "What just happened?"

"I was so lost in my book," I said quietly, almost a whisper, as I looked down at the hem of my dress. I grasped it in my fingers and began twisting it, focusing all my attention on how it wrinkled beneath my touch. "I get really wrapped up in the characters and the setting sometimes. So, when you pulled into the driveway, it startled me. I got sucked back into reality, and it just took me a bit to adjust."

"That was more than just adjusting."

"Just stop, Nate." I sighed and pushed to my feet. I could feel my walls coming back up and closed my eyes, letting the shame in. I picked up my book, flattening the pages out. "I don't want to talk about it."

"Okay." I stood there, clutching my book to my chest, surprised that he was willing to drop it so easily. He was making it harder and harder to cling to old habits when he showed me how patient he could be. I watched as Nate picked up my library receipt as if in slow motion and looked it over. "You checked these books out under my name?"

"Yeah, about that..." I laughed nervously. "I went to the library with the full intention of opening an account, but I don't exactly live here. Once I told them I was staying with you, they said I could just check out the books under your name."

"Is that even allowed?"

"I don't know," I said honestly. "But don't worry, I've never been late on returning them, so I won't rack up fees for you."

"You keep these things?" Nate asked, his focus on the slip in his hands. "They send texts now to remind you when your library book is due, you know."

"It's my bookmark," I said as I snatched it from his hands, but he didn't seem to hear me as he reached forward and gripped my arm. My heart thumped heavily in my chest as I held my breath, watching as his thumb ran along the charm bracelet that dangled from my wrist.

He dropped my wrist but kept his attention on the bracelet, seemingly lost in his thoughts. I covered it with my hand, hoping that if he couldn't see it, he wouldn't ask about it. Did he remember the night he'd given it to me? Was he surprised that I still had it? Did he like seeing it on me? Or did it remind him of the night I'd brushed him off even though I'd been stunned at the thoughtful gesture? *Ugh, why do I even care?* It was just a bracelet. It meant nothing.

"Your bookmark?" Nate questioned, bringing me back to our conversation.

"Yeah, I don't dog-ear pages." I shuddered at the thought. People who destroyed books like that couldn't be trusted. "I just use whatever is lying around. Receipts, old gift cards, a piece of paper, a bobby pin…One time I used a leaf."

"I'm surprised you don't have a collection of fancy book-marks," he said as he walked past me to open the front door. Okay, guess we weren't acknowledging the bracelet. *Phew.* I followed him inside and closed the door.

"I lose them too easily to waste money on them, and besides, these work just fine." I sat down on the couch, stretching myself across the cushions. Opening my book, I flipped through the pages and tried to find where I had left off. The sounds of pots and pans clinking together reached me from the kitchen. I looked over the side of the couch, trying to see what Nate was up to. "What are you doing over there?"

"Making dinner," he said as he pulled out the ones he needed from the cabinet beside the stove. "Are you hungry?"

"No, I'm good," I replied, despite having not eaten all day. Finally finding the spot where I left off, I slipped my bookmark in and swapped my book out for the remote. "I'm really tired," I said through a yawn. My panic attacks had a way of making me crash hard. "Just gonna try to catch up on some of my shows before I inevitably pass out."

"I'll still make enough and put it in the fridge, in case you change your mind later."

"Thanks." I smiled at him. The flutters I felt in my stomach whenever Nate was around were back, but this time they felt more like a flock of birds. *Don't think too much into it, Maddie, you're just not used to a guy being nice.*

Yeah, that had to be it.

Something soft brushed against my hand, waking me up. I looked down and saw Tuna rubbing his head against my dangling arm. When I scratched him behind his ear, he looked at me and hopped up between my legs, purring and kneading his paws. I sat up in alarm, realizing I wasn't in my room and had fallen asleep on the couch. I reached over the arm of the couch, turning on the small lamp on the end table. The throw blanket that was usually folded at the end of my bed was draped over me, and my sound machine was plugged in and sitting on the coffee table.

I was at a loss for words. How did Nate even know I needed my sound machine? I glanced around the empty room and gripped the blanket in my fists, bringing it up to my face as I tried to process how this made me feel. I wanted to kick my feet and giggle from giddiness as I thought of Nate going to shut off the lights, noticing that I had fallen asleep on the couch. I wondered what he thought as he draped the blanket over my body.

I looked over to the coffee table, seeing my cell phone resting atop my library book. I lifted my legs over the cat and sat up, reaching over to turn off the white noise. I grabbed my book from under my phone and noticed that my library receipt was nowhere to be found.

"Great," I groaned. I tried to remember the last thing I read, but when I opened the book, there was a new bookmark in the exact spot where I'd left off. With shaky fingers, I lifted the index card that was covered in Nate's handwriting.

Do something that makes you smile today.
The only thing more incredible than
your smile is... Nope. Never mind.
Haven't found anything yet.
—Nate

ten

Olivia didn't hesitate to merge me into her life. Even though I'd only been back in her life for a little over 24 hours, she already planned a night out to meet her friends, Daniella and Zo. Daniella was Olivia's hairdresser and Zo was her assistant manager. I didn't know how to say no, especially since I didn't want to disappoint her so soon after reuniting.

I was anxious, more so than usual; I hated meeting new people and struggled to trust anyone new. As I slipped on my boots and looked in the mirror, my stomach dropped.

The last time I was at a bar, it had been Griffin's.

The last time I was at a bar, everything changed.

The last time I was at a bar, he'd taken things too far.

The last time I was at a bar, I didn't know if —

Don't go there.

"Okay, Maddie," I said to my reflection, tucking my bra straps underneath the poofy short sleeves of my blue gingham dress. I looked like Dorothy from *The Wizard of Oz* who'd traded in her ruby slippers for a pair of Doc Martens. "All you have to do is make it through a few hours tonight. Pretend it's just you and Olivia, let her do all the talking, and follow her lead. You can do this."

I locked the front door behind me and hurried down the porch steps. When I reached my Jeep, I stopped short when I saw that the front tire was flat.

"Are you kidding me?" I groaned, and not knowing what else to do, I kicked the tire and headed back to the porch to sit on the swing. Not wanting Olivia to think I was bailing, I pulled my phone out of my dress pocket and typed in Latte Da!'s address. Seeing that it was only a fifteen-minute walk, I opened my messages and sent Nate a text. He was already gone when I woke up this morning, leaving a sticky note on the counter saying he was going to be away most of the day filming. I didn't want him to worry if he came home and found my car parked in the driveway but the house empty.

> Me: Hanging out with Olivia tonight. Tires flat, so I'm walking to her place. Have a good night!

Now that someone knew where I was headed, I hurried down the porch steps and started down the driveway, keeping my phone clutched tightly to my chest. Even though it was still light out and I could see all my surroundings, I could never be too cautious.

"What took you so long?" Olivia asked, pulling me into a hug when I stepped into the coffee shop where she and her friends waited. "And why are you walking?"

"Flat tire." I sighed, pulling out of her embrace. "I didn't want to cancel on you, so I walked."

"Guys," Olivia shouted, pulling me toward her friends. "This is my best friend, Maddie. Maddie, these are my other best friends."

"Hi, I'm Daniella," said a girl with a sleek jet-black bob. She wore an oversized white T-shirt dress with a black belt around the middle. "I'm so excited to meet you! I'm the head stylist at The Chop Shop so if you ever want to do something with your hair, I'll give you the friends and family discount."

I nodded in thanks, taking in how her fingers wiggled in excitement at her sides. She was probably the type of hair stylist who spent the entire appointment talking, regardless of how clear you made it that you didn't want to be there. A diamond ring sparkled on her manicured finger, distracting me from whatever else she was saying.

"And I'm Zo," her other friend introduced themself, putting her fist out so I could bump it. I assumed she was going for a handshake, which resulted in some awkward gearshift-type greeting where my hand wrapped around her fist and shook. If she noticed how embarrassed I was, she didn't let on. "Olivia said you'll probably be spending a lot of time at the coffee shop, so I'm sure we'll be seeing a lot of each other."

Zo was the polar opposite of Olivia. Where Olivia was all curves and bright colors, Zo was all defined lines and neutral tones. She wore ripped jeans cuffed at the ankles, a white T-shirt, and a gray blazer on top. Her hair was cut short and was such a light blonde, that it almost looked white. I caught a sliver of her floral tattoo peeking out from the cuff of her jeans.

"They just got engaged!" Olivia squealed, grabbing tightly onto my arm. "They just told me like five minutes before you got here. Now we have another thing to celebrate aside from you coming to town!"

"Congratulations," I said, swallowing my nerves. *Great, now I feel like I'm imposing.* "That's so exciting."

"Thank you," Daniella gushed, looking down at the sapphire engagement ring that sat on her finger. "I still can't believe Zo proposed; she swore she'd never marry. I've been dropping hints for a year now and I guess my hard work paid off!"

"It's a beautiful ring." I glanced nervously at Olivia then. "So, where are we going?"

"The Garage," Olivia said as she linked her arm with mine and pulled me alongside her. Her two friends followed behind. "It's pretty much where everyone in town hangs out on the weekend."

"Only because there's nothing else to do here," Daniella piped in from behind.

"Don't listen to her." Olivia rolled her eyes, letting out a small laugh. "There's good food, good drinks, and overall, it's a good time. Plus, there's always live music on Friday nights."

When we arrived, I immediately understood why it was called The Garage. It looked like an old mechanic's shop converted into a bar. There were neon signs and car emblems hung on the walls, tables made of wooden pallets, and license plates from every state. The space was packed with people chatting and laughing, some playing darts in the corner, others dancing. On the other side of the bar was a small stage, where a band was set up playing cover songs.

Olivia made her way to the center of the room, wasting no time. I laughed as she spun in circles, her black-and-white polka dot skirt fanning out around her.

I tried to make tonight feel like old times with Olivia, but I couldn't get myself to relax. I tried to let go of every thought in my head and just dance, but even though my body swayed to the music and I looked like I was having fun, I couldn't stop looking at everyone around me. Any time the door opened, I expected Griffin to walk in; I expected to see him behind the bar pouring a drink. Any time I felt someone bump into me, I saw dark, menacing eyes and tattooed arms. I knew tonight would be tough since it was my first time back in a bar — or any social setting, for that matter — but it was at the point where I was seriously plotting my escape.

After dancing to a few songs, the four of us sat down and split a monstrous plate of nachos. While everyone pulled at the chips, gooey cheese dripping everywhere, I monitored my surroundings. I had no appetite. My stomach was filled with a heavy feeling that something was wrong. I knew it was just my anxiety talking like it always did when I was uncomfortable, but I couldn't stop it. No matter how many times I told myself that I was hours away from Griffin and that this wasn't *his* bar, my brain wouldn't believe it.

My phone buzzed in my pocket and I pulled it out, grateful for the distraction.

> Nate: You had a nail in your tire. I got it out and was able to plug it for you.

> Me: Thank you. You didn't have to do that. I could've brought it to a mechanic.

> Nate: Don't worry about it.

> Me: Are you sure? I can pay you.

> Me: When I texted you earlier, I didn't mean you had to fix it.

> Nate: Everyone deserves to be taken care of sometimes, even you.

> Nate: Especially you.

I slammed my phone face down on the table, trying to smother the fire that I felt burning under my cheeks. My heart pounded in my chest, and I tapped my fingers nervously on the table, gnawing at my lower lip. How was I even supposed to respond to that? Picking it back up, I stared at the screen. I'd told Nate just the other day that I didn't need to be taken care of, but now looking at his text again, I couldn't deny that maybe I *wanted* to be.

"Everything okay?" Olivia leaned over, whispering in my ear. Crap, how long had I been staring at my phone like a weirdo? I pressed it against my chest, hoping she didn't see who I was texting.

"Yeah," I said, trying not to sound suspicious at all. "I'm going to get some water."

"Cool. I'll come with."

Olivia grabbed my hand as she pulled me toward the bar and slapped her hand on the counter, grabbing the bartender's attention. I was about to playfully chastise her about how rude that was when the guy came over.

"Hey, Liv," the bartender said, resting against the bar and leaning toward us. When he turned his attention to me, I looked down at the floor, immediately avoiding his gaze. "Who's your friend?"

"Ben," Olivia said, yanking my arm and jostling me like a ragdoll. I really had missed this woman, even though she knew how to push my buttons. "This is my best friend, Maddie."

"Maddie?" There was something in the way he said my name, like recognition, that had my attention snapping to him. He was looking at me as if I were a puzzle he was trying to solve, and had I not been looking at him the same way, I might've taken offense.

Nothing about his short wispy brown hair or his five o'clock shadow rang a bell. His deep blue eyes and boyish grin did nothing, either. My eyes trailed down his body, taking in his white button-down shirt, its top three buttons undone to reveal a smooth chest. I swallowed, bringing my attention back to his face, but as I continued to take in his appearance, I couldn't figure out why he felt so familiar to me.

"Do you guys know each other or something?" Olivia asked the question I was dying to know the answer to, her eyes darting between the two of us.

"No," I said, not entirely sure if that was true. I focused on the way Ben gripped the bar, the tips of his fingers going white as they pressed into the countertop. Flashbacks of Griffin standing in the same position flooded my mind, and I anxiously grabbed a hold of the charm bracelet on my wrist, spinning it around. "It's nice to meet you, Ben. May I have some water, please?"

"And I'll take my usual," Olivia chimed in, turning around and leaning her back against the bar.

"One water and a vodka martini coming right up," Ben recited to us as he started pulling glasses out and setting them on the bar.

"Where'd you get that from?" Olivia asked, gesturing to the

bracelet I was still fidgeting with. She reached out and took one of the charms in her fingers. "This is cute."

"I don't remember," I lied, pulling my wrist out from her grasp and covering the bracelet with my hand. "Hey, Liv, is Ben from here? Like, has he always lived here?"

"Yeah, it's kind of a sad story," she said, moving closer to me so that no one could overhear. "His mom had him as a teen and she got into a lot of drugs. She decided to pack up and leave one day, leaving Ben for her brother to take care of. His uncle passed away and left him this place less than a year ago."

"Shit." I looked over my shoulder at Ben who was tapping away on his phone, before turning back to Olivia. "How do you know all this?"

"The librarians told me." She let out a giggle. "Why do you ask?"

"Just curious." I glanced back over at Ben who was back to making our drinks now, his phone nowhere to be seen.

"I know he's hot, but don't fall for any of his tricks." Olivia snorted a laugh, and I turned my attention back to her. "He's the town flirt, so don't be surprised if he makes a move on you by the end of the night. It's not very often we get fresh meat in Briar Oakes."

"I'm not interested anyway," I said, wrapping my arms around my stomach in an attempt to stop the nausea from building inside me. Why couldn't I shake this feeling?

"Good." Olivia paused and stared at me, tilting her head. "Nate wouldn't be too happy if one of his friends made a move on his girl, either."

"I am not Nate's girl." Was Ben a friend of Nate's? I felt my shoulders drop from my ears, already relaxing slightly.

"Sure, sure, whatever you say. Oh, I love this song!" Olivia squealed as the band started playing a pop song. "I'm going to dance. Bring my drink over to the table when it's done?"

"Sure," I said, even though I definitely was *not* okay with it. It was one thing being in the bar with Olivia and her friends, distracted by their conversations and dancing, but it was another thing being alone at the bar.

I watched as Olivia darted away, already moving with the music, and I settled onto one of the barstools. Taking a deep breath, I glanced down at my wrist, looking at each charm on the bracelet. Maybe if Nate were here, I wouldn't feel so uneasy. I bet he would've sensed that I was nervous and stayed by my side.

I slid my phone out and opened my Kindle app. Sighing, I thought about how I was *that* girl; the one who brought a book with her everywhere she went. If I was expected to stand here and not have a shattering panic attack, then I needed to mentally not be here.

"You must be Maddie," a woman's voice announced, pulling me away from my book. I looked up, coming face-to-face with a woman who was probably ten years older than me. "I heard there was someone new in town, and I was just telling my husband that it had to be you."

"Yup." I looked around, trying to locate the husband she was referring to, but found multiple people looking in my direction instead. "That's me."

"How are you liking Briar Oakes so far?" she asked, taking a seat next to me.

"Good?" It came out more like a question and she pouted. "I mean, I've only been here a short while, so I don't know."

"I have no doubt that Briar Oakes will work its magic on you." She beamed, showing off the red lipstick that was smudged on her front tooth. I was going to gesture to her about it, but before I could, she kept on talking. "How's Nate? I hope he's treating you like a gentleman should."

"Nate?" I questioned. "I'm here with Olivia."

"Don't worry." She giggled, taking another sip of her wine. "Your secret is safe with me."

"What secret?" I asked, eyes locating Olivia and hoping for a rescue, but she was too captivated by the music.

"That you and Nate are together," she urged, clearly annoyed that I wasn't keeping up. I watched as she chugged the remainder of her wine and placed the empty glass on the bar. "Nate isn't the type of guy to let just any girl stay with him. He's been living in this town for a few years now and nobody's ever seen him with a girl. You must mean a lot to him."

"What are you talking about?" I asked, tamping down my irritation. "Nate and I aren't dating. Who told you otherwise?"

She leaned in closer and whispered, "The librarians know everything."

"Clearly they don't."

"You're so cute." She reached forward and pinched my cheek. I turned my head to release my poor cheek from her grip. "Ah, to be young and in love again."

My jaw dropped as she hopped off and walked away, back into the arms of her husband. What the hell just happened?

"Maddie." Ben's voice rang in my ear, startling me. "Your drinks."

"Uh..." I glanced down, pointing to the one closest to me. "We didn't order that one. It was supposed to just be the water and martini."

"I know." He smirked again, causing a chill to run down my spine. "But someone asked me to make it for you."

Someone? I looked at the drink in front of me, taking in its amber color and orange slice garnish. I knew that drink. In fact, it used to be my favorite. *He's here.* I placed my hand on my leg, gripping my thigh as I stared at the cocktail like he might somehow come out of it. I pressed down on my scars, reminding myself that I got away. I was safe. I made it. This was just a drink. Just a coincidence.

"I don't want it," I snapped, sliding it back to him. I must have used a little too much force because the glass slid clear off the bar and shattered on the ground. I glanced around nervously to see if anyone had noticed, but the sound of the music must have masked it. No one was looking in our direction. "Who told you to give me that drink?"

I looked around the bar, scanning every single person that occupied the room, looking for the face that haunted my thoughts and nightmares. I scanned the tattoos that were visible on some of the people, but none of them matched his. I could practically hear the blood rushing through my veins, trying to make it to my furiously beating heart. If Ben answered, I didn't hear him.

With my phone clutched to my chest, I shouldered my way through the crowd and escaped to the bathroom. Tears fell freely down my face, and I stumbled into one of the stalls, locking it behind me. With shaking hands, I started a new text to Nate, typing the one word I never thought I'd need and hitting send.

Me: dinglehopper.

eleven

"Maddie?" Olivia's voice was soft as she knocked on the stall door. I hadn't heard anyone walk into the bathroom. "Can you come out and talk to me, please?"

When I unlocked and opened the door, Olivia didn't hesitate to pull me into an embrace. I felt the weight in my shoulders drop as I collapsed into her arms, the sobs coming out at an embarrassing level. She rubbed my back slowly as she continuously whispered that everything was fine. That I was okay. I wanted to believe her, but I couldn't. Something wasn't right. And that drink...who had ordered me that drink?

"I'm sorry." I lifted my head off her shoulder, spying Daniella and Zo leaning against the sinks. "I am *so* sorry. This is the worst first impression, and I ruined your engagement celebration."

"Don't be silly." Zo waved her hand in the air, dismissing me gently.

"Why didn't you come get me?" Olivia asked, pushing me off her chest but keeping me at arm's length. "I had to find out from Nate that something was wrong. The codeword, Maddie...really? We've never used it before."

"Is he here?" I asked, not knowing who I was referring to. Griffin? Nate? Some creepy man who happened to know the signature drink from The Big House?

"Yeah, Nate just got here." She reached out and brushed a loose strand of hair behind my ear. I closed my eyes as she wiped the tears from my cheek. "He called as soon as he got your text, demanding to know where we were and what was going on. I've never heard him sound like that before. It was scary. He's going to take us all home."

"No," I protested while more tears spilled down my cheeks. "Please stay. Don't end your night because of me. I've already caused enough trouble. I'm just going to go to bed when we get back, anyway."

"I want to be there for you." I looked at Olivia, taking in her worried expression and realizing the weight those words carried, for both of us.

"Please, don't leave," I begged. "I'll feel even worse knowing I ruined this night for all of you."

"I'm just worried about you, Maddie," she said, giving my hands a gentle squeeze.

"I'll be fine," I promised, stepping us toward the bathroom door. "It was just a panic attack. Happens all the time. I just need to sleep it off."

Olivia kept her hand on mine as we walked out of the bathroom, Daniella and Zo following behind in silence. When we turned the corner and were back in the bar, I stopped short, sensing the commotion. I followed everyone's attention and my jaw dropped. Nate was leaning over the bar, shouting at Ben who stood terrified, both hands up in surrender. I walked closer as though in a trance.

"Don't make me ask you again," he growled, his back stiff and head lowered so he could look directly into Ben's face. My eyes traveled down those muscular arms to his hands, which appeared relaxed despite the rigidness of his posture and the anger that visibly shook through his body. "What the hell happened?"

"I'm sorry, man," Ben said, his voice hitching noticeably. "I wouldn't have given her the drink."

"Who bought her the drink?" he demanded. If his hands weren't so relaxed, I'd have expected him to be grabbing Ben by the collar. In the past, I loved seeing Griffin get protective over me and showing that via his strength. But now, seeing Nate stand up for me and not coming off as a threat, I realized that Griffin wasn't protecting me; he was being possessive.

"I didn't know she was with you," Ben answered, avoiding his question.

"I'm not *with* him," I interrupted, suddenly at Nate's side.

Nate turned my way the second the words escaped my lips, looking just as shocked to see me at his side as I was. His eyes dragged over me, as if checking for any physical harm, and then back to my face, taking in my tear-streaked cheeks. All the hardness in his eyes that was directed at Ben vanished. His eyes flashed to my hand, which had let go of Olivia's and now gripped his arm as if it were the last life vest on my sinking ship.

"Hey, it's okay," Nate said, leaning down to whisper in my ear. His breath skated across my skin, raising the hairs on my arms. I leaned forward, my hands sliding down to his wrist, getting so close to him that my chest pressed against his bicep. "I'm here. You're safe."

I clung to those words, letting the safety blanket drape over me once again. How did he manage to do that every time he said them to me?

"Nate." His eyes moved down to my hand, and before I could even realize what I was doing, my thumb ran along one of his bulging veins. I marveled at the feel of his skin beneath my fingers. I let go of his arm reluctantly and whispered, "Get me out of here. *Please*," into his ear.

He nodded as he stood at my side, placing his hand gently on the small of my back. It'd been so long since I allowed a guy to come close enough to touch me like this. I wasn't sure what surprised me more: the fact that Nate's hand on me didn't make me jump or the fact that I liked how it felt. I straightened my back as Nate guided me through the crowd. His thumb lightly brushed against my spine, encouraging me to relax. I looked over my shoulder, finding Olivia watching as Nate led us toward the exit. She gave me a smile, lifting her hand in a small wave, and I returned it, letting her know everything would be okay.

When we made it outside, I stepped out of Nate's grasp and turned to look at him. He was staring down at me with such intensity, and I could tell he wanted to ask me what the hell happened. I held his gaze, hoping he would be the first to say something. When I sent him that text, I was only thinking about needing an escape and not what I'd do once he was here. How could I explain my "bad feeling" in a way he would understand?

"Nate," I started, despite being unsure of what I wanted to say. "I'm sorry."

At the sound of my voice, everything in him softened: his posture, his eyes, his voice, even the way he scratched his jaw was gentler. "Never apologize for using the codeword, Maddie." He paused, looking back at the bar before bringing his attention back to me. "Come on, let's go home. I'm parked around the corner."

He gestured to where he was parked, and I began walking, Nate following close behind. I wasn't sure why I expected him to place his hand on my lower back again, but I did. And when he didn't, I couldn't help but feel slightly disappointed. I didn't have time to linger on my pity-party before turning the corner and gasping loudly. There was no way you could miss the monstrosity of his truck, and it wasn't until I was standing in front of it that I realized my mistake.

Crap.

"You brought the Beast?!" I shrieked, taking a step back toward the building.

"The Beast?" he questioned, giving me a sideways glance.

"Well, I debated calling it the Behemoth" — I looked at the

truck and how it took up the same amount of space as two parked cars — "but the Beast is just easier to say."

"Right." He chuckled, shaking his head at me. "And how else was I supposed to get here?"

"I don't know...my Jeep?"

"Why would I take your car?" he asked as he opened the door for me.

I stared at his hand that was now stretched outward to help me inside. Crap, how was I going to get myself out of this one? I'd had enough embarrassing panic attacks in front of Nate, so I really didn't want to have another one. All the possible worst-case scenarios started infiltrating my mind and I had to close my eyes, willing them to disappear. How was I going to survive this? I thought back to some of the techniques my therapist had provided me with.

What's the worst that could happen? Nate could get behind the wheel to drive us home, but instead, we'd get into a car accident and die. Okay, maybe that was a bit extreme. Next option: I could get in the truck, but then have a panic attack.

How could I cope with that? I could ask Nate to pull over and walk the rest of the way home.

What's the best that could happen? I get in the truck with Nate, get home safely, and go to bed with a smile on my face over the fact that I did it.

What's most likely to happen? I get in his car, I panic, but survive. I'd survived everything that'd been thrown at me so far, so why would this be any different?

While I'm waiting for this outcome, how can I smooth my anxiety or comfort myself? I could focus on my breathing and on the fact that Nate wasn't Griffin. That he wouldn't purposefully put me in danger. That I would be okay. It was only a five-minute drive to Nate's house. In five minutes, I'd be back in the safety of my bed. I could do anything for five minutes.

I opened my eyes at where Nate still stood, arm outstretched

— my way to safety. When I slid my hand into his, I marveled at the size of his hand. My stomach flipped as his fingers wrapped around mine and he helped lift me into his truck.

"You can do this," I whispered to myself after Nate closed the door. I watched as he walked around the front of the truck. "It's just five minutes."

He's not going to hurt you, I told myself as he climbed into the driver's seat and turned his key in the ignition.

Nate gripped the steering wheel, turning around in the middle of the street. I gripped the hem of my dress and let out a deep breath. Keeping my eyes on his hands, I watched for any sign that he might jerk the wheel.

He's not Griffin.

My hand slid up my thigh, pressing down on the scars hidden beneath my dress.

You're safe.

"Everything okay?" Nate asked, and I snapped my attention to him. He glanced down at my trembling hand.

"Keep your eyes on the road," I said in a shaky voice.

Nate turned his blinker on and the ticking of it momentarily filled the truck, but it wasn't enough. It was too quiet. I couldn't stop my thoughts and memories from attacking me. Griffin's voice was in my ears, rough and commanding, as the sounds of tires screeching along pavement rang through my mind like nails on a chalkboard. The shattering of glass exploded in my ears as I pushed my head against the headrest, bracing myself for impact. The deafening sound of the airbag deploying —

No.

"Can we put on some music?" I asked, reaching for the radio before he could answer. I needed a distraction. I looked over at Nate as I hit one of his preset stations. Classic rock played softly through the speakers, so I cranked up the volume enough that I had to shout. "Is this station good?

"Yeah," he answered, looking at me quizzically as I continued to raise the volume. I glanced at his right hand, which dropped from the steering wheel and fell into his lap. My heart rate picked up as I nervously looked from his hand to the road, to his face, and back again. He flexed his fingers, catching my attention, before gripping just above his knee, as if stopping himself from reaching out to me. Could he tell I was spiraling?

"Can you please put both hands on the steering wheel," I murmured. Ignoring the look of concern on his face, I turned my attention back to his hands that were now both resting lightly on the steering wheel, his thumbs tapping along to the beat of the music.

When we turned onto Nate's street, I reached down and grabbed the seatbelt, fully prepared to unlatch it and fly out the door as soon as we parked. The song ended as we pulled into the driveway, and Nate turned off the radio, letting the sound of the gravel beneath the tires replace the music. As soon as he put the truck in park, I freed myself from the seatbelt and went to unlock my door.

I did it.

"Wait," he said, wrapping his hand around my wrist. I jumped, twisting my body so that my back was now pressed against the door. I pulled my hand out from his and stared at him with wide eyes. His hand hovered in the air as he watched me, distress palpable in his eyes. My heart pounded in my chest.

It's Nate. He wouldn't hurt you.

"I'm sorry," I whispered, shaking my head back and forth. "I just thought — "

"What happened?" Nate asked, interrupting me, but I wasn't sure what he was referring to.

"I want to go to bed, Nate," I said with a sigh, wary of the emotions threatening to expose themselves at any moment. "Please, I'm exhausted."

"Why did you use the code word?" He pulled his keys out of the ignition, and we sat in silence for a few moments. "The one night I assume you're safe at Olivia's, watching a movie and eating your weight in ice cream...that's the night you need me."

"I'm sorry," I whispered. "Nate, I — "

"What if I wasn't around, Maddie?" he snapped, cutting me off before letting out a deep breath. "This is why I always had you two tell me when you were going out, so that I could make sure I was there."

The way he was talking to me right now reminded me of all those times I heard him fight with Olivia. He was just saying all this because he cared for me like a little sister. God, I felt so stupid. The amount of butterflies that'd been swarming my stomach these past few days...maybe I misinterpreted everything. He was only treating me the way he'd treat Olivia.

"I don't want to talk about it." I shook my head as tears welled in my eyes.

"I know I told you all those years ago 'no questions asked,' but it's killing me seeing you like this." He pressed his palms into his eyes and rested his head back. "I want to help you and I don't know how."

I took a deep breath, in through my nose and out through my mouth. Biting down on my lip, I tried to think of what part of me I was comfortable sharing with him now. I wasn't sure if I was ready to talk about everything yet, but I wanted to give him something.

"Griffin and I got into a car accident." I swallowed over the lump in my throat as the memories forced their way into my mind. Wincing, I shook my head as if it were an Etch-A-Sketch and I could erase them. "It was...bad. Aside from my dad, I haven't been able to get in a car since, unless I'm the one driving."

"Why didn't you tell me? I would've let you drive home."

"It's cute you think I can drive the Beast." Despite the tears falling down my cheeks, I laughed. "I doubt I'd even be able to see over the steering wheel."

"Hey," he said, and I held my breath as he hesitantly reached out to me. Swallowing over the feelings lodged in my throat, I nodded my head and Nate cupped my jaw in his hand. His thumb was gentle against my cheek as it swiped at my tears. "I'm proud of you."

That makes one of us.

Feeling proud of myself was something Heather and I worked on a lot together in our sessions. Now, whenever I caught myself feeling differently, I'd glance down at the scars on my body. A physical reminder that I survived. Proof that I had something to be proud of. But despite not always feeling proud of myself, I couldn't ignore the way my stomach flipped at his words. Nate was proud of *me*. I bit down on the inside of my cheek, keeping the corners of my lips from pulling up into a smile.

We sat in silence for a moment before he asked, "Are you hungry?"

"Starving," I said as I looked back at him, glad that he didn't press the subject. It was like he knew exactly when to pull back.

I followed him into the house where he proceeded to turn on every light he passed on his way to the kitchen. Kicking off my boots and leaving them next to his shoes, I took a seat on a stool. There was something about seeing him maneuver through the room, grabbing the necessary tools and ingredients and placing them on the counter, that captivated me.

"I hope you like grilled cheese," he said as he walked over to the fridge, pulling out even more ingredients.

"Mm-hmm. Does this mean I finally get to try one of Nate's Grates?" I said, leaning my elbows on the counter and taking in the fresh mozzarella, tomatoes, basil, garlic, balsamic glaze, olive oil, salt and pepper, and sourdough bread in front of me.

"For the real experience, you'll have to visit the truck," he said, giving me one of his famous winks. He began slicing the tomatoes in front of me with one hundred percent focus. "But for now, this will do."

"What kind of grilled cheese requires this many ingredients?"

"A Caprese Grilled Cheese." Seeing him in his kitchen, smiling and moving with such confidence, was enough to make me stare... but that smile? Game. Over.

Not wanting him to see the blush that was creeping on my face, I turned on the stool and hopped off. What the hell was that all about? Why was everything Nate doing affecting me like this?

"I'm going to get changed," I announced as I made my way down the hallway, ignoring the sound of Nate chuckling.

When I got into my room, I shut the door and leaned against it. I let the solid door at my back ground me as I collected myself, then walked over to my dresser and pulled out Nate's shirt and shorts. I slipped out of my dress, rolled it up into a ball, and shot it across the room so it would land in the hamper. Glancing down at my wrist, I unclasped the bracelet and placed it on top of the dresser. When I was dressed in my pajamas, I tightened the shorts so that there was no chance of them falling and made my way back to the kitchen.

"It's almost ready," he said, not even looking up as he flipped one of the sandwiches over and rubbed garlic on top.

"It smells amazing," I gushed. If these sandwiches tasted half as good as they smelled, I didn't think I'd survive.

"Why don't you put on a movie?"

"Sure, what do you want to watch?"

"Whatever you want." He smiled and I took that as a challenge. Did he really mean that? After staring at him for probably a stupid amount of time, Nate gestured to the living room with his spatula. "Go on, it's your choice."

I plopped down on the couch and pulled the throw blanket over. Stretching my legs out as far as I could, I took up most of the couch. Tuna, who must have been hiding underneath the couch, emerged and hopped onto my lap. I scratched behind his ears, and his purr vibrated through my body.

"He's really taken with you," Nate said as I turned on the television and started scrolling through his streaming devices.

"He normally hides out in my room whenever I have people over."

"I guess." I hummed as I continued scrolling through movie options until I found exactly what I was looking for. Grinning, I selected the movie and waited as the blue filter took over the screen.

"*Twilight?*" Nate sighed. He was standing at the end of the couch now with two plates balanced in one hand and a glass of water in the other. "I hate this movie."

"Nobody hates *Twilight*," I stated, freeing him from one of the plates. I tucked my feet in closer to my body so that Nate would have room to sit. "And if someone says they do, they're in denial."

He sat down and rested his plate on the arm of the couch, then reached over and placed my feet on his lap. I swallowed nervously as he began rubbing my feet through the blanket, trying not to make this a big deal. I was going to pull back and curl into a ball like I usually did when I felt uncomfortable, but then those thumbs started working their magic and I couldn't. If his grilled cheese career didn't work out, he definitely could make it as a masseuse.

I took a bite out of the sandwich and let out a satisfied moan. Never mind, grilled cheese was definitely his calling. Nate looked over at me, one eyebrow raised. I paused mid-chew and glanced down at his hands on my feet. *Oh my god,* did he think I was moaning because of his hands? Frantically I shook my head and gestured to the sandwich.

"Oh my god," I said, my mouth full of gooey deliciousness. "This is amazing. Like, borderline orgasmic."

"The sandwich or my hands?" he asked, winking again. That wink was going to be the death of me.

My heart stopped and I choked on the bite in my mouth. I continued coughing, beating my fist against my chest, as I placed my plate down on my lap and gestured to the water glass on the table. Nate kept laughing as he leaned over my feet, passing me the glass. He continued to rub my feet as I chugged the water, finally gaining some control over myself. "It's so easy to get you all flustered."

"It is not," I mumbled, pulling my feet away from him and letting my hair fall across my face. "Just watch the movie."

twelve

I stared at my planner, opened to today's date, in disbelief. Sitting on my bed with Tuna nestled between my legs, I rubbed the scar that ran across my ankle with the pad of my thumb. I'd known this day was coming, and I had avoided looking at my planner since arriving at Nate's, hoping it would pass without me realizing, but... that wasn't the case.

Nate knocked on my door this morning, but I pretended to still be asleep. It wasn't until I heard his truck pull out of the driveway that I ventured out of my room. I went into the kitchen to get a glass of water and found a plate of French toast waiting for me. Smiling, I tore off a piece and popped it into my mouth, letting out a satisfied moan at the taste. I grabbed the iced latte from Latte Da! sitting next to the plate and took a sip, picking up the tiny slip of paper that was tucked underneath, letting me know that he was going to be at his food truck all morning. He also said I should stop by if I wanted the *real* Nate's Grates experience.

I tried to suppress the smile that was threatening to grow. I wanted to squeal, I wanted to jump, I wanted to call up my best friend and pick apart every part of last night, but I couldn't. I shouldn't. Nate was Olivia's older brother. I couldn't risk our friendship, not when we had just made up. I couldn't break the ultimate girl code, so...that meant he was off-limits. But I had no idea if there was anything to even overanalyze. Nate had always been the sweet, nice, caring guy. What if his offer to cook dinner, watch my favorite movie despite hating it himself, massage my feet, and get me my morning coffee was a normal thing?

Here I was grinning stupidly at a piece of paper with my stomach all in knots over a guy that might just be...nice. Sure, he left me a note that sounded flirty, but what if it was platonic? I thought back to what the girl said in the bar about Nate never being seen with women. Maybe he simply didn't have the time in his life for anything more than friendship. I set the note down on the counter, thinking about how amazing his grilled cheese tasted last night. Could his cooking really be any better at the food truck versus here? Maybe I should go and find out...

Yeah, not happening. With the sounds that came out of my mouth when I took my first bite, the last thing I needed was to be moaning in public.

Taking my latte with me, I headed to the laundry room and stripped out of Nate's clothes. I darted to the bathroom and adjusted the shower's knobs until the water was perfect, then stepped inside. I let the water relax my muscles and hoped I could find something to distract me from where I was a year ago.

I forced everything that happened last night into my mind. Why was I such a mess? Sighing, I turned off the water and stepped out, grabbing a towel off the hook and wrapping it around my body. Holding on to my towel, I opened the bathroom door and stepped into the hallway, not realizing that Tuna had laid down in front of the door.

"Tuna!" I screeched, tripping over his sleeping body. I shot my hands out in front of me, reaching for the wall to stop myself from flying into it as my towel fell to the floor. Tuna scattered down the hall and disappeared into Nate's office. Wait, why was his door open?

Letting out a slew of curses in the direction Tuna ran off in, I took a few steps backward and crashed into something hard. A set of warm hands grabbed me from behind, preventing me from toppling over again. My heart skidded to a stop and a chill ran through my body as I thought about the fact Nate wasn't home. Everything started to spin, and if I wasn't currently being held, I would have already been on the ground.

I whipped around, fully prepared to scream, but instead found myself face to...chest. My eyes shamefully trailed up the perfectly sculpted muscles until they landed on Nate's face. His eyes widened as he took me in, dropping to my naked body before snapping back to mine. *Shit.* I looked down, trying my best to cover myself with my arms and hands as I twisted my body in every way possible. The air in the hallway seemed to disappear as his eyes moved away from mine and devoured every inch of bare skin on my body.

I remained frozen, unable to figure out how to make my body move in order to grab the towel at my feet. It was like I lost all brain function. I couldn't process my thoughts, move my body, or even remember how to breathe. Not being able to handle the heat in his eyes, I slowly let mine roam back down his chest to the ridges of his abs. I swallowed — hard — as I continued down the trail of hair that disappeared behind the waistband of his gray sweatpants. Not able to stop my eyes from doing their own thing, they landed on the bulge that appeared to be growing larger each second I lingered.

Holy fuck.

"Maddie." His voice was husky and captivating as his eyes dragged down my body. I stood still, unsure if I was even breathing at this point, as I took in the sudden change in his expression. His eyes narrowed, his brows pulled together, and his mouth pressed into a hard line. He leaned in, reaching forward, and my eyes widened. Oh god, this was really happening. But then he straightened, my towel in his outstretched hand, his eyes looking anywhere but at me. "You should get dressed."

I looked down, trying to figure out what was so repulsive about my body that made Nate want me to cover up, when my eyes landed on the scars on my thigh. *Shit.* I bit down on my lip, trying to stop it from quivering, as I held back the tears already clouding my vision. This was exactly why I always made sure I was covered, why I always tugged on my dresses and shorts to make sure only what I wanted to be visible was seen. The one time I slipped up and forgot about my damn scars...and now Nate probably thought I was repulsive.

I accepted the towel from Nate's hands and turned my back to him, cursing under my breath as I tried to wrap it around me with shaking hands. No matter how hard I tried to tuck it under my arm to keep it from falling, it wouldn't stay. My voice shook in embarrassment as I said, "I am *so* sorry."

"Are you covered?" he asked, and I held my towel tightly in my fist and turned back around. Nate stood there, staring up at the ceiling. Great, now he couldn't even look at me?

You know what? This is good. I need this. At least now I knew all my thoughts about Nate could only be that. He'd never see me as more than his little sister's best friend. I blinked back the tears before letting out a shaky exhale.

"Y-yes," I stuttered and Nate's eyes fell back onto mine, not once moving from my face. I took a step back, shaking my head slowly. "This is so embarrassing. I need to go."

"No, Madds, wait," Nate said, but I had already pushed past him and went into my room, slamming the door behind me.

When I was safely behind the locked door of my room, I walked over to my closet and grabbed a dress, yanking it over my head. I collapsed onto my bed, letting the tears fall. How could I have been so stupid? I'd been so careful not to let anyone see the scars on my thighs, and of all people, Nate had to be the one.

There was a soft scratching at my door and I knew it was

Tuna. I also had a feeling that if I opened the door, Nate would be there too. Not wanting to face him yet, but also wanting the comforting snuggles from Tuna, I didn't know what to do. Sighing, I stood up and made my way over to the door and opened it. Sure enough, Nate was leaning against the wall across from me. At least he was wearing a shirt now.

"You weren't supposed to be home," I sniffled, wiping the tears off my cheeks with the back of my hand. I didn't even feel embarrassed about the tears, especially not after how he reacted to seeing me naked. No one had ever looked at me the way he did.

"Tyler and Ben are managing the truck for the rest of the day. I came home to shower before I go check out a new restaurant for an episode, but then..." He trailed off, scratching the back of his head. "I didn't mean to startle you. Madds, I — "

"Please, just forget about it." Maybe if we ignored what happened, it would be like it never happened. Tuna walked into the room and weaved through my legs, rubbing his head against my calf. I bent down and scratched him behind his ears, smiling as he purred into the palm of my hand.

"What the hell did he do to you, Maddie?" I heard Nate ask, his voice firm. I stood up quickly, my heart racing. His eyes were narrowed, looking down at my legs where my scars were now safely hidden behind my dress. "How'd you get those scars?"

I gripped the doorknob, prepared to shut it, but Nate blocked it with his hand. The sound of his palm hitting the wood caused me to jump back, and I let go of the door immediately, taking a few steps closer to my bed. When the backs of my knees hit the edge of the mattress, I fell back onto it. Tuna jumped up and curled into a ball at my side.

"Maddie." Nate sighed and removed his hand from the door to run it down his face. I tracked his movements as he closed his eyes and leaned against the doorframe. When he opened them, he was close to tears. "It's *me*. You're safe. I would never hurt you."

"I know," I whispered, keeping my focus on Tuna. His gray

fur was soft against my fingers as I ran them from the top of his head to the tip of his tail. It was easier to talk about it if I kept my hands busy. "Sorry, it's just that today...it's not that...I'm just extra jumpy today." I rolled my eyes internally, thinking about how badly I wished it *were* just today. But the truth was...I was jumpy every day. And I was tired of it.

"Can I come in?" When I looked up, he was still leaning against the doorframe, but his eyes were softer. I bit down on my lip, trying to figure out what I wanted to do. It wasn't that I didn't trust him or thought he'd hurt me, but I just couldn't stop thinking about how he'd reacted. He certainly hadn't been disgusted by the scars on my face when he saw me for the first time. At least, I didn't think he'd been. So why were the ones on my thigh any different?

My phone rang on the nightstand, and I sighed as I walked over to it, seeing Heather's name flash across the screen.

"I'm sorry. I have to take this call. It's my..." I hesitated, debating on whether I wanted Nate to know. *Let him in, Maddie.* "It's my therapist. I have an appointment."

"Oh." He nodded slowly, his Adam's apple bobbing as he swallowed. "I'll give you some privacy then. I should get going, anyway. We'll talk later?"

I nodded, clutching my phone to my chest.

I called Heather back once I heard the sound of the shower starting. I'd scheduled an appointment with her months ago for the one-year anniversary of the accident, knowing I would need someone to talk to. But to be honest, I wish I'd allowed myself this day to just stay in bed and shut out the world. Maybe I should have paid a visit to Nate's food truck this morning. Cheese could fix anything, right? At the very least, it would have prevented the whole towel fiasco from happening.

But then nothing would improve. I'd still be stuck in my old habits. I'd still be hiding behind my fears. And I *wanted* to be better.

"Hi, Heather," I said when she picked up. "Sorry I missed your call."

"Maddie?" Olivia shouted through my locked door, which shook as she pounded her fist against it.

Reaching for my phone, I saw that it was a little after 7:00 p.m. The sun was almost gone, I could hear the cicadas singing outside my window, and thanks to the many hours spent in bed today, I was wide awake. My appointment with Heather was tough, to say the least. I filled her in on how I started writing again, where my inspiration came from, and the direction I was going in. She was proud of the fact that I took her homework assignment seriously, but she could also tell I was holding back. I'd thought long and hard about what I wanted to talk to her about today, and ulti-mately, I decided it was time. I couldn't get the help I needed, espe-cially not today, if she still didn't know the whole truth. So, I told her about the journals and what happened the night of the accident.

"I really thought she'd open the door for you," I heard Nate say quietly. I sat on the floor, leaning against the door with my ear pressed against it. "I don't think she's eaten anything today."

My stomach growled in agreement.

"How would you know?" she questioned. I could just imagine her standing there, hands on her hip, with her judging eyes.

"Would you quit trying to figure out if something is going on between us? Nothing's going on. We live together; I notice things. That's all." Nate sounded slightly annoyed. Then he sighed and I knew that Olivia wasn't giving up. "I made her French toast for breakfast and it's still there. She told me they're her favorite, so why would she leave them? Plus, there are no dirty dishes in the sink."

"I'm still on to you guys."

"Well, you're going to be disappointed, Liv, so I suggest you stop wasting your time and keep your nose out of my business." There was another soft knock on the door. "Maddie, I brought home pizza if you're hungry."

"Seriously?" Olivia chastised, clearly frustrated. "You're going to bribe her with food?"

"It's not like your plan of banging so hard on the door it almost fell over worked," Nate grumbled.

"At least the door would be open then."

I let out a laugh, breaking my silence. I never had a sibling growing up, so I'd always secretly enjoyed hearing them bicker. It was like no matter what one sibling did, the other would find fault with it somehow. It was comforting.

"Did you hear that?" Nate asked, and I could picture the two of them, ears pressed against the other side of the door, trying to catch any sign of life from me.

I stood up, not bothering to be quiet now that they'd heard me, and walked to my nightstand. Turning on my sound machine, I raised the volume to drown out their conversation. At least they now knew I was alive. If I was going to hide out in my room for the rest of the night, unable to sleep, I might as well be productive.

Grabbing my box of journals, I tossed them onto my bed and grabbed my laptop. I sat down on the bed, scooting myself back until I was resting against the headboard. I already tackled telling my story to Heather today, so I wanted to see how far I could get with telling the world.

title to be determined

By Madison Williams

Something is happening between me and Olivia. She's never home anymore, spending more and more time at her brother's apartment instead. Nate is four years older than us, single, and lives for his job. When he isn't busy making sure we're safe, he's working on his YouTube channel or playing video games with his friends. So, I was surprised to find out Olivia's been crashing with him.

"Are we going out tonight?" I ask her now, trying to take advantage of the fact that she's here, sitting on the couch, scrolling through Netflix.

"I don't know," she mumbles, not looking away from the screen.

"Come on, Liv," I pout, not that she can see with her back to me. "We used to go out all the time."

We used to do everything together: trips to Target, trying out new restaurants, playing board games every night until we were ready to fall asleep, jamming out to Disney music while we cleaned the apartment, pretending to be Mary Poppins by snapping our fingers at the laundry we didn't want to put away. But now I can't even get her to look at me for more than five seconds.

I hate that I can feel our friendship changing, but I can't get myself to blame it on my relationship with Griffin. She hates him, but I don't understand why. Griffin claims she's jealous and isn't used to sharing me with someone else, but I know Olivia and I can sense her hurt.

"Please?" I ask again, fully prepared to beg. "I feel like I never see you anymore."

"I don't feel like being babysat tonight."

"What are you talking about?"

"Seriously, Maddie?" She turns off the television and glares at me over the back of the couch. "We're only allowed to go to the bar Griffin works at. I'm not allowed to flirt with anyone because heaven forbid a guy comes near you, even if they're there for me. He watches every move we make."

"That's not true," I say defensively, crossing my arms.

"Whatever." She turns back around so I can't see her face.

"What is your problem?" I drop my hands to my sides and walk into the living room. "I honestly don't get why you have such an issue with Griffin. You were so excited when I first showed interest in him — hell, you were the one who initiated it! But now you avoid him like the plague."

"He treats you like dirt, Maddie!" She raises her voice and stands up. "He's like a drug and you're stuck in this fog that makes you think that he's this amazing guy when he's not."

"Please?" I ask again, not wanting to have this argument. "I really wanted to go out tonight."

I don't really care about going to the bar, but I have a feeling I won't be getting many other opportunities. Trying to please Griffin and Olivia is like being between a rock and a hard place; to make one of them happy, I have to lose the other. I don't want to do that. And I already miss her. I miss dancing with her. I miss having her dress me up. I miss seeing her face light up when one of our favorite songs came on. I miss walking arm in arm down the sidewalk, carefree.

"We'll have so much fun, I promise. We can do whatever you

want. We don't even have to go to The Big House. If you want to flirt for free booze, then go for it. I won't stand in your way."

"Fine," she relents, pointing a finger at me. "But this is the last time. He can try and control you all he wants, but not me."

"He doesn't control me."

"Right," she says, rolling the R and her eyes.

We still go to The Big House despite my offering to go somewhere else. Anywhere else. But Olivia insists, claiming she doesn't want to cause any problems for me. After Olivia sends Nate a text about where we are, we slip past the line of people waiting to get into the bar and make our way past the bouncers. One of the perks of dating an owner is that we don't have to wait to get inside on a busy Saturday night anymore. When we get inside, I beeline for the bar and flag Griffin down, giving him a quick kiss.

As soon as his lips crash against mine, I grab him by the collar of his shirt and pull him close, ignoring the fact that a bar separates us. Maybe Olivia is right and Griffin really is like a drug to me. His smell, his taste, the way he touches me, the way he makes me feel when he puts his arm around me...everything about him always leaves me craving more when he stops. Mike, Griffin's business partner, clears his throat, interrupting us.

"Hey." He pulls away and glares at Mike, then turns his attention back to me. Olivia let me borrow one of her dresses again and I can tell by the way Griffin's eyes are devouring me that he likes what he sees. "You said you weren't coming tonight."

"Change of plans." I smile, looking over at Olivia who's already setting her eyes on her target for the night.

He's tall, has skin that reminds me of rich chocolate, and stubble on his chin. Dressed in a suit like he just stepped out of a meeting, he stands out amongst his friends who appear to be dressed more for a bachelor party. I am surprised to see that he's the one she decided to go for. She usually goes after more of the college frat boy type. You know, someone with no respect for themselves or for her. Any easy target who doesn't get attached, she always says. She never wants to spend the night working hard to get attention or have to worry about someone wanting to get to know her outside the bar.

"Go easy on her," I say as I look up at Griffin, noticing that his body has gone rigid. He's now drying a whiskey glass in his hands rather aggressively. "And that cup."

"You should go home, Maddie."

"What?" I recoil, clearly confused. "Why?"

"If she's going to be doing that — " He jabs a finger in her direction and I follow with my eyes. Olivia is standing in the middle of the group, giggling as she latches on to the man in the suit. "Then you should go home."

"No. I promised her we'd have fun tonight. I can't just leave a few minutes after we show up."

"Maddie," he warns. His tone is hard, catching me off guard. Is this what Olivia always sees? I shake my head as if to clear this new vision of my boyfriend. He's just being protective. He sees so many girls being taken advantage of while working, and he doesn't want that happening to us. He isn't doing anything that Nate doesn't do; Olivia just doesn't understand that. "Go home."

It feels like I've somehow managed to swallow a bowling ball and it's sitting in my stomach, pulling me down to the ground as I look up at Griffin. His eyes are something I've never seen before. They're still their usual dark color, but instead of being soft, they're almost metallic. Like black ice. My bones feel frozen by them. I part my lips, about to protest, but the look he's giving me makes me rethink.

"Babe," I manage to say, my voice raspy. He turns his head to look in Olivia's direction again, but I reach over and turn his face back to me, holding his chin in my trembling hand. "You have nothing to worry about. *She's* the one flirting, not me. I'm standing right here, next to you. You're the only one who's going to be taking me home tonight, okay?"

I drop my hand from his face and look back at Olivia, trying to grab her attention, but instead make eye contact with one of the other guys in the group. He's standing there, leaning against a table with a beer in his hand. He has this *I'm too good to be here* presence about him, causing me to roll my eyes. I hate cocky people. I turn away as soon as our eyes meet and focus on the floor by my feet.

"What the hell was that?" Griffin asks, and when I look up at him, he is *seething*.

"What?" I ask, alarmed and unsure of what to make of that tone or the look on his face.

"*That.*" He juts his chin toward the group of guys around Olivia. I want to look away from him, but can't. His eyes hold me captive, despite feeling like daggers, puncturing every spot of my body they land on. "Did I interrupt something between you two?"

"Interrupt?"

"Don't act like you're not guilty, Maddie."

"The only thing I'm guilty of is being confused." I blink my eyes rapidly at him. Seriously, what the hell is he talking about?

"You like that guy," he growls, his hands clenched into fists on top of the bar.

"And you came to that conclusion how?"

"If you didn't, you wouldn't have looked away." Griffin proceeds to tell me about his crazy theory. Apparently, if you make eye contact with someone and look away immediately, it means you are guilty of something. Guilty of feelings. Guilty of judgment. Guilty of being wrong. Guilty of murder. Guilty of flirting. Guilty of anything. And apparently, I am guilty of finding that guy attractive.

"Everything okay here?" Olivia interrupts, suddenly at my side. Griffin's gaze shifts quickly to her hand, now gripping my arm, and then back to me.

"Never better," I mumble, shrugging free from her grip and then lacing my hand in hers. "Come on, let's dance."

We spend the next four or five songs dancing like we always do. Dare I say, things almost feel normal. Suit Guy hasn't moved from his spot, but watches as we twirl around. I can tell Olivia is trying not to pay attention to Griffin watching us. And to be honest, I'm doing the same. His stupid theory leaves me feeling uneasy.

"So, what's Suit Guy's name?" I ask, gesturing to the bachelors across the room, purposely not making eye contact with any of them.

"Dave, I think." She shrugs. "Who knows?"

"Not your usual type."

"Figured I'd try something different." She turns and gives him a flirtatious bat of her eyelashes, to which he turns his attention back to his friends. Griffin's theory floods my mind. If it's true, then he *likes* her. "But I don't think he's the type to do anything."

"You could always go for one of his friends," I suggest. "I'm sure they won't pass you up."

"Yeah, maybe," she considers, but doesn't continue the conversation, going back to dancing.

Suit Guy and his friends finally make their way over to us just as Olivia starts to lose hope that they're even paying attention to her, which is something neither of us is used to. Normally guys flock to her, demanding her attention, but tonight she's had to work for every glance. She blames it on the fact that I am no longer single and the bartender's scaring everyone off. But now that multiple guys surround her, her bright smile is back on her face and it's contagious.

"Hey." The guy I made eye contact with before steps in front of me, trying to get my attention. He slides his free hand into his pocket and takes a swig of his beer. "I'm Dylan."

I give him a quick smile, making sure to not look up at him, but instead over his shoulder. I try to find Griffin, but he isn't there. The bar isn't any more crowded than it usually is, but right now I feel like I'm suffocating.

"Can I get you something to drink?" Dylan asks, despite my clear lack of interest. I shake my head, craning my neck around him as I try to figure out where Griffin went.

Not even two minutes after Dylan offers to get me a drink, Griffin appears with the bouncers. Suit Guy and his friends are removed from the premises immediately. And if Olivia's eyes could kill, Griffin would be chopped up and stashed away in someone's basement freezer. Mike suggests we all go home after that, including Griffin. He senses something is going on between us and doesn't want to risk it escalating more.

"I'll just text Nate and let him know to come pick us up." Olivia's visibly deflated, and I'm at a loss for how to fix this, devastated that she'd been right in her predictions. I doubt she'll ever go out with me again.

"Don't," Griffin growls, tugging on my wrist to pull me to his side. Olivia's head snaps up, her eyes flashing between us. "I'll get you two an Uber."

I watch as Olivia rolls her eyes before glancing back down at her phone.

"Babe," I say quietly, looking up into his dark eyes. "It's fine. I'll just get a ride home with them and meet you there."

"You think I'm going to let you get in a car with another guy after what I just saw?" he huffs as his hand tightens around my wrist. "You think I don't see the way Nate looks at you when he thinks I'm not watching?"

"Griffin, please," I beg as I try to wiggle my wrist free from his grip.

"It's fine," Olivia says, and I turn my attention to her. Her eyes are glued to Griffin's and her jaw ticks. "I told Nate you don't feel well and that Griffin's taking us home."

"Liv, you didn't need to do that," I say, but she slings her purse over her shoulder and walks between us, causing Griffin to let go of my wrist so she can pass through. I turn around to face her, feeling Griffin's body pressed against my back.

"I don't want to give him another reason to be mad at you, Maddie," Olivia spits, glaring at Griffin. "Let's just go home."

Griffin pulls up on his bike in front of our building just as we're stepping out of the car. The entire Uber ride home, Olivia was silent. I tried apologizing, but no matter what I said, she didn't respond. I follow behind her as she walks into our building without a word, Griffin hot on my trail.

"Olivia, please talk to me," I cry as I step through our door, rushing ahead so I can stop her from going to her room. "I'm so sorry. I promised you that tonight would be different and I ruined it. Please, just look at me!"

"Maddie, shut up," Griffin groans, dropping his keys on the table. "She's not worth the apology."

"You're a dick, you know that, Griffin?" Olivia yells, turning on her heel to face him. In my seven years of knowing her, I have never heard her curse before. Not that the word *dick* is a curse word, but for Olivia, it's close enough. "Maybe Maddie can't see it, but I sure can."

I swallow the lump in my throat as Griffin steps around Olivia to stand by my side. His fingers circle around my wrist for the second time tonight and I hiss in pain.

"Griffin, let go!" I want to pull free, but can't. I try wiggling my fingers, but he only tightens his grip. I bite down on my lip to distract myself from the pain. Maybe if Griffin sees, he'll let go of my hand to pull my lip free like he always does.

"You're hurting me," I say, but they don't hear me over their shouting.

I wrap my other hand around Griffin's wrist, trying to pry his fingers off me, but they don't budge. He and Olivia continue shouting, and my heart pounds in my chest. I close my eyes, trying to tune them out as I struggle to get out of his hold, but it's no use.

"Stop!" I yell, so loud that I am pretty sure everyone in our apartment building can hear, but at least I finally have their attention. "I can't stand this anymore. You guys are always fighting."

"She's not good for you, Maddie," Griffin says, turning his attention to me. His eyes are just as dark as they were at the bar earlier. I shut my mouth and swallow, my throat suddenly dry.

"*I'm* not good for her?" Olivia screams, jabbing her finger into her glitter-dusted chest. "You're joking, right?"

"Right now, neither of you are good for me." They both glare in my direction and I instantly want to take back what I said.

"I mean..." I hesitate, biting down on my lip again. "I love you both so much. I can't handle you two constantly fighting anymore."

"You love him?" Olivia chokes. "Geez, Maddie. Out of all the guys to fall in love with, it had to be with someone like him?"

"You're the one who pushed me toward him!" I remind her for the second time tonight.

"Oh, so this is my fault?" She gives me a pleading look, then places her hands on her hips. Her eyes cut through me. "I don't even know who you are anymore, Maddie."

"Why?" Griffin shouts, pulling me closer to his side before I can say anything else. "Because now she isn't controlled by *you*?"

"*Controlled* by me?" Olivia laughs. "Maddie, do you *hear* him? He's twisting everything I say so that I'm the bad guy."

"Olivia, please." I wish Griffin would just look at me and see just how badly this is hurting me and stop. But he doesn't.

"I can't do this anymore," Olivia says, shaking her head in disappointment.

Without looking back, Olivia walks out of the living room and to her bedroom, slamming the door shut behind her. Tears well in my eyes and I look at the ceiling, trying to blink them back. I haven't cried yet in front of Griffin, and I don't want tonight to be the night I finally do. Especially when it's over someone he hates.

"I'm sorry," Griffin whispers in my ear from behind, brushing my hair over my shoulder and pressing a kiss on the back of my neck. "Did I mention how sexy you look in this dress?"

"Griffin, I — " I can't hold the tears back anymore, and he turns me around, pulling me into his chest as I let them flow freely. "Tonight was supposed to be different. I promised her it would be fun."

"I'm sorry she's treating you like this," he mumbles into my hair, running his hand up and down my back in soothing strokes. "Did you have fun?" He tilts my chin up and looks into my eyes. They're back to that black licorice color I love. "Because that's all I care about."

I shrug.

He presses his lips against mine, and my heart starts to race again, making me forget about the chaos of the night. His hands slide down my back to the hem of my dress and slip underneath. I try my hardest not to let his touch affect me, but I can't. He knows what he does to me. He knows I can't stay mad at him. Not when he's touching me like this. Every time he kisses me, touches me, or smiles at me, nothing else matters.

I am his.

He is mine.

And I love him.

title to be determined

By Madison Williams

Olivia left.

She hasn't responded to any of my calls or messages. I know she's staying with Nate, only because I texted him after a week went by without hearing from her, so at least I know she's safe. But I also know she wants nothing to do with me anymore. Nate wouldn't go into detail, saying he doesn't want to get in the middle and that I should give her time. *Time?* For what? I didn't do anything. She's the one who left.

So aside from Griffin, my blog is all I have and I let it consume me. My viewer count is rising every day and I'm making a decent salary through advertisements and affiliate links. Sure, it isn't the nine-to-five job that my dad wanted for me, but at least I'm able to support myself with it and have enough left over to put in savings. Which is important because my relationship with my dad has managed to get worse, so I can't rely on him for financial support anymore.

Griffin doesn't "do" parents. When my dad found out that I was in a relationship, he wanted to meet the guy who managed to sweep me off my feet. After spending weeks begging and making promises that it would be quick and painless, Griffin finally agreed to have dinner with my dad, so tonight we're meeting him at one of his favorite steak houses.

"Hi, I'm Griffin, it's nice to meet you," Griffin says, firmly shaking my dad's hand. My dad always told me that you can tell a lot from a person by the way they shake your hand. And the way my dad's eyebrows arch as he looks down at their joined hands in approval tells me he's at least passed that test.

I glance between the two of them before finally stopping on my dad, who's standing there with his lips pressed in a hard line, his eyes narrowing as he looks Griffin over again.

I wish I could say the dinner is going well, but then I'd be lying. I'm convinced by the time our drinks come out that no matter what Griffin says, it'll be wrong. If Griffin was a brain surgeon, my dad would find fault in it. If Griffin donated all his earnings to charity, he still wouldn't be good enough. If Griffin rolled out a red carpet in front of me everywhere we went, he still wouldn't appreciate me enough in my father's eyes.

"This isn't right, Madison," my dad says when Griffin excuses himself to use the restroom. My father makes it clear that he wants me to think hard about the choices I'm making, which is odd, considering he's never shown any type of interest in the choices I've made before. So when I make it clear to *him* that I have no intention of leaving Griffin just because he doesn't like him, he doesn't hold back his disappointment. "I will not stand here and watch you throw your life away over that boy."

"Then don't," I offer, before muttering under my breath. "It's not like you've been an active part of my life since Mom died anyway."

Okay, maybe that was a low blow. But it's true.

"How's your writing coming along?" he asks, changing the subject. Leave it to him to avoid any difficult conversation.

To answer this million-dollar question...it's not going well. If I have any time left over before Griffin finishes work, I try my hardest to get some pages in. I'm excellent at brainstorming and outlining, but actually writing the book? Something just hasn't been clicking. It doesn't help that my inspiration always strikes late at night when I'm with Griffin, so I can't exactly pull out a laptop and start writing. He doesn't like when I do that.

It's like you're cheating on me when you do that, he'll complain, closing my laptop without bothering to ask me if I've saved my work. *If you really love me, you wouldn't need to create fake boyfriends and live out your fantasies through them. You'd be busy living it with me.*

But, of course, I don't tell my dad any of that, knowing he wouldn't understand.

"It's going great," I say, smiling through the lie and picking up my wine glass. I catch a glimpse of Griffin exiting the bathroom and sigh with relief, draining my glass in a single gulp. All I have to do is make it through dessert and then this horrible night will be over.

When we make it back to my apartment later, Griffin makes it clear that he never wants to be around my dad again. I don't bother arguing because I don't want to go through that again either.

"I can't believe it's been three weeks," I say, taking a sip of my coffee while Griffin stands in front of the stove, flipping pancakes. Griffin moved in despite me not being completely on board. It's not that I have anything against living with him, it's just that I was holding out hope that Olivia would come back. According to Nate, though, that won't be happening anytime soon. At least not until Griffin is out of the picture. But now that it's been almost two months since she left, I've lost hope that she'll ever walk through the door again, even just to visit me. "Why didn't I have you move in sooner?"

"Do you really want me to answer that?" he says over his shoulder, cocking a brow.

"Nope," I say, placing my cup down on the counter. I've avoided the topic of Olivia since he's moved in. "Can you add chocolate chips to my pancakes?"

We've started transforming Olivia's room into an office for me. Which means I have a pile of boxes with her name written in black Sharpie that I'm procrastinating telling her to come get. Griffin offered to help me pick out a new desk and whatever else I may want, but I can't get myself to do it. I normally love decorating and designing spaces, and I had so much fun putting our personal touches on this apartment when Olivia and I moved in, but I can't seem to shake that I'm messing with Olivia's bedroom. It's becoming too real that she's gone. Both from the apartment and my life.

"Anything for you, babe." He reaches over and grabs my hand, giving it a little squeeze. I smile back, picking my coffee mug up and tracing over the engraved *breathe* with the pad of my thumb, and focus on the positives.

Just like the rest of my life, we've fallen into a routine. I spend my days working on my blog, doing some chores, and cooking dinner. When Griffin comes home, I spend the rest of the evening with him. Every day is the same. And, as much as I love him, sometimes I wonder if I even *am* happy. I've been so focused on masking my sadness about the Olivia situation that I've let things start to creep into our relationship.

It was a few days after Griffin moved in when I noticed the change. His grip on my hand became tighter whenever we'd run errands, his fingers would dig into my hips when he held me close, his kisses grew harder and needier, and his insistence on knowing where I was at all times hit new peaks. Every weekend, he insists that I go to The Big House with him while he works and takes my car instead of his bike, saying he feels safer driving me home in my car than on the back of his bike.

"Want to watch a movie?" I ask, grabbing my plate of pancakes from him. "We can eat on the couch. There's a new movie that just came out on Netflix and I heard it's pretty good."

"Maybe next time," he replies, and I watch as he crosses over to the couch, pancakes and cup of coffee in hand, and turns on the television to his favorite show.

"Come on." I put my plate of pancakes down, taking a seat next to him, and snuggling up under his arm. "We never watch anything I want to watch."

"That's because I don't like your shows," he says before taking a sip of his coffee. His newly tattooed knuckles tighten around the mug in his hand, and I suck in a breath.

"Well, I don't particularly like yours, either," I mumble.

"You're home all day." He turns his attention to me, tucking a strand of my hair behind my ear. My traitorous skin tingles underneath his fingers. "You can watch your shows then."

"Yeah, I guess," I agree, despite the uneasiness I feel in my gut.

"How about this?" He shifts his body slightly, pulling me onto his lap and giving me a slow kiss, his lips tasting like maple syrup and coffee creamer. "You can watch one of your shows *if* you give me one of your amazing massages at the same time."

"How will I eat my pancakes?" I question. "Kind of need my hands to do that."

"I'll feed you," he says breezily, pressing his lips against mine again. When he pulls away, he moves me off his lap and scoots forward. "Come on, get behind me and tell me what you want to watch."

It's moments like these where Olivia's voice pops into my head the most. *He's controlling. You let him do whatever he wants. Does he ever care what* you *want to do?* I can't help but wonder if she's right, and I find myself shrinking into myself. But then Griffin will reach over and rub my back or free my lip from my teeth, and the effect of his touch will shoo her voice away. Sometimes I feel like

I'll let him do whatever he wants as long as it means he never stops touching me.

I love Griffin. And he loves me. Our relationship is just...different. It isn't something you'll find in a Hallmark movie or romance novel. We don't go on typical dates, instead spending our time going for rides on his bike or taking photos for my blog. He might not hold my chair out at fancy dinners or take me to the movies, but *my god*, when he touches me, none of that matters.

title to be determined
By Madison Williams

Every Sunday morning, I wake up just as the sun is about to rise and tiptoe into the kitchen with my planner materials. Griffin always closes the bar on Saturday nights, so he needs to sleep in. Despite always being with him at the bar and being exhausted myself, I savor the quiet of these mornings. Our kitchen table is positioned in front of a window seat, and I love to curl up against it with the blinds open.

With my planner, colored pens, highlighters, and sticker pack arranged neatly in front of me, I'm ready to tackle the upcoming week. Today, my favorite mug is filled with my favorite tea. Sometimes I imagine the steam is filled with courage, strength, and hope. I try to fill my lungs with as much of it and keep it there as long as I can before I exhale, hoping I absorb one of those things.

After all the important times and details are filled in, I press my planner flat against the scanner in our printer and send it to my laptop. After converting it to a PDF, I email it to Griffin so he can have it since he likes being able to see what I am doing wherever he is. I often find him peeking inside my planner at night, as if to make sure nothing changed. It bothered me at first, but now, I find comfort in it. Or I at least learned to. I just have to keep reminding myself that he's interested in my life. I should be lucky, honestly.

Staring down at my planner and seeing Olivia's name circled under today's date, I remember why I am a little anxious. She's coming to finally get the last of her things, which means after today, she will be officially out of my life. Griffin pressed me all week to reach out to her, claiming he was tired of walking around her stuff, but I wanted to push it off as long as I could. If her stuff is still here, then I can ignore the fact that she's gone.

None of that mattered to Griffin though. He sent her a text through my phone last night telling her she had until this afternoon to get her things before they were thrown out. I was furious, but he was quick to dismiss me. Apparently, he did it for my own good. Olivia never responded, so I'm not sure she'll be coming, but I'm hoping. And by putting it in my planner, it makes me believe that she will be. I mean, it's written right there in sparkly purple ink, so she *has* to come, right?

Griffin is still asleep in our room, and since he typically sleeps until noon, I have a few more hours to myself. I close my planner and walk over to the couch, fully prepared to put on my favorite show, when there's a knock at the door. Olivia still has the key to the apartment, so why would she knock? I wrap my arms around my stomach, feeling nauseous as I realize how far our friendship has fallen.

I walk over to the door and peer through the peephole. When I see who it is, I gasp and jump back, throwing my hand to my chest. *What is he doing here?* He knocks on the door again and I glance down the hallway, begging whoever might be listening that Griffin hasn't woken up. When I hear a muffled snore, I grasp the doorknob and pull it open.

"What are you doing here?" I whisper, looking up at Nate.

"I'm here to get Olivia's things," he says, walking in without an invitation.

"Where is she?" I question. I'm tempted to step out of my

apartment and look around the corner to see if she's hiding, but then that means leaving Nate alone in the apartment with Griffin.

"She's not here." I turn sharply on my heel and face him, taking in his black jeans, black Vans, and white T-shirt that hangs loosely on him. His brown hair looks freshly cut, his green eyes bright and focused on mine. Feeling uncomfortable, I focus on his hands, which rest on his hips.

"What do you mean she's not here?" I ask through gritted teeth, making sure to keep my voice down as I look him straight in the eyes. "She was supposed to come. Not you. I was supposed to fix everything. You're not supposed to be here."

My heart races in my chest and I'm not sure what's happening. I push past Nate and take a seat on the couch, clutching my chest with my hand. Why can't I breathe? This has been happening to me a lot lately, and I'm not sure what it means. Am I going to faint? I lean forward, putting my head between my knees, hoping it will help. That's what you're supposed to do, right?

"Madds, are you okay?" Nate asks, the sound of his footsteps coming closer. The couch cushion sinks as he takes a seat next to me, causing my body to lean into his. Nate drapes his arm around me, pulling me into his side. I know I should put some space between us, but his touch is so comforting.

"I can't breathe," I mumble into my knees as I continue to hug them.

Nate moves his arm from around me and places his hand on my back. I can feel the warmth through my clothes as he lightly rubs up and down. I try to mimic the pattern with my breathing, but nothing is helping slow the beating of my heart.

"Hey, look at me, Madds," Nate says, his hand coming to rest on my shoulder. I let him pull me up into a sitting position, but don't look at him. My hands fall into my lap and I close my eyes. "You're okay, I promise. You're having a panic attack."

"A what?" I ask, looking over at him, taking in how concerned he is. His hand is still on my shoulder, keeping me from bolting off the couch. Not because his grip is firm, because it isn't. Nate has always done everything with a certain gentleness. His touch keeps me there because of the feeling it gives me. I don't want to lose it. It's the only thing keeping me from spiraling out of control. As long as I can feel him, I know I'm safe.

"A panic attack," he repeats. "Have you ever had one before?"

"I don't know, maybe?" I shrug, and his hand slips off my shoulder. "My heart won't stop racing and I feel like I can't breathe."

"Try something with me, okay?" he asks, and I nod. "I want you to tell me five things that you can see."

"Five?" Nate nods and I take a deep breath, glancing around the room. "Okay, I see our television."

"What else?" he says, encouraging me to go on.

"I see the candle on our TV stand." Another breath. "It smells like sunscreen and reminds me of summer, and I hate it."

"Okay." He chuckles. "What else?"

"I see Griffin's leather jacket and my denim one on the chair." I look around the room for one more thing to point out. "Oh, and I see Olivia's sparkly nail polish on the shelf over there. Don't forget to take that when you leave."

"Good," he says, sounding proud. "How do you feel now?"

"My heart is still racing," I note. "Maybe I need to go to the hospital. Am I having a heart attack? Oh my god, will I need a heart transplant?"

"Take a deep breath, Maddie," Nate says. I watch the way his chest rises and falls with each breath as he guides me through it.

"It doesn't hurt to breathe anymore."

"At least we can rule out a lung transplant then." He chuckles softly as he runs his hands down his jeans. "Now, what are four things you can feel?"

"Nate," I say, rolling my eyes. "What are you doing?"

"Trust me, this helps." He grins, and something inside me flutters. *What the hell, Maddie?* Griffin is literally in the other room and here I am, turning into a puddle for a guy because he showed me a breathing technique. Shit, *Griffin*. I'm about to stand up and insist that he leave, but his hand lands on my thigh, freezing me to the spot. "What are four things you can feel right now?"

"Feel?" I ask, blushing at the fact it sounds like a wheeze. "I don't feel anything."

"It can be anything. For example, I can feel the pillow behind my back, an itch on my neck, and the goosebumps on your leg."

"Stop it," I say, pushing his hand off me. "I told you I don't feel anything. I can't. It's like I'm numb."

"Maddie. It's me. You're safe. We can work through this, okay? I just need you to trust me."

"No," I say a little too loudly, standing up in front of him. "You shouldn't be here. Just take Olivia's things and go."

I glance down the hallway nervously. I can just make out the sound of Griffin snoring on the other side. *What am I thinking?* If Griffin wakes up and comes out to see Nate's hand on me, he will freak out. No, that's an understatement; he'll become murderous.

"Is he here?" Nate asks, looking down the hallway and then back at me. I nod.

"You need to leave," I whisper, shaking my head slowly. "You shouldn't be here."

He must notice how scared I am because he doesn't argue. Instead, he gestures to the boxes stacked against the wall. I give him a thumbs up, glancing back at our bedroom every few seconds as I watch him move the boxes. I sit back down on the couch and pull my phone out of my pocket, flipping it in my hands. He picks up each box one by one and moves them out to the hall; it's like he's dragging this out. Doesn't he know I need him gone?

When the last of her things are moved into the communal hall-way, Nate crosses the living room, walking past me. I watch as he grabs the bottle of nail polish I mentioned before. Yup, he is defi-nitely dragging this out on purpose. As he walks past again, I stand up and follow until he stops short in the entryway. I watch as he turns around, glancing at the door that separates us from Griffin before he slides his phone out of his back pocket and begins typing. When he puts his phone down, mine vibrates in my hand.

Nate: dinglehopper?

My stomach drops as I read our code word on my screen. What is he getting at? I look up, noticing how his eyes are glued to mine, as if looking for some sort of reaction or sign that I need him to rescue me. Well, he's wrong. I don't need him. I don't need Olivia. I *want* my friend back, but I don't *need* her. And who does Nate think he is, showing up at my door and pulling something like this?

I narrow my eyes and shake my head. I watch as he digs through his pockets, finally pulling out a crumpled receipt from his wallet. Patting down his jeans pockets once more, he glances around the space until he lands on a permanent marker on the table. I watch impatiently as he scribbles something onto the back of the receipt, my heart in my throat.

When he finishes, I watch as he folds it and walks over to me. He grabs my hand and pushes the folded receipt inside, closing my fingers around it.

"This is my new address," he says softly, looking me directly in the eyes. He moved? Did Olivia go with him? I swallow, taking in how serious he is. "If you ever need somewhere to go, you're always welcome. No questions asked."

"I won't," I say once he makes it to the front door, causing him to turn around and look at me. "I won't need it."

"I hope you won't, Madds." His eyes dart to my bedroom door and then back to me before he finally leaves. The look on his face before he shuts the door is a look I'll never forget, like he'll never see me this way again.

My heart shatters as a voice screams that he probably won't.

thirteen

I knew I couldn't stay hidden from the world forever and I'd have to eventually leave my room. I pressed my ear to the door, trying to hear if Nate was home. There was no sign of him in the kitchen or working in his office, and no sign of Tuna's nails scratching against the hardwood floors. There was no sign of life at all.

"Nate?" I shouted down the hallway, my head poking out from the doorway. No response.

I dragged my feet into the kitchen, finding another note from Nate saying he took Tuna to the vet and would be at the food truck for the day. He also told me there was a breakfast sandwich waiting for me in the fridge, followed by the heating instructions. After eating my sandwich, I quickly got dressed and headed to Latte Da! with a book tucked under my arm. Making sure to not look in the direction of Nate's Grates, I kept my head down, staring at my boots as I walked in.

"Hey, Maddie!" Olivia said from behind the counter, waving enthusiastically.

"Hey," I said, making my way over as I took in her hair. It was no longer purple, but instead a deep auburn shade. How Olivia hadn't lost all her hair with how many times she'd dyed and bleached it was seriously a miracle. "What's with the new hair color?"

"I had Daniella change it up yesterday, do you like it?" she asked, twirling a piece around her finger in front of her face. "I can't figure out how I feel about it."

"You can pull off practically anything, Liv. See how you feel about it in a few weeks and then decide. You can always switch it up again."

"Iced decaf vanilla latte?"

"Yup," I said, popping the *P*. "With cinnamon sprinkled on top."

"Coming right up," she sang, making her way to the espresso machine. "So, about yesterday..."

"Ugh," I groaned, taking a seat at one of the barstools along the counter. I'd been hoping Olivia wouldn't bring up yesterday's door incident. But it was a new day and I was ready to start facing things...so long as she hurried up with my coffee. I was already finding things to fidget with on the counter. "I'm sorry about that. I was a bit dramatic."

"Did something happen?" Olivia questioned, looking over at me hesitantly. "I don't want to pry, but we're just worried about you."

"Yesterday was the one-year anniversary of the accident," I said softly, dropping my hands to my lap and pressing softly along the scars. "I had a therapy appointment and it was hard, so I wanted to be left alone."

"You should've said something," Olivia said softly, handing me my drink. "Now I feel bad for pounding on your door."

"It's fine." I followed the trail of condensation down the side of the cup. I knew Olivia wouldn't press me if I didn't want her to, but Nate on the other hand...there was the towel fiasco we still needed to talk about *and* me locking myself in my room. And once Nate came home from work, there would be no way of avoiding it. Unless... "Hey, do you want to come over tonight?" I'd have plenty of time to be the bigger person; I didn't say I had to start *today*.

"Me?" Olivia asked, making a show of looking over her shoulder.

"Yes, you," I laughed. "We can order takeout and have a game night. It'll be fun! I don't know if Nate has any — "

"I can bring some games!" she chirped, getting excited. "I have Scrabble, Life, Monopoly, UNO, Cards Against — "

"Bring whatever you want," I said, taking a sip of my coffee. "When do you usually wrap up here?"

"We close at five, so I'll take a shower and then head over."

With Olivia coming over, I wouldn't have to worry about Nate bringing anything awkward up. I doubt he'd want to mention in front of his sister that he saw me naked. The bells above the door chimed as more customers walked in, and Olivia headed over to the register. Picking up my book, I turned to the first page.

Later that day, I made a trip to Target, picked up some face masks and snacks, and then grabbed our dinner. I offered to pick up Olivia so she wouldn't have to ride her bike over, but she said Nate would give her a lift. My hands felt clammy as I sat on the couch, a buffet of snacks and Chinese food spread out over the coffee table, waiting for them to arrive. As soon as I heard the keypad ding on the front door, my heart started to race.

Olivia barreled through the door with Nate close behind, cat carrier in hand. He lowered it to the ground, opening the door for Tuna, who took it as his chance to bolt down the hallway and out of sight. I watched as he dropped his car keys next to mine on the table before taking off his Vans.

"Yay, snacks!" Olivia cheered as she kicked off her heels, rushing over to my side. I laughed as she bit off each end of a Twizzler and placed it in her can of sparkling water like a straw. "What game do you want to play??"

"Uhh," I fidgeted in my seat, looking at her empty hands.

"Oh, hamburgers!" Olivia shouted, turning to face the door. "Nate, I forgot the games! It's okay, I'll just walk back and get — "

"No!" I said a little too loudly. The whole point of inviting Olivia over was so that I didn't have to be alone with Nate. "I mean, it's fine. We can just watch a movie." I grabbed the remote off the coffee table and turned on the television, hitting the wrong button. Static noise blared through the speakers, causing me and Olivia to jump. I frantically tapped at the buttons, but no matter how many times I lowered the volume or tried to change the channel, nothing happened.

"I've got it," Nate shouted over the noise. I twisted in my seat, holding the remote over the back of the couch. Even though I was holding the remote by the very end, Nate still managed to brush his fingers against mine as he took it from my hands. I swallowed, my gaze falling to his calloused fingers lingering over mine as he took it from me. With the click of a few buttons, Nate had Netflix running and the house was silent.

"Hey, Madds." Nate cleared his throat, bringing my attention to his lips. "Can I talk to you for a second?"

"Now?" I glanced over at Olivia quickly before widening my eyes at him. "But Olivia just got here."

"It'll be quick," he promised, nodding down the hallway.

I mumbled an apology to Olivia before standing up and following him to his office. He held the door open for me and I squeezed past him in the doorway, immediately being hit with the scent of rosemary, mint, and rich butter. He smelled just like a grilled cheese sandwich. Once inside, Nate turned on the light and shut the door.

"Maybe we should keep the door open?" I suggested, staring at his hand on the doorknob. "I don't want Olivia to think anything — "

"Can we talk about yesterday?" He let go of the doorknob, and I nodded.

A silence fell over us as we stared at each other. Tuna sat by the window, perched on his pillow, his purring filling the silence. I walked over to him and reached out a tentative hand to stroke his fur, enjoying the rumbling under my hand. Whenever I was alone with someone, I'd obsess over what the other person was thinking. But standing there with Nate, it felt...fine. Even after he'd seen me naked.

"I know I said no questions asked," he said, scratching his chin through his beard. "But I'm worried about you. You know you can talk to me about anything, right?"

"I know." I swallowed, averting my eyes from his. Should I open up to him? Was I ready to reveal everything? I couldn't even speak the words to Olivia, instead making her read my journals. But Nate had already seen so much, and I wasn't just referring to my body. Every panic attack I'd had since coming to Briar Oakes had been in front of him, and every *single* time he'd been so patient and understanding. "Thank you."

"Why do you do that?" Nate asked, gesturing to my leg where I was rubbing my thumb in circular motions. "I've seen you do that a few times."

"I do this when I'm nervous or anxious," I said, meeting his warm eyes. "It reminds me of what I've been through. That I made it out."

"The scars?" Nate asked and I nodded, looking away from him again. "What did he do to you, Maddie?"

I didn't have to be looking at him to feel his helpless energy emanating. I sucked in a breath through my teeth as I contemplated my next move.

"I'm sorry." I shook my head and chewed on my lip. "I'm just not ready to talk about it."

Honestly, I just didn't want to give him another reason to look at me differently.

"Okay," he said, even though I could see him losing all confidence in me ever opening up and trusting him. I gave him a small smile, hoping it conveyed everything I wasn't ready to say. That I was glad that he never pushed anything with me, that I wanted him to keep trying, even though I wasn't making it easy for him. "Can you tell me what happened yesterday, and why you locked yourself in your room?"

"Yesterday was...it was the anniversary of my accident and the last time I saw Griffin." I paused, all my attention on his knick-knack shelf. "My therapy session drained me, so I slept most of the day away."

"Maddie and Nate, sitting in a tree," Olivia shouted from the living room. I threw my head back and groaned. "K-I-S-S-I-N-G!"

"I should get back out there," I said, gesturing toward the door. "Before she gets any more ideas."

"Mind if I join you two after I take a shower?"

"Of course, it's your house, Nate. You don't even have to ask." I laughed nervously, wondering how I was going to make it through the night now.

*

"Is it a Disney or vampire night?" Olivia asked as she tried to push her egg roll through the mouth hole of her face mask. Maybe we should have waited to put the masks on until after we ate. Tuna had taken one look at us earlier and scampered down the hall, taking cover in Nate's office. I didn't blame him, though. We looked absolutely terrifying.

"Disney," I said, pointing to our faces before taking a bite of my chicken and broccoli. When I saw the Disney Villain face mask collection while shopping, I knew I had to grab them for tonight. I was sporting Cruella De Vil while Olivia was Ursula. The face masks came in a pack of three and we hoped we could convince Nate into being The Evil Queen. "Obviously."

About ten minutes later, we heard the bathroom door open and Nate made his way into the living room. Olivia and I both turned in unison, looking over the couch at Nate who stood frozen next to the couch.

"What the fuck?" he shouted, his eyes widening in alarm. Olivia and I laughed so hard at his reaction we had to clutch our stomachs to keep from toppling over. "You two look..." He trailed off, shaking his head.

"Relax," Olivia said, pulling off her Ursula face mask and massaging the excess product into her skin. "Come join us, Nate!"

"Yeah." I kept my mask on, having finally gotten the hang of eating through it. "We saved you The Evil Queen."

"I'll pass." He took one more look at us, shook his head, and then walked over to the couch, stepping over our scattered snack wrappers.

When he sat down next to me with wet hair and that delicious body wash scent clouding around him — *and* wearing a shirt this time, thank god — we shared a quiet look, and I mouthed the words "Thank you," to which he gave me a genuine smile and nod. He might be the best guy I'd ever known. And that wasn't just the post-shower-mussed-Nate effect talking. Probably.

When I felt the tickle of his leg hair brush against mine, I scooted over so I was closer to Olivia. Nate let out a soft chuckle before grabbing the container of fried rice. Feeling like an idiot being the only one wearing a face mask, I peeled it off and massaged my face with the tips of my fingers.

"So," Olivia mumbled over a mouthful of chicken lo mein. I laughed, watching as a piece fell from her mouth and landed on her lap. "Have you dated at all since you and Griffin ended?"

"Olivia," Nate said in a warning tone before turning his head to face me. "You don't have to answer — "

"It's fine," I said, taking a sip of my Dr. Pepper and placing it on the coaster on the coffee table. "But no, I haven't. Griffin kind of ruined relationships for me."

"Just because you dated one bad guy doesn't mean you're destined to be alone the rest of your life."

"I'm not alone, Olivia."

"So you *do* admit it!" she shouted, pointing her fork at me and Nate. "You *are* together."

"I meant I have *you*." Why did Olivia even feel the need to bring this up? "And I have all my lovely book boyfriends."

"I'm going to tell you the same thing I used to tell you in college, Maddie." Here we go. "A book boyfriend might make your heart all happy and fill you up with butterflies, but can you sit on his face?"

Nate choked on his food, rice erupting from his mouth and... nose? "Oh my god, are you okay?" I shrieked, slamming my palm between his shoulder blades.

"Don't be so dramatic, Nate, you're the one joining girls' night." She rolled her eyes and leaned back against the couch. "Have you even thought about dating recently, Maddie?"

"You mean, aside from Nate?" I asked sarcastically and she nodded. "Not really. I mean, don't get me wrong, if I see a cute guy, I still get all the butterflies." Out of the corner of my eye, I saw Nate's grip on his fork tighten. "But I have no desire to pursue anything."

"I hate that he ruined love for you."

Me too.

But honestly, I wasn't even scared of someone hurting me. No, I was scared of *me*. What if I met someone and we really hit it off, and yet again, I was blind to the signs of abuse? Or what if I was so messed up by my relationship with Griffin that I overanalyzed every situation and sabotaged the relationship before it even started?

"Griffin was like a drug to me, which I know you told me over and over again, but I never believed it until recently. Or at least, I didn't think it was a negative thing." I looked down as I twisted my charm bracelet around my wrist. "Yeah, he treated me like shit — "

"That's an understatement."

" — but it wasn't always bad," I continued, giving Olivia a pointed look. I thought back on the flowers and sweet kisses he'd give me in the mornings leaving for work. Part of me missed his daily text messages, telling me how much he missed me. Okay, maybe I didn't miss *him* sending them, but just having something like that to look forward to.

"Don't feel the need to defend him, Madds," Nate finally chimed in. He reached over, placing his hand over mine to stop me from fidgeting with the charms on the bracelet. I was just about to overthink his gesture when a warbled sound exploded from Olivia.

"Wait!" Her eyes went wide as she stared at me, slamming her hands down. "Was Griffin the last person you slept with?"

"Seriously, Liv?" I exhaled loudly, placing my elbows on my knees and dropping my head into my hands.

"No wonder you're locking yourself in your room!" she shrieked, taking in my lack of answer as confirmation. "I would be, too, if I hadn't had a proper orgasm in over a year."

"Oh my god, Liv." I ignored the feeling of Nate's eyes drilling into the back of my head. "Shut up!"

"Well, is it true?" She rolled her hands to encourage me to answer. "Or have you been taking the self-guided tour?"

"No!" This time I was the one raising my voice. "I am not doing that. I'm living with your *brother*. Who is sitting right next to us, in case you forgot."

"So?"

"I'm not having this conversation."

"I did it all the time when I lived here. The jets in his tub are fan-tas-tic."

"I did not need to know that." I sunk lower into the couch as I covered my face with my hands. I invited Olivia over to avoid being alone with Nate, and instead, I was dealing with this. I peeked through my hands to gauge Nate's reaction and could see him feigning being sick.

"Me neither," Nate agreed.

"You're honestly telling me that you haven't" — she lowered her voice and waggled her eyebrows — "visited your safety deposit box?"

"No!" I shouted again, not even attempting to hide my frustration. "Do I really have to remind you again that I live with your brother?"

"Oh, so he's been petting the kitten?" Olivia smirked.

"Jesus Christ," Nate muttered.

"I'm not sleeping with your brother, and for the last time, I am *not* having this conversation." I stood up and gathered my garbage.

"I'm so getting you a vibrator," she shouted over the back of the couch. "The one I have is waterproof, has four speeds, and twelve different patterns! You'll love it."

I glanced at Nate, watching as his jaw dropped. He looked just as uncomfortable as I felt. I slapped my palm against my forehead, dragging it down my face as the urge to die filled me. That was it, I'd never be able to look at him again. It was safe to say Olivia and her word-vomit condition hadn't changed one bit.

"Please excuse me as I have lost the will to live," I mumbled against my hands, pretty confident that they couldn't understand anything I just said.

Nate cleared his throat, and I dropped my hands from my face at the gravelly sound. "Just remember my room is across the hall for whenever you feel the need to use that."

My eyes widened at his comment and I glanced at Olivia, whose eyebrows seemed to have taken residence in her hairline.

"No, no, no," he said, shaking his hands in front of him. "I didn't mean it like that! I just meant that if you're going to be using that while I'm home...that I can probably hear it. Not that you should find me."

"Why me?" I looked up at the ceiling and spoke directly to God. "Please forgive me for murdering Olivia."

"I doubt you'd hear it anyway," Olivia shrugged, not bothered at all by this conversation. "You never heard me."

"For fuck's sake, Olivia," Nate muttered. Now he was the one covering his face with his hands.

"Oh, come on." She rolled her eyes, looking at her brother. "Don't pretend that you never oodled your noodle while I lived here."

"I'm never joining your girls' nights again," Nate groaned, standing up and gathering his garbage. "And oodled my noodle? What are you, five?"

"Okay." I clapped my hands once in the way my mom always did when I was younger to signal the end of a conversation. "Excuse me while I use the bathroom and then go to bed. Nate, can you take Olivia home?"

"Wait," Olivia said, hopping off the couch so she could block me from going down the hallway. "You should take a bath and test the jets."

"Goodbye, Liv," I said as I shoved her to the side and walked down the hallway, pretty sure my face was as red as the shirt Nate was wearing.

"I'm never taking a bath again," I heard Nate mutter before I slammed the bathroom door shut behind me.

fourteen

Nate had been away for four days at a food truck festival, and I was grateful for the alone time, knowing I needed to get these feelings brewing inside me sorted out. And it worked. I thought. Well...I at least convinced myself that I was only feeling the flutters in my stomach (fine, they felt more like bowling balls bouncing than gentle butterflies) because it'd been over a year since I'd even been near a guy.

And of course, Nate had to have a glow-up since the day he showed up to my apartment to get Olivia's things. Okay, maybe that was a bit harsh. He was never hard on the eyes, but I'd always just seen him as Olivia's older brother. Now I was seeing him differently and part of me wanted to know what types of things this man could do...

I pinched myself, stopping my thoughts from going any further.

Okay, so maybe my feelings were still a work in progress.

Nate came back late last night, giving me a heads-up text before he pulled into the driveway so that I wouldn't attack him again with Lysol.

"Maddie, you got a package," Nate's voice called from outside my door. I glanced at my phone and saw the time, wondering who delivered packages this early in the morning. You would think, with Briar Oakes being such a small town, they'd wait until later in the day to deliver. It's not like they had an insane amount of stops to get through.

"Are you sure it's for me?" I shouted back. I hadn't ordered anything and no one knew where I was staying, aside from Olivia. I hadn't even given my dad Nate's address.

"Uh, yeah," Nate said, sounding a bit uncomfortable. "It's definitely not for me."

Unsure as to why Nate sounded off, I walked over to the door and opened it just enough to poke my head through. Nate stood in the hallway, holding a hot pink box and looking anywhere but in my direction.

"I thought it was for me, so I took it out of the box it came in. But once I saw what it was, I double-checked the label and saw it was for you. I'm sorry. I swear I wasn't being nosy."

"It's fine, Nate." I stepped out and looked down at the lid, my eyes widening at the bold black font. "What the hell is *The Intimidator 3000?*"

"No, you don't need to open..." I didn't even hear him as I lifted the lid of the box and reached inside, wrapping my hand around...silicone?

"Oh my god!" I shrieked once I realized what I was holding, dropping it to the floor. "I'm going to kill your sister!"

"Be my guest." He chuckled and scratched the back of his neck, eyes on the vibrator lying between our feet. "Just a friendly reminder, I'm right across the hall."

"I am *not* using that!" I continued to shout. I quickly snatched it off the floor and shoved it back in the box, my face burning with embarrassment.

"What you do in your spare time is none — "

"I'm not!"

"Okay, fine," he said, the tips of his ears turning a bright shade of red.

"Let's just add this to the never-ending list of things we will not be talking about again."

"Sounds good to me." He started sorting through the rest of the mail in his hands. "What are you doing today?"

"Nothing planned." I smiled, grateful for the easy subject change. "What are you doing?"

"I'm supposed to go to this restaurant not far from here. They reached out, asking if I'd be willing to feature them in one of my videos." I watched as his throat bobbed as he swallowed. I found it cute how obvious he was when he was nervous. "So, if you're up for some good food, and you don't mind the drive, you're more than welcome to — "

"Can I come with you?" I asked, surprising both him and myself. Why was I asking to spend time with the man that I continued to embarrass myself in front of? "I've been wanting to see what goes into filming for your channel. Olivia used to make fun of me when we were in college because I always watched your videos as soon as they were posted."

"You did?" Nate asked, his voice raising an octave. I couldn't help but smile as he cleared his throat. "I mean, yeah, you can come. Honestly, it's probably not as fun as you think it'll be. There's a lot of technical stuff and retakes, but the food is usually good."

"I don't mind. Hold on a sec." I turned around and threw the box on my bed, running over to my dresser to get ready. Quickly, I threw my hair up into a half ponytail and clasped the charm bracelet around my wrist. "But can I drive?"

"Yeah, that's fine," Nate said, pulling his phone out of his pocket and glancing at the time. "We need to leave in about thirty minutes if we want to get there on time."

"Sure, sounds good." I rushed over to the door, grabbing my bag off the knob. I left Nate in my room as I dashed into the living room to grab one of the books from my ever-growing stack and shoved it into my bag.

"I'm ready!" I shouted down the hallway. Nate's answering laugh sent a shiver zipping down my spine.

I pulled my Jeep along the curb outside of Off the Leash. When I asked Nate what type of food they served, he told me it was best if I went in blind. When I saw the smirk on his face, I knew I was in for more than your typical restaurant. Off the Leash's facade immediately reminded me of The Big House's, but rather than let my anxious thoughts overrun me, I chose to remind myself Nate would never take me somewhere that would make me uncomfortable. As I stepped out of the driver's seat, I took in the brick exterior that was painted black and the giant hot dog spray-painted to the right of the door in bright colors. Aside from that, it was dark and mysterious, giving away no other clues.

"I'm assuming we're having hot dogs?" I asked as Nate began to unload his equipment. "You could've just told me that, I don't see why you had to keep that a secret."

"You'll see." He laughed and winked at me over his shoulder. "Just don't get weird, okay?"

"Who me?" I gasped and threw my hand against my chest. Nate shook his head and chuckled, but there was a lightness to it that zinged through me. I stood there like an idiot, staring at him, as his smile grew wider. My heart stuttered at the single dimple on his right cheek and the way the sun reflected off his green eyes. I was suddenly very glad I came.

I followed Nate inside, arms filled with my tote and one of Nate's bags. Nate stopped at a table that was reserved for him and I watched as he started placing his bags down.

"What is all this stuff?"

"That bag over there has my camera, mic, memory cards, and extra batteries," he said, gesturing to one of the black bags on a table. "The bag you brought in has my tripod and that big one over there has my light kit in it."

"A light kit?" I raised an eyebrow at him. "Like those ring lights that beauty influencers use when they show how they apply makeup?"

"Not quite." He laughed. "The lighting is different in every restaurant, so I always bring it just in case."

"Hey, man," a deep voice called from behind us. "Sorry I'm so late."

"Nah, we just got here ourselves," Nate said, grabbing the guy's hand and pulling him close. I rolled my eyes as they bumped chests, patting each other on the back with their other hand. Why couldn't guys just have a normal handshake? "Maddie, you remember Ben, right? He's the bartender at The Garage."

"How could I forget?" I said sarcastically as I looked over at Nate, who smiled at me apologetically.

"Ben's been my friend since I moved to Briar Oakes," Nate chimed in, taking a step between us. "I met him through Tyler since they grew up in Briar Oakes together."

"Cool," I said shortly, hating the way Ben was looking at me. There was something about him that made my stomach feel queasy. I was sure it was because I associated him with my panic attack at the bar, but something still niggled.

"I really am sorry," Nate said once Ben was out of earshot. "It completely slipped my mind that I had asked him to help. I can see if I can reschedule and take you home if you want."

"No, Nate. Seriously, it's totally fine," I said, placing my hand on his arm. "You just do your thing."

"Are you sure?" he asked, eyes flicking to my grip which I loosened and dropped, cheeks flushing. "I don't want you to feel uncomfortable."

"Really, it's fine," I said, taking my book out of my bag and waving it in the air awkwardly. *Why am I like this?* "Just let me know where to go so I'm not in the way."

Ben was talking to one of the employees, who giggled a little too loudly at whatever he was telling her. She glanced over in Nate's direction, and I rolled my eyes as I watched her ogle him next. I took a seat at one of the tables closest to the door and dropped my bag onto the table. Pulling my book out of my bag, I forgot how revealing the cover was. I turned the book over on my lap, feeling my cheeks heat as I realized the back cover had a close-up of the model with a hand down his pants. When I opened the book and an index card fell onto my lap, I knew my heated skin was beyond concealing.

It's a great day
to be proud of how far you've come.
I know I am.
-Nate

"Oh my god," I whispered, looking over at Nate who was focused on setting up. I glanced back down at my book, taking in the suggestive cover, and groaned. Nate had seen this. I could only imagine what he thought I was reading.

But he was right. I *had* come far. And I should be proud of myself. A year ago, I was lying in a hospital bed, drugged up on painkillers, having just come out of emergency surgery. I left a toxic relationship. Sure, I still had my moments. I still cried. I still got scared. I still doubted my progress. I still didn't believe in happily ever after. I may have spent the entire day of the anniversary in bed.

But I also went to therapy. I found the right medication to help me. I learned how to go out into the world despite being afraid. I left the safety of my home and found Nate and Olivia. I stepped out of my comfort zone and went to a bar for the first time since Griffin. Yeah, I had a panic attack and had to leave, but I still went. Just because I'd had some hard moments didn't mean that all the progress I made disappeared. I *was* proud of how far I'd come.

Looking down at the index card that shook in my trembling fingers, I realized that Nate really did want to be there for me. He wanted to cheer me on through whatever life throws my way because I matter to him.

"Maddie," Nate called, snapping me back to reality. His eyes moved from mine to the bookmark in my hands, a soft smile appearing on his face. "Can you come here for a minute? I want to introduce you to someone."

Nate was at the counter standing next to Ben, the woman he was talking to before, and another man. Ben picked up the camera and pointed it at Nate, its flashing red light indicating that he was now recording.

"Hi, everyone," Nate started, shooting a smile at the camera. "Welcome back to another episode of *Nate's Gratest Food Finds!* I've got some new friends with me today that I'd like to introduce you to. Maddie?"

Oh, shit. Was I going to be in this episode? I looked down at what I was wearing, smoothing my now clammy hands over my white eyelet lace dress as I checked for any stains or wrinkles. Before I could freak out more, Nate stretched his hand out and I stared at it, contemplating whether I should take it. If I did, then I'd be in his episode. If I didn't, then he'd just have to do a retake. I mean, that was fine, right? He said he did it all the time.

Smiling, I placed my hand in Nate's, allowing him to pull me to his side. My eyes drifted down to where his hand wrapped around mine, his thumb toying with the fork charm on my bracelet. A warmth spread through me, all the way down to my toes.

"Maddie, this is Felix. He's the owner of Off the Leash." He let go of my hand, gesturing to the man standing to his right, who stretched his hand out to shake mine. Giving me a supportive smile, Nate slid his hand around my waist and tucked me in closer to his side, his eyes telling me, *You're safe,* before dropping his hand back to his side.

"It's nice to meet you," I smiled softly at Felix, placing my hand in his and giving it a shake. The corner of Nate's mouth lifted in a smile, causing another wave of warmth to course through me. Nate's fingers brushed lightly against mine. I looked down at his hand, which was centimeters away from mine, and swallowed. Was he asking for me to hold it again? No, that would be crazy. But the need to reach out and touch him, to lace my fingers with his, trumped the panic that had taken over me seconds before. If I leaned to the left just the slightest, I could...

"And this is his daughter, Abigail." His voice snapped me out of my thoughts as he gestured to the brunette that was practically drooling over him earlier. "She's the one who reached out to me about my channel."

Of course she was.

"We're so happy to have you here at Off the Leash," Felix said. I stood awkwardly at Nate's side, not sure of what to do while Felix continued to talk about the restaurant's history and how it once started as a food truck. Knowing that Nate recently started up his own food truck business, I wondered if he had any plans to open a storefront one day. It made me realize how little I'd spoken to Nate about his business and his life since I got to Briar Oakes, and I made a mental note to rectify that ASAP.

"I hope you're hungry," Abigail said, her voice light and playful, as she stepped around her father. I gritted my teeth as she grabbed on to Nate's other arm. My hands twitched at my sides as I fought the urge to pull Nate back to me, letting her know that he wasn't for the taking. But I had no claim over Nate, so instead, I plastered the sweetest smile across my face as I made eye contact with her. "Because we sure know how to handle a wiener around here."

You've got to be kidding me. I looked up at Nate, hoping he wasn't falling for these innuendos, but he showed nothing beyond his confident, professional charm. Abigail directed us to the menu, but I kept my eyes locked on him.

"Our most popular items are the Dil-Dog, Naughty Dog, and Doggie Style," she said, pointing to the chalkboard menu that hung above the counter. Nate moved his hand to my lower back, turning me so that I was facing the menu, but all I could focus on was where he touched me. Even through the material of my dress, I felt his rough, calloused fingers. Trying to distract myself from this feeling, I glanced up at the menu and my eyes widened as I took in the other item names. There was the DTF, the Magnum, the Gagger, and the Naked Dog. "But my favorite is the Deep Throat."

Nate cleared his throat and I glanced up at him. The tips of his ears turned the lightest shade of pink as he scratched the back of his neck. Okay, at least I wasn't the only one uncomfortable by all of this. How were you even supposed to order these without laughing? Were names like these even legal? What if you brought your children with you? I guessed this was what Nate meant when he said "Don't get weird" earlier. I stifled a snort and decided to play along, proud to be standing by his side regardless of the circumstances.

"So, what'll you have?" Abigail asked, keeping her attention solely on Nate.

"Everything looks amazing," he remarked, keeping his focus on the menu and not on Abigail. Not that I was keeping track of that or anything. "So I'm going to try it all. Maddie, how about you?"

"Oh, I don't know." I blushed and looked back at the menu. "I guess I'll just take the Naked Dog?"

"I had a feeling you liked to play it safe," Abigail said, smirking at me before she turned her attention back to Nate, giving him a wink. "And don't worry, I'll take care of you, Nate. You won't leave here disappointed."

Seriously, how was she getting away with this? Her dad was literally standing right next to her! But then, he was probably the one who named all these hot dogs, so maybe it didn't faze him that she was being highly inappropriate.

Ben stopped recording and went back to where all of Nate's things were set up. Not sure what had to be done next, I started to make my way back over to my table when Nate grabbed my wrist lightly.

"Hey, where are you going?" he asked, and my lips pulled up into a smile. He was so touchy with me all of a sudden, and it surprised me that I hadn't freaked out once today. Instead, every touch left me feeling all warm and cozy on the inside. "You did a great job. Don't worry, I can edit out anything you don't like."

"Me? Worried? Nah, I'm fine." I laughed and tried to make myself sound as convincing as possible. "But there's no way you're going to get me to eat a hot dog on camera. Especially not ones that are named like that."

"Fair enough. Hey, I hope it's okay that I pulled you into the video. It just felt right."

"Don't worry about it." I waved my hand in the air, dismissing his concerns. "I'm just going to go back to my table, okay? Call me over if you need me."

"Yeah, go enjoy your book," he said, waggling his eyebrows at me. Yup, he definitely thought I was reading porn. *Great.* "You'll have to tell me all about it on our ride home."

"Don't count on it."

fifteen

Nate was sitting at a table, tasting and reviewing the entire menu, while I sat with my book pressed against my face, trying to ignore him. Abigail had dropped off my food first, letting out a dramatic sigh as she asked me if there was anything else I needed. I debated on having her get me an assortment of things like napkins, mustard, utensils, and a straw for my water just to keep her away from Nate, but realized that meant I'd have to interact with her more than necessary so I decided against it. She certainly was pleased that she could forget about me and bring all her attention back to Nate.

Ben had set the camera up on the tripod and let it record on its own, only getting up occasionally to check the battery life, memory card space, or to get a different angle. My body stiffened as he took a seat next to me, but he was too engrossed in his phone to pay me any mind. If Ben really was a threat, Nate wouldn't have let him stay and I trusted him enough to allow myself to relax. I tried my hardest to focus on my book, but not even the sexiest billionaire could pull me away from the show Abigail put on.

She really pissed me off. The way she kept finding excuses to walk behind Nate just so she could get into the shot, the way she popped her chest out just a little farther, and the way she batted her eyelashes every time he glanced in her direction — I wasn't sure if Nate was picking up on her not-so-subtle hints. He didn't show he was interested or flattered by her, but it wasn't like he was stopping it either.

"So, what's the deal with you and Nate?" Ben whispered, pulling my focus away from Abigail.

"Sorry?" I asked as I turned a page, keeping up with the illusion.

"Keep it down or the mic will pick us up," he said quietly, pointing to Nate who was taking a bite out of the Gagger. "Are you two a thing or something?"

"What makes you think that?" I mumbled, glancing at him before turning back to my book and keeping my eyes glued to the pages.

"You haven't taken your eyes off him since we got here," he noted, slouching farther down in his chair and stretching his feet out, crossing them at his ankles. "And anytime Abigail comes near him, you get this violent look in your eyes."

"I'm just surprised you haven't swooped in and tried going after her. You know, since you're the town flirt and all."

"Town flirt, huh?" Ben questioned, glancing at me with a smug look on his face.

"I haven't been in Briar Oakes long and even I know your reputation." I rolled my eyes, glancing down at his phone as it buzzed yet again. "You can't possibly tell me you didn't know?"

"Oh, I know." He winked and I had to hold back a grimace. Only Nate could wink at me and get away with it. "I'm just surprised you do, considering you never leave Nate's house."

"I leave his house!" I whispered.

"You've gone to the library and The Garage once." I looked over at him just in time to catch him rolling his eyes. "Other than that, you only come out of hiding to visit Olivia."

"How would you know?"

"The librarians." He shrugged and turned his attention back to Abigail, who was now leaning forward, exposing her cleavage to the camera.

"So why haven't you made your move on Abigail?" Even her name felt sour on my tongue.

"Because it's far more entertaining watching her get under your skin."

"I don't know what you're talking about," I said, turning yet another page in my book that I hadn't read. "I've been reading the entire time."

"You do realize your book is upside down, right?"

I focused on the words in front of me for the first time, noticing he was right. *Shit.* Slamming it shut, I placed it on the table and crossed my arms. Ben's phone vibrated on the table, but before I could get a look at the name that flashed across the screen, he grabbed it and turned it face down on his lap.

"You're awfully popular today," I teased. "I don't think your phone has stopped buzzing since you sat down."

"Jealous?" He raised an eyebrow at me. "I can give you my number...if you want."

"No, thank you," I replied, looking at the time on my phone. We'd been here for about two hours and I was starting to get antsy. Nate had said we might be here a while and I'd been fine with it, but that was before I knew Ben and the Queen of Perverted Hot Dogs would be here.

"Why not?" He grinned, slouching down in his chair and crossing his arms behind his head. I hated the way he was looking at me right now, like he had me figured out.

"Because I'm not interested." I sighed, sliding my book into my bag and grabbing my car keys from the front pocket. "If Nate asks, tell him I'll be waiting in my car."

I clearly wasn't going to get any reading done here with Ben's probing questions and Nate just...existing. I needed to escape.

Packing up my things, I stood up and headed out the door as quietly as I could so I wouldn't distract Nate.

Less than an hour later, Nate and Ben walked out of Off the Leash, carrying all the equipment.

"All set?" I asked as Nate hopped into the passenger seat and closed the door, sighing as he put on his seatbelt.

"Yeah," he said, unbuttoning his jeans. I averted my eyes from his waist as I caught a glimpse of his boxers, focusing out the window instead. "Just wish I brought a pair of sweatpants to change into."

I looked over at him, watching as he adjusted himself in the seat. My eyes lingered on his arms and the way his muscles seemed to strain against the sleeves of his shirt. I had the urge to reach out and squeeze them, just to see how hard they were.

Nate cleared his throat and I just knew I'd been caught staring. I looked up and his grin widened.

"Why?" I questioned, turning to adjust the rearview mirror for no apparent reason. I put the Jeep in drive and pulled out onto the road, trying to take the quietest deep breaths I could manage.

"Wasn't expecting to eat everything on the menu," he said through a yawn, reclining his seat back as far as it could go without crushing his equipment behind him.

"Wait." I laughed and looked over at him, taking in his relaxed state and then quickly bringing my eyes back to the road. "You ate *all* of them? I thought you were just going to take a bite of each for the camera and then call it a day."

"They were good, it would've been a shame to waste it. I would've offered to share them with you…" Nate paused, looking out the window. "But you left." He yawned again, but it wasn't lost on me that he sounded a bit agitated.

I'm sure Abigail would've been happy to taste your hot dog.

"Excuse me?" Nate said, snapping his head in my direction.

Shit, did I just say that out loud?

"You sure did." Nate chuckled and I grimaced, gripping the steering wheel tighter. "Who's Abigail?"

"Oh, come on." I huffed, turning the radio on as Nate pulled his seat up to its upright position.

"No, we're talking about this," he said, turning the radio back off and angling so he could face me. "Who's Abigail and why would she want to 'taste my hot dog?'"

I couldn't hold back my laugh as Nate mimicked me, his voice shrill and ridiculous.

"Okay, first of all, I do *not* sound like that," I said, holding up one finger. "And secondly, she was the owner's daughter that *you* introduced me to, so don't act like you don't remember."

"I have so much running through my mind when I'm filming that I hardly remember my own name, Maddie."

"She spent the entire time practically drooling over you," I added, not loosening my grip on the steering wheel as her face came to mind. I'd never met someone whose pure existence bothered me so much, and I wasn't sure what to do about it. "Any chance she could get, she'd find a way to get in the shot. I'm also pretty sure that her shirt somehow managed to get smaller in the time it took for your hot dogs to come out."

"And here I thought you were reading your porn." He crossed his arms over his chest and I looked over at him, noticing his crooked smile had appeared again. How I wished I could smack it off. This was good. Maybe if I just stayed angry at him then the butterflies would disappear, too. "Is that why you left?"

"I'm surprised you even noticed." I rolled my eyes, knowing how childish I sounded.

"Of course I noticed." He sighed, clearly frustrated. At what? I wasn't sure. "I notice everything when it comes to you."

What the hell did *that* mean? Suddenly feeling hot, I adjusted the vents so they were pointing directly at my face and blasted the air.

"Whatever it is that's making you angry right now," he said, reaching across the center console and placing his hands on top of mine lightly, "don't take it out on your steering wheel."

I looked down at his hand, trying to ignore the warmth it always ignited when it touched my skin. Despite the heat, goosebumps scattered across my arm, and Nate smirked. I shook his hand off mine, repositioning mine on the steering wheel.

"Fine," I said, letting out a breath I'd been holding. I kept my eyes on the road and swore they wouldn't stray from it the rest of the way home. I tried to convince myself that what I felt when his hand touched mine was because I wasn't used to being touched by a guy. But I knew the truth. That touch meant something. "Can we please talk about something else?"

Nate reached out again and I was certain he was going to place it over mine, but instead, he brushed his fingers over my bracelet. My breath hitched in my throat as he gently unclasped it, catching it in the palm of his hand as it fell from my wrist. Not wanting to take my eyes off the road, I watched out of the corner of my eye as he inspected every charm on the bracelet.

"I can't believe you kept this," he said softly, keeping his eyes on the bracelet.

"It's beautiful," I whispered. I knew that Nate noticed me wearing it, he'd made it clear a few times, but this was the first time he'd acknowledged it out loud.

"I was so nervous to give it to you on your birthday," he admitted, continuing to toy with the charms. I bit down on the inside of my cheek, trying to hide my face from revealing too much as I silently begged him to continue. "I think I went to four different stores that week trying to find the perfect gift. But as soon as I saw it and those charms, I knew I had to get it for you."

"I don't know if I ever thanked you for it," I said softly, tapping my thumb nervously along the steering wheel. "It's probably the most beautiful gift I've ever received. I'm glad I found it and can wear it now."

"Found it?" he questioned, clasping the bracelet back around my wrist. I glanced down, taking in the different charms sparkling in the afternoon light.

"Well, I didn't exactly lose it." I glanced at the GPS and took a sharp right turn. "I knew Griffin would have had an issue with it, so I couldn't wear it. I kept it inside a box of memories I have and came across it the day I left my dad's."

"I'm sorry, Madds." Nate shifted in his seat again. "I didn't even think about that. I should have known it would cause an issue."

"Nate, stop." This time I was the one reaching out, grabbing hold of his hand and giving it a reassuring squeeze. I looked down at our joined hands quickly before pulling my hand back and placing it on my thigh. I ran my thumb over my scars and took a deep breath.

"What's wrong?" Nate asked, eyeing my fingers.

I shook my head lightly. I could never hide anything from him, even if I wanted to. But to be honest, I couldn't think of another reason to keep me from telling him everything.

"The scars on my leg, um..." I paused, turning my head and giving him a weak smile before looking back to the road. "Griffin burned me. More than once."

"Madds — " Nate winced, but I cut him off.

"Please." I tilted my chin. "Let me explain. And when I finish, don't tell me that this wasn't my fault. Not putting the blame on me is something I'm still working on, but I need to do that on my own, okay?"

Nate nodded.

"The first time was an accident," I continued, trying to fight the memory from flooding my mind. "He had a bunch of his friends over for a cigar night."

I breathed through the pain in my chest.

"He got mad at me and asked to talk to me, so we went out onto the balcony. He accused me of making eyes at one of his friends. He said I wore my shortest dress on purpose to impress them. The only thing I could think to do was remind him that he was who I wanted. So...I sat down on his lap and started to kiss him."

I shook my head, trying to hold back the tears.

"I managed to get him to forget why he was mad at me, but also that he was holding a lit cigar. It fell out of his hand and landed on my thigh. And that was the first time."

"You can't be telling me that all of those scars were accidents, Maddie." Nate's voice was strained, his hands clenched into fists on his knees.

"Just the first one." I swiped at the tear that managed to escape off my cheek with the back of my hand. "When the cigar landed on me, I screamed, but I guess Griffin took it as more of a...like I enjoyed it?" My hand shook as I reached over to adjust the vent. "He shut me up by kissing me, not letting me pull free."

"Maddie — " Nate's voice broke on my name. I kept my focus on the road, knowing that if I saw him breaking, I'd fall apart, too.

"Griffin thought I was just playing along, acting like I didn't like it because I was ashamed or something. Turns out he was into that sort of thing, and from then on, I was only allowed to wear dresses because of the easy access. And every time he had cigar night, he'd pull me out onto the balcony and burn me."

"Fuck." Nate made a pained sound and leaned forward to rest his elbows on his legs. "I am so sorry I wasn't there for you, Madds."

"Nate, no. You did more than you could to try to help me."

"I could have done more. I wish I had done more."

We sat in silence for a while, nothing but trees and the open road passing us by. My heart was racing in my chest from what Nate had said. He wished he had done more? Aside from throwing me over his shoulder and physically removing me from the relationship, he did all that he could, and that fact alone broke my heart. From the moment I met him, he'd done the *most* to make sure I felt safe, but unfortunately, there were just some things you couldn't protect someone from. Not when they weren't ready to be saved.

"I found the note you left in my book," I said, breaking the silence. "And I want you to know I *am* proud of me, too. But mostly, I'm thankful for you."

"Why?"

"Because you gave me an out, Nate."

sixteen

Days turned into weeks, and I fell into a routine. I spent most of my time working on my manuscript, turning Nate's dining room table into my temporary desk. Every night I sat on the porch swing, escaping into my books. Summer was coming to an end, so I was thoroughly enjoying the cooler nights. I even found comfort in the chirping crickets and the singing cicadas that normally drove me crazy at my dad's. When I'd spoken to my dad last, he'd asked me if I was ever planning on coming home.

To be honest, I didn't have an answer for him.

I was comfortable here, and Briar Oakes was starting to feel like home. When Nate and I were both at the house, we spent all our time together. On Sundays, I'd wake up to the smell of waffles, eggs, and bacon, as well as my decaf latte from Olivia's waiting for me on the kitchen island. Almost every night after dinner, we'd find ourselves on the couch together: me snuggled up with a book while Nate played video games. Some nights we'd pick a movie to watch together, and I'd find myself smiling at the way he laughed at the dumbest things on the screen.

But the more comfortable I became at Nate's, the louder Ben's voice became, whispering, *You never leave Nate's house*, over and over in my head. It was time to prove him wrong. I pulled my Jeep along the curb on Main Street, coming to a stop in front of a hardware store. I couldn't believe people were actually talking about the fact that I preferred to stay at Nate's rather than socialize with the rest of the town. *Well, look at me now, Briar Oakes!*

I knew I needed to start making an effort with the town...but now that I was here, I wasn't sure I was ready. Drumming my fingers nervously on the steering wheel, I sighed and pulled my phone out of the cup holder, opening a new text.

> Me: Hey! Are you closing today? I was thinking maybe we could go shopping.

There. If she was available, I had a reward for socializing.

> Olivia: Sure! Zo should be coming in soon. Want to pick me up in an hour?

> Me: Sounds good!

Before I could give myself a chance to change my mind, I yanked the keys out of the ignition and climbed out of my Jeep. The sun was hot on my bare shoulders as I stepped onto the sidewalk. Reminding myself to keep my head up and not trained at the ground, I ignored my reflection in all the store windows. I'd rather not see if I looked as awkward as I felt.

I crossed the street, passing a mom pushing a stroller while chatting animatedly on the phone. I smiled at her, hoping it came across as friendly and not forced, before waving at the toddler snacking on Cheerios in her seat.

Okay, that wasn't too bad. I can definitely do this.

I flexed my fingers at my side and stood tall as I continued down the sidewalk, unsure of where I was even headed. There were so many people out and about — did I have to introduce myself to everyone or just until someone notified the librarians that I was making an effort to be a part of Briar Oakes? I looked straight ahead, my eyes locking on Nate's food truck. The nerves stirring in my belly lessened at the sight of it.

"Good afternoon!" A cheerful middle-aged man greeted me on the sidewalk, stopping me in my tracks. "Welcome to Briar Oakes!"

"Thanks," I replied, not pointing out the fact that I'd been in Briar Oakes for quite some time now.

"Are you Maddie? I was wondering when we'd meet." He chuckled, coming even closer to me. I took a step back, trying to put some space between us. "Where are you headed to?"

"Yup, that's me," I replied as I stretched on my toes and peered over his shoulder to Nate's. I could just make out his silhouette as he faced the grill. "I'm just taking a walk through town."

"Ah!" He seemed pleased as he hooked his thumbs into the belt loops of his jeans. He was incredibly chirpy, slightly red-cheeked, plump around the edges, bearded, and bald. Not to mention, overly excited to be in my presence. "I was heading over to Nate's, why don't you join me?"

"Sure," I said through a plastered smile as I shifted on my feet uncomfortably.

"I'm Lou Reynolds." He shot out his hand and I hesitantly took it in mine. "Mayor of Briar Oakes."

Lou draped his arm over my shoulder and my body stiffened at the sudden contact. He spun us so that we both faced Nate's and he fanned his other hand out as if presenting the town to me. A playground and splash pad were behind the gazebo and you could hear the children laughing all the way down the street. Park benches and potted flowers lined the sidewalk leading around the park and up to the gazebo. I remained silent at his side, trying to ignore the fact that I could feel the sweat forming between my shoulders and his arm. *I'm not ready for this.*

It's okay, Maddie, I prompted myself, as we began to walk towards Nate's. *This man is just welcoming you to the town. Keep your smile on and make it to Nate's. Everything is fine.*

"Briar Oakes is just so happy that you came," he gushed, removing his arm from around me. I wanted to laugh at the fact he was referring to the town as if it were a person, but I figured it would be best not to say anything. If he could be this happy, I could only imagine how he'd be if he were offended. He seemed like the type of person who felt every emotion to the extreme. He reminded me of Olivia, actually, and I laughed, picturing Olivia's face if I ever told her she and the mayor were one and the same.

We got in line behind the others and I glanced around, taking in the small table and chairs Nate had set up on either side of his truck. A group of teens had pushed the tables to the left together to make one large table and to the right, my eyes passed over unfamiliar faces before landing on the librarian, Margaret.

As if she could feel my gaze, her eyes locked with mine, and I suppressed a groan as I saw her stand up and make her way over to us. Lou had already exhausted my socialization skills for the day and I wasn't confident in myself to prevent another rumor from spreading about me.

"Maddie!" she exclaimed, pulling me in for a hug. It was a relief when she took a step back from me. Why did people like physical contact in this sort of heat? Margaret turned over her shoulder, signaling to the woman she was sitting with. "Lara, can you come over here for a second? I want to introduce you to someone!"

Come on, Nate. Can't you speed up the line a bit? My plan for today was to stroll down Main Street, put in some effort to be a part of the community, then hightail it to Olivia's and get out of here. I wasn't planning on having lunch with the mayor or the librarian.

A red-haired woman, maybe a year or two younger than me, stood up and my attention immediately fell to her round belly. She dragged the back of her hand over her forehead, wiping away the sweat that glistened her skin.

"Maddie, I want to introduce you to my niece, Lara." Margaret reached out to the two of us, placing a hand on one of our arms and giving it a gentle squeeze. Her *niece*? Was this the niece she had tried setting up with Nate? I swallowed, letting my eyes trail over Lara's body from head to toe. She was gorgeous. Why would Nate turn her down?

"It's way too hot to be touching right now," Lara complained, shrugging her arm free from Margaret's grasp before resting a hand on her bump. My lips twitched at the corners as I caught Margaret glaring at her. "I'm sorry," Lara turned her attention to me. "I don't mean to be rude. I'm seven months pregnant and this heat is just too much for me. When Aunt Maggie told me she knew of just the place for one of my cravings, I was picturing something indoors with blasting A/C."

"No worries." I waved my hand in the air, giving her probably my first genuine smile of the day. "Was the food worth it at least?"

"Oh yes," Lara said, nodding enthusiastically. "That was probably the best sandwich I've ever had."

"Any suggestions on what to get?" I asked, glancing at the three of them. "It's my first time here."

"Nathaniel West!" Margaret hollered, causing both me and Lara to jump. Even Lou threw a hand over his chest. The line in front of us cleared as she plowed through to the front. "Did I just hear that this sweet girl, who's been *living* with you, hasn't had one of your delicious sandwiches yet? I thought you were more of a gentleman than that!"

I groaned, covering my face with my hands. This was exactly why I preferred to stay indoors.

"I can assure you I am, Margaret." The sound of Nate's voice had me removing my hands from my face. "I've just been keeping her all to myself, I'm sorry."

"Aunt Maggie." Lara waddled over to her aunt's side, placing a hand on her shoulder. "Let's not cause a scene, okay? Come on, let's go home. I'm sure Derek is wondering where I am."

"Good, let him wonder," Margaret muttered under her breath. "Hope to see you at the library again soon, Maddie."

"Thank you," I mouthed to Lara as she steered Margaret past me.

"Mayor Lou, I've got your order right here," Nate said as he stretched his arm out the serving window, holding a styrofoam container out.

"Thanks, Nate. I'll see you at the same time tomorrow." Mayor Lou took the container into his hands before turning to me. "It was nice meeting you, Maddie."

I nodded at him as he walked by, not waiting another second to open the container and take a bite out of his food.

"Well, well, well." Nate beamed as he leaned out the serving window of his food truck, giving me his undivided attention. "Who do I have to thank for this visit today?"

"I'm going shopping with Olivia in a few." I told him part of the truth, not wanting to admit that Ben's words had gotten under my skin. I smiled up at him before glancing at the menu. "Figured I'd fill up on some Nate's Grates beforehand. I'll try the number five, I think."

"One sharp cheddar with pulled pork and caramelized onions coming up." I watched as he threw a white apron over his head, admiring the way his muscles flexed as he tied it around his back.

I took a step back, grateful there was no one in line behind me so I could get a better view of Nate in his element. I'd seen him cook in his house plenty of times, but this was totally different. Seeing him in the truck, a white apron draped over him, hair pulled back into a neat bun, I couldn't help but be in awe of him. He looked so happy and confident while he cooked. I could clearly see how passionate he was about it.

My mouth went dry as I zeroed in on the way his forearm flexed as he moved the spatula. I fanned myself with my hand, unable to handle the heat. Nate turned his head over his shoulder, his mouth curved into a grin, as he watched me watch him. "You okay?"

"Yup, I'm fine," I squeaked, tugging at the neckline of my dress. "It's just really hot out here. Are you okay? Do you need water? What about a fan?"

"Yup, I'm fine," he chuckled, throwing my words back at me. "How's the writing coming?"

"Okay, I guess," I said, shrugging my shoulders and grateful that he changed the subject so easily. "It's not coming as naturally as it used to, but I'm getting there."

"Are you going to tell me what it's about?"

I looked down at my boots as I dug the toe into the ground. It was hard enough for me to let Olivia in, but...I guess I was making today all about stepping outside my comfort zone.

"It's about my relationship with Griffin," I said, glancing up just in time to see Nate's hand freeze over my sandwich. "My therapist suggested that I should rewrite my ending, to give myself the happily ever after I wanted."

"And what is that?" Nate asked, just loud enough to be heard over the sound of the food sizzling on the grill.

"That's what I'm having a hard time with." I leaned my back against the exterior of the food truck. "I'm not sure what it would be. It's kind of hard to write one when you don't exactly believe in them."

"Still?" he asked, his voice suddenly a lot closer than before. I glanced up to my left, seeing Nate resting against the serving window. He placed my sandwich on the counter and slid it toward me. "I'm surprised Briar Oakes hasn't turned you into Little Miss Romantic again with its small-town charm."

I grunted, grabbing my sandwich off the plate and taking a generous bite. My eyes rolled to the back of my head as I sighed. Nate's eyes moved to my mouth as I licked my lips, ready for another bite. "This is delicious. Seriously, what's your secret?"

"Just these guys," Nate smirked suggestively, wiggling his

fingers in front of him. I followed the movement of his hands and found myself imagining what his fingers laced through mine might look like, how his calluses might feel against my — "Are you ready for today?" Nate snapped me out of my thoughts.

"What?" I asked, blinking rapidly.

"You can't go in blind shopping with Olivia." Nate shook his head as he leaned forward on his elbows, clasping his hands together. "I got stuck doing it a few times when she moved here and it lasted hours. It's best if you know what you want, go straight for it, and then run."

"Oh, I remember." I burst out a laugh and then grabbed a wad of napkins from the holder. "I should probably get going, though."

"Right," Nate said, dropping his hands to the counter. "Well, thanks for stopping by. I'll see you at home? It's your turn to pick the movie tonight."

"You always say it's my turn." I shook my head, waving as I walked away. "See you later, Nate."

My pillow was cool against my cheek as I buried my face deeper. Goosebumps skated across my skin as Nate traced patterns lazily from my shoulder down to my elbow and back up again. I scooted back into his warmth when I felt something hard press against my back. I gripped my sheets tightly as Nate's breath tickled my skin, his lips brushing softly along the curve of my neck. I grinded myself against him harder and Nate stifled a groan, his teeth sinking into the crook of my neck.

I let out a gasp of pleasure. Grabbing his hand, I slid it lower until it reached my hip. His fingers toyed with the waistband of the shorts I wore. The ones I borrowed that first night and couldn't seem to part with. I didn't think I'd ever be able to sleep in anything else again. I let out a whimper, wishing that his hand would explore a little farther so he could see how wet I was for him. Giving him a little nudge with my elbow, I let out a satisfied moan when his hand slipped under my cotton panties and teased my entrance.

"Shit!" A car horn blaring outside the window had me jolting up in bed. My heart pounded in my chest as I glanced down at my empty bed.

What. The. Fuck. I just had a sex dream starring Nate. No, no, *no.* This couldn't be happening. I racked my brain, trying to unravel my thoughts from my racing heartbeat. Trying to get to the bottom of why I should've been more horrified than I was...

Annoyed with myself, I changed into a pair of jean overalls and the short-sleeved shirt I'd bought with Olivia during our shopping trip. Fall hit Briar Oakes early, and I was ready to ditch my summer wardrobe. I grabbed my tote bag with my laptop, planner, and current read and stormed out of my room. I stumbled over Tuna, who was sitting right outside my door, glaring up at me with judgmental eyes like he knew what I'd been up to on the other side of it. I rolled my eyes at him and said, "Oh, don't look at me like that."

Knowing I needed the fresh air and hoping that it would clear all these thoughts from my head, I decided to walk to Latte Da!. Three bells jingled as I pushed the door to the cafe open. Olivia's head popped up from behind the counter and a huge smile spread across her face.

"Oh, good, you're here." She blew out a big breath, swiping the back of her hand across her forehead. "I was hoping you'd come in this morning. Want to give me a hand with the fall decorations?"

"Sure," I said, dropping my bag at an empty table. I glanced around the coffee shop, noticing that every table was empty. Well, that was different. There were always a few groups of teens hanging out with their frozen sugary drinks. "But can I get a pumpkin spice latte first?"

"You got it." She threw me a thumbs up and I smiled, excited to get my first pumpkin drink of the season. "School started today, so I probably won't get another rush until later this afternoon."

We spent the next two hours covering her cafe in leaf garlands, decorative pumpkins, and fall flower bouquets. While Olivia started working on her chalkboard menu that displayed her seasonal drinks, I pulled out my book, grateful for the fact that the cover didn't have a shirtless man on it. Flipping through the pages quickly, another index card fell onto my lap and my stomach flipped.

Aww, no naked man?
Is it bad that I'm a little disappointed...
I'm just here to say
I hope something good happens for you today.
Can't wait to hear all about it later.
—Nate

After an hour of reading, I closed my book and set it down on the table. Out of habit, my eyes drifted over to the gazebo. Seeing Nate's Grates parked in front wasn't a surprise, but seeing Nate set up a few tables and chairs next to the trailer...my eyes were drawn to him like a magnet. My throat dried and I swallowed over the sandpaper feeling as Nate pulled his black hoodie over his head in one swoop. Even from where I was, I could make out the lines of his abs as his shirt, clinging to his hoodie, rode up to his chest. As if he could sense my eyes on him, he glanced in my direction, locking eyes with me. His crooked smile appeared, and lo and behold, those bouncing bowling balls returned to my stomach.

Picking my book back up, I hid my face behind it. My phone

vibrated next to me and I glanced down, seeing I had a new text from Nate. I kept the book in front of my face while I picked it up.

Nate: How's the porn?

I bit the inside of my cheek, trying to stop my cheesy smile from spreading across my face.

Me: It's called smut, not porn. If you're going to call me out on it, at least get it right.

Nate: My apologies.

Nate: Is it even legal to read that stuff in public?

Me: That's the beauty of cute cartoon covers. No one knows.

Nate: Your secret is safe with me ;)

Nate: But I can't back you up when you carry around a book with a half-naked man on it.

Me: Jealous?

Nate: Of a fictional man? Please. They've got nothing on me.

Me: Clearly you've never read a romance novel.

Nate: You sure about that?

Thoughts of Nate lying in bed, skimming through the pages of my spicier books, filled my mind. I thought of him placing the book down on his nightstand, rolling to his side to face me, his hands gently caressing my skin as he promised to do all the things he read about. My stomach clenched and I crossed my legs in an attempt to smother the ache forming between my thighs.

"Hey, Liv," I shouted over my shoulder, knowing she was somewhere up in the loft decorating. Not wanting to read into this conversation with Nate and fuel the intrusive thoughts, I dropped my book into my bag and slipped my phone into my pocket. "I'm heading out. I'll text you later."

"Sure," she shouted back. "Thanks for all the help!"

I couldn't stay here, knowing that Nate was just across the way, and expect to get any work done. The vibrator Olivia bought me popped into mind and maybe...*maybe* if I squeezed in one orgasm then I'd finally be able to break free from this spell Nate had me under. Maybe then I'd know if I was reacting this way only because it'd been a year since any guy had paid attention to me...or if I was developing feelings for Nate.

I stepped outside of Latte Da! keeping my focus on anything but Nate as I turned to where I parked my Jeep.

"Maddie, wait up," Nate called, and as was totally normal behavior for a twenty-seven-year-old woman, I picked up my pace. Suddenly at my side, he grabbed my wrist and stopped me from stepping off the curb.

I looked down to where his thumb pressed against my pulse. His touch felt electric, sending shivers down my spine and causing that ache between my thighs to return. He gently tugged on my arm, pulling me closer to him. My breath hitched in my throat as I imagined his fingers trailing along my jaw. The tip of his tongue tracing the seam of his lips and me melting into him.

I swayed on my feet and Nate's hand moved from my wrist to around my waist, pulling me flush against him.

"Hey," Nate whispered, using his other hand to tilt my chin up to him. His eyes searched mine, his eyebrows furrowed in concern. "You okay?"

"Yes." I let out a sigh, pressing where I needed him most against his body. "Totally fine."

Nate cleared his throat and I froze. *Oh my god, what am I doing?*

"Nate!" I gasped, coming to my senses and slipping out of his hold. I took a step back, putting a few feet between us. Ugh, I *really* needed to get home. I bit the inside of my cheek, focusing on the pain instead of the need in my core. "You can't be doing that."

"Doing what?" He raised an eyebrow, placing his hands on his hips.

"You know what," I said through gritted teeth, glancing around at the mostly empty street. I felt my shoulders relax as I saw no one looking in our direction. "It's a small town. People are going to get ideas."

"So?" he questioned, keeping his eyes on mine. Was that a challenge? "If people are that bored and pathetic that they need to make something out of nothing, then that's their problem."

Something out of nothing. His words echoed in my head, causing the tingling feeling I felt before start to fade.

This was good. This was the reminder I needed, despite my heart cracking at his words. Nothing was going on between us. He didn't see me that way. I had to remember that. Everything that I was feeling had to be because it's been a year since I'd felt anything. I was just overwhelmed. Which was why I really needed to get home and give my body what it needed.

"Are you done working for the day?" I asked, eager to get out of this conversation.

"No," he said, raising an eyebrow at me. I smiled in relief. "Why?"

"No reason." I pulled my car key out of my tote bag. "What time do you think you'll be home?"

"I'll probably stick around for the lunch rush and then see how things go," he said, looking over at his food truck. "I'm supposed to check out another restaurant in the next town over this afternoon for another episode, too."

"Great. Awesome."

He chuckled at me, finding my impatience amusing. I watched as he pulled his hair back into a bun. God, that bun was like kryptonite. I crossed my ankles, squeezing my legs together as the throb between my legs intensified. Nate's eyes flashed down to my legs and then eyed me curiously. Knowing that my time was limited, I took a few steps toward my Jeep.

"Hey." He followed after me, causing me to stop in my tracks. "Where are you off to in such a rush?"

"Oh, nowhere." I gave a short, half-suppressed laugh, fanning myself with my hand. It's like the temperature increased twenty degrees in the last five minutes. My hands shook as I opened my door. I needed water or a cold shower or *something*.

"Are you sure you're okay?" Nate asked, taking another step closer. "You don't look too good."

Crap, what could I even say that would get him to stop asking me questions? Knowing that what I was about to say would embarrass me, I climbed into the driver's seat and said in a rush, "I just *really* need to use the bathroom. I love a good pumpkin spice latte, but they don't particularly like me back. Bye!"

seventeen

Not wasting any time, I barged into the bathroom and hurried over to the tub. I turned the faucets on, watching it fill with warm water, before running back to my room. I stripped out of my clothes and grabbed the pink vibrator from its box, double-checking that it was waterproof. Back in the bathroom, I slipped into the tub, sighing as the warmth pulled me in like a hug.

Sinking down so that the water came just above my shoulders, I powered up The Intimidator 3000 and my eyes widened at how powerfully it began to pulse. And this was the lowest speed? There were still three more after this! Trying not to think too much about it, I slipped it under the water, appreciating the way it muted the sound, and guided it between my legs.

Just remember, my room is across the hall. Nate's voice suddenly filled my head, causing me to glance at the closed bathroom door.

My nipples peaked under the water at the thought of his voice in my head. Knowing it was wrong but too far gone to stop, I rested the vibrator against myself, parting my legs more so that it hit my clit, and jumped at the powerful sensation rushing through me.

"Holy shit," I gasped, sitting up and removing the vibrator

immediately. I slid my thumb over the pink silicone frantically as I tried to find the power button. Once I found it, I pressed so hard on the button that I was surprised I didn't snap it in half. This was all too overwhelming. Maybe I needed to take this slowly at first, and explore before jetting off to the finish line. Bringing The Intimidator back under the water, I angled it toward my entrance and slowly slid it inside. I slouched down in the tub, trying to get comfortable.

Don't forget to try out the jets, too! Now Olivia's voice echoed in my ears.

"Nope," I said out loud, shaking my head back and forth. Definitely *not* thinking about her. I'd get nowhere with that, but... maybe she was on to something. I shifted my body to the right and propped my feet up on the tub in front of me, positioning myself so... *Oh.*

My room is across the hall. Nate's voice appeared again. I closed my eyes, imagining his crooked smile while my hands slid the pink vibrator slowly in and out. Too bad he *wasn't* in his room across the hall. Sighing, I gave in to my thoughts and let Nate take over. I wasn't going to get myself anywhere on my own, but maybe he could help. It wasn't like I had to admit any of this to him. It would be my little secret.

My mind transported me back to the other day, when I stood naked in front of Nate, watching as his eyes roamed over my body. I licked my lips as my eyes devoured the ridges of his muscles, following the trail of hair to the waistband of his sweatpants. Ugh, those sweatpants. How I loved those sweatpants. My left hand gripped the edge of the tub as my mind's eye continued farther down his body, taking in his poorly hidden bulge. My hips began to move of their own accord as I imagined how he'd feel against me.

A sound I'd never made before rumbled through my body and up my throat, escaping my lips as I imagined his hard length entering me instead of the toy I held in my hand. My toes curled on the edge of the tub as I felt an overwhelming clenching feeling overtake me. It was as if all my organs were tangled up inside me like a bunch of Christmas lights. I was breathing hard now, picturing Nate hovering over me as he pumped inside me, his breath matching my own against my neck.

"Nate," I moaned, arching my back in the water. "Fuck, yes."

Maddie. Nate's voice was comforting and safe as he said my name, encouraging me to relax and let myself lose control for once. I held back another moan, picturing Nate's large hand cupping my breast instead of my own, tracing my pebbled nipple with the pad of his thumb.

"Nate." I continued to say his name just above a whisper, over and over. Keeping my eyes closed, I slid my thumb over the vibrator and found the power button, contemplating on whether I could handle it. "More, give me more."

"Maddie." Nate's voice came from the other side of the door, startling me. *Oh shit. Was that not my imagination before?* "Are you okay in there?"

"Y-yes," I stuttered, grateful at that moment that I hadn't hit the switch yet. The panic rushed through me quickly and I froze in place, my hand still gripping The Intimidator that was deep inside me. I was afraid to take it out. To make any movement. To make any noise that could potentially reveal what I was doing. "I'm fine. I'll be out in a minute."

I'll be out in a minute? What was I thinking! I needed way more than a minute to figure out how to get myself out of this situation. Did I *want* out of this situation though? The thought of him standing outside the door while I was...*nope.* It was bad enough that the only way I could get myself to relax before was by thinking of him. I couldn't continue while he stood outside that door, probably leaning his head against it with his palm pressed flat along the wood, hearing every moan that escaped my lips.

I whimpered softly, thinking about how he'd look if I got out of this tub and walked over to the door to unlock it. If I stood there in front of him, water dripping down my skin and into a puddle on the floor...would his eyes slowly roam my naked body like a kiss or devour me greedily? Would he want to help finish —

"I brought you some things," he went on, and his voice, soft and caring, spurred me to start moving under the water again. "I know how much it sucks to feel like crap, so I went to the store."

He went to the store? I forgot I told him I was in a hurry because my pumpkin spice latte didn't agree with me. Great, as if I had more of a reason to be embarrassed. My hand began to slow under the water again...but he went to the store for me... My heart swelled inside my chest and I felt my body begin to melt. I slid farther down in the tub, unable to stop my pace from quickening again.

"What did you get?" I managed to ask, my voice shaky as I barely held on. I was desperate to hear more of his voice.

"Uh..." I heard the rustling of a plastic bag. Come on, Nate, just say anything. He could recite the alphabet to me right now and I'd probably explode. "I wasn't sure what you liked, so I got Gatorade, crackers, ginger ale — "

"*Fuck*," I exhaled loudly, my thumb slipping and powering the vibrator up, causing me to moan loudly. I slapped my hand over my mouth but had no hope of stopping what I now knew felt *so* good.

"Maddie?" He said my name again.

Yes, keep saying it, I begged. *Don't stop saying my name.*

"What was that?"

Crap. Why did I keep thinking out loud around him?

I held the vibrator in place, feeling the pressure build up inside me, begging for release. No, I couldn't stop now. I already dug my grave, so I might as well get comfortable. My thumb frantically ran along the exposed part of the vibrator, desperately trying to find the speed controls. Once my thumb came across the button, I pumped it up to full speed.

Nate's voice teetered on panic. "Are you — you're not...is that...are you in the — "

"Oh my god," I shrieked, my legs straightening out above the tub, positioning the jets perfectly on my bud. My eyes rolled to the back of my head as I let my body explode.

I stood in the middle of the bathroom, staring at the door while wrapped in a towel, and The Intimidator tucked away safely in my designated drawer. My heart pounded in my chest, each thump growing more painful with each beat. *Was it hot in here?* I needed air. Fanning myself with my hand, I walked over to the window and cracked it open, but frowned when I was met with warmth instead of a cool breeze. I needed to get out of this room before I passed out.

But how was I supposed to do that when Nate was out there? There was no denying that he knew exactly what I was doing in here and who I'd been thinking about while doing it.

"You're such an idiot," I groaned, slapping my palm over my face as I held on tightly to my towel.

Glancing around the bathroom, I realized I didn't bring any clothes in here with me. My eyes landed on a pile of Nate's balled-up clothes in the corner of the bathroom right next to the hamper. Was it really that hard for a man to put his clothes inside the hamper? I tossed his jeans to the side and lifted a plain white T-shirt, giving it a quick sniff. Well, this would have to do.

"Maddie." Nate's muffled voice startled me and I clutched my chest. Surely he hadn't been standing out there the entire time...

"Please go away," I muttered, running my hands through my damp hair. Turning around, I leaned against the bathroom sink and nervously tapped it. What was I supposed to do now?

"Open the door." His voice was calm as he knocked lightly.

"It's just me, Maddie, you have nothing to be embarrassed about. You're safe."

There were those two little words again. It's like he knew they were the key to breaking through my panic. My fingers shook as I unlocked the door and opened it. Nate stood there, leaning against the wall with a bag at his feet. I could see all the supplies he mentioned before, plus a bunch of bananas and a hot pink bottle of Pepto-Bismol. My throat went dry. I'd never be able to look at the color pink the same way again.

"Did you get this all for me?" I said, barely above a whisper, as I gestured to the bag at his feet. I kept my focus on the bag, nervous about what I'd see if I looked at him. Would his stupid crooked smile be there? Would he be angry? Would he be flushed with embarrassment, too?

"I hated that you didn't feel well." His voice was husky and, dare I say, sultry? I glanced up and watched as the tip of his tongue slowly ran over his lower lip. His crooked smile slowly stretched across his face. That stupid smile. He found this hilarious. He found *me* hilarious. I was nothing but a joke to him. My stomach twisted in a knot and I felt like I was going to puke. "But clearly that wasn't the case. Do you feel better now?"

I stood there, wearing nothing but his worn shirt and wanting to melt through the floor with embarrassment. His eyes roamed over my body, taking in my bare feet first, dragging over my legs, then lingering on his shirt that clung to my damp skin, before settling on my face. I held my breath, waiting for that same look of disgust to flash across his face, but it never did. He stepped forward, and my breath caught in my throat as his hand reached out to cup my jaw gently. His thumb slowly swiped away the tears that I didn't realize escaped on my right cheek before moving over to the left.

"Come here, Maddie," he whispered, dropping his hand from my face.

Pushing away all the fears I had about giving in to my feelings,

I closed the distance between us. It suddenly hit me that this was what I wanted. When his arms wrapped around me, I realized I was wrong. It wasn't what I wanted. It was what I needed. I needed to feel his hands on me, I needed to feel that warmth I always felt when he touched me, and I needed to feel safe.

Nate was always that.

My stomach flipped as his arms pulled me closer, not leaving any space between us. All I could focus on was the way my body touched his. I snuggled into him deeper, fully aware of the fact that my tears were leaving wet stains on his shirt. Without even thinking, I sniffled and rubbed my nose into it.

"Did you just wipe your nose on me?" I froze, but Nate just snorted, fighting back a laugh. His hands moved to my shoulders, pushing me away to get a better look at me, but I tightened my grip.

"No," I mumbled, keeping my eyes on anything and everything but his.

"Please stop crying," he said softly, and I could swear I felt the lightest touch from his lips on the top of my head. "You have nothing to be embarrassed about."

I intertwined my fingers behind his back as if I were pinky promising myself that I wouldn't be the first to let go. I could have stayed there forever, wrapped in his strong arms, safe from the world. It was like his hug was this giant protective bubble.

"Do you feel better now?" he asked again, his voice deep and raspy. My grip tightened around his waist and he rested his chin on the top of my head. He chuckled as I somehow found a way to bury my face even deeper into his chest. I could feel his breath against my scalp, and it caused a shiver to run down my spine.

"Yes," I said with a smile. And I did feel better. He somehow always made everything feel better. "Thank you."

"What for?" He shifted his arms around me so that he supported most of my weight with one hand. With his thumb, he tilted my chin so I was looking at him.

"For always being that safe place for me," I said softly, not believing what I was about to say. "Even back when Olivia and I were in college, I always knew that I could count on you. That you'd always be there for me. It was like you were *my* big brother, too."

"Is that how you still think of me?" He raised an eyebrow and then that smile was back, inches from my face. My eyes dropped down to his mouth and my heart stopped as I watched his mouth move around his next words. "Because what I heard in that bathroom didn't seem like something you'd be doing while thinking about a brother."

"I don't know what you're talking about," I said, trying to squirm out of his hold, but he only held on tighter. I gasped, freezing in his arms as I felt his erection against my waist. His name slipped easily from my lips. "*Nate.*"

"Were you thinking of me?" His hand slid behind my ear, tangling itself in my hair as he slowly brought my face closer to his. I never knew it was possible to feel dizzy just from a simple touch.

"N-no," I said, not sure how I was still breathing.

"Don't lie." He shook his head, pressing his forehead against mine. "Not to me."

I swallowed and nodded, unable to find my voice. My stomach felt like those old-school bingo ball cages. Nate was the one cranking the lever, making all the balls spin in my stomach. The air in the hallway thickened and I found myself taking in deeper breaths.

"Say it." Even his demands were gentle and soothing. How was that possible? "Say it out loud."

With his forehead pressed to mine, Nate's gaze moved down to my lips and my heart raced as his mouth moved closer to mine. Was he going to kiss me? I tracked his every move. The way he slowly moved closer, the way the tip of his tongue licked his lower lip before his teeth grazed over it, and the way his eyes slowly began to flutter closed. Was I going to let him kiss me?

I smiled, not able to stop the laugh from bubbling out of me. "Vampire."

He groaned, throwing his head back. "You did not just quote *Twilight*."

"You started it." I shrugged, unable to hide my relief that suddenly the air felt significantly lighter.

"Maddie."

"Sorry." I giggled anxiously, pressing my face into his chest again, my new favorite hiding place. Leave it to me to ruin the moment. "I got nervous."

"What am I going to do with you?" He sighed, tilting my head back up. "You were just touching yourself while you thought of me. You screamed my name. Then you walk out here wearing nothing but my T-shirt. You're making it so hard, Maddie."

"Making what hard?" I asked, but then immediately shook my head at how that sounded. "Never mind."

"You have no idea the effect you have on me, Madds." He let out an exhale. "Living with you has been..." He rubbed his finger along my jaw. "Do you not realize how hard it's been to see you walking around the house wearing my clothes every night? Having to see you obsess and drool over all your book boyfriends when I wish that could be me?"

I stood there, stunned. I wasn't used to hearing Nate sound this way. I took a deep breath, trying to calm my racing heart, and leaned back to put some distance between us. I didn't understand what was happening. One second, I was orgasming to him and the next he was telling me how turned on he was by me? I shook my head, taking another deep breath. *Come on, you can do this.* "I just feel..."

"Feel what, Maddie?" Nate sounded impatient.

"Confused," I said, finally settling on a word. "I don't know what's going on, Nate. Maybe I'm jumping to conclusions, but..." I trailed off, trying to collect my scrambled thoughts. "It's like one second I think you're flirting with me and maybe like me, but then something happens and I second guess everything."

"Shit." He paced the floor in front of me, his fingers flexing at his sides. "I've made such a mess of things. I am so sorry for putting you through this."

"No." I shook my head, confused as to what he was talking about. "Nate, you've been perfect. It's me," I said, making my way toward my bedroom. Once I made it inside, I went straight to my closet to get dressed. I looked over my shoulder, noticing Nate standing in the doorway, and slipped inside the small closet so I could get changed.

I balled up Nate's shirt in my hands and stormed out of the closet. Shoving it into his chest, I pushed past him and made my way to the kitchen.

"What are you talking about?" Nate asked, following after me. He reached out and wrapped his hand around mine.

"First you see me naked and..." I closed my eyes tight as Nate intertwined his hand with mine, pulling me closer to him. Goosebumps spread along my skin and I knew there'd be no way to explain them if he asked. "At first, I thought maybe you *liked* what you saw. That maybe...*ugh*. But then you looked so disgusted, Nate. You made me put clothes on."

"Maddie, that's not — "

"I might not have the most confidence," I said. "But I know I'm not that bad. Yeah, I have scars, but I don't think that's reason enough to look horrified."

"Maddie, I — "

"In fact, I'm proud of my scars," I continued. His thumb started massaging my hand as I let the words tumble out of me. "They're a reminder. Of what I survived."

Nate remained silent, continually brushing his thumb against my skin, giving me the space to continue.

"And then" — I swallowed, keeping my eyes on the floor beneath us — "you said to me, 'if people are that bored and pathetic that they need to make something out of nothing, then that's their problem.' Something out of nothing, Nate? If *this*," I gestured between us, "is nothing, please tell me now so I can stop trying to figure out why my stomach flips every time I see or think about you."

"I shouldn't have said that," he said, his hand letting go of mine. He cupped my face. "Look at me Maddie, please."

I sighed, bringing my watery eyes to his.

"I can't believe how bad of a job I've done over the past few years showing how I feel about you," Nate said, looking at me earnestly. "You are beautiful, Maddie." He swallowed as his eyes flitted to the scar above my eyebrow, down to the one on my chin, and then back to my eyes. "Scars and all."

I sniffled, wiping my nose with the back of my hand. *Real cute, Maddie.*

"I thought you were beautiful the first time I saw you." Nate brushed away a tear that slowly strolled down my cheek with his thumb. "And I think you're even more beautiful now."

"Then why did you act that way when you saw me naked?"

"I asked you to put a shirt on because if you stood in front of me looking like that for one more second, I wouldn't have been able to hold myself back. You really don't know what you do to me, do you?" He leaned forward so that his forehead was resting against mine. "And then when I saw the scars on your leg, it hurt me. The fact that you had to go through that...it hurt me so much. I felt like I failed you. I was disgusted at *myself*, but never you, Maddie."

"What are you talking about?" I whispered. "You didn't do anything wrong."

"I should have tried harder to get you to leave that day when I came to get Olivia's things." Nate closed his eyes as though in pain as he continued. "You have no idea how many nights I lost sleep, wondering if you were safe."

I pulled back, reeling at the thought that I had a lifeline all those nights I spent scared and alone, and I hadn't thought to use it.

"I'm sorry," I said, my voice breaking. "I just...I can't do this."

Nate's arms dropped immediately, respectfully, even though his eyes were storm clouds. I swayed, feeling unbalanced without his touch. I hesitated, wondering if I should walk away or walk straight back into the safety of his arms. In the end, I ignored what my heart wanted and moved to the front door, feeling his eyes on me as I left the house.

eighteen

I drove around Briar Oakes, noticing little things I hadn't taken the time to before. Rolling past quaint little houses with their perfectly manicured lawns, I smiled to myself as I took in the calmness of the town. An elderly man was trimming the hedges along the perimeter of his property with a large pair of shears, a mom was sitting in her driveway a few houses down while her toddler scribbled all over the pavement with sidewalk chalk, and the mail carrier turned to wave at me with a friendly smile on his face as I drove by.

This was what I wanted for my life. I wanted to see the world's beauty. I wanted to be a part of a community that was so genuine and welcoming. I wanted to be brave. I wanted to make changes for the better and start allowing myself to truly be happy. My mind was already feeling clearer than it was when I stormed out of the house. I turned down a random street and parked along the curb, my tires scraping along the concrete. I rested my head back and let out a deep breath.

You have no idea what effect you have on me. Nate's words echoing in my mind had my heart galloping in my chest all over again.

I'm pretty sure you don't know what effect you have on me, *Nate,*

I thought, laughing quietly to myself. But honestly, did *I* even know? Glancing down at my phone sitting in the cup holder, I grabbed it and pulled up my contacts, my thumb hovering over Olivia's name. I had no idea what to make of what almost happened with Nate and I needed to talk about it with my best friend. But...I couldn't. How was I supposed to tell my best friend that I might have feelings for her brother and that we may have almost kissed?

Not knowing who else to call, I scrolled up in my contacts and landed on Heather.

"Maddie." Her voice was alert but soft. Placing the call on speaker, I dropped my phone into my lap. "Is everything okay?"

"I'm sorry for calling, but I have no one else to talk to about this. Is it a bad time?" I rushed everything out in one breath.

"No need to apologize, Maddie, this is what I'm here for." I could hear the smile in her voice and my shoulders relaxed in response. "What's going on?"

"I feel like this is something people normally share with their best friend," I scoffed, feeling more ridiculous by the second. "But I can't do that. Not about this."

"Did something happen between you two?"

"No..." I looked out the passenger window. "But something almost happened with Nate...I think. I don't know. But I can't talk about it with Olivia because that would just be weird. I mean, she seems receptive to us...maybe? I don't know." A couple was walking their dog and I smiled at them, waiting for them to pass before I continued.

"Explain to me what happened, Maddie," Heather said.

So I did. I told her about the past few weeks. How Nate and I ended most of our days on the couch, feet intertwined. How Briar Oakes had started to feel like home and I wasn't sure how that made me feel. I even told her about the Intimidator 3000 incident from earlier that afternoon, much to my chagrin.

"And then..." I swallowed, not sure why this was harder for me to say than admitting I got off to thoughts of him in the bathtub. "I'm pretty sure he was going to kiss me...and I bolted. I literally ran out of the house, Heather."

"Why do you think you felt the need to do that?" Heather asked.

"I was scared," I said quietly, tracing my fingers along the rubbery part of the window to my left. "I'm making such a mess of things." I let out a frustrated sigh. "I've sabotaged everything. I've been so afraid of the future that I've let my second-guessing take over."

"What exactly are your fears?"

Geez, where did I even start? "I guess I'm scared of how he's making me feel. It's been years since I felt even remotely close to this and...well, look at how that turned out. I got so wrapped up in getting my happy ending that I lost sight of what I deserved. Griffin took advantage of me in every possible way. I can't put myself through that again."

"Is it fair to project someone else's behavior onto Nate?"

"No." I pulled my hand back into my lap and closed my eyes. "Especially not Nate. He's been..." I smiled at the thought of his kind eyes, his gentle touch on my cheek a mere hour ago. "Nate's been so patient and understanding. I couldn't have asked for a better person to be by my side as I figure things out. But..."

"But?" Heather probed.

"I don't think I'd survive getting hurt again." I sighed, and tears suddenly flooded my eyes. I rested my head back, trying to blink them away as I stared at the ceiling. "Nate would never hurt me in the ways Griffin did, but in other ways...I think he could hurt me more. I'm just not sure if I'm up for that risk. And then there's Olivia." I took a few breaths, trying to wrap my head around those thoughts. "I just got her back as a friend, and I don't know if pursuing things with Nate will create too much change."

Heather was silent for a moment, absorbing this. When she spoke again, her voice was soft, but I hung on to every word.

"Sometimes what we might gain by being brave ends up being more valuable than what we risked in the first place."

I entered the passcode to the front door and pushed it open, summoning all my bravery. Nate sat on the couch, playing a video game. My eyes lingered on his bare back, watching his muscles flex with every movement. He leaned forward, his thumbs moving the right and left stick buttons in slow circles. I bit down on my lip, heat forming in my core again as I imagined him doing those exact movements on my body. I squeezed my legs together, trying to relieve the feeling I felt between them.

Shaking my head, I turned to shut the door, trying to be as quiet as possible so as to not break his concentration. Bending down, I unlaced and took off my boots, placing them to the side with lethal precision.

"Oh, come on!" he shouted into his headset, slamming his controller onto the coffee table. I jumped back up to my feet, my back straight, as Nate cursed again. "I'm on your team! Why would you shoot me?"

A giggle slipped out and I slapped my hand over my mouth, hoping he hadn't heard. Nate grabbed the remote and turned off the television, twisting around to face me. He ripped the headset off and ran his fingers through his long wavy hair, his deep green eyes wide as he searched my face.

"You're back," he exclaimed as he stood up and walked around the couch.

My eyes trailed down his body, taking in the muscles of his chest, and — oh crap, he was wearing those gray sweatpants again. My cheeks felt hot as I remembered the last time I saw him like this. My eyes dragged back up his body, taking their time on his chest, admiring every single dip and curve of muscle. I wondered how often he worked out to look like that and how he did it without me noticing. Those muscles couldn't be just from flipping grilled cheese sandwiches.

Nate let out a laugh and leaned against the back of the couch. I looked up at him, hoping to hold his gaze, but instead, my eyes kept drifting to the trail of hair disappearing behind the waistband of his pants. My fingers itched at my sides as I struggled to keep them there instead of letting them reach out and run across his torso.

"I went for a drive," I said, digging deep to remember how to form words, "and called my therapist."

"Your therapist?" He repeated, sounding nervous. "Did I overstep earlier? I'm sorry if I did, that wasn't my intention."

"No, Nate. You didn't do anything wrong," I assured him. "I just needed help sorting some things out in my head." I stopped and finally let myself meet his eyes. "I need to ask you about something you said earlier."

"You can ask me anything," Nate said, his hand coming up to rest on his chest.

"You said you wished you tried harder to save me that day. But what I don't understand is...what more do you think you could have possibly done?"

"So much, Maddie. So much." He dropped his hand and I felt the need to reach out and catch it, to comfort him, feel his pain as though it were my own. "I should have thrown you over my shoulder and made you leave, but it was all so complicated. I didn't want you to hate me for taking you away from him." His voice cracked on the last word. "I never changed my phone number, just in case you needed it. I checked it constantly, wanting to see your name pop up on my screen, but at the same time, was relieved it never did."

"Why?"

"Honestly? I knew if you texted me, it would have meant you were in danger." The rawness in his voice broke my heart. I pulled him into a hug, wrapping my arms around his waist tightly.

"*Nate.*" I took a steadying inhale, letting his scent fill my lungs. "I don't know how to get you to believe that there was nothing more you could have done. I wasn't ready to leave back then, regardless of how much I saw that I needed to. Hindsight is a bitch." I huffed a laugh, but it sounded tortured even to my own ears.

"When you and Olivia stopped being friends, it killed me. How was I supposed to keep you safe then?"

"Why were you so obsessed with keeping me safe, Nate?" I asked, pulling out of the embrace and letting my head drop back. "I thought it was just because of Olivia, but if this is how you felt when — "

"You really had no idea?" he said. I stared at him, my mind blank.

Nate slipped his fingers around my wrist and pulled me gently until I was flush against his body again. He wrapped his right arm around my waist, and I shivered at his touch, despite the warmth it radiated through my body. I held my breath as his hand slid into my hair and he pressed his forehead to mine.

"Nate," I whispered as he tugged me closer. I placed my hands on his chest, running my fingers through his soft curls as I slowly traced each dip of his muscle.

"I'm going to kiss you," he whispered so close I could feel his breath on my lips. "Like I've wanted to from the moment I first laid eyes on you."

"You are?" I asked, my throat suddenly dry. I swallowed as I looked down at his mouth, admiring the crooked smile that always graced his face. "How?"

"First," he said as his grip around my waist tightened. I gasped and my body molded against where he was now hard. I wanted to take a peek down, but his eyes held me captive. "I'm going to pull you so close that every single inch of your body is touching mine."

"And then?" My hands slid up his chest to his shoulders, not once lifting off his skin. I could keep them there forever.

"Then" — he slid his thumb over to my chin, tracing my scar and coaxing a shiver out of me — "I'm going to bring your face closer to mine, but not too close. Just close enough until my lips are hovering over yours."

"Go on," I whispered, wanting more.

"Then I'm going to kiss you." He smiled and my eyes fluttered closed. Nate's lips pressed against mine so softly that I wasn't even sure I felt them, and then he made his way to my chin, kissing my scar. My body trembled as he grazed my skin, leaving a trail of kisses along my cheek to my temple. A single tear slipped and strolled slowly down my face as his lips rested on the scar above my eyebrow.

His breath tickled my skin as he pulled back, his eyes drifting from mine to the tear on my cheek. I sucked in a shaky breath as he gently brushed away the tear with the pad of his thumb, exhaling softly as his eyes dropped to my mouth. When he leaned in, his lips were soft on mine, his beard even softer as he continued to press the lightest kisses against me. I stood still as my anxiety started to bubble inside me. The last guy I kissed was Griffin, and I tried my hardest not to let thoughts of him ruin this moment.

"Get out of your head," Nate whispered against my lips, sliding his hands from the nape of my neck down to my hands. I let him lift my arms, placing my palms flat against his chest.

Nate kept his forehead glued to mine as he stared down at my lips. My hands explored his chest and his broad shoulders, stopping only when they met at the back of his neck. I took a deep breath, imagining that the air I exhaled was every doubt and insecurity blocking in my path. I couldn't keep letting other people sabotage my future, not when there was no way to change my past. I pulled down on his neck, bringing him closer.

This time I kissed him.

Nate deepened the kiss and I gasped, breathing in his air. He took advantage, sliding his tongue against mine lazily, gauging my reaction. I pulled him closer to me, letting him know with my touch that I was okay with this, as the butterflies exploded in my stomach. Even while he was kissing me, he wasn't doing anything without taking my comfort in mind. I melted into his arms, forcing him to hold me tighter, letting all my senses linger.

Nate's hands slid down my waist to my thighs, hoisting me up. I wrapped my legs around his middle and tightened my arms as he moved us to the couch. A soft giggle escaped me when I crashed against him on the way down, and I loved feeling Nate smile against my lips. With my knees on either side of his body, I wiggled against him, seeking friction.

"You have no idea how much I love these sweatpants," I said between kisses, trying to hold back the moan that threatened to escape every time he shifted beneath me.

"I'll wear them more often, then." He chuckled and then gripped my hips, pressing me harder against him. When the moan building inside me slipped out, Nate let out a groan. "Mmm, make that sound again."

"Make me," I challenged, despite feeling incredibly insecure.

Nate's hands moved from my waist to my butt and I squealed as he lifted me again, flipping us over so that I lay on my back. He pressed his body against mine, parting my legs with his knee so that he could settle between them. A deep groan rumbled through his body as I wrapped my legs around his waist, pulling him down on me so that there wasn't any space left.

The sound of his moan filled me with joy. I couldn't believe this was happening. I was kissing Nate. Nate was kissing me. He pulled back, and I pouted in protest, causing him to chuckle.

"What?" I leaned forward, trying to get more of him, but he stopped me, tracing my swollen lips with his thumb.

"I'm going to make you fall in love with me," he whispered, leaning forward so that our noses touched. He was so close that our breathing became one.

What I didn't tell him was that I already was.

I stood in front of the bathroom mirror, tracing my now swollen lips as I replayed everything that happened over the past hour. Holy fuck. And what was more, he had feelings for me. Actual feelings. Feelings that'd sprouted years ago. All those nights I thought he was being overprotective because of Olivia...but it was really because of *me*. It was his way of showing me that he cared.

My pajamas, which still consisted of Nate's clothes, were folded neatly on the counter. Nate was having friends over for video game night, so I made sure to bring everything I needed to the bathroom. He'd asked if I wanted to join him and his friends, trying to bribe me with the promise of good food, but I couldn't. I wasn't ready to brave a guys' night. I knew I was safe with Nate, but old instincts were harder to quell. I made him promise not to let his friends in on our kiss, in fear of Olivia finding out from someone else before I mustered up the courage to tell her myself.

I slipped the shirt over my head and let myself luxuriate in the worn cotton that smelled faintly of rosemary, mint, and that delicious hint of butter. Once I was completely dressed, my hair brushed, and my skincare routine done, I stepped out of the bathroom and into the hallway. Not wanting to be rude, I walked down the hall and into the living room where Nate, Tyler, and Ben sat on the couch with their backs to me, a controller in each of their hands. I cleared my throat to let them know I was there and all three turned together to face me. My eyes remained on Nate as he took in the clothes I was wearing, and my stomach fluttered at the grin that stretched over his face.

"Finally," Tyler said, putting his remote control down on the coffee table before turning back to Nate. "You really need to find a house with more than one bathroom if you're going to live with a girl."

"Hey, Maddie," Ben spoke, his voice pulling me away from Nate's gaze.

"Hey, Ben." I nodded.

"You sure you don't want to hang out with us?" Nate asked. "We ordered a few pizzas and wings; they should be here soon."

"No, thanks," I said, giving Nate my brightest smile. "I've got some work to do and I'm going to get to bed early. It's been a long day."

"All right." His eyes trailed along my body once more before landing on my mouth. A blush crept onto my face as his eyes practically screamed how badly he wanted to kiss me. "Goodnight, Maddie."

"Night," I said through a yawn, turning around to head back down the hallway.

"Are you tapping that?" I heard Ben ask once I made it to my room. I paused in the doorway, closing it only halfway so I could hear how Nate would answer.

"She's my little sister's best friend, dude." Nate sighed, but when he spoke again, his voice was firmer. Almost threatening. "She's off-limits."

"Was that your shirt she was wearing?" What was his deal? Always so many questions.

"How should I know?" Nate answered, sounding unfazed. He was so good at acting like I meant nothing to him. "And quit talking about her, she can probably hear us."

I closed my door and locked it behind me. Turning on my sound machine to drown out the guys yelling at their games, I plopped down on my bed and went to grab my laptop off my nightstand when the book I was reading caught my attention. Smiling at seeing an index card poking out from within, I grabbed it and turned to the page it was holding. Picking it up in my hands, I ran my fingers over Nate's handwriting.

Remember how I told you I hadn't found anything more
incredible than your smile?
Well, I finally did. You kissing me.
You should keep doing that.
—Nate

Blushing, I tucked the card back in and wondered what happened to all the other bookmarks. Every time I opened my book, I found a new one to replace the previous one. I wished I had thought to keep them for my harder days. Putting the book and my ruminating aside, I grabbed my laptop and box of journals.

title to be determined
By Madison Williams

I'm finally starting to feel like myself again. The girl who dances despite looking like an idiot, the girl who smiles, the girl who has fun. I go to The Big House like I used to with Olivia on Saturday nights, even getting dressed up. Normally I hang out with Griffin for a bit, have a beer or two, and then head to the back and wait for his shift to end. But tonight? I have plans to have fun.

"Hey, babe." Griffin smiles as I take my usual place at the end of the bar. The Big House is busier than usual tonight. I watch as he pops the top off an IPA for me and slides it my way. A group of women come up to the bar, and Griffin goes to pour their shots.

"Can I get you something?" I turn in my stool to find the newest bartender. I keep my eyes on him, knowing that Griffin's watching.

Don't look away, I prompt myself. *Hold his gaze until he looks away first.*

"No, thank you." I lift my beer, cheersing with the air before taking another sip. "Already covered."

"What's someone as pretty as you doing sitting alone at a bar?"

I roll my eyes and take another sip of my beer, letting the smoothness of it coat my throat.

"I'm Griffin's girlfriend." Only then do I look away from him so that I can gesture toward Griffin, who's watching me as he lines up more shots. I give him a quick wave before turning back to the bartender. "And he tends to be a bit protective, so I suggest you get back to your job."

"Good thing I'm not afraid of a challenge."

My eyes widen in alarm. Is this guy serious? I'm not sure whether I should keep my eyes on him or look at Griffin for help. I'm definitely uncomfortable with how forward he is, but if I look at Griffin for help...well, that would be the end of this guy. And nobody deserves that.

"You're disgusting," I mutter, rolling my eyes and chugging the rest of my beer.

I stand up and head toward the door before he can say another word but stop as the group of girls from earlier catch my attention. They're on the dance floor, singing at the top of their lungs. I smile, watching them dance as they let the song take them away from the world, just like it did when I came here with Olivia. Without even glancing back to see if Griffin's watching, my feet move beneath me and I'm sidling up next to them. One of them smiles at me warmly and it's all the invitation I need.

I have no idea who they are. We never exchange names or stories. All I know is that it's one of the girls' birthdays because she has a giant pink button pinned to the collar of her jacket. I tell them I'm dating the bartender and can guarantee us free shots for the rest of the night, so they're more than willing to let me join in on their celebration.

"*Madison.*" I wince at the sound of Griffin's voice over the music. He sounds just like my dad does when he's upset with me; it's disapproving and sour. I watch as he pours us our fourth round of shots. "Don't you think you've had enough?"

"Nope." I shrug and somehow manage to scoop up the four shots in my fingers. Mr. Jim Beam, I thank you for providing me with the confidence to be this dumb.

"Okay, well I think you've had enough," he warns, but I just roll my eyes. "I'm cutting you off. No more after this."

"That's fine." I turn slowly, careful not to spill the whiskey. Priorities. The girls are waiting for me at a high-top table off to the side. "I'm sure your new bartender over there won't turn me down."

As soon as the words escape my lips, I know I've messed up. But it's too late. I quicken my pace to the table and set the shots down. I don't have to look at Griffin to know that his eyes are on me. I can feel them. Whenever his hands touch me, it feels like fire. But his eyes? My body goes cold as ice. We continue the rest of the night as we have been, dancing, singing, laughing, and taking turns getting shots. I already dug myself into a hole, so I figure it can't get any worse and I might as well have fun while doing it.

All the girls took their turns getting rounds, so now it's mine. I was hoping they'd call it a night before it got to me, but boy, can these girls party. "I knew you couldn't stay away from me." Mr. Cocky shoots me a dopey grin. I debate on asking his name, but I probably won't remember it in the morning, so what's the point? "What can I get you?"

"That," I say, nudging at the bottle in his hand. Normally I'd roll my eyes or gag at a cheesy comment like that, but there's too much alcohol in me at this point to care.

"If you give her any more, you're fired." I jerk back at the sound of Griffin's voice. He comes to stand next to a slightly shorter Mr. Cocky, but his looming presence is all I can see or feel. Griffin grips the bottle of tequila from him and yanks it back toward his own body. I look up at Griffin and meet those black-ice eyes. I feel the blood draining from my face and an invisible fist wrapping around my lungs, squeezing hard.

Fuck, I messed up.

"What the hell are you doing, Maddie?" His voice is sharp and I can't tell what hits me harder, his voice or his eyes.

I can't get any words out, so I just swallow the lump in my throat.

"Come with me." He walks out from behind the bar and pulls me along behind him by the elbow, leading me outside.

"Griffin, let go of me," I shout, trying to wiggle away as I stumble to keep up. I can feel his fingertips pressing into my skin between my bones. He's leading me to the alleyway behind the bar where staff take their cigarette breaks. "You're hurting me."

But instead of letting go, he spins me around and slams my back against the wall. I wince as the roughness from the bricks scrapes my bare shoulders. He paces back and forth in front of me, breathing heavily. I stand motionless with my back still against the building. I've never seen him like this before and I am terrified.

"I thought this shit would end once Olivia left," he yells, stepping forward so he's right in front of my face. His palm collides with the brick wall next to my head, and I'm so shocked that I cower, raising my hands to form a shield over my head. "But you just find a group of her clones and decide to do it again? The drinking, the dancing, the singing, the flirting."

I remain silent, my eyes pinned on the rusty green dumpster over his shoulder.

"Maybe I was wrong about you." His hands go wide on either side of his body. "You always told me it was Olivia who wanted all of that. The attention from random guys, free booze, making a fool of herself. But you're just as bad as her, aren't you? Were you just using her as an excuse?"

"Shut up," I say through gritted teeth. I hate when he talks about Olivia like she's the shit on the bottom of his shoe. Yeah, maybe she doesn't care what people think about her or what she does and how it looks, but I always admired that. She knows what she wants and she goes after it.

"What did you say?"

I don't have time to react. His hand moves to my neck and grips hard. I try to swallow, but can't get it down. I try kicking and pushing and squirming away from him, but the more I move, the tighter his grip gets. I look up at him, tears burning in my eyes, hoping he'll see my pain and stop. But when I look at him, I don't even recognize the guy standing in front of me.

The neighboring restaurant's back door opens and Griffin's hands loosen and drop to his side immediately. One of the employees steps out with a bag of trash and drags it to the dumpster.

"Everything okay here?" he asks.

"Yup," Griffin replies, giving him a quick smile. "Just on my break and spending it with my girl."

I look over at the man and notice he's looking straight at me. His eyes fall to my neck and I reflexively reach to cover it.

"Tell him you're fine," Griffin whispers in my ear as he nuzzles my neck.

"W-we're fine," I say weakly.

When the guy goes back through the door he came, Griffin holds out his hand and demands my phone. Afraid of what might happen if I refuse, I pull it out of my dress pocket and hand it over.

"I want you to go straight home, I'll call you an Uber." He clicks around on the screen, the backlight revealing a bulging vein in his temple and reddened eyes. "Don't go anywhere else, got it? I shared your location with me so I'll know if you do. We need to talk when I get home."

"You're tracking me?" I say incredulously as he slips my phone back into my dress pocket. "You're insane, Griffin."

"I don't know where all this talking back to me came from, but it ends now."

"Okay, *Dad*," I grunt, trying to make light of this situation that's shaken me to my core.

"Save that talk for later," he says as he cages me in with his arms, both palms flat against the brick.

I want to tell him to fuck off. I want to tell him that he'll never touch me like that again. I want to tell him that he's lost me. But I don't. Instead, I let Griffin come closer and wrap his arms around me. I let his mouth glide over my neck where his hands previously held me captive. I let him wipe my memory with a kiss.

Maybe I do deserve this. I know he hates it when I dance. I know he hates it when I drink too much. I know he hates it when I speak to guys. Maybe this is my fault. I know he'll get mad and I do it anyway. What type of person does that to someone they love?

"Okay," I whisper between kisses.

nineteen

I slammed my laptop shut and pushed it to the end of the bed, out of reach. I remembered that day like it was yesterday. The way his hands felt around my neck, the way his voice had terrified me. But what haunted me were his eyes, black as ice on a winter road. Taking a deep breath, my breath shaky as I exhaled, I reached over and turned my sound machine off, letting the sounds of the guys playing video games fill the room.

"All right, pause the game guys," Ben said, and my heart sped up at the sound of his voice. I heard the springs in the couch groan as he stood up. "Anybody want another slice of pizza?"

"Nah, I'm good," Nate replied. "I might go check on Maddie though. See if she's hungry."

"Is she really off-limits?" Ben's voice was muffled, like he was talking through a bite of pizza. "Like off-limits for you or off-limits for me?"

"To anyone," Nate growled in response. "Now drop it."

I smiled to myself as I sat on my bed, knees curled up against my chest. I'd only ever seen Nate jealous one time, and it was when I met Griffin and he'd told him not to count on ever seeing me again. If only that were the case.

"I know that look," Nate said, and I wished I could see what he was referring to. "I'm being serious, Ben. Olivia just got her back. She's had a hard time. She doesn't need another guy getting in the way."

"It's a small town, man." Ben laughed. "If she stays here, she's going to fall for one of us eventually. She doesn't have much to choose from. And besides, something tells me she likes guys who aren't afraid of a challenge."

Holy shit.

I grabbed my laptop and threw it open, pulling up my manuscript and scrolling until I found the last chapter I wrote, rereading the words.

"Good thing I'm not afraid of a challenge."

My hand flew to my mouth.

Ben was Mr. Cocky.

Of course he was. It was why he looked and felt familiar. I thought back to the first night I saw him at The Garage, *his* bar, and felt instantly anxious. He'd looked at me like he recognized me, like he knew me. He'd known the entire time who I was: *Griffin's girl.* And now he was sitting in that living room. Next to Nate. In the same house as me.

I shoved my journals back into the box and slid it underneath my bed. I couldn't be here. I needed air. Grabbing my cell phone off my dresser, I headed out of my room, slamming the door behind me. All three guys turned around at the same time, watching as I stormed over to the front door where my sneakers were.

"Madds? Where are you going?" Nate asked, but I couldn't even get myself to look at him, let alone answer. I bent down to grab my shoes, sliding them on without untying them first.

Nate was at my side, his hand resting on my arm and pulling me up. I jumped, sliding out of his grip as the panic began to build inside me.

"I'm going for a run," I said, my voice as unsteady as my legs. "Please, I need to get out of this house."

"Everything okay?" Ben asked from the couch while Tyler stood motionless in the kitchen.

I glared at Ben, unable to hide my anger, before I flickered my attention back to Nate. Did he know that Ben knew Griffin? Did he know that the moment Ben saw me he knew who I was and said *nothing*? Did he know that Ben caused me to have a panic attack in his bar because someone bought me a drink...but not any drink. *The* signature drink at The Big House.

"Wait," I said, shaking my head and turning to face Ben. "It was him, wasn't it?"

"Uh...what?" Ben looked at Nate, eyes wide.

"Who bought me that drink, Ben?" I snapped, taking a step forward, my fists clenched at my sides. "It was him, wasn't it?"

"Maddie..." Nate's voice was somehow calm, despite the tension in the air. "What — "

"Answer me!" My heart pummeled my chest as I waited for his answer. Ben looked between me and Nate, questions in his eyes. "Oh, all of a sudden you have nothing to say? Ever since I met you it's been one question after the other. 'So, what's the deal with you and Nate? Are you two a thing? Are you tapping that?' Yeah, I heard you. Were you asking all these questions for your own personal benefit or *him*?"

"Who are you talking about?" Nate asked, not giving Ben a chance to answer.

"Was it Griffin?" I asked, saying his name to fill in Nate, through gritted teeth. "Or shall I inform Nate of how much shit you caused me?" I gestured to the scars on my body.

"He did that to you?" Ben asked, his eyes widening as they trailed over every visible scar from the top of my head to my ankles.

"He tried to kill me!" I was seeing red now, clenching and unclenching my hands at my side, ignoring the ache in my fingers. I took a few steps forward.

"Can someone please fill me in on what's going on here?" Nate's hands were heavy on my shoulders now.

I knew that if I turned around and looked into his eyes, I'd fall apart. The tears would start falling. The panic would take over. And only his words of "You're safe" would be able to snap me out of it. But I couldn't do that here. I couldn't let Ben see. I couldn't take the chance that he'd tell Griffin. I had to leave.

"I can't do this." Tears clouded my vision as I shrugged out of Nate's grip and ran out the door.

I shouldn't have taken my anger and hurt out on Ben without knowing the full story. I'd hardly been thinking straight after making the connection, but that didn't excuse my outburst. I hated that Griffin was still driving my emotions like this, more than a year after I'd escaped. I called Heather and filled her in on what had happened. She encouraged me to go back and talk to Ben, to get his side of the story, but I couldn't do that yet. I'd made a fool of myself and Nate in front of his friends and needed to get myself together.

"Maddie," I heard someone shout, slicing through my rapidly deteriorating thoughts like a knife. I turned around, trying to locate who it was, but couldn't see anyone in the dark.

"I have pepper spray!" *Lies.* I spun in a circle, trying to figure out where the voice was coming from.

"It's Nate," he shouted back, suddenly at my side. Where did he come from? "Where the hell have you been? I've been running around town since you left."

With all the fight draining from me, I let out a small laugh. "It's not that big of a town, Nate. Either you're lying or you're a really terrible runner."

"I went to Olivia's first, figuring you'd go there," he panted, clearly out of breath. "What the hell happened?"

"You didn't talk to Ben?"

"No, I kicked them out as soon as you bolted and went looking for you." He ran a hand through his hair and then down to his beard before placing it on his hips. "Please, Maddie. You need to talk to me. I can't help you if you don't tell me what's wrong."

Glancing down, I stared at the charms on my bracelet, spinning it nervously around my wrist. I wanted to shout that I didn't need his help, to just turn around and go back home. But it was time that I learned to not only start asking for help when I needed it but to accept it as well. I didn't need to heal on my own. Looking into his deep green eyes, I reached out and laced my fingers through his. "Let's go for a walk, this could take a while."

When we got back to the house, Ben was waiting on the porch. Nate was about to charge up the stairs, but I pulled him back by his arm. I needed to get his side of the story.

"You found her," Ben said, sounding relieved as he looked at us. "After you kicked us out, I made it one street before I turned around. I figured someone should be here in case she..." — he looked away from Nate to meet my eyes — "in case *you* came back. I'm so sorry, Maddie."

"I don't even know where to start, Ben." I took a seat next to him on the swing, tucking my feet underneath me. "There's so many things I want to ask you, but part of me isn't sure I even want to know."

"How about we just start at the beginning?" Nate offered, climbing up the porch steps and leaning against the railing. "When he saw you at The Garage."

"I knew it was you the second I saw you," Ben admitted. "But you didn't seem to recognize me, so I didn't want to say anything." He rubbed his hands down his jeans nervously. "I couldn't believe that you were there, standing in *my* bar and without Griffin. The last time I saw you was the night of the accident. I haven't even seen Griffin since then. I was gone before he was released from the hospital."

"But you kept in touch?"

"Yeah, we've texted quite a bit," he admitted. "My uncle passed away about a month after your accident and left me The Garage, so he's been helping me out."

"Wait, did you say a month?" I asked, my head turning sharply to him. "How long was Griffin in the hospital for?"

"Uh..." He winced, scratching his brow. "A while. He was in a coma for a bit. We almost lost him a couple of times."

"Wow." I let his words simmer. Sure, I wasn't in love with him anymore, but it still hurt, knowing that someone you once cared about almost died. But then I remembered what he did and shook those thoughts away.

"I texted him after you and Olivia ordered your drinks, telling him that he'd never believe who just walked into my bar. That's when he told me to make you that drink." He looked down at his hands, shaking his head. "What happened to you...he told everyone it was an accident. He was so upset when he found out you were gone. I felt *bad* for him. If I had known he had hurt you...Maddie, I never would have contacted him."

"What else have you told him?" I asked.

"He asked me to keep him updated whenever I bumped into you. He also wanted to know if you were seeing anyone." He rubbed his hands together between his legs, clearly uncomfortable. "I'm so sorry, Maddie. I had no idea what I was doing. He just helped me out so much with running The Garage that I felt I couldn't ignore him."

"Does he know where I am?" I asked the one question I was most terrified to know the answer to.

"He knows where my bar is," he said nervously, glancing at Nate.

"What about Nate?" I asked, my stomach dropping at the thought of how Griffin would react if he knew who I was with. "He was always sensitive about him. Does he know you're friends with him or that he's here, too?"

"No, I don't think so." He glanced at Nate before focusing back on me. "When he asked if you were seeing anyone, I said I wasn't sure, but that I'd keep my eye on you."

I felt my shoulders sag in relief. That meant Nate was still safe. I just had to find a way to keep him that way. To keep Griffin from showing up here. Maybe if I left and Ben let Griffin know? But even just the thought of that made my stomach twist. I didn't want to leave, but something told me it was my only option.

"Okay." I moved off the swing and onto my feet. I knew I probably should have said more or tried to figure out where to go from here, but I needed time. It was like my body was on auto-pilot and I needed reality to hit. "I'm going inside, Nate."

I didn't wait for Nate or Ben to say anything before I hurried inside. Once I was back in my bedroom, Tuna scurried in after me and I shut the door. I slipped into a clean shirt of Nate's and crawled into bed and stared up at the ceiling. Not long after, there was a knock at my door.

"Come in." Tuna moved from the bottom of the bed to the pillow next to mine, curling up into a ball.

"Hi." He smiled sheepishly, his head poking through the crack in the door.

"Did Ben leave?"

"Yeah, I told him he should go home, and give you some time." He scratched the back of his head, looking nervous. "Can I sit down?"

I nodded and he took a seat at the foot of my bed, reaching over to place a hand on my feet. I closed my eyes and sighed deeply as he began massaging them through the blankets. Despite the smile taking over my face, my heart began to break as I mustered up the courage to say, "I can't stay here."

"You're not leaving." Nate's voice was firm and his hands stilled on my feet. "You're safe with me, Maddie, I promise."

"Nate, you travel for work. You aren't always here," I said as I sat up and crawled over the blankets, getting closer to him. His hand moved from my feet to my knee, where they gave it a reassuring squeeze.

"I've only had to leave once since you showed up," he replied, looking down at his hand covering my knee and his thumb drawing circles over my skin.

"You think I haven't noticed?" I laughed softly, despite not finding it funny. "You can't stop what you're doing because of me. I know you think your sole mission in life is to keep me safe, but that doesn't mean you have to drop what you're doing and become my bodyguard."

"You're worth it, Maddie."

Even though I was scared out of my mind and frustrated with him, I couldn't hold back my smile. No matter how hard I tried to stop it by biting on the inside of my cheeks, it still managed to take over my face. I rolled my eyes at myself. Knowing that his words affected me, he leaned forward and gave me a soft kiss on my forehead.

"Stop distracting me, Nate. This is serious."

"So am I, Madds," he said, and I watched as he rose to his knees, leaning his body over mine so that I had to lay down.

"Nate," I groaned. Ignoring my pathetic excuse of a protest, Nate took my hand in his and placed it on the nape of his neck, lowering his head. His face was so close to mine that his breath tickled the tip of my nose with each exhale. Slowly, I pulled his face down closer to mine and pressed my lips against his. He kissed me slowly, taking his time and making my mind dizzy in the process. I pulled away, my breath heavy as I freed his hair from the elastic holding it in a bun. He shook it out, letting it fall over his face.

"This is still so weird." I giggled softly as I ran my fingers through his silky hair.

"What is?" he asked, laying soft kisses along my scars. God, I loved it when he did that. "My hair?"

"No, I love the bun, don't ever cut it." I smiled as I trailed my hand down his jaw, my palm brushing through his facial hair. "And your beard."

"Then what's weird?" he questioned, turning his head in my palm so that he could kiss it.

"Kissing you." I lifted his shirt over his head. "Touching you."

"You'll get used to it." His eyes darkened as he dipped down to my jaw, kissing it until he reached the back of my ear. I squirmed beneath him as he hit my sweet spot. A soft moan escaped me, and I grabbed him by the pockets of his jeans and pulled him closer, lifting my hips so I could press him against me. "You're going to be the death of me, Maddie."

"Seriously, Nate," I gasped, pushing on his chest to put some space between us so that he had to lift his head and look at me. "We need to talk about this. I can't have you backing out of work. I'm not worth it."

"Yes, you are." He held my gaze as he cupped my cheek.

"Nate," I groaned, closing my eyes for a moment so I could collect my thoughts. "Until this afternoon, I had no idea you even thought of me this way. That you felt something for me all these years. I didn't even know I felt this way about you. You're not going to jeopardize everything you've worked hard on just because we kissed."

Nate just stared at me as I took another deep breath.

"It's not like we're even together," I carried on, bolstered by his silence. "You haven't even taken me out on a date yet. Where would we even go? There are eyes everywhere in this town and I wouldn't want Olivia to see and get uncomfortable, and I don't even know if I'm ready or if I'm looking too much into this. Ugh, I'm being ridiculous."

"Are you done?" He laughed at my rambling, gently pushing Tuna away so that he could claim the spot next to me. I nodded and brought my fingers to my lips, miming zipping my lips shut. "First, I was hoping this would be more than just a kiss. Second, you haven't even given me a chance to take you on a date. And third, I was really hoping that this would be more than a kiss."

"You already said that." I sighed as he snuggled me in his arms. I placed my hand across his chest, feeling his heart beating just as quickly as mine through his shirt.

"Because I really mean it," he said, kissing the top of my head.

"So, what are you saying?" I asked, pulling away from him so I could look him in the eyes.

"I'm asking if you'd take a chance on us." He looked at me nervously. "And be my girlfriend."

His girlfriend?

My heart skidded to a stop. I rolled out of Nate's arms and stared up at the ceiling. He wanted me to be his *girlfriend*. What was I thinking? I should have never let him kiss me. Kissing led to dating which led to relationships which led to someone falling in love which led to disappointment which led to breaking up and someone getting their heart broken...and I just couldn't do that again.

No. I couldn't do that to Nate.

He deserved someone who could give him that happily ever after. Someone who *believed* in it. I couldn't even read a romance novel without wanting to throw the book against the wall. I couldn't even watch a rom-com without bawling my eyes out at the end because it was a reminder that those endings didn't exist. I slid my hands out from where I'd tucked them under my arms and covered my face with them, letting out a soft groan.

"Madds," Nate whispered, uncovering my face with gentle hands. "Get out of your head."

"I can't." I shook my head, refusing to look at him. "I know earlier I ran you through what life was like for me over the past few years, but there's something else I want to show you. That I need to show you. I kept journals and documented everything. Olivia's the only other person who's read them, but I want you to read them, too. Once you do, you might change your mind about me."

"Nothing could change the fact that I want to be with you, Maddie."

Nate's hands moved to my shoulder, inching me closer to him and sliding his hand up my back to smooth my hair. I tried to match my breathing to his. Why was I so nervous about being with Nate? He never made me feel unsafe or unworthy. He never went out of his way to hurt me. The entire time I'd known him, his only goal was to make sure I was happy and safe. He wouldn't treat my heart any differently.

Taking a deep breath, I realized that if I was already feeling all these things, it would probably be worth it. Worth the nerves. Worth the scariness. Worth the risk. I looked up at Nate, whose eyes were taking in every freckle that scattered the bridge of my nose and cheeks. Giving him a small smile, I strained my neck so I could kiss him softly.

"We'd have to take things slow, Nate. Like, *really* slow. Tortoise speed." I looked away, but he caught my cheek and pulled me back so I was looking at him again. "I'll need you to be patient with me."

"Of course." He pushed a stray hair off my face and tucked it behind my ear, not wasting a second before kissing me again. "I'll be whatever you need me to be. If you want me to be your boyfriend, great. If it's too soon, then I can wait. If you want to date first and not have any titles, I'm okay with that, too. I'll meet you wherever you're at, okay?"

I turned his words around in my head. "I'm not sure what I'm ready for yet, but I like the sound of that. Let's just take it day by day and see how this goes."

"Whatever you want, Maddie."

"I want to talk about this whole Griffin thing," I said, bringing us back to our original conversation. "You can't distract me with all this kissing and girlfriend talk. This is a serious thing, Nate. You're not quitting your job and staying home to be my personal bodyguard."

"Fine." He rolled his eyes dramatically and I snorted. I rested my head against his chest as his fingers trailed up and down my spine. "I don't want to come across as controlling, so if I am let me know, but how about you come with me when I travel, and while we're home, avoid The Garage unless you're with me? And I promise I'll read those journals."

I had to stop myself from immediately saying no, but also from immediately saying yes. I didn't want to feel like a burden, but part of me also knew I wasn't. Not to Nate. So, taking a deep breath, I said, "Deal."

Climbing out of bed, I grabbed my journals and held them out to Nate. "Take your time with these, okay? You're not going to like a lot of what you read. Just...when you're done, bring them back into my room. I'm using them for my book."

"Okay." He sighed, climbing out of my bed and walking over to kiss me one more time. "Thank you for sharing these with me."

"Of course." I yawned. "Now, get out and let me go to sleep. I'm tired."

"Yes, ma'am." He took the box of journals from my hands. "Sweet dreams, Madds."

twenty

I had a date tonight.

Yup, a *date*. With *Nate*. After weeks of him being patient and never pushing anything with me, I told him I was ready and he asked me out. But now that the night had finally arrived, I was second-guessing if I really was ready. It wasn't that I didn't *want* to go on a date with him, I just didn't know what I'd be agreeing to. Was I signing myself up for something I wasn't ready for? Just the thought of losing the two people who meant the most to me in the world again had me breaking out in hives.

After vetoing all the outfit choices I'd laid out, I decided on a pair of black leggings, an oversized cream-colored sweater, my boots, and a pink braided headband to pull back my hair. I usually resorted to throwing it into a half ponytail, so I figured this would step my game up. I had no idea where Nate was taking me because he wanted it to be a surprise, but at least he told me to dress in something comfortable.

I looked out the living room window, letting the curtain drop as Nate pulled into the driveway a few minutes later. Nate's foot-steps echoed on the porch as he made his way over to the front door. I walked over and unlocked it, slowly opening it so I could greet him.

"I thought I was supposed to ring the doorbell." Nate stood there, scratching the beard that covered his jaw. A bouquet of daisies was in his other hand. "You know, pretend like I don't live with my date and all."

"Do you want to try again?" I laughed, taking the flowers from his outstretched hand. "I can shut the door and sit back on the couch, nervously waiting for my date to show up. I can even put my dad on speakerphone, so that you can tell him you'll have me home before midnight and promise to treat me with respect."

"Your dad?" Nate questioned, placing his keys on the entry table. I brought the flowers to my face, inhaling the fresh scent and hiding my smile. It'd been so long since someone gave me flowers and the butterflies in my stomach were taking flight. "When was the last time you talked to him?"

"He makes me text him every few days," I said as I made my way over to the kitchen, not wanting to get any deeper into the complicated relationship between us. I placed the flowers on the kitchen island and worked my way through every cabinet, searching. "Do you even own a vase?"

"Probably not," he said, suddenly behind me by the kitchen sink. I gripped the edge as Nate's body moved closer to mine, pressing my front against it. His chest was hard against my back as he dragged his hands down my arms until they reached my own, interlocking our fingers. My breath hitched in my throat as he rested his chin on my shoulder, his beard tickling the side of my neck. "Can't we just fill up the sink and stick them in?"

"No!" I laughed as Nate spun me around so that we were now facing each other. I reached up and linked my hands around his neck, feeling Nate's hands rough against my hips. He pressed me even more against the sink, dropping his forehead to mine.

"Have I told you how beautiful you look today?" Nate asked, his green eyes darkening. I swallowed. Hard. A warmth spread through me as Nate's thumbs tucked themselves under my sweater, tracing the bare skin just above the band of my leggings.

I shook my head, unable to formulate words as his eyes drifted to my lips, unconsciously licking them. I held my breath, hoping he'd kiss me. And soon.

"Please," I whispered, unable to handle the tension building between us.

Without any hesitation, Nate's mouth was on mine. His hand moved from my waist to the back of my head, tilting it back to gain better access. I gasped as his other hand wrapped around my thigh, lifting me. Wrapping my legs around his waist, Nate's grip tightened as he spun us around, placing me on the kitchen island. Spreading my knees wide, Nate stepped between my legs. My mind zeroed in on every part of him that was touching me.

"Nate," I moaned as his lips left mine to trail along my jaw, finding their way down my neck. I leaned back, hands on the counter to support my weight. Nate pressed kisses all along my sensitive skin. My jaw. My neck. My collarbone. He didn't leave a single exposed part of me untouched.

"Forget the date," I groaned as he nipped at my skin.

"Nope," Nate said, breathless. "I want to know what a date with Madison Williams is like. Don't deprive me of this."

"Fine," I groaned again, dropping my forehead to his shoulder.

"Are you ready?"

"Yes," I said, moving my hand to the back of his head where I ran my fingers through his soft waves. "Are you?"

He planted one more soft kiss against my lips. "I need a minute."

Nate took a few steps back to lean against the counter, and my eyes darted down. I bit down on my lip and fought a grin as I saw *why*.

I sat in the passenger seat of the Beast, gripping the edge with both my hands. Nate was insistent on having our date be a surprise, which I pretended to have a problem with in hopes he'd clue me in, but it didn't work. I closed my eyes, trying to focus on the music coming out of his speakers and not the fact that he was driving us somewhere that was an hour away from home.

An hour.

I could barely handle the five-minute drive from The Garage to his house, but I focused on the fact that we wouldn't be wining and dining in town, where everyone would see.

"You okay?" Nate asked, reaching across the center console to place his hand on my thigh. I jumped in my seat, causing him to bring his hand back to the steering wheel.

"Sorry." Tucking my hands into my arms, I rested my head against the headrest and closed my eyes. *Great job, Maddie. You haven't even made it to the real part of the date and you're already freaking out.* "How much longer until we get there?"

"Fifteen more minutes," he answered as he reached a hand up to change the station. "Do you need me to pull over?"

"No, I just need some air," I said, lowering my window and letting the cool autumn night air toss my hair around my face. *Okay...I survived forty-five minutes of this ride, I can make it another fifteen.* "I'll be fine, promise."

I turned my head to the side and looked at Nate. He glanced over at me quickly, giving me an encouraging smile before looking back at the road. But despite how brief that look was, I could see the concern in his eyes. *I really am blowing this date, aren't I?*

"No, you're not." Nate sighed, his hand briefly letting go of the steering wheel as if he were going to reach out to me again, but then hesitated. I watched as his hand dropped to his leg instead, sliding up and down his jeans.

"Crap, did I say that out loud?" I laughed nervously. "I'm sorry."

"You have nothing to be sorry about." He turned his signal on so he could merge into a different lane. "I just wish I made you feel safe enough to be in the car with me."

"If I didn't feel safe, I wouldn't have gotten in the car." When we headed out the door for our date, I immediately turned toward my Jeep, assuming that I'd be the one driving, but he grabbed me by the waist, spinning me so that I was facing the passenger seat of his truck instead. I tried to protest, but he said that his truck was part of the date. Since I was still too afraid to drive something this big, I had no real choice but to let him drive. So that was how I found myself shaking and gripping my seat for dear life while every bad possibility raced through my mind. "I'm not scared of you driving, necessarily. Just not being in control of the vehicle myself."

"I have no problem pulling over." I watched as his hand slowly made its way over to me, finally resting on my thigh. This time, I let myself relax in the seat. I smiled at the way his fingers felt wrapped around my leg, giving me a comforting squeeze before returning to the steering wheel. Even though I loved his hands on me and my skin felt too cold as soon as they left, I was grateful for their ten and two positions. "Just let me know what you need."

My stomach fluttered as I continued to remind myself that I was going on a date with Nate. As long as I pushed aside my nerves, I couldn't deny how right this felt.

My phone buzzed in the cupholder between us and I grabbed it, grateful for the distraction.

"It's your sister." I laughed, rolling my eyes as I opened her text. "I guess she's ready for her play-by-play."

Olivia: So...how's it going?

"How'd she take it when you told her who you were going out on a date with tonight?" Nate finally asked the question I'd been dreading all night.

"Yeah, about that." I winced and typed out my reply. "I didn't exactly tell her."

> Me: Still don't know where we're going. I'll text you when we get there.

"Why not?" I could feel his eyes on me, but I kept my focus on my phone, my thumbs hovering over the keyboard. "I thought you told her you were going on a date tonight."

"I did." I shrugged, watching as the three little dots appeared at the bottom of my screen. I'd gone to Latte Da! earlier today in hopes of getting some writing done, and Olivia knew instantly something was up. When I told her I had a date, she insisted on knowing who the lucky guy was, but I refused to let on. I wanted to keep this thing between Nate and me to myself for a little while longer. "But, for some reason, she thinks it's with someone else."

"Like who?" Nate said with an edge to his voice. Was he jealous?

"Ben," I whispered as I finally looked over at him, nervous to see how he'd react. His face remained expressionless, despite the previous edge to his voice, as he stared at the road. He turned his signal on so that we could merge off the highway before letting out a dramatic exhale. I bit down on my cheek, trying to suppress a giggle. "Which I did not confirm. Or deny."

> Olivia: Who knew Ben was such a romantic?

I already felt guilty keeping whatever was going on between me and Nate from Olivia, but now I was letting her think I was on a date with Ben? Ugh, I truly was the worst friend ever. My thumbs hovered over my screen, trying to come up with something to say back. Anything I thought of either confirmed or denied who I was with.

"She's going to find out eventually, Maddie," he said, turning us down a side road once we were off the highway. The paved road came to an end and we were now bumping along, heading for a field up ahead. "Might as well just rip the Band-Aid off and get it over with."

"Oh my god," I squealed, turning in my seat so I faced Nate. I grabbed his arm as his "surprise" came into view. "You took me to a drive-in theater?"

Now the whole comfy clothing suggestion made sense.

"I'm surprised you didn't guess." Nate chuckled and pointed to the backseat. "I was sure the basket of junk food, blankets, and pillows was a dead giveaway."

"I've been in the Beast exactly once before, *and* I was fighting a panic attack," I said matter-of-factly. "I wasn't exactly paying attention to what you kept in your truck. You could always have emergency blankets and pillows in here. You do travel for work, so it's not too crazy of a thought."

We got in line behind a few other cars, waiting for them to pay for their movie. I leaned forward in my seat and took in the three large movie screens spaced out over the field, trying to control my excitement. "What are we seeing?"

"That's up for you to decide." He smiled and reached over to tuck a strand of my hair behind my ear. I shivered at his touch, despite his fingers always being warm against my skin. "But I think I know which one you'll choose. The movie listings are right over there."

I looked to where Nate was pointing and gasped. "*Twilight*? I can't believe you found a drive-in theater playing *Twilight*! I knew you were just in denial. You're totally a secret fan, aren't you? Now tell me, are you Team Edward or Team Jacob?"

"They're also playing *Star Wars* and *Toy Story*," Nate added, avoiding my question, as he pulled his wallet out of his back pocket. "So, what will it be?"

"*Star Wars*, for sure," I said, completely deadpan. Nate turned toward me and raised his eyebrows. "Just kidding. Bring on the sparkly vampires, Nate!"

twenty-one

"I can't believe you're still hungry," Nate said, reaching over to squeeze my hand as we turned onto Main Street. "I don't think I'll be able to look at popcorn the same way again."

"No one told you to eat the jumbo bucket of popcorn all by yourself." I laughed through a yawn. Despite eating my weight in M&M's, I was really craving one of Nate's famous grilled cheese sandwiches. "There was enough butter in that tub, you could've swam in it."

"Did you at least have fun?" Nate asked. Although I felt more comfortable being in the passenger seat of his truck now than I did a few hours ago, I still tracked every movement he made, and I noticed his hand fanning out over the wheel as if he was nervous about what my answer would be.

"You can't dangle sparkly vampires in my face and expect me to not have a good time. And the company wasn't bad either," I said, nudging him with my elbow. "It was the perfect first date. But if I don't get some of Nate's Grates inside of me shortly, I might have to deduct some points."

He turned his head in my direction quickly, and thanks to the streetlights, I was able to catch his suggestive wink.

"I meant a grilled cheese sandwich." I hid my grin behind another yawn. "Pervert."

"Hey, the night is still young." Nate cocked a brow as he pulled the Beast along the curb in front of the town's gazebo, right next to his food truck.

"Didn't I call them orgasmic?" I giggled and felt myself blush. "Maybe it'll put me in the mood."

"Tortoise speed, remember?" He smiled at me as he unbuckled his seatbelt, and my stomach did a cartwheel at the reminder that he was respecting my boundaries.

"I know, I'm just teasing you." Nate reached over, giving my thigh one more comforting squeeze before hopping out of the truck.

Before I could even get my hand on the handle, he was outside opening my door. I slipped my hand into his as his other arm wrapped around my waist, lifting me out of my seat and spinning me before planting my feet on the curb. He pulled me close, pressing our chests together as he left the lightest kiss against my lips. Butterflies fluttered inside me as his lips touched mine. And unfortunately, we didn't do a lot of it at the drive-in.

Tonight was perfect. I wasn't lying when I told him that. I spent the majority of it looking at the screen, but instead of being locked in on Edward Cullen, I was focused more on how nervous I was.

We had all the cozy blankets, pillows, and snacks, and Nate even had some twinkly lights running along the perimeter of the bed of the truck. We started off with some space between us, but by the time we met the Cullens for the first time, I was curled up against Nate, running my fingers over the soft light brown hair that dusted his arms. Occasionally I'd feel a kiss on my hair, but I never found the courage to turn around and meet him halfway.

"Please tell me your food truck has heat." I shivered and let my teeth clatter loudly as Nate's hands slid underneath my sweater, finding their place against the bare skin of my waist. The nights were getting chilly as we crossed over into October, the promise of a crisp fall in the air.

"The grill will warm it up quick," he said, planting a kiss on my forehead and giving me a little squeeze before sliding his hands out to grab ahold of mine. "Come on, let's get you inside."

Nate held my hand as he unlocked the food truck, opening the door for me. I stepped inside and waited for him to turn the lights on, taking in the large griddle, stove top, refrigerator, cabinets, and sinks. Nate pointed to the countertop, which ran along the entire length of the trailer with the serving window. "You can sit up there while I get everything ready."

"You mean I don't get to learn how to make a Nate's Grates grilled cheese?" I feigned being disappointed as I hopped onto the counter, sliding back until the back of my knees hit the edge.

"And share my secrets?" He laughed, and I watched as he made his way over to the fridge, pulling out all kinds of ingredients and setting them down beside me.

"What are you making me?" I asked as I picked up the bottle of Worcestershire sauce.

"I'm trying out a new recipe." He shrugged, turning around so he could fire up the grill. "I'm not sure what I'm going to call it yet, but it's similar to a Philly cheesesteak."

"That sounds delicious." I smiled at the same time as my stomach growled.

Nate was like a machine in the kitchen, grabbing different tools and ingredients, cutting up everything, and throwing them together, never taking a moment to breathe. He didn't stand in one place for more than five seconds before moving on to something else. It didn't take long for the inside of his trailer to smell amazing, and my mouth watered as I inhaled the combination of cheese, peppers, and onions.

I watched as the muscles of Nate's arms strained against his gray shirt as he stood in front of the grill, browning the meat. My eyes trailed down his arms to his hands, which gripped a spatula tightly, and all I could think about was how I wished those hands were on me instead. My eyes trailed back up to his face just in time for Nate to look over his shoulder, giving me a wink before focusing back on the food in front of him.

"So," I said as I kicked my shoes off and pulled my feet up onto the counter, crossing them in front of me. "Do you plan on doing the whole food truck business forever or do you have plans on opening a restaurant at some point?"

"You sound like my mother." He glanced over at me again before grabbing some more ingredients. I watched as he added some butter to the grill and tossed in the peppers and onions, cooking them until they were brown and caramelized. "She's always bugging me to quit traveling and open up a restaurant so I can find a wife and settle down."

"What every girl wants to hear." I laughed softly, grabbing a raw green pepper strip and taking a bite. "That they remind their boyfriend of their mother."

"Boyfriend?" Nate whirled around to face me, spatula mid-air. "Is that what I am?"

Crap.

"Ugh," I groaned, lifting my head to face him again. "Nate, I'm sorry. I don't know why I said that. Tonight's been a dream, seriously. But I need to talk to Liv before we put a label on this."

"*Are* you going to talk to her?"

"Of course." I gave him a smile despite the pit forming in my stomach. My gut was telling me she'd be happy as long as we were happy, but I couldn't forget about how she was so against the idea of us when we were in college. There was also a voice in my head that warned me she might not think I was ready. I'd grown a lot since losing myself in Griffin, but I was still healing. Would our friendship survive if me and Nate's relationship didn't?

"Promise?" he asked, closing the distance between us. He rested his hand on my cheek, his thumb brushing back and forth across my skin.

"I promise that as soon as I talk to her, we can come back to your food truck during the lunch rush, stand on top of the roof, and shout to all of Briar Oakes that we're officially a couple." I smiled, imagining all of this going down in my head.

"Or," he countered, leaning in to give me a soft kiss on the lips. "We could just go to the library and tell Lorraine and Margaret and let them spread the news. It'll probably get around a lot quicker."

"True." I pushed him away from me gently. "Now go finish my sandwich, I'm starving."

I spent the next twenty minutes watching Nate make our sandwiches and admiring the way he moved about the kitchen. There was just something so mesmerizing about watching him cook. He was so happy. So confident. So full of joy. Watching him cook was like foreplay. I closed my eyes and let out a deep breath, trying to control my thoughts.

You said you wanted slow, Maddie. Tortoise speed.

"All done," Nate said, and my hand flew to my chest. I opened my eyes, finding Nate standing less than a foot away from me with a plate in hand.

He set the sandwiches down on the counter and leaned over me, his hard stomach pressed against my crossed legs as he reached behind me to grab some utensils. When he pulled back, he paused with his face just inches from mine. My gaze dropped to his lips and lingered. I swallowed, moving my gaze to his, taking in how his forest green eyes darkened as they dipped to my mouth and back. It was as if all the air in the food truck evaporated, leaving only the smell of Nate luring me closer. But just when I got close enough to feel his breath against my skin, he let out a soft laugh and pulled back, bringing his attention back to the sandwiches he made.

He cut them diagonally before lifting one of them, pulling the two halves apart in the air. I watched as the cheese pulled apart slowly, my eyes widening at the ooey-gooeyness of it. He held up the half sandwich and I took a generous bite. Nate blinked, moving his attention from my eyes to my mouth as I slowly chewed my bite, savoring every flavor that overwhelmed my tastebuds.

"Oh my god," I moaned, my eyes rolling to the back of my head. I reached for another bite, but Nate pulled the sandwich back. "Nate, stop it."

"Make that sound again," he said in a raspy voice, sending a shiver through my body.

"What sound?"

"The same sound you made the first time I cooked you a grilled cheese sandwich," he said, his voice guttural as he tucked a stray piece of my hair behind my ear. "That moan gets me every time."

"Well..." I cleared my throat, trying to unscramble the feelings bursting inside me. "I can't if you don't let me have another bite."

Nate's hand dropped to my leg, settling just above my knee. I grabbed the sandwich and took another generous bite, letting the moan rumble through my stomach, up my throat, and finally escape my mouth as I chewed. Both of Nate's hands were now on my legs, sliding down until they hooked themselves behind my knees so that he could uncross them, letting them dangle off the edge of the countertop. I gasped as his hard length pressed against the apex of my legs, letting my eyes bounce between us and then back up to his face.

"Nate," I whispered, feeling his hand travel back up my thigh, over my hip, and underneath my oversized sweater. His hands were warm against my bare back, his knuckles slowly trailing up and down my spine. I leaned forward, resting my hands against his chest and grabbing his shirt, inviting him even closer.

He freed one of his hands from beneath my sweater and moved it to the back of my neck, fisting my hair gently. I held my breath as he leaned down, kissing my forehead, the scar above my eyebrow, my nose, the scar on my chin, and then finally resting on my lips. I melted against him, every part of my body he touched liquifying.

Nate's hand tightened on my back as he tilted my head, angling me so that he could deepen the kiss even more, fusing us together. His tongue traced the seam of my lips and I opened for him, letting his collide with mine. The ache between my legs became more powerful as Nate pressed himself against me, proving just how badly he wanted me, too.

Nate's lips trailed my jawline until it reached the back of my ear. I let out another gasp as he pressed the softest kiss against the skin of my neck and nipped at my earlobe. His tongue danced around my earring until I was arching my back and moaning shamelessly. He turned my head toward his quickly and pressed his mouth back on mine as if devouring the moan that just escaped me.

Fuck, I was in trouble.

"Maddie," Nate groaned, pulling away from me slightly, but keeping his forehead pressed against mine. "I want you so bad but I don't want to rush you."

"It's fine, Nate," I panted, keeping my eyes on his mouth. Taking it slow had felt like the right decision, but here in this moment, Nate was all I wanted. "Maybe we can be like tortoises on roller skates? Speed it up just a bit?"

"Tell me what you want," he begged, closing his eyes. He let out a slow breath and I felt it tickle my nose. "Please."

I wanted to savor every second of this moment. He leaned against the counter, one hand on either side of me. Not knowing what to say, I swallowed and decided maybe I could show him.

Taking a deep breath, I hooked my thumbs under my sweater and slowly raised it over my head, letting it fall to the counter behind me. Nate's eyes dragged over me, studying each part of my skin as if it were a touch over my collarbone, past the swell of my breasts covered by my black lace bra, down to my belly button, and then back up to my face. I covered Nate's hands with mine, bringing them to my hips, and played with the waistband of my pants, letting Nate know that I wanted him to slide them off.

Nate's throat bobbed as he swallowed, and his fingers slowly peeled my leggings down my hips. His fingers lightly skimmed my skin as he dragged them lower, and a rippling fire ignited inside me. My heart hammered inside my chest as I watched every careful move he made. He dropped my leggings to the floor and closed the distance between us, stepping between my open legs once again. His lips were on mine in an instant, his teeth grazing over my lower lip as he lightly nibbled against it.

"Kiss me," I whispered against his lips, finally knowing what I wanted from him and how to tell him.

"I am," he replied, and I felt him smile against me.

"No." I shook my head the smallest amount, not wanting to break away from our locked lips any more. "Kiss me everywhere."

Nate growled as he pulled away, moving his mouth to my neck.

I leaned back on my hands as Nate's mouth made a path down my neck and over to my shoulder, where he pressed a featherlight kiss against it. I shivered as Nate's hand rested over my bra, his thumb skating over my cleavage before going around to my back. He continued leaving kisses on my skin, moving from one shoulder to the other, while his fingers unclasped my bra and freed my breasts. Nate shut his eyes and took a deep breath before opening them again, admiring my body as I sat in nothing but my black panties.

"You have no idea how hard I'm trying to control myself right now, Madds." His lips were back on my neck before whispering in my ear, "You have no idea how many nights I've dreamed of this. Having you here, in my arms. Being able to touch you, kiss you, make you happy. I want to taste every part of you, savor every little bite and lick, make you moan my name."

"You've already done that," I reminded him, arching my back as his lips trailed down my chest and over my right breast. Nate's tongue swirled around my peaked nipple, and I gasped.

He groaned, rubbing his thumb over my other nipple as he continued to suck on the one in his mouth. "But this time I'm *making* you moan, instead of just the thought of me. You have no idea how badly I wanted to bust down the bathroom door when I heard you getting off to the thought of me."

"Show me what you would have done," I whispered.

"My pleasure," he said, releasing my nipple from his mouth with a pop.

Nate's eyes held mine as his thumb traced my seam over my panties. Before I could even react, his mouth was on mine again and he was moving in small circles over my center. He pulled back as his fingers hooked in the fabric. I held my breath, watching him kneel in front of me, slowly peeling them off and letting them fall to the floor. Looking down at Nate, his head positioned right between my bare legs...I couldn't believe this was happening.

"Nate." The panic in my voice was clear and I winced, not wanting to ruin this moment but unable to stop it. "*Nate.*"

My hand covered the scars on my left thigh. My heart pounded in my chest and it felt like a gorilla was trapped in my rib cage, banging against the bones. Deep down, I knew I had nothing to be self-conscious about, but I couldn't stop covering myself up.

"Maddie." His voice was calm as he continued to trail kisses from my knee up my thigh. His lips moved over my fingers, giving each one a soft kiss. He pulled away, placing his hand over mine as he looked me in the eyes. "You're safe with me, I promise. If you want me to stop, just tell me and I will."

And I was. I knew I was safe with him. Nate kept his eyes on me as he lifted my hand and laced our fingers together, and then brought his lips to my scars. I fought back the tears that threatened to spill, swallowing over the lump in my throat. This was all too much. Nate was too much. He was too good. How did I deserve him?

I shoved the thoughts away, mindful of staying in the moment. My past didn't get to take over, not now. I deserved someone good. I deserved Nate.

"Okay," I breathed, my voice shaky as his mouth moved over my entrance.

Nate's tongue took over where his thumb had circled me before. I threw my head back and mumbled a few nonsense words before letting my mind drift.

And this time, it wasn't the grilled cheese making me moan.

"Don't stop."

Nate groaned deeply and I felt the vibration through my entire body. It was like he'd never tasted something so good in his entire life. Like he was deprived of sugar and was finally getting his first taste of it. I ran my fingers over his head until I reached the elastic holding his hair back in a bun. I released it, letting my fingers tangle themselves in his loose waves. Nate's moan deepened as I pushed his face farther into me.

His hands were on my knees, holding me open for him. The fact that my pleasure was causing him to moan was enough for me to lose myself, but I held on as long as I could. I wasn't ready for this to end yet.

"*Fuck.*" I dragged out the word as Nate's hand slid off my knee and his fingers found their way into me. He pulled back, looking me in the eyes as he slid one, then two fingers inside me. Knowing I wasn't going to be able to last much longer, I fisted his hair and pushed his head down, feeling the overwhelming sensation build up between my legs and rapidly take over the rest of my body.

"Don't. Stop," I begged, my voice unsteady.

"Let go, Madds." His breath was hot against me as his fingers pumped in and out, quickening his pace. His tongue was back on me, trying to keep up as it swirled around my clit.

"Nate," I cried as my walls tightened around his fingers. Nate's hand pushed against my knee and he continued pumping his fingers, chasing my orgasm. Time seemed to stand still as I came back to earth, registering the cool metal surface beneath my legs and the sounds of our breathing in the tight space.

"God, you are so beautiful," Nate whispered as he stood up and pressed his mouth against mine, letting me taste what he did to me on his lips.

twenty-two

Oh my god.

I covered my face with my hands, hoping it would turn me invisible as the panic began to build up inside me. My face flushed as I thought of everything Nate did, every part of me he touched, every sound I made. I clenched my teeth and pressed my lips together, holding back the moan that so badly wanted to slip out as I remembered exactly how everything felt.

Holy fuck.

Nate just had his head between my legs.

I pulled my legs up to my chest, bringing my face between my knees.

Breathe, Maddie, just breathe.

"Hey," Nate whispered in my ear, wrapping his arms around my curled-up body. "What's going on?"

How was I supposed to tell him that I was letting my thoughts sabotage everything again?

"I just — " Three bangs echoed in the trailer, cutting me off. The metal of the closed window behind me rattled with each pound. I lifted my head, my eyes opened wide, as I stared up at Nate in alarm. His eyebrows drew together and formed a set of wrinkles between them before he glanced at the door. "What was that?"

Nate let go of me, reaching down to grab my underwear and leggings off the floor before tossing them at me.

"Put those on," he whispered, taking the three short steps to the door. The handle rattled as whoever was outside tried to open it. I remained frozen, watching as Nate gripped it tightly to keep the door closed. "Quickly."

I hopped off the counter, slipping my clothes on. I was pretty sure I put them on backward. Turning around, I grabbed my sweater off the countertop. "Nate, where's my bra?"

"I don't know." He scratched his head, eyes darting around wildly. Whoever was outside pounded on the door again. "Don't worry about it, just get dressed."

I slipped my sweater over my head and nodded at Nate, letting him know I was ready. Holding my breath, I stood behind him as he unlocked the door and swung it open.

"Where is she?" Olivia's voice rang through the air, her pint-sized body blocked by Nate.

Shit.

"I know she's in here, Nate," Olivia said, and I could hear her heels tapping on the two steps as she climbed into the trailer.

Nate reached behind him, tucking me in closer. Was he really getting all protective of me over his sister? What did he think she was — some crazed dog about to attack? Nate was six feet tall and Olivia barely stood at five. All he had to do was poke her and she'd fall over. But despite how ridiculous he was being, I couldn't stop the grin from forming at how protective he was.

"Hi," I said, stepping out from behind Nate, holding on to his arm as I took my place at his side. "What are you doing here?"

"What am *I* doing here?" Olivia glared, letting out a maniacal laugh. Great, she was mad. I gripped Nate's arm tighter, waiting for her to blow. "Do you know where I went tonight, Maddie?" she asked, but didn't give me a chance to respond. "The Garage."

My eyes widened as I realized what that meant.

"And guess who else was there? Ben." Olivia crossed her arms over her chest, the shimmery threads of her sweater sparkling under the lights in the trailer. "And guess who *wasn't?* You."

"I never said — " I started, but Olivia held up a finger to silence me.

"Yeah, I realized that." She leaned against the doorframe, blowing a piece of hair out of her face. "I was about to accuse him of standing you up, but then I realized you never did say it was with him. You didn't deny it, either, though."

"You didn't give me the chance to," I said softly, flicking my eyes between her and Nate.

"I was just so excited that you were going on a date that I didn't care who it was with, you know? And he just...kind of made sense. Once I realized all this, I tried to figure out *who* you could be on a date with." Her eyes flitted between us, and I could tell she was trying her hardest to fight a smile. But...why was she smiling?

Nate's grip tightened around me as he gave me a reassuring smile. Olivia huffed as she walked past us, hopping up onto where I was sitting moments before on the countertop. I bit down on my cheek, trying to stop the giggle from coming. If only she knew. She grabbed my half-eaten grilled cheese off the plate and took a bite. "Oh, this is good, Nate."

"Thanks, I'm thinking of adding it to the menu."

"When did this whole thing start?" Olivia asked around a mouthful of cheese.

"What thing?" I asked, playing dumb.

"Please." She waved the remainder of the sandwich in our direction. "I've been watching you two, trying to see when one of you would crack and confess, but you surprised me. I honestly thought it would be you, Maddie."

"Me?" I slapped my hand over my chest. "Why me?"

"Because Nate's managed to hide his giant crush on you since the day you two met." She gave me a look that said, *Duh.* I grabbed a hold of Nate's hand and laced my fingers with his, giving it a squeeze. "You, on the other hand...you've never been able to hide anything from me."

"Are you mad?" I finally asked, not wanting to drag this conversation out any longer. The suspense was starting to be too much and I wasn't sure how much longer I could stand here, watching her eat a sandwich so calmly while I stood here sweating from nerves.

"That depends." She shrugged and hopped off the counter, putting the empty plate in the sink. "Are you two together or not?"

Nate gave my hand a squeeze, and I knew he was going to leave that question up to me to answer. Were we together? My stomach churned at the thought of giving in to my feelings and giving him a chance to hurt me. But Nate was Nate, and I knew exactly the kind of person he was. So even if he did break my heart, I'm sure he'd be so gentle about it that I wouldn't even realize it was happening.

I glanced up at him, his eyes soft on mine, his thumb rubbing back and forth across my hand. If I said no, would I lose this? Would I lose the comfort he gave me? The sense of safety? Would he be so disappointed in me that he'd kick me out of the house?

No, I couldn't lose that. I couldn't lose him. Just the thought of it was making me feel worse than the fear of having my heart broken into a million pieces again. I'd let it happen if it meant Nate was the one doing it. Taking one last deep breath, hoping the air was filled with the confidence I needed, I looked over to Olivia and said, "Yes, we're together."

"Yes?" Nate whispered and I swear I saw a sparkle in his eye, a lightness that wasn't there before. His shoulders relaxed and he turned his body toward me. I giggled as he pulled me closer to him, pressing me against his body.

"Well, hallelujah!" Olivia let out in one loud breath, hopping off the counter to wrap us into a group hug. "It's about dang time. I'm so happy!"

"You are?" I asked, utterly surprised. Nate shrugged us out of her embrace, but still kept his arms around me. "But you were always on my case about him throughout college. I thought you'd be upset."

"I was just being stupid and territorial back then. I didn't want to lose my best friend to my brother." She smiled at me. "But you deserve it, Maddie. He's one of the good ones."

Yeah, he was.

I beamed at her, feeling the happiest I'd been in a long time. Standing here, in Nate's arms, with Olivia's approval — whether or not she wanted to be watching us right now — was just what I needed. Bending down, Nate pressed his lips against mine, and I felt his shoulders sag in relief.

"Right, now that this is all cleared up," Olivia coughed and I tried to pull away, but Nate ignored it, his grip moving to the back of my head to hold me in place, "I'm going to go. I might approve of this, but that doesn't mean I want to see it."

"Bye, Liv," Nate said between kisses.

"Oh, and by the way, your bra is dangling over there."

I managed to pull away from Nate to look where Olivia was gesturing, noticing my bra hanging loosely off the handle of a cabinet in the corner.

"Even if you two lied about what's going on, that gave it away the second I walked in here." Olivia rolled her eyes at us. "Not to mention the sounds. You should really figure out a way to sound-proof this place if you plan on using it for things aside from cooking..." She paused, bursting into a fit of giggles. "And maybe put your Lysol skills to work and disinfect this place, Maddie."

My cheeks flushed and I turned back to Nate, burying my face into his shirt. Nate's chuckle rumbled through his chest as he yelled, "Get out, Liv."

twenty-three

Freshly showered, I padded into the living room with a book and my laptop. We were supposed to get a bad storm today, so I planned on staying inside, eating too much junk food, and getting lost in writing or reading. I was almost done turning my journal entries into chapters, and I just needed to figure out how I wanted this book to end so that I could be finished. I still had no idea what my happily ever after was. Heather continued to ask me about it during our sessions, but I wasn't any closer to figuring it out.

Thunder boomed, and the sound had me jumping out of my skin. I stood and ran to the window, peering outside. Rain pelted against the glass and I bit down on my lip, glancing at the empty space in the driveway where Nate's truck usually was. I paced the living room floor, shooting a text to Nate to see when he'd be coming home. Tuna sat on the arm of the couch, watching as I practically paved a ditch into the floor. More thunder rumbled in the sky, shaking the house, and a crack of lightning stopped me in my tracks. I raced over to the window again, but Nate was still nowhere in sight.

I looked at the time on my phone and groaned. Ten minutes had passed since I texted Nate and I still had no response.

"Where is he?" I asked Tuna who continued to watch me. Not knowing what to do, I collapsed onto the couch face-first into a pillow. Tuna let out a soft meow as he crawled over my legs and settled onto my lower back. Sure, I could text him again, but I didn't want to be that clingy girlfriend who watched the clock and needed to know where her boyfriend was at all times.

I guess one more text wouldn't hurt, right? Just as I was about to open my messages, I heard Nate's truck pulling up the driveway, his headlights illuminating the darkness in the living room. Forgetting that Tuna was resting on my back, I hopped to my feet and raced to the door. When I swung the door open, a gust of wind barreled into me, causing me to stagger back a step or two. The front door flew from my grasp and slammed against the wall, and I saw the cat leap into the air and scurry under the couch in my periphery.

Nate stepped out of his truck with his arms filled with shopping bags and ran to the front porch. Once he made it to the door, I grabbed the bags from him as he locked the Beast with the click of a button; two deep beeps were barely audibly over the rumble of the clouds above.

"You went to Target?" I asked, plopping the bags down onto the kitchen island.

"Yeah," he replied as he hung up his wet jacket in the closet. "I wanted to grab a few things just in case we get stuck here for a while."

"You can't hang that up in there soaked like that." I rolled my eyes, walking over to it and taking it off the hanger he just put it on. "Come on." I tugged him by the hand toward the bathroom, ignoring the squelching sound his socks were making on the floor.

I let go of Nate's hand and started up the shower, loving how the sound of the water matched the pattern of the rain outside. I turned the knobs until the room started to fill with steam, and before I could turn around, Nate's arms wrapped around my waist, pulling me against his firm body. I tried to squirm out of his arms, shivering as his cold wet clothes pressed against my back.

"Nate." I giggled as his hands slid down to my hips, spinning me around so my chest was pressed to his. I looked up at him just as he shook his wet hair, water droplets flying and landing on my face. "Stop, you're getting me all wet!"

"Mmm, is that so?" Nate growled, tilting my chin up so he could see my face completely. His thumb traced the seam of my lips as his eyes darkened, trailing over every freckle and scar on my face. He lowered his face, pressing his lips against mine. "Shower with me."

"Tempting," I whispered against his lips, squeezing my thighs together. I stole a few more kisses before trying to pull away. "But there's this book I need to get back to."

"How about I tell you how it ends instead?"

"You read the book?" I slapped my hands against his chest, prepared to push him away, but Nate grabbed a hold of my wrists and kept them there.

"I've read all your books," he admitted, and my jaw dropped as I stared up at him.

"Even the spicy ones?"

"*Especially* the spicy ones." He raised his eyebrows, and it was all I could do not to faint on the spot. "I want to know what my girl likes when I get the chance to please her."

My cheeks instantly felt like they were on fire and I tried to hide my face in his chest, but Nate made that impossible. He cupped my jaw, pulling my face to his again. His forest green eyes held mine captive, and I couldn't pull away even if I wanted to. His voice was huskier than before as he said, "Do the characters in your book blush as much as you do when they're being flirted with?"

I pressed my lips together and scrunched my nose, trying to force the heat in my cheeks away. I wasn't sure what made my heart explode more, the fact he called me his "girl" or the fact that he'd been thinking of "pleasing" me. Just the thought of Nate touching me had me squeezing my legs together, making me reconsider his offer to shower with him.

He dropped his forehead to mine and let go of one of my hands to tuck a stray piece of hair behind my ear. "I pay attention, Maddie. When I catch you giggling, I know whatever is happening makes you happy. The opposite makes you roll your eyes. When I see you lick your lower lip and then bite it, I know you're imagining it was you in the character's shoes. And when I see you trying to act out facial expressions, you're trying to visualize what's happening but can't. That's my favorite."

Groaning in embarrassment, I buried my face into his wet sweatshirt.

"Did you know the library has an app? It's amazing." His chest shook with a laugh. I felt his lips in my hair as he pressed a kiss on the top of my head. "Every book I've caught you smiling and biting your lip at, I borrowed the audiobook and listened to it while cooking. I'm taking notes on how to be the perfect book boyfriend."

"You're too much," I said into his chest, still not ready to look at him. *I can't believe he reads my books.* Nate was reading smut. *Smut.* What I would have given to see Nate's expression as he read my favorite spicy scenes. Before I had the chance to say anything else, he lifted me off the ground and threw me over his shoulder.

"What are you doing?" I squealed as I pounded on his back, his muscles firm as he held on to my wiggling body. He said nothing as he kicked off his shoes before walking into the shower. The water was warm as it pelted against my back when he stepped inside. "Nate, you're getting my clothes wet!"

"So?" He laughed, putting me back on my feet. "I have to throw mine in the dryer anyway, what's a few more? And besides, isn't that my shirt?"

Nate lifted my arms in the air, telling me to keep them there, while his fingers slowly lifted my drenched shirt over my head and let it fall to the floor. Lowering my arms to my side, he spun me around so that I was facing the wall of the shower. My heart rate picked up like a jackhammer in my chest as his fingers brushed my hair over to one shoulder. He pressed his warm lips against my neck and I leaned my head to the side, giving him better access. His tongue trailed down my neck and along my shoulder, and my body shivered under his touch, goosebumps pebbling my skin.

He unclasped my bra in one move, my breath hitching as he slid the straps down each arm. He closed the distance between us, pressing his front to my back. I gasped when I felt his hardness against my lower back. He walked us forward, not allowing any space to come between us. His hands came around me to cup my breasts, and his thumbs rubbed against my peaked nipples until I was pressed against the wall of the shower. Nate let out a groan as I recoiled from the cold tiles, pressing myself harder against him.

Nate placed my hands against the wall and I dug my nails into the grout as he slid down my body, stopping once they reached the top of my shorts. I held my breath, feeling his fingers trail along my exposed skin until they reached the tie that held my pants up. Nate left a trail of kisses down my back as he lowered himself, shimmying my shorts and underwear down until I could kick them off.

His hands were back on my hips, spinning me so that my back was flush against the shower wall. Down he went to my thighs, his right thumb grazing over my scars. I closed my eyes, resting my head against the tile, as he kissed each one softly. When I felt his lips make contact with the last one, I looked down at him, and a wave of emotion like I'd never felt before flooded through me, making it hard for me to breathe.

Not liking the fact that I was once again naked and he was fully clothed, I cupped his jaw, letting my fingertips graze over his damp beard before pulling him up so that he was standing in front of me.

"Arms up," I whispered, peeling his sweatshirt and shirt over his head. My eyes took in his chiseled chest, water droplets clinging to the light brown hair that dusted his pecs. I took my time running my hands over him, each finger tracing along the ridges of his muscles as if memorizing them like they were trails on a map.

Nate's hands pressed against the tile wall as he caged me in. With the tip of my finger, I traced the line of hair from his belly button to where it disappeared behind his jeans. Shaking despite the steam encircling us, I unbuttoned them and slowly pulled down his zipper. Looking up, I softened when I saw his dark eyes already on me as if they'd been devouring me whole throughout all of this.

"Fuck," I groaned as I struggled to get the wet jeans of him. "Why did you have to wear jeans today?"

"Sorry." He laughed, his breath cool against my forehead as he leaned over me. "We can keep them on. I don't mind making this all about you."

"No." I shook my head as I dropped to my knees. "I want to hear you moan my name for a change."

"I've waited too long to get my hands on you, Maddie," he said just as I managed to get his pants down to his ankles. I brought my gaze to his black boxer briefs that were plastered to his body, leaving nothing to the imagination.

My eyes widened as I rolled down his boxers, freeing his dick, and noticed how it seemed to grow even larger now that it had more room to breathe. *My god, how am I supposed to take that?* I reached toward him and held his length in my hand. I traced the vein underneath his shaft until it reached the head, where I swirled the bit of precum around it.

A guttural moan escaped Nate's lips, filling me with enough confidence to lean forward and taste him. I swirled my tongue around his head, looking up at Nate as I moved my mouth over him, taking him inch by inch until he hit the back of my throat. Slowly making my way back down his length, I released him with a pop, feeling Nate's body shudder above me as he let out a deep groan.

"Get up here." His voice was husky as he pulled me to my feet, not wasting a minute to press his lips against mine. He moaned into my mouth and I felt the vibration through my core, his hot breath filling me as he pinned me against the wall. His hard length pressed against where I so badly ached for him. His tongue tangled with mine as he deepened the kiss until I had to pull away to gasp for air.

"Nate, please," I said the words in desperation, his teeth grazing over my jawline and his tongue trailing down my neck, making me wonder why we hadn't been doing this forever.

"Please, what?" he whispered against my skin.

"I need you." I swallowed, trying to smother the butterflies that took over my stomach with what I was about to say. Not once had I felt the need to beg for someone to be inside me.

Nate pulled away, his lips leaving my skin the second those three words left me. His eyes were the darkest I'd ever seen as he searched mine, trying to see if I meant what I said. I held my breath, afraid that if I exhaled too hard, it would blow this feeling between us away. "Are you sure?"

"Positive." I wrapped my hands around his neck to pull his mouth back to mine. He reached behind me to shut off the shower, and I squealed as his hands moved to my waist and lifted me up. Neither of us had the presence of mind to reach for a towel. Instead, he slammed his lips against mine, our wet bodies leaving a trail of water from the bathroom to his bedroom door.

His room was dark when we entered. Nate lowered me onto his bed, not caring that it was getting wet.

"Scoot up," he said. I dragged my body back until I reached his pillows, lying back as he kneeled on the edge of the bed. I licked my lips, taking in the way his muscles flexed with each move he made as he crawled to me, hovering his body over mine.

His mouth was against my neck, his kisses harder than before, hungrier, as he made his way down to my chest. He cupped my breast and pulled it into his mouth. I let my head fall back, a moan escaping me like a soft breath of air, as his tongue circled my nipple. I gasped as his thumb and pointer finger lightly pinched the other and the vibration from his chuckle traveled through my body. I wiggled against him, urging him to continue. His tongue left a trail as he made his way down until he reached the wetness between my thighs.

"Mm, look how wet you are for me," Nate growled, and I threw my head back harder into the pillow. "So delicious."

"Nate, no," I gasped, trying to pull him off me. "I'm not going to last if you keep doing this. I need you, *now.*"

He opened the drawer of his nightstand, digging around until he pulled out a foil wrapper. Without hesitating, he tore it open with his teeth as he sat back on his heels. I watched as he rolled the condom down his length before positioning himself at my opening. He leaned himself over me, one hand still on his dick, and the other just above my left shoulder.

"Are you sure?" he asked again, keeping his eyes on me.

"Never been more sure," I whispered back.

Nate remained where he was, his face a few inches from mine, as he slid himself inside me. I let out a sharp gasp as he filled me, inch by inch. Once he was fully settled, I gripped him by his backside, my nails digging into muscle as I adjusted to him.

"Fuck, Maddie," Nate groaned, moving the hand that he used to guide himself into me to the other side of my head. "You're so tight."

I'd never felt so...full before. I grasped the comforter on either side of me, twisting the fabric into my fingers, as he pumped himself in and out.

"Shit," he hissed, pressing a soft kiss against my forehead and searching my face. "You're perfect."

I squeezed my eyes shut, trying to hold myself together as his pace picked up. He shifted between me, adjusted my legs, and placed them on his shoulders. I let out a soft scream as this angle allowed him to go even deeper, hitting a sweet spot inside me that I didn't know existed.

When I opened my eyes, I caught sight of the scar on my ankle before flashing down to my thigh and automatically shot my hands forward to cover it.

"Don't," Nate demanded as he continued to pound into me, placing his hands over mine and moving them to my side. "Let me look at you, all of you."

I swallowed, moving my gaze to his face, taking in the sheen of sweat that glittered his forehead, the way he looked at me so appreciatively...like I was a work of art. His hands skated over my skin, trailing over my scars with a featherlight touch.

"You're beautiful," Nate said, his hand moving back between my legs, rubbing me in tight circles.

My orgasm coiled in my center and I could feel myself tightening around his cock as his thrusts became harder. He gripped my legs tighter and I let out a sound I wasn't even aware I could make as I shattered around him. Seconds after I felt my release, I watched as his back arched and his body shook, and Nate came undone above me.

twenty-four

I lay on Nate's bed, staring up at the ceiling as I tried to hold in my emotions, rigid as a pencil. Sucking my lips under my teeth, I clamped my mouth shut, not wanting Nate to see my lips quiver. The mattress dipped beneath Nate's weight as he rolled onto his side to face me. His thumb brushed along my cheek and I could feel his eyes roam over my face. Could he tell something was wrong? I closed my eyes, not wanting them to give anything away, and waited. For what? I had no idea. I needed time to stop so I could figure out what the hell was happening.

"I'm going to deal with the condom," Nate said in a soft voice, just barely above a whisper. "Do you need anything?"

Somehow, I managed to shake my head.

"I'll be right back, promise." He pressed a kiss to my temple and left the room.

I sat up in bed and scooted back until I reached the headboard. Tucking my feet under the comforter, I gathered it in my arms and hugged it to my chest. It felt like all these different feelings were zapping my heart like little lightning bolts. I was scared, I was excited, I was sad, I was happy. I felt lost, I felt safe, I felt wrong, but also so, so right.

I tucked my face into my knees and closed my eyes, trying to keep my tears from falling. I was not going to ruin this. Nate was amazing. He didn't deserve this. Each and every one of his touches were gentle and comforting. The way his eyes stayed locked on mine as our bodies became one. The way I felt absolutely, without a doubt, safe in his hands, my heart exploding in my chest as I climaxed around him...I had never felt this way in my entire life.

So why was I on the verge of breaking down?

Closing my eyes, I took in a deep breath, my nose overtaken with the smell of him, letting it soothe me. I heard the toilet flush down the hall, and not wanting Nate to see me upset over this, I stretched out my legs and smoothed the comforter over me. I ran my fingers through my hair, hoping it made me look like I wasn't on the verge of collapse. My heart skipped a beat as the doorknob turned. I wanted to slap myself for being like this. This was *Nate*, for crying out loud. He'd do anything to make me happy. To feel safe. To feel wanted.

Nate walked into the room, a clean blanket in his hands. His eyes landed on mine, not once dipping to my exposed chest, and his eyebrows raised in concern. Without saying a word, he replaced the wet comforter with a clean one and climbed under it with me, wrapping his arms around my waist. I exhaled, not realizing that I had been holding my breath, and rested my head against his chest. I listened to the steady beat of his heart, a sound I could easily fall asleep to.

The second his lips pressed against my hair, I lost control and the tears fell. I wasn't talking about a single tear that managed to escape from the corner of my eye and slowly make its way down my cheek. I was talking full-blown tears, uncontrollable, complete with the sounds of sobbing and hiccuping.

"Hey." Nate's arms tightened around me, his hands rubbing up and down my spine. His lips landed in my hair, pressing a few soft and soothing kisses. "What's wrong, sweetheart?"

I shook my head against his chest, not able to get any words out.

"Did I hurt you?" he asked, then tilted my head up to look at me. His thumb ran over my cheek, wiping away the tears that soaked my skin. "Did I do something wrong?"

"N-no." I sniffled, tucking my face back into his chest. I needed to hear his heart beating, to feel his arms wrapped around me. Who knew if this would be the last time? The last thing he probably wanted was a sobbing mess in his bed. "You were perfect. I'm just...I'm not."

"What are you talking about?" He was running his hands through my hair now, leaning back and cradling my face in his hands. "Look at me, Maddie. There is nothing wrong with you."

"I'm not worth it, Nate," I said, barely above a whisper, as my eyes dropped to his mouth. His breath was like a gentle warm breeze against my skin as he exhaled softly.

"I hate that he made you feel like you're not worth it." He sighed. "I wish you could see yourself the way that I see you. Every freckle, every curve, every scar...there's not one thing I would change about you, Maddie."

Nate continued to rub his thumbs over my cheeks, as if on a mission to catch every tear that fell. I shook my head as I let out another whimper, my chest rising and falling in a static pattern. Even if I wanted to explain to him what was going on, I couldn't. I had no idea what was happening inside my head. I was feeling too many things, things that I'd never felt before, and I was so overwhelmed.

"I'm so...s-sorry," I said between sobs, raising my hands to cover his as he cupped my face. "You don't deserve this."

"You have nothing to be sorry for, Maddie. Just please, let me know what's going on inside this pretty little head of yours. I can see your mind reeling. I want to help you. What do I need to do to show you that you have nothing to be worrying about right now?"

"I'm overwhelmed," I whispered. Shaking my head again, I sighed. "I don't know, it's stupid."

"No, it's not," he insisted, brushing a strand of hair off my forehead. I closed my eyes at the warm touch of his fingers across my skin. "What's overwhelming you, Madds? You can tell me. Nothing's going to change the way I feel about you."

My stomach flipped at his words. I knew Nate had feelings for me and that he had them since we met, but he never said how strong those feelings were. Wait, how did *I* feel about Nate?

Since coming to Briar Oakes, Nate had been nothing but patient and kind and that constant safe place for me. He let me share what I wanted, how I wanted, and when I wanted to. He encouraged and motivated me to follow my dreams of becoming an author, supported my love of reading, helped me work through my anxiety without making me feel bad about it, and helped me build up my confidence again. He not only showed me what I was worth but made me believe it, too. Nate never made me feel like I had to be someone different, or that I had to push away my feelings to make others feel more comfortable.

He always met me where I was at.

"My first time was with Griffin..." I trailed off, not sure where I was headed with this and what I wanted to say next. "I always imagined it to be this magical, amazing moment. I knew it would be messy and most likely wouldn't be enjoyable, but I at least thought I'd feel...something."

"And you didn't?" Nate asked after I fell silent for a few moments.

"No." I let out a soft laugh despite the tears still falling from my face. "When we were done, all I could think was...wow, that's it? That's what I waited for?"

Nate pressed a kiss to my head, giving me time to process my thoughts.

"Afterward, I cried," I continued. "I guess I looked similar to how I just looked when you came into the room, but he didn't comfort me. He got mad. He said girls always got emotional when they had sex for the first time, and he didn't want to deal with it."

"Why were you crying tonight?"

"Because...because this was how I imagined feeling. What I just felt with you...what we did...*that's* what I've always dreamed of."

A feeling so strong that I'd never felt before rippled through me. Sure, I'd told Griffin that I loved him. And, at the time, I believed it, too. But being with Nate, I was starting to wonder if I ever did love Griffin or if it was just the idea of him. I was so desperate to experience a real relationship that I ignored all the red flags and convinced myself it was love. I sniffled against his bare chest, feeling a fresh wave of tears coming.

"I'm so sorry," my voice was muffled as I spoke into his chest.

"Don't be silly, Madds," Nate said, taking my face in his hands and swiping away the freshly fallen tears with his thumbs. "If you need to cry, then cry. If you need to laugh, then laugh. If you need to sleep, then sleep. Whatever you need to do, you won't go through it alone. I'm not going anywhere."

"Thank you." I smiled up at him through blurry eyes. "Not just for tonight, but...for everything. You've always been there for me, and I don't know what I would have done without you."

Nate tilted my head and left a soft kiss lingering on my lips. They were soft and gentle against mine, and everything felt right. My legs relaxed, my arms loosened their grip around him, my head felt light, and I swore my heart beat a tad gentler, too. Nate was like magic.

The house was quiet when I woke up, and there was no sunlight shining through the blinds. Not even my sound machine was going off. That was weird. I hadn't been able to sleep without that since I came home from the hospital. I rolled over onto my back, stretching my arms above me as I let out a soft yawn, taking in my surroundings.

"Oh my god," I gasped, jolting up in bed, feeling Nate's gray comforter slide off my chest.

Nate.

I looked to my left at the side of the bed where he slept last night. The book I fell asleep reading rested on his pillow with a light blue sticky note on top, telling me he went into town early to see if there was any damage from the storm. *Oh my god, I slept in Nate's bed.* I dragged my hand over my face, pulling my knees up to my chest as I curled myself into a ball. Images of everything that went down last night, every touch, every kiss, every tear, all flashed through my mind like some montage. I uncurled my body and rested my head against his headboard.

Grabbing my book, I flipped through the pages until I landed on where I left off. A new index card held my place.

Good morning, beautiful.
Every second, minute, and hour spent with you will
always be my favorite part of the day. From now on,
I'm making it my mission to make you smile as soon as
you wake up and before you fall asleep at night. So be
prepared for your cheeks to hurt.
−Nate

Smiling already, I looked around the room, trying to find where I left my phone. Spotting it on Nate's nightstand, I crawled over to his side of the bed and grabbed it, clicking on his name with a smile on my face.

"Mornin', sleepyhead." Nate's voice was smooth as butter over the line.

"Mission accomplished," I said, bringing my face up to pat my flushed cheeks. "I haven't stopped smiling since I woke up."

"Glad to hear it." I heard him give directions to someone, and I took the chance to shuffle back to my still-warm spot. "I should be home later this afternoon. Are you going to Liv's at all?"

"I want to get some writing done first, I think, but I'll stop by to grab some lunch."

"What chapter are you working on today?"

Nate had read through all my journals the night I found out who Ben really was. We hadn't talked about it much, to be honest. When he handed me back my journals the next morning with dark circles under his eyes, he didn't apologize. He didn't show me pity. He didn't treat me any differently. Instead, he pulled me into his arms and whispered against my hair how proud he was of me and how I was the strongest person he knew.

"I'm on the last of my journal entries." I bit my lower lip and tugged on the edge of the comforter. "And then, I have no idea. I'll have to really start trying to figure out what I want my happily ever after to be."

"I believe in you, Madds," Nate said, and I could practically hear him smiling through the phone. "I know how difficult this chapter might be for you to write, so if you need me, just call and I'll come home."

"Thanks, Nate," I said and hung up the phone.

Not wanting to leave his bed but needing my laptop to write, I dragged myself back to my room. I debated bringing everything back into his, but I didn't want to take my journals in there, so I plopped down on my bed. With my journals fanned out around me, I opened to my last journal entry, preparing myself to relive my worst nightmare.

title to be determined
By Madison Williams

"I thought we already went over this," Griffin says, irritation rising like smoke off his tone.

"We *have* gone over this. Multiple times a day for the past week, Griffin. I wasn't flirting with him," I grit out, so done with this topic. "How many times do I have to tell you?"

"You couldn't even pretend for one weekend." His grip tightens on the steering wheel. "You promised me you wouldn't do this again. That you were done with the dancing and drinking and flirting. And look what happened tonight. You couldn't even make it one week. I'm tired of you embarrassing me at work." I narrow my eyes, wanting nothing more than to point out to him how *he* is the one who insists I come to The Big House practically every night, only to be left sitting around the bar bored and not even allowed to speak to anyone.

"I wasn't flirting with him," I say again instead, keeping my eyes on his grip around the steering wheel of my car. My heart races at the sight of his hands twisting around the leather. We don't have the radio on and all I can hear is the sound of the road beneath the tires and Griffin's agitation.

I want to tell him that I never promised those things. That I never said I wouldn't dance again. Or flirt again. Or drink again. He demanded it. But I'm already screwed enough as it is and I don't want to add fuel to the fire. So I let it go.

"He fucking had his hands on you," he growls, turning his head toward me. His eyes are as dark as the night sky and I have to turn away from their intensity

"I can't control what other people do, Griffin," I say, looking out the window and watching the trees pass by. I sit up straighter in my seat, gripping my seatbelt across my chest with my hands when I realize I don't recognize where I am. "Where are we going?"

"People don't go around just touching people," he snaps, ignoring my question. "What did you do to make him think he could do that?"

"Nothing!" I raise my voice, focusing on the speedometer and seeing that we're going fifteen miles over the speed limit now. My heart continues to race, pounding rapidly in my chest. "He's been a tool to me ever since I met him."

"You think I'm going to believe anything that comes out of your mouth?" He turns his focus back on me, raising an eyebrow as if daring me to respond.

I remain silent, not sure if anything I say will even matter.

"You do realize I could end our lives so quickly, right?" My stomach twists at how maniacal he sounds. "All I'd have to do is turn this steering wheel and — *bam!* — we're off the road, upside down in a ditch."

"You're psychotic," I say shakily as I pull my cell phone out of my pocket, trying to shield it with my body so as not to alert him. "Let's just go home, okay? We can talk about all this then."

Griffin keeps muttering things under his breath, and without any music coming from the radio, the tension in the car's cab is a living nightmare. Not wanting to waste this opportunity when he isn't focusing on me, I pull up my contacts and scroll until I find Nate's, getting ready to send him my location and our codeword.

I'm too slow, though, and Griffin is too fast. My phone is in his hands before I can even blink.

"Nate?" he shouts, chucking my phone at the windshield. I flinch, squeezing my eyes shut while I wait for the next blow. "You're a fucking bitch, you know that?"

"Stop!" I shout, opening my eyes just as Griffin yanks the steering wheel to the right. I reach out to stop him, but I'm not quick enough. I'm not strong enough to fight him. The sounds of tires screeching along the pavement rings through my mind like nails on a chalkboard. The shattering of glass explodes in my ears and I slam my head back against the headrest, bracing myself for impact. All I hear next is the deafening sound of the airbag deploying, overpowering the crash.

"Don't move." Someone is speaking close to my ear, and I groan as I turn my head toward where it's coming from. I don't recognize his voice...but it's stern, so I obey. I want to speak, but it feels like I haven't had a sip of water in days. I try to reach for my throat, but my arms are trapped. Something's holding them down. No, some*one* is holding them down. "I need you to try to stay as still as possible."

Who are you? I want to say, but nothing comes out. *Where am I?*

I can feel the panic surfacing in my chest, and my breathing becomes quick and shallow. My head feels like it's going to explode and I swear my heart is beating inside my forehead. Why does my entire body feel rearranged? With all the strength that I can muster, I flutter my eyelids open but am instantly blinded by flashing red and blue lights. The passenger door is gone and a firefighter is crouching next to me. The sound of metal crushing is loud in my ear, but before I can look to see where it's coming from, the firefighter pulls my attention back to him.

"Keep your eyes on me." Despite all the ear-piercing noise going on around me, I can hear the firefighter perfectly as he continues to talk. "My name is Wyatt and I'm going to help you. Can you tell me what hurts?"

Say you're fine, tell them everything is okay. Griffin's voice infiltrates my mind and I squeeze my eyes shut to push it away. How is he inside my head? Where is he?

"No, no, no," the firefighter continues, but this time his voice sounds panicked. My head feels like it weighs fifty pounds, and I'm struggling to keep it up. I can feel it rolling to the side, but then something stops it — the weight that was on my arms before is now on my head. Something is being strapped around my neck to keep my head up. "I need you to stay with me. Open your eyes. Can you do that?"

"I'm fine," I lie, opening my eyes just the slightest to look at him. I try to make out his features, but everything is blurry. My lips start to shake. Something warm is flooding my face, and my head feels like it's going to burst. My mind goes blank. How did I get here? Why can't I move? I don't know where to look. The sirens in the distance are coming closer and the lights seem to get brighter, causing my head to hurt even more. How is that even possible?

"You were in an accident," he tells me. "Can you raise your arms?"

I lift my right arm with no issue, but let out a stifled scream when I try to move my left. I close my eyes and coach myself to breathe. *You can do this.*

"My leg is stuck," I gasp, panic taking over my body. I reach for my seatbelt with my right hand, but am stopped. Another person crouches behind the firefighter. "I can't move it. Why can't I move it?"

"I need you to remain as calm and still as possible. We're going to get you out of here, but it's very important that you don't move."

"We need to get her to the hospital," the other person says.

The pain that comes next is excruciating, and I try to focus on the fact that if every part of my body hurts, then that means it's still there. I'm still in one piece. As soon as I'm on the stretcher, I'm carried into the back of an ambulance.

"What's your name, miss?" An officer stands over me, a leather notepad in his hand. I try to make out a name on his badge. None of this feels real. I close my eyes, hoping that if I squeeze them shut hard enough, I'll be transported to my bed at home. That this is some crazy nightmare.

Madison, I want to say. *Where's Griffin?* But nothing comes out.

The sirens and the voices murmuring around me fade.

The world fades.

Everything goes black.

A monitor beeping to my left wakes me up. My eyes take a while to adjust to the bright lights above me, but when they focus, I see that I'm alone. I lift my right hand and notice an IV, and my left hand is tucked in a sling at my side. I pull up the thin blanket that is draped over me and see my right leg in a cast. What the hell happened? My head throbs as I try to remember anything that could have brought me here, but everything feels distant. I move to run my hands through my hair out of frustration, but instead, wince as my fingers press down on bandaging across my forehead. I look to my right and see the call button on my bed rail, and I press it frantically.

"Hi, Madison." A young woman in blue scrubs walks in with a

clipboard in her hand. "We've been waiting for you to wake up. How are you feeling?"

"Where am I?" My voice is raspy. I try to swallow, but it feels like my mouth is full of cotton and my throat is sandpaper and everything's just getting caught. The nurse gestures to the water pitcher and full glass of water resting on the nightstand beside my bed. I reach over and grasp the pink plastic cup, slowly taking a sip of the ice-cold water.

"You're in the hospital. Your father just stepped out to get some coffee," she informs me. "He's going to be so upset that he missed you."

"My dad?" I ask, bewildered. Why is he here? "What happened?"

"I'm sure you have a lot of questions," she says as she adjusts the IV bags and then jots something down on her clipboard. "I'll let the doctor know that you're awake."

I'm alone for fifteen more minutes before the doctor walks in, my dad not far behind. My heart rate on the monitor begins to rise as I make eye contact with her.

"Hello, Madison." The doctor's voice is friendly and warm, taking my attention away from the sight of my father, who's now sitting in the armchair across the room. "I'm Dr. Paula Kinsley."

I give her a weak smile as I fidget with the thin thermal blanket draped over me.

"You must have so many questions." She walks over to the end of the bed and lifts the clipboard, flipping the pages as she reads them. "Do you remember how you got here?"

I shake my head, but wince in pain.

"You were in an accident three days ago," she informs me, and I can feel Dad's intense stare on me as I process this.

Three days ago? I look at the whiteboard on the wall with its *Rate Your Level of Pain* chart followed by eight different emojis. Just above that is today's date, written in red. That means the accident happened on Saturday...so we must have been coming back from the bar.

"You suffered a lot of injuries. The worst of the damage was in your leg. You had multiple fractures and we needed to perform surgery. You'll need to keep weight off it as much as possible and will be in a cast for six to eight weeks, depending on how you heal. We will schedule a follow-up appointment to monitor your progress, and then discuss physical therapy."

I nod, encouraging her to go on, but hope my dad is paying attention and taking notes. I'll never remember all of this. My mind is still spinning on the fact that I have been here for three days.

"Your left shoulder was dislocated, but you should expect to regain full function of your shoulder within a few weeks."

I nod again.

"Your forehead required twelve stitches." Using the pen in her hand, she drags it across her own skin to indicate where my stitches are. I watch as her pen starts at the center of her left eyebrow and slides to her hairline. "Our plastic surgeon is hopeful scarring will be minimal, but it will require proper upkeep."

"Is that all?" I whisper, noticing how weak I sound.

"Yes, do you have any questions for me?" I shake my head as she places her pen back into her lab coat pocket and crosses her arms. "How are you feeling?"

"I don't know." I sigh as I look over at those stupid emojis on the whiteboard.

"Understandable, you've been through a lot." The doctor pauses before continuing, as if unsure if she should. "There are some officers who would like to ask you some questions now that you are awake."

"Questions?" I look over at my dad, suddenly nervous. He always told me to never answer any questions unless he or a lawyer were present. Is that why he is here? Did I do something wrong? "Why would they need to ask me questions?"

"That can wait." My dad's voice is stern, but I can hear the exhaustion in it still. "She needs her rest."

"I have to let them know you're awake." She looks back and forth between us, clearly uncomfortable by his tone. "You and the driver were both unconscious when you arrived at the hospital, so they need to get as much information as they can about the accident."

"Griffin? Is he okay? Where is he? Can I talk to him? Can I see him?" I can't hide the panic in my voice as the questions pour out. "I need to see him. Is he awake?"

"I cannot disclose that information, Madison." She sounds apologetic. Ugh, this is a nightmare come to life. "But when you arrived, we noticed some scars on your left thigh. Could you tell us what they're from? Some are older wounds, but there are a couple that are newer."

I swallow as I fight the urge to rest my hand over my thigh like I always do when someone looks too closely. I can feel my dad's eyes on my leg as if he has x-ray vision and can see through the fabric of the blanket.

Lie. Griffin's voice pops into my head and I flinch, eyes darting around the room.

My mind spins. It's not the first time I've heard his voice like this. It happened the night of the accident. I remember now. There was a firefighter and he asked me if something hurt, and Griffin told me to lie. But was Griffin even there? Did he actually say that? I squeeze my eyes shut again as I rest my head back on my pillow, trying to force something else to surface.

Lie. His voice is sharp and it sends a shiver down my spine. *Do not tell them anything.*

"They're chicken pox scars," I whisper, avoiding eye contact. "From when I was six."

"Madison, those — "

"That'll be enough, Dr. Kinsley." His voice is now aggressive, and I know he's switched from distraught father to attorney Mark

Williams, the highest paid lawyer in the tri-state area. "There will be no further questions until her lawyer is present."

I don't even think about the scars that marr my left leg. I never forget about them, but of course, they couldn't have missed them. There is no way to miss them. How am I supposed to get myself out of this now? My chicken pox lie is always my go-to, but that's usually when someone catches a glance of them while I'm swimming or if the wind ruffles my dress up. But how long was I on an operating table? How long were these doctors examining them?

"Dad..." I sigh once Dr. Kinsley leaves the room, shutting the door behind him. "What are you doing here?"

"What am I doing here?" he roars as he runs his hand through his hair and paces the floor. "I haven't heard from you" — he throws his hands in the air — "for who the hell knows how long, and then I get a phone call that you're being taken to the hospital. I thought you were dead, Madison. Do you not understand what that did to me? I can't lose you, too."

I swallow, taking in the sight in front of me. My dad stops pacing the floor and moves to the side of my bed, and I have to turn my attention away from him, but more specifically from his eyes. The last time I saw him looking like *that* was when I was a few weeks shy of turning thirteen and my mother had just died.

"Why do the police need to question me?" I ask, trying to distract myself from my thoughts.

"Is there anything that happened the night of the accident" — I watch him take a few steps closer to me, glancing back down at my legs — "or during your relationship that would warrant a police investigation?"

"What happened to Griffin?" I ask, not wanting to answer his question. "Is he okay? He's not...is he?"

"No." I know he isn't sure what to tell me from the way he's looking at me. "He's still alive. I don't know the extent of his injuries, but he's been in and out of surgery since you both were brought in."

"Will he be okay?"

"I don't know, Madison, and frankly, I don't care. You need to tell me what happened so that I can help prepare you for when the police come. Can you remember anything?"

I close my eyes, trying to remember something, *anything*. But all I can think about is the sound of Griffin's voice in my head, telling me to keep my mouth shut.

"They think you hit a pothole while speeding," my dad says, sitting down on the edge of the bed, mindful of my injured leg. "Does that ring a bell?"

"I don't know."

"Why were you outside the city?"

"What?" I ask, opening my eyes in alarm. "What do you mean?"

"That's where they found you. Where were you going?" he says, not bothering to hide his frustration anymore. His words are getting sharper, clearer.

Wait, I remember asking him where we were going. There were trees. Too many trees for us to still be in the city. He was mad at me. We were in a fight. He thought I was flirting with the new bartender. He was gripping the steering wheel so tight. He was so angry. He said the craziest thing... *You do realize I could end our lives so quickly, right? All I'd have to do is turn this steering wheel and — bam! — we're off the road, upside down in a ditch.*

Holy shit.

He tried to kill me.

Lie. Griffin's voice was in my head again. *Lie, and I won't finish what I started.*

"N-no." I look away from my dad. "I don't remember anything."

twenty-five

"Are you *sure* you don't want me to help with the festival?" I said through a yawn, curled up against Nate's naked body. Today was Briar Oakes's annual fall festival, and Nate had been working hard organizing food trucks to attend.

"It's your first fall festival in Briar Oakes and I want you to enjoy it." He smiled as he tilted my head up, pressing his lips softly over the scar above my eyebrow. "There's going to be great food, music, a corn maze, and other cheesy fall things."

"*Cheesy.*" I laughed as I played with the smattering of hair on his chest. "You mean aside from your food truck?"

"Ha-ha." He rolled over so that he was on top of me, his lips traveling down my jaw to my neck. I closed my eyes and gasped when his mouth found its way between my legs, his tongue teasing my entrance.

The past few weeks had been nothing short of a dream. There were even times when I found myself believing in true happiness again. If I told that to my therapist, she'd think I was having a breakthrough and Olivia would jump up and down, holding onto my hands as she spun us in a circle. It hadn't even been long since Olivia found out about me and Nate, but she was convinced we'd be sisters in no time. Every time I stepped inside Latte Da! and those damn bells chimed above me, she'd say something along the lines of, "Are those wedding bells I hear?"

But this wasn't a breakthrough.

And those weren't wedding bells.

And this wasn't my happily ever after.

As much as I felt safe and happy in Nate's arms, I was still waiting for the other shoe to drop. I couldn't shake the feeling that this was temporary. I knew Nate wouldn't hurt me like Griffin had. But there was a part of me that hated to admit that he could hurt me even more. Sure, my body was covered in scars and my mental health went to shit, but Nate had the power to break my heart in ways no one else could. I knew one day he'd get tired of my panic attacks, of me constantly being in fear of my own shadow, of needing to protect me from the world.

"Nate," I groaned, reaching under the covers and cupping his jaw. Slowly, I guided his head back up until it popped out from under the covers. "As much as I'm really enjoying this, and the three other orgasms you gave me last night, you need to get going. The festival starts in a few hours and you need to set up."

"They can wait," he grumbled, shaking free from my grip. "This can't."

"Come on." I gave him my biggest eyes and blinked rapidly, planning on using his words against him. "This *is* my first Briar Oakes Fall Festival, and I have very high expectations. I'm imagining every square inch of Main Street decked out in foliage and pumpkins, everyone wearing flannels, and you serving up some orgasmic grilled cheeses."

"Fine." He dropped his head to my shoulder, kissing me there softly before getting out of bed.

I reached over to the nightstand so I could grab my book. Flipping to the page where I had left off last, I frowned. "Hey, no new bookmark?"

"I was a bit preoccupied last night," he said over his shoulder, giving me a wink. I watched as he slicked his hair back into a bun. God, I loved that bun. He yanked a shirt over his head, his muscles flexing with the movement. "I'll see you at two?"

"Yeah, I'll be there."

"Bye, Madds," he said as he came to the side of the bed, kissing me on the top of my head.

"Bye, I — " I stopped mid-sentence, my body freezing. Was I just about to say *I love you*? I swallowed, and my heart pounded in my chest as Nate turned to face me.

"You what?" he asked, the tiniest smile appearing on his face.

"Nothing." I slinked back under the sheets and lifted my book. I didn't even know how I felt, so I certainly couldn't trust my face to portray the right emotion. "I'll see you later."

Wearing a pair of dark jeans with rips at the knees, an oversized cream sweater, my hair in its usual half ponytail, and my Docs, I locked up the house and headed to the festival. Not knowing what to expect, or if I'd even find parking, I decided to walk from Nate's house.

Today was the perfect fall day for the festival. The leaves had already started changing colors and falling, crunching in the most satisfying way beneath my steps.

"Maddie!" Olivia squealed, running around her booth near the gazebo and pulling me into a hug. "You made it!"

"I wouldn't miss it." I extracted her black hair out of my face and grinned. With the way the sun was hitting her hair, it almost looked blue. "You changed your hair again?"

"Yeah, you know I can't commit. It's amazing I'm not bald, right?" She pulled away and stepped back, looking me up and down in appraisal. "*You* look cute. Did we get this outfit when we went shopping? I want to borrow it."

"Really?" I looked down at my sweater. "It's not too plain for you?"

"That's what accessories are for," she said as she headed over to her booth to stand next to Zo. "Come here, you have to try this! I was saving this recipe specifically for the festival. It's pumpkin spice hot chocolate and it's delicious."

"Sure." I shrugged. "Hey, Zo. How's the wedding planning going?"

"Ugh, don't even talk to me about that." She started making my drink, swaying her hips to the live music we could only just make out. "Daniella's subscribed to every bridal magazine, and I feel like I'm drowning in pages covered in blonde twigs wearing lingerie and calling it a wedding dress."

I laughed, taking a look around the park. "If I ever get married, I want something super small. I'll probably find a random dress off the rack, hope it fits, pick some park, and then say 'I do.'"

"Wow," Olivia gasped, raising her hand to her chest. "Is Madison Williams, the girl who swears happily ever afters don't exist, talking about getting married?"

"N-no." I kicked at a small pile of maroon leaves and clasped my hands behind my back. "I was just saying *if* that were to happen."

"Maddie, don't you lie to me!" She raised her voice and pointed a freshly manicured finger at me, the pink a stark contrast to her black-as-night hair. "Holy macaroni, I cannot believe it! My brother, of all people, is turning you back into a romantic."

"Olivia," I warned, taking my hot chocolate from Zo. "Stop or I'm going home."

"Fine, you're no fun." She untied her apron and set it on the back of a milk crate. "Zo, I'm going to show Maddie around and then I'll be back. You're okay handling the table for a bit?"

"Sure thing," she replied as she straightened out the supplies. "Take your time. Enjoy your first fall festival, Maddie. If this doesn't make you want to stay in Briar Oakes, then nothing will."

Kids dressed up in their Halloween costumes ran around us as they waited for the parade and contest to begin. Young couples pushed their babies in strollers, taking in all the foliage and freshly fallen leaves. Smells of cinnamon and fried dough filled the air, and my mouth watered as we passed a booth selling donuts. I definitely needed to stop back there after I grabbed a bite at Nate's. I could see the abundance of food trucks stationed in the parking lot down the way and couldn't wait to try something from each one.

We moseyed through the park and around the gazebo, covered in pumpkins and decorated hay bales, until we reached the street. A fire truck was parked along the curb with a swarm of children and their parents. A firefighter in his gear stood in front, holding out a hose for a few toddlers to touch while another stood at the door, lifting kids in so they could sit in the driver's seat.

"Good golly." Olivia stopped and grabbed hold of my arm. "Look at that guy." She pointed a very conspicuous finger to the fireman lifting the kids into the driver's seat. Whoever that man was, he clearly did not want to be there. It was like his face was stuck in a permafrown. Even when the parents shouted "Say cheese!" his face didn't budge. "Who thought letting that grouch be in charge of a children's activity was a good idea?"

I laughed, but then someone coming toward us caught my attention. "Hey, isn't that Tyler?"

"Oh, yeah," Olivia said, waving as he stepped onto the curb in front of us. She reached out and gave him a quick hug. "Any open apartments in your building yet?"

"At least let me say hello before you ask," he teased and then nodded hello to me. I returned it before glancing back at Olivia, who had her focus back on the grouchy fireman. "And no, not yet. But like I've told you countless times already, I'll tell you when I do. I think one of my older tenants is planning on moving in with her daughter once her lease ends, so I'll let you know as soon as she gives notice."

"You're moving?" I asked, snapping Olivia out of her trance

again. Did she think he was attractive or something? I glanced back at the firefighter, but he didn't seem to be her type. He didn't even look approachable.

"Tyler owns one of the few apartment buildings in town," she said as she started walking, hooking her arm into Tyler's. "I've been waiting for one to become available so that I can move out of the studio apartment above Latte Da!"

Olivia kept peering over at the firefighter as we passed the truck, the kids' laughter and excitement preventing any real conversation from breaking through.

"Hey, Ty," I asked once we passed the firetruck. "Who is that?"

"That's Wyatt Payne," he said, nodding in his direction and capturing Wyatt's attention. "He's one of my tenants."

"He is?" Olivia crossed her arms over her chest and grumbled under her breath. When Tyler nodded in the distance, she said, "So you're telling me that you're letting the Grinch have an apartment in your building but not me?"

"He keeps to himself."

I looked over my shoulder at Nate's Grates, seeing a line of at least ten people waiting to place an order. In fact, all the food trucks had a line. My stomach growled as if on cue, reminding me that I'd skipped lunch in preparation for this.

"I'm going to grab something to eat, I think," I said to the two of them, but only Tyler was paying attention. Olivia had her back to me, her focus solely on the firefighter. Giving her a nudge, I said, "Get back to work, Liv. I'll stop by before I head back to Nate's. And you're fooling no one, by the way." I shot her a couple of eyebrow waggles as I nodded toward Wyatt before turning and bolting.

twenty-six

"I've got two originals for Caroline!" Nate shouted, waving a slip of paper in the air. Ben handed Nate some more orders before turning back to the grill.

"That's me," a young woman said. "Thank you."

"Hey." I smiled up at Nate as I took a step forward.

"Come inside and I'll make you something." He gestured toward the door, his eyes bright from the adrenaline of a busy rush. "It won't be too long."

"No, I don't want to get in the way." I eyed the other food trucks. There were so many and I wanted to try them all. And even though Ben and I sort of made up, I still wasn't too comfortable being around him yet. Who knew what he'd relay to Griffin? "I was hoping to try out some of the other trucks unless that's against the rules. I know they're technically your competition." I shot him a playful look.

"I can make you a grilled cheese sandwich any day, but today's the only day you can get Mac n' Cheese in a cone, rice balls, empanadas, and milkshakes with pieces of cake on top all at once. Although, I don't recommend that." He reached into his pocket to pull out his wallet. "Here, my treat."

I looked at his outstretched hand that had his credit card in it and shook my head, taking a step back. "No, I couldn't, Nate."

"Please?" he said, reaching out to grab my hand. He closed my fingers around the plastic and gave them a kiss before letting go. "It's bad enough I can't spend the day with you at the festival. Let me at least treat my girl to some good food."

There he went with the "my girl" again. This man was going to turn me into a puddle. *Okay, heart, don't melt.*

I dipped my chin, lowering my hand down to my side. "I'll see you later?"

"Have fun, Madds."

With my stomach filled with fried macaroni and cheese, chicken fajita tacos, and garlic knot chicken parmesan sliders, I took a bite of my birthday cake milkshake and immediately knew I'd made the right decision. Olivia had to try this. Slipping Nate's credit card into the back pocket of my jeans, I headed over to the Latte Da! booth. I slurped my milkshake as I walked, trying my hardest to take a bite of the cake without knocking it off the top.

The sound of an engine revving startled me, and I almost let the plastic cup slip from my hand. I whipped my head around, trying to find where it was coming from. People walked past me, some asking if I was okay, but I couldn't respond. My heartbeat competed with the sounds of the festival, overwhelming me. I clenched a hand into a fist and slammed it against my chest as if I could jumpstart my lungs. This all felt too familiar.

I closed my eyes, taking a deep breath as I focused on my feet touching the ground. Wiggling my toes, I tried to concentrate on how they felt in my boots, how it felt to dig my heels into the concrete...but the engine turning off snapped me out of my grounding techniques, and my eyes frantically searched until they landed on Latte Da! and the bike parked in front.

I'd recognize that bike anywhere. The familiar steel-gray paint with red accents, looked harsh in comparison to the cheerfulness of Olivia's coffee shop. Griffin was here. But where was he? I looked down the sidewalk and found it empty. My stomach roiled, and I had to fight to keep from vomiting. I tossed my milkshake into the nearest bin and ran my hands through my hair, gripping it at my roots.

Fuck.

I backed away, one hand covering my mouth, eyes still fixed on the motorcycle. Before I could turn, a hand locked around my upper arm, fingers digging into my flesh.

No.

"Maddie." The word was like a knife scraping along a plate, sending chills down my back.

The scent of tobacco and leather that I once loved now made my stomach churn. My head spun and I felt myself fall forward. Griffin's grip shifted from my arms, wrapping themselves around my body as I collapsed against him.

"Let..." I squeezed my eyes shut to keep the world from spinning. "Go."

Everything went black.

The ground was hard beneath me and every part of my body ached. My eyes fluttered open but I remained still, trying to situate myself. I focused on the fans slowly oscillating above me before flicking my attention to the wall on my right. *The Garage.* Why was I in Ben's bar? I groaned and pulled myself into a seated position. I lifted my head at the sound of ice clinking in a glass. My heart didn't know whether to stop and play dead or fight for its life.

"Griffin," I breathed, crawling back a few feet. No, this couldn't be happening.

He sat on a stool, his back against the bar, swirling a glass of whiskey in his hand. I swallowed as he leaned forward, resting his elbows on his knees. *Fuck.* I hated how he looked so casual and confident while every organ in my body seemed to be working at hyperspeed. A smug look was plastered across his face as he took me in, his eyes slowly roaming over my body.

"What's with the pants?" His voice was rough like sandpaper in my ears. I ground my teeth together, trying not to let any emotion flicker across my face. "I thought I told you to only wear dresses."

"The day you tried to kill me was the day I stopped giving a shit about what you wanted," I said sharply, surprised by my own words. I held his gaze as his eyes narrowed, turning from brown to nearly black with rage. I tried remembering all the techniques Heather gave me to calm myself, but I was coming up blank. What would she even recommend in a situation like this?

I patted my pockets, trying to find my cell phone so I could call for help. "Where's my phone?"

"You won't be needing it." He took a swig of the amber liquid in his glass. I remained frozen on the floor, paralyzed by my fear. A silver piercing in his left eyebrow caught the light from above, distracting me for a moment. I let my eyes scrape over his body, wishing my gaze were a blade, slicing through every centimeter of flesh it trailed over. "Not when you're with me."

"Someone will notice I'm missing," I said, finding my voice. "They'll come looking for me."

"That's highly unlikely." Griffin snickered, but it held no humor. "The Garage is closed all day, so even if they do notice you're gone, they won't look here."

He pushed off the stool and took a few steps to close the

distance between us. I held my breath as he stood less than a foot from me and his eyes landed on my forehead. He lifted his hand and I used every ounce of strength in me not to flinch, as his calloused fingers traced over the scar above my eyebrow, trailing down to the one on my chin.

"It's a shame you have to live with these scars on your pretty face, babe." I swallowed, not saying a word as his hands moved to my hair. He twirled a few strands around his finger and my eyes drifted to the vile grin stretched over his face. "You cut your hair."

"What are you doing here?" I asked, and I hated myself for the wobble in my voice.

"I wanted to see you," he said simply. I grimaced as he looked me over again, but despite the hungry, feral glimmer in them, his eyes were cold and cruel.

Without warning, Griffin bent his wrist and threw his empty glass at my head. I ducked, but was close enough to feel a few drops from the dregs of the glass against my skin as it flew over me. The sound of glass shattering against the wall erupted into the space, and I screamed.

I glanced down at his hands which were clenched into fists so tight his tattooed knuckles were white. "Do you know what it was like waking up in a hospital bed, with all these wires hooked up to me and not being able to move, only to find out that my girlfriend was gone?"

"You tried to kill me," I whispered, unable to make eye contact with him. I kept my focus on his hands, trying to anticipate their next move. "Why the fuck would I have stayed?"

"Because you love me, Maddie." He laughed. God, he sounded insane. "And when you love someone, you stay by their side."

"No." I watched that damn grin slowly turn into something sinister. "I don't love you."

"Don't say that," he said through clenched teeth. I managed to take a step back, hoping he'd keep the distance between us. "Not when I still love you."

"No, you don't." And this time I was the one laughing. "You're only capable of loving yourself, Griffin."

"Don't be so fucking dramatic, Maddie," he shouted, and I flinched. He reached into his pocket, pulled something out, and held it in front of his face. "Nathaniel West. I should've known." I struggled to breathe as I got a glimpse of Nate's credit card in his hand before he snapped it in half. "And I'm here to take back what's mine."

My mind raced, taking note of everything in arm's reach, and locating where the exits were. No part of me doubted Nate would come. He said he'd keep me safe. That he would protect me. I just had to make it until he realized I was missing.

I needed to keep him talking.

"No," I said firmly, shaking my head at him. The walls felt like they were closing in on me, threatening to suffocate me. I pulled on the collar of my sweater, suddenly too tight. "You're insane to think that I'd ever go anywhere with you again."

He took another step forward, standing so close that if I took a deep breath, my chest would brush against his. My brain was telling me to move, to run, but I couldn't. It was like my feet weren't getting the message.

"You're coming back home, Maddie."

I shook my head and sucked in a breath.

"Why the fuck not?" His voice exploded in the empty bar and I flinched as he reached out, his large hand wrapping around my throat.

"We're over, Griffin," I said, tears pouring down my cheeks. My hands shook as they wrapped around his hand, trying to break free. "Let go."

"There's no you without me," he growled, tightening his hold even more. I followed the movement of his other hand, watching as he reached behind him. My eyes widened in alarm as he pulled a gun out of his waistband. The sound of it clicking echoed in the bar as he held it to the side of my head.

"No," I sobbed as I tried to free myself from his hold, but the more I moved, the tighter his grip became. "Stop!"

"Since you won't admit you still have feelings for me" — he pressed the metal harder against my head — "I'm finishing what I started."

I let out a whimper, clenching my teeth as I waited for him to pull the trigger. He adjusted his grip around my neck, and despite everything in me saying to close my eyes, I looked straight into his. He narrowed his eyes, pressing the gun deeper into my temple.

"Please," I croaked, my voice barely audible over how heavily Griffin was breathing.

"Let go of her!" A voice I'd recognize anywhere boomed from the back of the bar, startling me, but Griffin didn't even flinch.

"What did you do?" Griffin hissed. I inhaled sharply as he spun me by my neck so my back was now on his front, his gun never dropping away from my head.

Keeping me pressed against him, he turned us around and dug the barrel of the gun deeper into my skin. I let out a garbled sound as Nate came into view.

"Oh, look," Griffin scoffed, adjusting his grip around my neck. "Prince Charming came to save the day."

"Put the gun down," Nate said, and my heart sank at the tremble in his voice. He took a step forward, his hands held up to show no harm. "Please."

"Well, since you asked nicely." Griffin laughed, his stale breath hot against my skin. "*No.*"

My lips quivered as tears flooded my eyes, obscuring my vision. If Nate kept showing how much he cared for me, who knew what Griffin would do? How was I supposed to get out of this? Seeing the fear laced with determination in Nate's eyes, I knew I had to do something.

He took another step forward and Griffin dug the gun deeper into me. "Take one more step and I'll shoot."

"You don't want to do that," Nate said, keeping his eyes fixed on Griffin. "You can control how this ends. No one has to get hurt."

I knew he was talking to Griffin, trying to de-escalate the situation, but maybe, just maybe, I could attempt to gain control instead. I was torn between wanting to help and knowing I couldn't live with myself if Nate was hurt.

Sometimes what we might gain by being brave ends up being more valuable than what we risked in the first place. Heather's voice echoed in my mind and I set my shoulders.

That was it. I had to be brave; I had to do something. And if it didn't work out, at least I tried.

Without hesitation, I jammed my head back, hearing the crunch of bone as my head collided with Griffin's face. He let out a string of curses, dropping his hand from my neck. I inhaled sharply, taking in my first full breath of air, and stumbled forward, landing on my knees. I climbed back to my feet as Nate rushed past me and turned just in time to see him collide with Griffin.

"You bitch," Griffin shouted, spitting the blood pooling in his mouth at my feet.

Three police officers barged into the bar, guns drawn. At first, I was relieved they'd found us, but then the panic came back at full force when I saw their weapons aimed at us. I stood frozen in place, my eyes wide as they ran past and dropped to the floor next to Nate, taking over. As soon as the officers had their hands on Griffin, handcuffing him behind his back, Nate was at my side.

"Maddie, let's go," he said, but my feet felt like they were stuck in cement. He picked me up and carried me outside, his thumb making tiny circles on my back.

My body shook as he set me on my feet on the sidewalk. Blue and red lights flashed around me and I collapsed to the ground, a sob escaping my chest. Nate dropped to his knees beside me and shifted my shaking body into his lap.

"Shh," he whispered as he cradled my head into his chest. "It's okay, Maddie. You're safe now."

twenty-seven

Once Griffin was in custody, the rest of the day was a blur. After I'd calmed down enough to stand, Nate brought me to the EMTs. In bits and pieces, he filled me in on what had happened before he burst into The Garage.

Ben had received an alert on his phone that someone had broken into his bar, and when he checked the security camera, he saw Griffin carrying me inside. Ben alerted the police while Nate took matters into his own hands. I couldn't imagine what would have happened if Ben hadn't checked his phone when he did.

While I sat with the EMTs, Nate called my dad to fill him in on what had happened. With my permission, he also asked him to come to Briar Oakes. It was time my dad knew the whole story anyway. I was tired of hiding.

While my dad stayed with us, I showed him my journals, as difficult as it was. I let him in on the dark secrets of my past that I had never felt comfortable sharing with him. He left Nate's shortly after Griffin's hearing was over and we knew he'd remain at the county jail until the trial started. My dad was confident that he'd be found guilty of multiple offenses, but until that took place, he said he'd check in on me daily and planned to return once the trial started. Even though we didn't have the closest relationship, it was nice having him around, especially now that there were no more secrets between us.

I talked to my therapist daily and learned new techniques to pull me out of this new state of panic I found myself in. I wasn't leaving the house. I couldn't sleep. Every time I shut my eyes, I felt Griffin's hand around my neck and the cold metal of the gun against my forehead, and I'd wake up screaming. Nate was the only one who could calm me, and he'd rock me in his arms until I fell asleep again.

I spent as much time as I could with Nate when he was home, clinging to that sense of security as much as I could. When he was at the food truck, I'd escape into my books until he returned. And when he worked from home, editing his videos and uploading them to his channel, I joined him in his office. My favorite time of day was when I'd set my book down and he'd log off his computer, and we'd crash on the couch together or tackle a new recipe in the kitchen. The more time I spent with him, the more I felt like myself again.

A week after my dad left, I sat on the couch with Nate, my laptop open, attempting to figure out the ending to my story. Nate turned the page in the book he was reading and I watched as his eyes scanned over the words. He crossed his ankle over his knee, sinking back in his seat to get more comfortable. I bit down on my lip, my need for him growing in my core, as I watched him turn the page. Forget sunsets and waves crashing along the shore, I could watch him read all day.

"Are you going to stare at me all day, or are you actually going to write?" Nate chuckled as he looked over at me.

"You're just so distracting." I sighed dreamily, batting my eyelashes at him. He was shirtless and wearing his famous gray sweatpants again, knowing exactly what effect they had on me. "How do you expect me to concentrate when you look like *that*?"

"I can go in the other room if that helps," Nate offered.

"No!" I sat up straight, slamming my laptop shut and gripping it tightly to my chest. "Don't leave me."

"I'm not going anywhere, Maddie," Nate said reassuringly, placing his hands over mine so he could pry my laptop from my hands and place it on the coffee table. I let out a deep breath as he tucked me in at his side, his fingers trailing over my arm in soothing patterns.

"I'm sorry," I whispered as I buried my face into his shirt, inhaling his scent. "Guess I'm not as okay as I thought I was."

"How *are* you feeling, Maddie?" he asked, placing a light kiss on the top of my head.

"I don't know." I burrowed into him, inhaling his comforting scent.

I avoided opening up to Nate, preferring to keep him as my escape from the real world, especially since I spent an hour every day talking to Heather about how I was processing and handling everything. I hated that I was essentially keeping him in the dark, especially since he'd been so kind to me. He never complained about having to hold and comfort me back to sleep when I woke from a nightmare in the middle of the night. He didn't even hesitate to stay home with me after my dad left until I felt comfortable being alone again. He knew I wasn't okay, that I was having a hard time dealing with the aftermath. I was grateful for the fact that he wasn't pushing it with me. He knew I'd talk when I was ready.

"How are you doing?" I asked as I chewed on my lip, pulling away from him just enough to look into his forest green eyes. "I've been so wrapped up in myself that I never thought to ask how you're handling everything or about how it might have affected you. I'm so sorry, Nate."

"It's fine," he murmured, pulling me back into his side and running his hand up and down my arm.

"I've said that enough times to know that's not true." I laughed weakly, rubbing the back of my hand across my nose and sniffling.

Nate let out a breath, his hand stilling on my arm.

"What is it?" I asked, pulling out of his arm and sitting up. I turned so that I was facing him and crossed my legs in front of me, his hand in mine.

"I was terrified," he said, his voice barely above a whisper as he closed his eyes and rested his head back against the couch. "I've never been so scared in my life. I always promised that I would keep you safe, that you wouldn't be in harm's way as long as I was around..." He trailed off, sliding his hand out of my hold to cover his face with his. "I don't know what I would have done if he had — " My heart broke at Nate's unfinished sentence.

Uncrossing my legs, I crawled onto his lap and pulled him into a hug, feeling his chest shake as he held back a sob. He tucked his head into the crook of my neck, wrapping his arms tightly around me.

"Nate," I whispered, running my hands through his soft waves and massaging his scalp. "You can't beat yourself up over this. I know you'll do whatever you can to keep me safe. To make me happy." I rested my cheek against the top of his head. "And that's what I love most about you."

"Love?" Nate asked, rearing back so he could look me in the eyes. I held his stare as his eyes glistened, damp with tears that had yet to escape. He dropped his forehead to mine, his hand tangling itself in my hair as he cupped the back of my head.

"Yes, love." I let out a breath before continuing. "I love you, Nate," I said against his lips, desperate to kiss them. "You make me feel so protected and understood. You're so patient with me and I don't deserve it. I don't deserve *you*. You make me feel like I can get through anything...as long as I have you."

Running my thumb over his beard, I smiled and closed my eyes as I pressed my lips against his once more. I parted my lips for him and let out a soft moan as his tongue traced my lower lip. Nate's mouth moved from mine as I gasped, kissing me from my jaw to my ear and down my neck. It was like he was trying to devour me.

"I love you too, Maddie." Nate smiled against my skin and I felt his entire body relax with those words. He pulled away, running his thumb over the scar on my chin, and I watched as his face fell.

"Hey, what's wrong?" I gave his palm a comforting squeeze. "This is supposed to be a happy moment. I love you, Nate."

"So does that mean you're going to stay?" he asked, sounding nervous. He looked down at our joined hands, watching as my thumb ran over his knuckles.

"Stay?"

"Yeah, you know, after you finish your book."

"Nate, you are my home," I said, tilting his face up. "I don't want to be anywhere if it doesn't include you. I want our Sunday morning waffles and French toast. I want to keep finding new bookmarks from you. I want to spend my nights curled up at your side, learning how to play video games or laughing at some dumb movie with you. I want to get coffee at Olivia's and visit you at your food truck. I want your kisses and foot rubs and to wear your clothes to bed. I want forever with you, Nate."

I let out a squeal as Nate wrapped his arms around me, pulling me up off the couch with him. I wrapped my legs around his waist, leaning forward and bringing my mouth to his. The kiss started gentle, our lips barely touching as we shared one breath. Nate's tongue traced the seam of my lips and I parted mine for him, letting him deepen the kiss.

A groan vibrated through me as Nate's mouth pressed against mine. He stepped forward, his hands cupping my ass, as he brought us down the hallway to our room. I kept my focus on every inch of him that pressed against me, wanting to savor his touch. He pressed me against the door, his tongue tangling with mine, and used his leg to support my weight so he could turn the handle.

"Tuna, get out," Nate said between kisses, plopping me down on our bed. When Tuna didn't move, I giggled as Nate let out a sigh and scooped him up, putting him on his feet just outside the door and closing it on him.

In one fluid movement, Nate stripped his shirt over his head, and I raked my eyes over his body, lingering on the bulge in his sweatpants. He was by my side then, hovering over me. I stared into his eyes as his hand explored my body, pausing at the swell of my breasts. His thumb rubbed over my nipple through the thick fabric of my sweater and I let out a soft moan, wishing I could feel his hands on my skin. I moved my hands to his hair, tugging him forward and devouring his mouth in a kiss.

He moved his hands down lower, his fingers curling on the hem of my sweater. In one slow movement, he lifted my shirt and dragged it over my head, causing a shiver to ripple through me. He dropped his head to my shoulder and left a trail of kisses over my exposed skin.

"Nate," I gasped. He let out a moan, his eyes dark with need as he dragged them to my face until they locked with mine.

"Maddie." He ground his erection down on my core and my eyes fluttered shut in bliss. "I love you."

"I love you too, Nate," I whispered. "Always."

"If you feel uncomfortable, stop me, okay?" I nodded and he palmed my jaw. "Despite knowing how strong you are, it's been a crazy time and I don't want to push you too far."

"*Nate.*" I pulled his head down to mine so our breath mingled. "If you don't touch me right now, I'm going to lose my mind."

Nate wet his lips before leaning forward and capturing my mouth with his. I couldn't contain my happiness; it was beyond anything I could've imagined. His touch, his smell, his overall presence — it was as if I was drunk on him...drunk on a feeling I couldn't even begin to describe. He ground his hardness against me once more and I threw my head back, lifting my hips to press harder against him.

He moved down to my jeans, making quick work with the button and zipper, before tugging them and my underwear down to my ankles. I kicked them off, letting them drop to the floor, as Nate hovered over me. He locked eyes with me, his chest rising and falling with his heavy breathing.

"As much as I love those sweatpants on you" — I slid my hands between us and tugged on the waistband of his pants — "they need to come off. Now."

Nate spun us around so that he was now beneath me and I was straddling his waist. Reaching behind my back, I unclasped my bra, letting my breasts spring free, and Nate's eyes flared. I held my breath as his eyes roamed over my naked body. He looked at me like he just realized what love was. Like I was the one who put the sun in the sky. The one who put the twinkle in the stars at night.

His hands moved to my hips, his thumbs brushing over my freckled skin, and I shuddered.

"No, Nate," — my voice sounded breathless — "me first."

I ran my fingers over his chest, feeling the softness of the curls that dusted his skin. I licked my lips and trailed my fingers over each ridge of muscle, memorizing the way it felt. Grabbing the waistband of his pants, I crawled back as I slid them off with his boxers. Running my hands up his thighs, I gripped his erection, hard and ready, and stroked him with a fervor.

Nate let out a guttural sound, giving me the confidence I needed. Leaning over him, I took him in my mouth and swirled my tongue around his head. Keeping my hand wrapped around him, my hand and mouth worked in rhythm until Nate trembled beneath me.

"Maddie." I looked up at him as I continued stroking and sucking him. "Fuck, you need to stop. I'm going to come."

I pulled back, releasing him with a pop. Sitting back on my heels between his legs, Nate twisted his body to the side and dug into his nightstand for a condom. Tossing the foil wrapper to me, I tore it open and slowly slid it on him, marveling at his length.

I straddled him, running the tip of his dick along my entrance, causing him to suck in a sharp breath. Slowly, I eased myself down, taking him inch by inch. When I was fully seated on him, I leaned forward and angled my mouth over Nate's, pulling him into a kiss. He snaked his fingers into my hair, pulling me closer to deepen the kiss. I moaned into him as I began moving up and down on his shaft, overcome by the fullness.

Nate sat up, and I let out a moan as my clit rubbed against him with the new angle, picking up my pace. Unable to control my breathing, Nate pulled away, keeping his forehead pressed to mine, and watched as I chased this high. My sharp little pants filled the room, our bodies slick with sweat as we moved as one.

"You feel so good," I said between breaths, unable to keep my eyes open anymore. "I'm not...I can't, I — "

"I know," Nate said, sucking on my lower lip like a man possessed. "I've got you."

He flipped me over in one fluid movement, positioning us perfectly so the back of my head rested on the pillows. With one hand braced behind me, he hooked one of my legs around his waist and thrust into me harder. The string of curses I let out as he reached unknown territory inside me would've impressed many a sailor. He palmed my breast, lightly pinching my nipple between his forefinger and thumb. Grabbing the spare pillow next to me, I threw it over my face and let out a scream.

"No," Nate said, the roughness in his voice giving away just how close he was to coming undone. He tore the pillow from my face, his deep green eyes filled with pleasure. "I want to watch."

His hand moved between us, his fingers gliding through my wetness as he rubbed small circles over my bud. His pace picked up and he thrust harder into me, the sound of the bed creaking beneath us shooting bursts of pleasure up and down my spine. Gripping his ass, I dug my nails into his cheeks, not caring if I was piercing skin. I was only focused on bringing him closer, wanting to feel our bodies mold into one.

With three final thrusts, we fell apart together, our mouths clashing in a passionate kiss. Nate unhooked my leg from around him and fell to my side, draping his arm over my stomach. I turned my head to my left, my eyes roaming over his naked body as it shook in pure bliss.

"You okay?" I asked as I wiped the sweat off his brow.

"Never better."

twenty-eight

"Nate, are you sure about this?" I fidgeted in the passenger seat of the Beast. I glanced at the GPS, which said our estimated time of arrival was in ten minutes. Despite claiming he could drive to his parents' house with his eyes closed, I made Nate program the address in so that I could anxiously watch the time shrink. "I haven't seen your family in years. What if they hate me?"

"I already told you they don't hate you." Nate smiled at me and gave my thigh a gentle squeeze before placing his hand back on the steering wheel. "My mom is thrilled that you're coming back home."

Home.

All throughout college, I had considered Mr. and Mrs. West's home my own. I spent almost every school break and holiday at their house in Pennsylvania, and they always welcomed me with open arms. Sometimes I felt more at home at their place than I did at my dad's.

But after Olivia left...I wasn't sure what they thought. How they felt about me. Did Olivia tell them everything, or only what she wanted them to know? Were they disappointed in me for choosing a guy over their daughter? Knowing how anxious I was about this, Nate never pressured me to reconnect with his family.

It was Thanksgiving weekend, and having spent Thanksgiving Day with my dad, we were on the way to his parents' house for the remainder of the long weekend. Olivia was already there and I wanted to kick back and relax like old times. We used to love drinking wine in their garden as we dreamed about our future.

"This is going to be a disaster, Nate." I dropped my head into my hands and rested my elbows on my knees. "I've disappointed them so much. I chose a manipulative, narcissistic, and abusive man over my best friend. I threw out years of friendship for someone I had known for only a few months. I ignored all your parents' calls after Olivia left and — " I sat up in confusion as Nate pulled the truck over to the side of the road, putting it in park. "What are you doing?"

"Madds." He turned his body toward mine, clutching my hands in his. "My parents are *not* mad at you and they are certainly not disappointed in you. Olivia and I didn't say a single bad thing about you to my parents after everything."

"But they know what happened!"

"Yes." He reached forward and tucked my hair behind my ear. "And that's why they kept calling you. They wanted to make sure that *you* were okay. They thought maybe they could get through to you when I couldn't."

"How am I supposed to walk into their home and act like nothing happened?"

"You don't." He raised a shoulder. "You don't need to hide anything, Maddie. Just be yourself. They already know and love you, so you don't have to worry about impressing your boyfriend's parents."

"Are you sure?"

"As sure as how I feel about you." His crooked grin flashed across his face before he leaned forward for a chaste kiss. "Can I start driving again or do you need more time? We should be there in less than five minutes."

Taking a deep breath, I smiled at Nate and said, "Yeah, let's do this."

I took a seat on the swing hidden within one of the many gardens in the backyard. Nate was right, I had nothing to worry about. Darla, Nate's mother, pulled me into a tight hug before I had both my feet on the ground, saying over and over again how it had been too long and that she'd been counting down the days to see me. I apologized repeatedly as she hugged me, but she told me to be quiet and to hurry inside because Olivia had been waiting for me to arrive.

Taking a sip of my sweet tea, I used my feet to push the swing gently back and forth. In the past month, this might have been one of the few times where I felt at peace.

"I thought I'd find you here." Olivia appeared, holding a chunky blanket and a glass of wine. "How'd you manage to escape the wrath of my mother?"

"Oh, stop." I chuckled quietly, scooting over to make room for her. Olivia sat down and draped the blanket over us, shielding us from the crisp autumn air. "Your mom isn't that bad."

"Not to *you*." She rolled her eyes and took a large sip of her wine.

"I've missed coming here," I admitted in an attempt to change the topic. I tucked my feet underneath me. "I was so nervous on the way over, I almost made Nate turn around. I thought everyone would be mad at me."

"We're just happy that you're happy and safe."

"That's all thanks to Nate," I said, looking down at my glass and tapping my fingers against it. "He's seriously one of the best."

"He's all right." She laughed, downing the rest of her glass before setting it on the ground in front of us. She reached over and patted my leg, giving me a comforting smile. "But don't underestimate yourself either. You got yourself out of a very toxic relationship, you put in the work with your therapist, and you're the one who showed up at Nate's door."

I let that sit with me for a while as we swayed back and forth on the swing. She was right, but why couldn't I believe it?

"How's your writing going?" Olivia finally asked, looking at me.

"I don't know." I swiped at the condensation on my cup. "I've been stuck on the ending for a month now and I feel like I'm not getting any closer to figuring it out."

"No, but you will." She scooted closer, resting her head on my shoulder. "We all believe in you."

I took another sip of my tea before placing it on the ground next to her empty glass. I pulled the blanket up higher over us and rested my head on top of hers.

"Remember when we used to come out here all the time?" I asked, staring out at the garden. "We used to talk about your coffee shop and me writing a book?"

"Among other things." Olivia grinned cheekily.

"Yeah, let's not get into that." I pushed us again, the hinges creaking beneath our weight as we met the chilly air head-on. "Want to know what else I dreamed about?"

"What?" Olivia asked, sitting up so she could look at me.

"This garden. I always thought it would be the perfect place for a wedding," I said dreamily as I stared out at the rows of perfectly landscaped bushes. In the spring and summer, the most beautiful flowers bloomed, and there was a wishing well that sat at the center of it. With the amount of pennies I tossed into there, wishing on my happily ever after, I could probably pay for that wedding. "I thought the willow tree would be the most beautiful backdrop for the ceremony. I always imagined myself standing beneath it, wearing a lace dress with the love of my life as we said our vows. We would have some tables set up under the pergola, but I always thought everyone would be too busy dancing and talking to sit down. There'd be waiters handing out hors d'oeuvres, and we'd have carrot cake to honor my mother."

"That sounds perfect." Olivia beamed and then glanced down at my ringless left hand. I could tell by the look on her face that she was holding back.

"Come on." I rolled my eyes. "Spit it out."

"Have you and Nate talked about getting married?" She gnawed on the inside of her cheek, trying to contain her excitement.

"No." I let out a laugh and now *I* was glancing down at my left hand. "It's too soon for that. I'm still processing everything that happened with Griffin. Nate's focused on his business and I need to finish my book. I'm still waiting for my brain to catch up on everything that's happened."

"You'll have your happy ending soon enough." She took one of my hands in hers and gave it a squeeze. "I promise."

"I'm living it right now."

We sat in silence on the swing, orange and red leaves floating around us. This — sitting here with Olivia, with Nate running an errand with his dad, my life back in Briar Oakes, Griffin behind bars — *this* was my happily ever after. I had finally found it.

"Oh my god," I gasped, jumping to my feet. "That's it!"

"*What's* it?" Olivia looked at me, confused but jumping to her feet as well.

"I need my phone." I spun around, frantically patting my pockets. "I need to write this down."

"Write what down? Maddie, calm down!"

"I can't," I said as I practically jumped up and down. "I need to go!"

"Okay..." She was clearly not picking up on my groundbreaking realization.

Leaving Olivia in the garden, I ran across the lawn, the fallen leaves crunching beneath my feet, until I reached the back patio. Nate's mom was doing the dishes when I barged into the house, the back door rattling as it bounced off the wall. Shouting out an apology to her over my shoulder, I didn't slow down as I headed to the stairs.

I didn't stop until I was in the safety of the room Nate and I were staying in. Pulling my bag onto the bed, I yanked my laptop out of it and turned it on. I anxiously tapped my nails on my legs as I waited for it to power up. My fingers itched to start typing, wanting to get the words that were flying through my head out. It wasn't until I had my manuscript open that I felt like I could take a real breath.

"Maddie?" Nate ran into the room, out of breath. I looked up from my laptop, having just typed the last word of the chapter. His eyes searched me, trying to find any signs of distress. "Everything okay?"

"Everything's great." I looked up at him, hardly containing my excitement. "Why?"

"I just got home from the store and my mom said you ran into the house like a bat out of hell. " He glanced from me to my laptop and then back again. "She was going to come up, but then Olivia came in and stopped her. Are you sure everything's okay?"

"Yes, Nate, I promise." I stood up and closed the distance between us, wrapping my arms around his middle. "I just finally figured it out."

"What did you figure out?" he murmured into my hair.

"I've read more romance books than I can count in the past year, and every time I got to the end, I was left disappointed. I haven't found one character yet who's been through what I have and still managed to find their happily ever after. Do you know what that means?"

"That you need to read more books?"

"No!" I let out an exasperated sigh, pulling out of his arms. "It means that there are also other people out there like me who might not have found a character that they can relate to. People who rely on words on pages to give them hope." I paused, smiling so hard that my cheeks ached. "I can be that person. I can show them that there's still hope. That we still deserve a chance at what we deserve."

"That's amazing, Maddie." He smiled back, rubbing my arm encouragingly. "Does that mean you figured out what *you* deserve?"

"I think I finally did."

He pulled me in tighter, tilting my head up by my chin as his thumb skated over the smile-shaped scar there. "What is it?"

"You," I said, my eyes growing wide. "I was outside talking to Olivia and she said something about me finding my happily ever after and...that's when I realized I was already living it, Nate. All of this — Olivia, your family, Briar Oakes, the food truck, writing. You."

"Me?" He stared at me and the uncertainty in my eyes told me everything I needed to know about the man he was. And how I would need to work harder to show how appreciated, cherished, and adored he was.

"Yes, you." I grabbed a hold of his hand and dragged him to the bed, pushing him down so that he had to sit. Picking up my laptop, I scrolled to the beginning of the last chapter I wrote and placed it in his hands. "Read this."

I paced back and forth in the room, keeping my eyes on Nate. My heart raced in my chest and my hands shook at my sides as I watched him eat up the words on the screen. When he was done, he slid the laptop closed on the bed beside him.

"I'm your happily ever after?" he asked, wrapping my hand in his and pulling me in to stand between his legs.

I considered his words. They were true, but it was also more than that. It was the fact that I found a home. I found a town with people I felt comfortable with. I found my passion for writing again. I found happiness. Now I could write it all down and share my story with the world, and maybe...maybe I could provide other people like me with hope. Hope that they, too, could find their happily ever after.

I looked up at Nate.

"No," I said, shaking my head with a smile on my face. "You're my *gratest* ever after."

epilogue

Six months later.

"I can't believe I finally have my own apartment," Olivia squealed, jumping up and down. "Like, I have a bedroom. And a bathroom. And a kitchen. And a living room. And they're not all in the same room! This is unreal."

I laughed and dropped the last of her boxes onto the floor of what would be her dining room if she had a table.

"I'm so happy for you, Liv," I said as I plopped down on the couch in her living room. "This place really is going to be amazing. I can't wait to see what you do with it."

"You're going to have to help." She sat next to me and draped her feet over my lap. "You were the real brains behind how our apartment was decorated when we lived together."

"Just let me know when and I'll be more than willing to help." I looked over at her and held a finger up in warning. "But I am *not* helping you unpack."

"Come on, Maddie, please?" She gave a full pout, hands on hips and all.

"No." I laughed, pushing her feet off me as I stood up. "I packed up everything you left at Nate's and brought it over here, but that's where I draw the line. I'll even help you put together anything you buy at IKEA if you promise to feed me, but that's about it."

"Fine," she grumbled, standing up so she could walk me to the door. "But you mean takeout, right?"

"Duh, I'd rather not die from poisoning."

"Don't be so dramatic." She rolled her eyes but then laughed. We both knew she was the worst cook. "Thanks again for helping me, Maddie."

"Anytime." I yanked her into a tight hug, inhaling the scent of coffee beans and vanilla. "Are you sure you don't have any idea what Nate has planned for today?" When I woke up this morning, Nate was already gone. There was an index card in my book, telling me he was going to take me out this afternoon and to be ready for something magical. When I texted him about it, he refused to give me any hints as to what he had planned. "He's never this secretive."

"Nope," she said, pulling out of the hug but keeping me at arm's length. With her hands on my shoulders, she looked over my outfit, which consisted of a pair of jeans and a loose-fitting short-sleeved shirt. "But you should change. Maybe a cute dress and do something nice with your hair? You know, just in case."

"Just in case what?" I raised an eyebrow at her. "I thought you didn't know what he was planning."

"Oh, be quiet." She huffed as she rolled her eyes again, starting to shove me out the door. "Just look cute."

"Fine," I groaned, walking out of her new apartment. "I'll call you later, Liv."

"You better." She giggled and shut the door in my face before I could ask any more questions.

Nate: Hey, I'm running a bit late. I got hit with a lunch rush. Want to meet me over here and then we can go together?

Me: Yeah, no worries. Need me to bring anything?

Nate: No, just your cute, perfect self.

Me: OK, be there soon. I love you ♡

I parked my Jeep in front of Latte Da! as I planned to stop in and grab an iced latte before I made my way over to Nate's food truck. But when I hopped out of the front seat and looked up, my heart skipped a beat in my chest and my hand flew to my mouth. I stood frozen in the middle of the street, staring at the town's gazebo. Taking a few tentative steps forward, tears welled in my eyes. White and pink flower petals lined the sidewalk from the street to the front of the gazebo steps. A flower garland filled with white and pink roses draped over the awning of it, framing Nate, who stood in jeans and a suit jacket, smiling at me.

Somehow, my feet brought me to where he was and I climbed the stairs to the gazebo, fully aware of what was about to happen. Behind Nate, a pink blanket and throw pillows were laid out for us, and a picnic basket rested to the side. A bottle of sparkling apple juice sat in an ice bucket with two champagne flutes next to my...

"Is that my book?" I gasped, shoving Nate to the side as I dropped to my knees on the blanket. Okay, maybe I didn't know what was about to happen. Clearly, Nate wasn't proposing. I picked up the book and tears fell down my cheeks as I read the title: *Gratest Ever After* by Madison Williams. My fingers ran over the illustrated cover, marveling at how well the artist nailed Nate's characteristics and the blonde girl in a dress and Docs standing next to him outside a food truck.

"It came in while you were at Olivia's." He took a seat next to me. "I'm so proud of you, Madds."

"I can't believe I did it," I whispered, unable to take my eyes off my book. "I published a book! Thank you, Nate, this is the best surprise ever!"

"It's not over yet." He chuckled and reached over so he could pull the picnic basket closer to us. "I have one more surprise for you."

I watched as Nate pulled a small box out of the basket and handed it over to me. I raised a brow at him suspiciously as I took hold of the box and placed it on my lap, lifting the lid. When I looked inside, my breath caught in my throat. "Nate, is this..."

"Every single one of them," he said, sneaking a quick kiss.

"I had no idea you kept them." I picked up the stack of index cards, flipping through all the bookmarks Nate had made me. "I just assumed you threw them out every time you wrote a new one."

"No, I just didn't want you to lose them." He tucked my hair behind my ear for a better view of my face as I read through them all. "I wanted them to be in a safe spot, this way if you ever doubted yourself or were having a hard day, I could pull them out and help you remember how great you are."

"Nate." I sniffled, swiping the tears from my face. "I love you so much."

"There's one more," he said, nodding at my book.

Pushing the box to the side, I lifted my book and flipped through the pages until an index card fell onto my lap. And there was Nate, kneeling in front of me, reading what he wrote out loud with shaking hands.

Madison Williams,
Thanks for being my "gratest" ever after.
Will you marry me?
—Nate

"Yes," I said, knowing the answer before it even left my mouth. It was the simplest word, and yet, I knew it would be the most important one I'd ever say. I looked up at Nate, who was holding out the most beautiful diamond ring. "Absolutely, yes."

acknowledgments

When I first started writing this book, I was struggling with my mental health. My anxiety was at the highest it's ever been and I spent my days fighting panic attack after panic attack. There were days where I couldn't even get out of bed. Days where I felt like I could never be alone or leave my house. I truly felt like I lost myself. Writing this book was the best therapy I could have asked for. In a way, I healed alongside Maddie. The conversations she had with Heather were similar conversations I had with my own therapists.

This book would not have been possible without the immense support from friends, family, and co-workers! I seriously had the best team ever and without you, Gratest Ever After would have never been possible.

A special thanks to my alpha and beta readers (Ashlyn, Jessica, Rebeccah, Casey W, Jesse, Katie, Casey R, and Melissa). You all are the reason that GEA is the way it is today. I loved hearing your feedback, reading your comments and reactions, and working with you throughout this process. Thanks for helping me feel confident in this book and ready to share it with the world.

Thank you to my amazing editors and proofreader, Britt, Kristen, and Jaime. Seriously, thank you for taking such great care of my work and helping me perfect Maddie's story. I am so lucky to have worked with you!

Monika de los Rios (riocovers on Fiverr), thank you for being my go to person for all my graphic needs. You brought my characters to life and I couldn't have asked for a better person to work with.

Ashlyn, an extra special thanks to you for being the brains behind all this (and for reading GEA a dozen times). I may have written the book, but everything else is thanks to you. I know you say that you're my unpaid assistant, but consider this your payment for all your support - I'm declaring that Nate is yours. Enjoy him - winks and all.

Rebeccah and Jessica - thank you for listening to my five-thousand voice texts, brainstorming with me, and convincing me to not give up every time I was overwhelmed and doubted myself. I'm so grateful that bookstagram brought us together and have no idea how I made it this far in life without you (I know, I'm so dramatic).

Molly, thank you for spending countless Sunday mornings in coffeeshops watching me write, making sure I stayed focused, and brainstorming with me. Also, thanks for being my photographer and videographer for all the embarrassing content I made. When we first met at 13, I never imagined you sitting on the Barnes and Noble floor taking photos of me holding books or lying in my grass while I pretended to jump inside a book wearing my wedding dress. You really are the bestest friend ever and I appreciate you so much!

Hoover, here is the moment you've been waiting for (and reminding me a million times about). Thank you so much for helping me rewrite the entire end of my book, answering my million and one questions regarding your career, and not questioning the hypothetical situations I threw your way (okay, at least not to me). You da best. Now don't let this get to your head.

Frank, thank you for all of your lawyer knowledge and giving me a play-by-play on what my imaginary lawsuits and trials would look like.

To all my bookstagram friends and my street team - I cannot tell you how much your support and friendship has meant to me. Thank you for making this book launch so much fun!

To Christie, Yuheini, and Mickey - thanks for being a part of my book club with me even though we never read any books together. You helped me make it through one of the toughest years in my teaching career and your support of my writing meant so much to me.

Thank you to my husband, Steven, for accepting the fact that I fall in love with fictional men hard and talk about them like they're real human beings. Oh, and thanks for acting out certain parts of my book with me so I could figure out how to accurately write it without questioning our marriage. Can't wait to act out book #2 with you!

And last but not least, I wanted to thank my son, Crew, for the endless snuggles and kisses throughout this entire process. And thanks for taking 3 hour naps so that I had time to write this damn thing.

about the author

Carissa lives in New Jersey with her husband and son. She's a special education teacher by day and creator of happily ever afters by night (and nap time). When she's not writing or reading, you can find her dancing and playing HotWheels with her son, drooling over cars, sipping on Pink Drinks, jamming out to Disney music, going to Target, and collecting book boyfriends.
Gratest Ever After is her first novel.

Find her on social media:
@hellocarissamay on Instagram and TikTok

Milton Keynes UK
Ingram Content Group UK Ltd.
UKHW020755080124
435661UK00018B/1222